AFRICA'S
HEART
THE JOURNEY ENDS IN KANSAS

BY MARK WENTLING

A PEACE CORPS WRITERS BOOK

AFRICA'S HEART
A Peace Corps Writers Book
An Imprint of Peace Corps Worldwide

Printed in the United States of America
by Peace Corps Writers of Oakland, California

For more information, contact peacecorpsworldwide@gmail.com.
Peace Corps Writers and the Peace Corps Writers colophon are
trademarks of PeaceCorpsWorldwide.org

ISBN: 1935925555
ISBN-13: 978-1-935925-55-2
Library of Congress Control Number: 2014957197
Peace Corps Writers

First Peace Corps Writers Edition, January 2015

An ambitious novel concludes Wentling's (*Africa Release*, 2014) African trilogy.

Letivi, chief of the Ataku village, is faced with a modern dilemma: wealth disparity is growing in the village between those families who have sent children to work in Europe (who then send money back home to their families) and those who have not. Letivi's goal of correcting this problem via a wealth-sharing agreement among the village is hindered by his own lack of a wife or child; as a clan leader says, "Chief Letivi is without a wife or children and thus knows little about the lives we live as we struggle to support our families." Letivi, a light-skinned half-caste, is also burdened by the secrets of his own parentage: he is the son of Bobovovi, an American Peace Corps volunteer chosen by the moon god and consumed by a sacred baobab tree 20 years before. A hemisphere away, a newspaper reporter named Robin is tracking down a mysterious man named J.B., whose disappearance shocked the town of Gemini, Kansas, and whose trail will lead Robin all the way to Africa. Destinies converge, and the generational saga that Wentling began in *Africa's Embrace* arrives at its conclusion…

With impressive scope and flourishes of magical realism, the book transcends what might seem to be mundane storylines to instead feel fully epic.

Kirkus Reviews
March 18, 2015

Dedicated to all those who went to Africa to help
for a few years and stayed a lifetime

CONTENTS

AUTHOR'S NOTE

The deed is done. My Africa Trilogy is complete. My three books stand as a testament to my forty-four years of being immersed in Africa, as well as my enduring Kansas connection. Yes, there is more to write, but I believe my three books with their thousand pages of words are more than enough for any reader.

My own story is not yet over. I am still in Africa trying to lend a hand. I feel other books about Africa stirring within me. There may be more to come. Much depends on the feedback I receive on my trilogy. For sure, I will not want to disappoint my book fans. Sincere thanks to all who have taken the time to read my books.

While it is best to read my trilogy beginning with the first book, any reader can gain much by reading these books out of sequence. Each book is designed to entertain, educate, and enlighten the reader independently from the other two. So don't worry if you have not read the previous books.

Some readers of my first two books noted their appreciation of my description of how Africa appeared years ago. My reply to this praise was that as far as I am concerned, most of what

I describe still applies. For me, rural Africa remains much the same, except there are many more people today than when I first arrived on the continent in 1970. I therefore see very little that is outdated in my books. I also believe my third book brings everything up to date and provides a good comparison of African and Western cultural values and views.

I believe I must say a few words about the baobab tree, which plays such an important symbolic role in my books. This tree, *Adansonia digitata*, is worshiped across Africa and is a symbol of knowledge and wisdom. The tree can grow to a very large size and can live for thousands of years. The oldest of the baobab trees in Africa can therefore be counted among the most ancient living organisms on the planet. The baobab can store water, and its bark, fruits, and leaves have a number of uses. This remarkable tree is associated with many local myths and mysteries. I urge readers not familiar with this unusual tree to learn more about it.

I admit that I cringe every time I use the word *Africa* to refer to a vast (three times the size of the continental United States) and very diverse continent. Nonetheless, common usage leaves me with no other choice. I hope the reader knows there is no single word that can sum up a continent composed of fifty-four distinct countries and an indescribable mosaic of hundreds of ethnic groups and languages, as well as dozens of ecological zones. Africa is more than a place—it is a whole, complex world of its own.

Perhaps one way to communicate the complexity of Africa is to share with you some of the names given to me over the years as I have moved around Africa. Upon my arrival in Togo in 1970, I was given the Ewe day-name *Komla*, which indicates that I was born on Tuesday. I still receive mail from Togo addressed to my full local name, *Agu Komla Amerika*. In the late 1970s, I was in

Niger for five years, and my colleagues gave me the French nickname *rigid et sec*. This was because I would succinctly say things as I saw them when I tired of the long African palaver.

In Somalia, where everyone has a nickname, I was called Red Beard, *gadhka cas*, because of the reddish color of my facial hair. In Kenya, I was tagged in Kiswahili as *mwasawali mingi* because I asked too many questions. In Tanzania, I was frequently called in Kiswahili *mzee kijana* because of my youthful way of behaving in spite of my age. In Congo-Kinshasa, I was referred to as 'Rainmaker' by people I did not know. They said they had given me this name because they had heard that everywhere I went, funds for projects were likely to follow. My latest African name here in Burkina Faso is the honorific in Mooré, *Naaba Toéga* (Chief Baobab). Of course, I am called in many local languages the word used to refer to white people. For example, some of these words are: *yovo, anasara, toubab, musungu, mondélé,* and *faranji*.

I could have used many words from African and European languages in my books, but I chose to make things easy for my readers and write only in English. I hope this choice does not diminish the desired impact of my books. Certainly, most of what my books describe did not occur in English.

I am very thankful for the privilege I have had to work and live in Africa for over four decades. I have had many close calls over the years, and it is only because of a matter of minutes or dumb luck that I am still here to tell the tale. I have escaped by a hair a number of traffic accidents. I missed being injured or killed by grenades and bullets by only a few minutes in Somalia. I barely missed stepping on a land mine in Angola. I have had guns stuck in my face in a number of countries. Through it all, I have always been impressed by how even in the worst of circumstances Africans could still laugh and find the courage to carry on. I will always be touched by all those Africans I have observed aiding others. There are many unsung heroes in Africa.

I would be greatly remiss if I did not mention the impact the films and writings of a famous Kansas couple had on me. I am referring to Martin and Osa Johnson. They courageously arrived in Africa fifty years before me and had many amazing adventures. As a child growing up in Kansas, I was inspired by their adventures. I have visited their Safari Museum in Chanute, Kansas, their hometown. Osa's book, *I Married Adventure*, was a best seller in 1940. I thought about naming my trilogy *I Married Africa* but decided to use book titles that reflect my different and much lengthier path in Africa.

As I have done in my previous two books, I must give the biggest possible thank-you to Richard Feutz, who, from his home base in Mount Horeb, Wisconsin, voluntarily edited multiple times my numerous book manuscripts. My book-writing journey would have indeed been much longer and lonelier without him. He has demonstrated repeatedly the inestimable value of a friendship that started in early 1967. Of course, I must take full responsibility for every word in this book. I remind the reader that this is a work of fiction; therefore, any resemblance to anyone alive or dead is pure coincidence.

I hope my books will be used for many years to come to promote a greater understanding of Africa. An underlying intent of my books is to communicate Africa's development challenges via a captivating fictional story that is rooted in my firsthand experiences. The best compliment I can receive is for someone to tell me he or she enjoyed my books and learned much from reading them. I hope my *Africa Trilogy* opens not only eyes but hearts as well.

Mark Wentling
Ouagadougou, Burkina Faso
January 2015

CHAPTER ONE
BOOK MANIA

Robin Fletcher had met his match. The landscape surrounding him was covered with books. His eyes feasted and his heart raced. His profound love for books and his lust for the knowledge they contained made his arrival at the annual Kansas Book Festival on the grounds of the magnificent old statehouse in Topeka a glorious moment for him. He could not wait to delve deeply into the thousands of books on display. There was not a moment to waste of this very special, bright, and sunny day in September 1990.

It was stressful trying to decide where to start looking at books and how to proceed to get the most out of this booklover's paradise. Robin had driven all night from his home in Chicago and taken a day off from his job as a journalist to return to his home state for this big book festival. He made the same trip almost every September. Although his tiny apartment was overcrowded with books, stacked from floor to ceiling, he continued to buy as many books as he could afford.

Robin grew up on a hardscrabble farm in a remote location on the windswept, desolate plains of western Kansas. His youth was filled with hard work. There was little free time for amusements. The nearest neighbor was over three miles away, and his parents did not believe in TV. His parents and especially his grandfather believed in reading as much as they could. The mounds of books stacked around their decrepit little house on the prairie testified amply to this belief.

Robin learned to read at an early age and developed the habit of reading more than one book a week. He read every book in his small rural high school and the Carnegie Library in the nearest town where his parents shopped every Saturday. He even read the big Webster dictionaries and the *Encyclopedia Britannica*. He devoured every word of an old Lincoln Library of Essential Information that his grandfather had given him. His photographic memory enabled him to remember all the information on every page he had ever read. Starting at a young age, he firmly believed in what his grandfather frequently said: "The only thing new under the sun is in the books you have not read."

Robin had a special penchant for old and used books. Hence, he gravitated to the display of these books on the second floor in the west wing of the vast rotunda area inside the historic statehouse. There, under the fierce scowl of the abolitionist John Brown, whose oversized image in a famous wall mural depicted him menacingly with a Bible in one hand and a rifle in the other as he stood wedged in between a tornado and roaring flames, Robin found what he called "many under discovered jewels of the past." He perused one old book after another in search of subjects that appealed to him. He made a mental note of any book he might want to come back to later.

He would read the title and check the copyright page for year of printing and the name of the publisher. He would then read the opening and last pages. If he liked what he read, he might read a few pages more before moving on mechanically to another book. There was one book that grabbed his attention and slowed his methodical book perusal process down. This was a slender book with an odd title *JB, Hero of Gemini, Kansas,* printed in 1985.

This novella intrigued him. He sat down on the floor and began to devour this little book published by an unknown press in Newton, Kansas. The more he read, the more he wanted to know about JB and Gemini. He asked the lady tending the book stand where Gemini was located, but she did not know. He then asked her where he could find a map of Kansas. He felt a deep need to know where Gemini was located. Already in the back of his mind, he was thinking he wanted to know more about this JB character and that maybe this would be a good story for him to report in his Chicago newspaper.

He read speedily and did not stop until he finished the entire book. It did not answer for him a few central questions: Who was JB, and what really happened to him? How did a flash of dry lightning relate to his disappearance in 1984? What about the rumors about him being abducted by aliens or having suffered some kind of trauma in Africa? He could see that this was worth some good investigative journalism. He was hoping he could persuade his editors to let him go to Gemini to ferret out the information he needed to write an interesting article on the life and disappearance of the mysterious JB. He was bound and determined to know more about JB—who he really was and what had happened to him. Although he did not hesitate to purchase the book, the answers he wanted were not in any book.

Robin rushed out of the statehouse and asked those tending each book stall he passed where he could find a map of Kansas. Nobody could tell him where Gemini was or where he could find a state map or road atlas. It became apparent that maps were not something anyone displayed at the book festival. He was torn. He wanted to spend the rest of the day looking at books and buying more books. Yet, on the other hand, he was eager to get his hands on a state map to see where Gemini was located. He finally decided to take a break and go to the nearest gas station to buy a Kansas road map.

He found a filling station a few blocks away from the expansive state capitol grounds and lost no time in buying a road map and unfolding it awkwardly on the hood of his car. He first looked at the index of towns and cities in the right hand margin of the map but could not find any Gemini noted. He then proceeded to examine every square inch of the map to see if he could find any place named Gemini. After about an hour of intense scrutiny, he spotted, in the smallest of print, the word "Gemini." He could see that this was a small town, off the main road, tucked away on the southern flank of the Flint Hills, on the north side of the highway between Beaumont and Piedmont in Butler County, Kansas' largest county in terms of surface area.

This exciting discovery had Robin's mind reeling. He could see that driving to Gemini could take a couple of hours. He wanted to take off for Gemini right away, but doing so would mean not returning to the book festival and, possibly, returning late to his job in Chicago. He told himself that he needed to settle down and calmly think of how he should handle this unanticipated situation. He forced himself to return to the book festival and continue working the book stalls as he had long planned. At the same time, his mind was preoccupied with how and when he would make a trip to Gemini to begin investigating the strange JB case. He decided he would call his boss in Chicago and ask for a few days off.

After the book festival had closed, he returned to his motel and called his boss. In a trembling voice, he explained as calmly as he could the interesting story of JB and how he wanted to take advantage of his presence in Kansas to pursue this story. His boss did not share his enthusiasm and thought any trip to Gemini would be a wild goose chase. Nonetheless, he liked Robin and could tell from the distressed tone of his voice that he really wanted to do this. With much hesitation, Robin's boss grumpily approved a one-week absence.

Robin lit up like a Christmas tree, spurting out repeated, over-generous 'thank-you's' to his no-nonsense boss. He decided he would lose no time and set out at dawn the next day for Gemini. He told himself that he would not leave any stone unturned in his pursuit of information about JB. He would begin by talking to as many of the town's residents as possible and looking through city records for any clues that would lead him to the true identity of JB. He was bound and determined to not leave Gemini until he knew all there was to know about JB.

Robin did not know that finding all the truth about JB would require much more than a quick visit to Gemini. JB's secrets could not be found in any archive or book anywhere in Kansas— or, for that matter, anywhere in the United States. Getting to the bottom of JB's baffling story would require much more work than Robin could imagine. He did not know it at the time, but going to Gemini would be the first step in a long and compli-cated journey that would take him on a thrilling adventure to Africa. He would find that there are many new things under the sun that are not to be found in books.

CHAPTER TWO
FUTURE WORRIES

Robin was not the only one fretting over the next steps to take on that day. Across the globe in Africa, the chief of the small village of Ataku in the tiny country of Kotoku was also worrying about how to maintain progress in his village. Chief Letivi was proud of all that his people had achieved in recent years, but he was concerned about their ability to maintain progress and sustain what they had already achieved. He feared that rising expectations for an ever-improving quality of life could not be consistently fulfilled and that failure to keep the development momentum moving at an acceptable pace would breed discontent.

Chief Letivi's days were filled with tormenting thoughts on what could be done to keep the village on an upward development track that could keep people happy and more prosperous. He was painfully aware of their weak capacity in many areas and the limitations often imposed by external factors. He was also acutely aware that much depended upon his leadership and managerial competency. He felt the weight of this burden on him growing every day. A breakthrough of some sort was needed soon if Chief Letivi was to lead the village of Ataku on to better and bigger things.

Everyone in the village wanted to know what more could be done to further reduce their still-high level of poverty. They believed they had done everything possible to help improve their lives and were much better off for all their efforts, but they remained too poor and deprived of much of what they wanted, needed, and were obliged to purchase. Their incomes had increased, but so had prices for all essential items. Thus, their purchasing power had declined. They had increased production of cocoa, their main cash crop, but prices for this crop had stagnated in the face of weak world markets and increased competition from other cocoa-producing countries. The demand for things they had to sell had fallen. Everyone complained about having less disposable income to procure nonessential items. They were worried that their prospects for sliding backward were greater than for moving ahead.

The villagers had found that their most profitable program was the training and support of their most promising youth. Many of their brightest young people had made their way to well-paying jobs in Europe. Every month these successful young people would send money orders to their families in the village. These families enjoyed a much higher living standard than those families who did not have one of their members working abroad. This gap was the source of growing dissension in the village.

The impact of this new "money-order phenomenon" stressed greatly the social fabric of the village. Poor families who had smart and hardworking children were now richer than the traditionally most prominent and royal families in the village. Envy and jealousy raised their ugly heads everywhere. The old habit of working to bring down anyone who succeeded was in resurgence. Families usually used the extra money they received from aboard for nonproductive luxuries. Much of the money was used frivolously. People bought more expensive clothes to show off, traveled to the capital and neighboring countries, imported food and alcoholic beverages, and paid fetish priests to undertake ceremonies to protect them against evil spirits and improve their destinies. Change had occurred in the village in undesirable ways that had not been anticipated. The unintended consequences of well-meaning development actions had Chief Letivi worried.

Very little of this additional money-order income went to improve child education and nutrition, nor was money invested in raising crop yields and new income-generating activities. Sometimes men would use the money to acquire more wives. People were more interested in using money to gain prestige than in using it for anything that would improve the standard of living of the village and ensure their well-being in their old age. Moreover, no thought was given to laying the groundwork for a better future for the upcoming generation. People lived too much for today and gave too little thought to what would be needed tomorrow. They failed to recognize how fragile their situation was. They lived without any safety nets. There were not any social security schemes or pensions for when they were old, sick, or without sufficient means of support. Homes for the care of the elderly were unknown. They were fond of quoting a Bible verse (Matthew 6:31-34) about letting tomorrow take care of itself.

Chief Letivi was happy to see the added income that was flowing into the village, but he worried about the uneven distribution of this income and the fact that the village was benefitting very little from it. He was determined to find a way to channel this income to benefit more fully the growth and prosperity of the village, not just some families who had relatives working abroad. He believed a share of this money should go to the village's development fund to help lift up the poorest families in the village. He decided it was time to discuss all these important issues in an assembly of elders and clan leaders so that some actions could be taken in the best interest of the community. He had no doubt that course corrections were needed in the village's development plan to achieve more desirable outcomes.

The chief's messengers fanned out into the village, beating with a short metal rod on loud iron gong-gongs, shouting for all to hear that the chief was convening a meeting after the first light of the next day to discuss the village's development plan. The elders and leaders were happy to respond to the convocation, and all were in their places in the large, circular meetinghouse in the chief's compound early the next morning. All stood when Chief Letivi entered with his senior counselor, Chief Gyasi. Chief Letivi was dressed in the brightest of old traditional clothes, while a contrasting Gyasi was in his usual modern safari business suit attire. The brightness of his clothes made Chief Letivi's half-caste whiteness look even whiter.

As Chief Letivi stood up to make his opening remarks, all became quiet and listened attentively to the words flowing melodically from the chief's smallish mouth: "Today, I would like to review with you where we are on every component of our development plan, noting our progress or lack thereof, and discuss with you possible solutions to any obstacles that are being confronted in the timely implementation of our development plan. We should be prepared to talk openly and frankly. We must search together for ways to accelerate progress in our village."

The dour Chief Gyasi dryly added, "We have made much progress, and we are much better off than we were before, but we need to continue working to maintain the progress achieved thus far while searching for new ways to improve our living conditions and hopes for a better future for our village."

At this point, the heads of various development committees were called on to report. The water and sanitation committee reported that all was well. Everyone had ample potable water and access to latrines, and the village trash collection and disposal scheme was working well. These actions had made the village a much healthier place to live. The village road maintenance committee reported that all was going as well as expected and the amount of road toll fees collected was increasing. The tourist and traditional welcoming committee reported a steady stream of expatriate visitors who always paid more than asked. The cocoa production committee reported great success in improving yields with the introduction of new tree varieties, but that total profit was down because world prices were low. There was nothing they could do about falling cocoa prices on the world market, but if the declining price trend did not reverse soon, some farmers would lose so much money that it would no longer be worthwhile to cultivate cocoa.

The education committee reported that it had an increasing number of top students who were going on to complete their secondary-school and university studies in the capital city, and a good number of these brilliant students had found well paid jobs in Europe. Many of these former students regularly sent money to their families in the village. It was expected that more young people would be finding good jobs abroad in the coming years. The committee had found that preparing high-potential students for jobs abroad was a successful approach to contributing to the village's prosperity.

The child-care and health committee reported that all children were up to date on their vaccinations and that no cases of child malnutrition had been identified. All lactating mothers were practicing exclusive breastfeeding, and all pregnant mothers were healthy and going to the clinic for their prenatal checkups. All births over the past year had occurred in the clinic, and all newborn babies weighed well above the national average birth weight of five and one-half pounds. All mothers of young children were now utilizing improved feeding practices. Many mothers were also realizing the benefits of spacing the births of their children. Families were sleeping under bed nets, and mosquito breeding areas were regularly treated with pesticides or destroyed. The incidence of malaria in the village had declined considerably.

Chief Letivi thanked all the committee heads and said, "I am proud of all of you and the work you have done to achieve so much progress in the village. I do worry, however, about sustaining this progress while keeping the village on an upward development track. There are many things that worry me. For example, we are overly dependent on cocoa production, which, as we have seen, is subject to the vagaries of world market prices, over which we have no control. We need to find a way to add value to our cocoa production and diversify into the production of other profitable cash crops."

Chief Letivi hesitated before going on to his next point. He was aware that it involved some sensitive issues. Nonetheless, he bravely continued. "I also see that income flowing into the village from former students working abroad is not evenly spread throughout the village. Therefore, the village derives minimal direct benefit from this income. I believe we must search for ways to optimize the use of this income for the village in a fair and equitable manner." The chief's words on this delicate subject had many of the men squirming on their benches and stools, as no family wanted to share any of the income its members were earning abroad.

The chief decided not to hold back any punches, saying bluntly, "I wish to remind all of you that it was the village that selected the students for further training and supported them in their studies and their search to find jobs abroad. These efforts used a high percentage of our development fund, and, thus far, none of these costs have been recovered. These costs need to be reimbursed to our village development fund so we can help more students with their advanced studies and job searches abroad. I must note that I lament the fact that there are many families who have not yet benefited from this program. What can we do? I welcome your comments on this challenging subject."

The room was very quiet following Chief Letivi's vexing remarks. Nobody wanted to say anything that might offend a neighbor, but clearly, there was a tense divide in the room between those who had children working abroad and those who did not. The former were against sharing any of their additional income and, thus, wanted things to stay as they were. The latter wanted the village to receive some of this income and they also wanted to benefit from this program.

Just when it seemed that no one dared to speak up, one man, Joseph, the middle-aged leader of the lowest-ranked clan, asked to speak. He spoke in a trembling, hesitant voice, apparently fearful of the reaction his words would generate. He simply stated, "I am a poor man with a needy family who humbly comes before you to say that our poverty is less than it was, but we are still too poor, and we have little hope of improving significantly our impoverished condition. We, too, would like to see some of our children selected for support for advanced studies and jobs abroad. We are certainly willing to pay back any money spent on our children with the additional income they are able to send home. Thank you for allowing me to say these words."

Following Joseph's sincere remarks, there was much murmuring among the group members. Heated arguments broke out between some clan leaders. Chief Letivi struggled to calm everyone down and bring order back to the meeting. He also struggled in his own mind about what to say and do next. For him, important equity issues were tearing at his heart, and they must be resolved peacefully. Yet, he knew it would not be possible to correct this situation to the satisfaction of everyone. He had to make a decision and ask that all adhere to it. This was the first real test of his leadership and his chieftaincy.

Chief Letivi stood up and tried to speak with authority, but in a tone of voice that projected deep understanding of the issues. "I can see that this is not an easy subject for us, and it will not be possible to reach a conclusion that will make everyone happy. As your chief, I must keep the best interests of our village in the forefront of my thinking. I strongly believe that every family should benefit from the progress we are achieving. Nobody should be left behind. These thoughts and many other factors prompt me to decide the following. Special efforts will be undertaken to give priority to selecting students from the poorest families for advanced studies and work aboard. Those families who have not yet benefitted will be given priority. Every family needs to benefit from this program, and every family benefitting needs to repay the village for any funds expended from its development fund to support their children. Money paid back can be used to support more children. I will appoint a committee to enact my decision in the most efficient and equitable manner."

The authoritarian manner with which Chief Letivi issued his decision did not abide well with some of the clan leaders. It was customary to enter into a long, consensus-building palaver that allowed everyone to speak. Chief Letivi's abrupt closing of the discussion was unprecedented. Obviously, Chief Letivi was not in the mood to spend hours in a long discussion that would not produce any results. He did not have the patience such a long palaver required. His hurry to achieve progress was more important to him than respecting custom.

Some of the more senior leaders were upset that the highly regarded Chief Gyasi had kept quiet. Chief Gyasi naturally wanted to avoid conflict and had remained quiet because he knew that what Chief Letivi said was necessary, although it would cause some resentment. He also did not want to undermine the authority of his grandson or make any sign that he favored his grandson. Of course, nobody knew that Chief Letivi was his grandson, as he had always been presented as the son of their former long-serving Chief Yofu. Only a handful of people knew about Chief Letivi's true origins. This great secret would need to be revealed to everyone in due time to avoid living a lie, even though it was undisclosed in the best interests of the village.

The former, long-sitting Chief Yofu was impressed with the brilliance of the young Letivi. Chief Yofu did not see any of his many sons as being suitable replacements for him. He had reached an agreement with Letivi's mother, Atibona, the formidable master of all plant knowledge, and her parents, Chief Gyasi and his wife, Evelyne, to have Letivi succeed him. Chief Yofu claimed to everyone that he had sired Letivi with a light-skinned, mixed-blood woman living in the capital city of Melomti. Chief

Yofu was comfortable with this big lie because he felt strongly that he had the backing of the grandfathers (ancestors). But the most important element of this monumental secret concerned the real biological father of Letivi.

The real father of Letivi was Bobovovi, a white man from America. Bobovovi had come to the village as a Peace Corps volunteer and became very popular with the grandfathers and the spirit world. He was chosen by the moon god to ride a moonbeam from the mountaintop to his house in the village and ended up being consumed by the most ancient baobab tree in the district. He was obviously a moon child who had been born under a full moon, as was his son, who was given the name Letivi to indicate that he was a moon child. It had been nearly twenty years since Bobovovi (Tuesday's white child) had disappeared inside the old baobab tree, never to be seen again. His miraculous transformation served as the shock needed to galvanize the villagers to put all conflicts behind them and work harmoniously together for the good of the village, just as Bobovovi would have wanted. Everyone now revered Bobovovi as a saint. Many offerings were regularly left in his honor at the base of the old baobab tree. Everyone wanted to please the spirit of Bobovovi.

Chiefs Yofu and Gyasi were afraid that if people knew Letivi was the son of Bobovovi, it would be difficult for Letivi to rule. They feared people would perceive Letivi as a demi-god and not a chief. Letivi went along with this grand mise-en-scène, as he strongly believed becoming chief was an important part of his destiny and that he could do much more good for the village. He knew that if he became chief, the ancient feud between Ataku and its nearby sister village of Aniko could be ended and that with his grandfather, Chief Gyasi, the chief of Aniko, he could unite the two villages. He strongly believed that uniting the two villages was a precondition to progress. All concerned were convinced that making Letivi chief of the village was the right thing to do, particularly as the grandfathers had communicated to Chief Yofu their support for making Letivi Ataku's chief. The grandfathers believed that having a moon child as chief was in the best interests of the village. It was what their first chief, also a moon child who had sat on the royal stool almost two hundred years ago, wanted. For them, Letivi's ascension to the royal stool had been written in the stars decades ago.

While there was still some grumbling going on among the clan leaders, Chief Letivi announced, "I think this is a good time to close this meeting. I will convene another meeting to discuss the important issue of how to add value to the production of our cocoa plantations. In the meantime, I will pray about all of this and consult with the grandfathers. We will meet again soon. Thank you for your participation."

Just as Chief Letivi finished speaking, Chief Gyasi felt compelled to say something. He rose and said in a loud voice a few closing words: "Our chief has spoken, and I know I can count on all of you to follow our traditions and obey without further comment the decision he has made today."

As the men filed out of the meeting room, they shook the hands of the chiefs, making with each handshake a loud snapping sound as they rubbed their forefingers together. When the head of the oldest and most powerful clan exited the building, he could be overheard by the chiefs telling another clan leader, "Chief Letivi is without a wife or children and thus knows little about the lives we live as we struggle to support our families."

After overhearing these remarks, both chiefs looked each other in the eye. Chief Letivi softly said, "What he said is true. There has never been a chief without a wife and children. Many people wonder about my virility because I do not have children. My wifeless and childless condition undermines my authority as chief. My dear grandfather, I ask that you advise me on what I should do."

Chief Gyasi did not hesitate to speak. "My dear grandson, this is a serious matter. We must find you a wife as quickly as possible and celebrate your marriage. Is there any woman you are interested in?"

Letivi surprised his grandfather by confiding, "Yes, there is one woman I would like to consider, but I must first talk to my mother, your daughter, before revealing the name of this woman. I think you will be pleasantly surprised by my choice of a first wife."

Letivi could not say it, but he also wanted to talk to the trees with whom he had grown up in his mother's off-limits forest retreat. Only he and his mother knew he had mastered tree talk and had become very close to many of the trees growing in and around his mother's botanical domain. The next full moon was approaching, and Letivi would spend the night at the base of the old sacred baobab that had consumed his father, as he always did when the moon was full. At this old tree, he would make offerings and pray and listen for anything this ancient living giant might have to tell him. This huge baobab tree was looked upon as the repository of all knowledge and wisdom, but it rarely communicated with humans.

The last time the old baobab had communicated was a number of years ago, when Letivi's white father, Bobovovi, was returned to the old baobab by the moon god. Letivi saw for the first and last time his aged father on that full-moon night. Bobovovi had been returned to the old baobab, which had taken him away to be joined for a few minutes with his son before dying. The only words the expiring Bobovovi could utter to his son were "I love you." After he said these words, the tree's trunk split open, and Letivi carried his father's body inside the tree to his final resting place. The tree immediately closed after Bobovovi's body was inside its cavernous trunk. Only Letivi and his mother knew that Bobovovi had returned and was buried inside the old baobab.

Letivi's words about knowing a woman he could marry made his grandfather very happy. All he could say was, "I look forward to learning about which village woman you have chosen to be your bride. As you know, you must have a child with this woman to consummate your marriage. I pray that by this time next year, you will be seen as a complete man capable of siring children. When this happens, you will be above all criticism."

Letivi smiled and nodded agreement when his grandfather said these words, but there was one word in what his grandfather said that alarmed him. That word was "village." This troubled him because the woman he was attracted to was not from his village. The possibility that love could not conquer tradition gave him more to worry about.

CHAPTER THREE
GEMINI OR BUST

R obin endured a sleepless night as he contemplated the trip to Gemini and all he would do to discover the truth about JB. He would leave at daybreak the next day and drive straight south along Highway 75 until it crossed Highway 54. He would turn right on Highway 54 and head west until he arrived in Gemini. That should take no longer than a couple of hours. Once he arrived, he would go door-to-door, asking for information about JB. He would not stop his investigation until JB's true identity was revealed.

The high flow of adrenalin running through Robin's veins obscured his vision of the true state of Gemini. It took him a while to free himself from his denial of the truth to see clearly Gemini as it really was. The rusty old sign pointing the direction to Gemini should have signaled to him the ruin he would behold in this small town on the Kansas plains. Gemini was nothing like he had expected. It was more like a ghost town. Most houses were falling apart and abandoned. The tall bluestem grass of the prairie had overgrown most of the town, and the streets were full of weeds and debris. Standing in solemn testament to the death of a once-thriving small town were the rusting remains of two oil refineries.

Robin feared that JB's secret had died with the town. He did not know where to begin. He threaded his way through the streets, looking for any inhabitants. A black-and-white cocker spaniel passed in front of him. In the hope that the dog would lead him to a living soul, he followed it. The dog ran to the front porch of a tiny house that seemed to be tottering on the brink of collapse. Someone opened the door to let the dog inside. Robin's heart beat faster as he drove toward the house and prepared himself to talk with a resident of Gemini.

Robin parked his old Honda sedan and quietly walked up to the front door of this crumbling old Sears house. He lightly knocked on the front door. Immediately the dog started barking loudly. The door opened a crack. A weak, wobbly voice struggled to put forth four words: "What do you want?"

Robin meekly replied in as polite a tone as he could muster, "Sorry for the bother. I'm a journalist, and I want to do a story on JB."

The door slammed shut, and there was only silence. Not even the dog barked. Robin did not know what to think or do. He waited for some time and was preparing to knock again when the door was swung wide open, revealing an old, miniature woman with a hunched back, stooped over a black plastic cane. She wore a black dress that had been popular generations ago. Her long, stringy, white hair fell in haphazard strands around her worn and deeply wrinkled face. Her puckered mouth indicated she was toothless. With her cane in her left hand, she extended her claw-like hand and cackled, "Welcome to my house, or what is left of it. Any friend of JB is a friend of mine. My name is Rebecca. You can call me Granny. Sorry for the delay, but I had to change into better clothes."

Robin shook her bony little hand as he searched for words to say. "Thank you for receiving me. Could I have a few minutes of your time to talk about JB?"

Robin accepted the offer of tea, and the little old lady hobbled her way to the back of the house, leaving him time to look around at his depressing surroundings. He could see everything around him was in disrepair, and there were many dusty, faded mementos of a distant, happier past. The humble sitting room was filled with ruin and neglect. Even the old dog lying at his feet appeared to be on his last legs. This somber environment gave Robin some pause, but it did not dampen his satisfaction over having found a person still in Gemini with whom he could talk about JB.

His whimsical, frail hostess returned, walking clumsily with a tiny porcelain cup of tea in one hand. She placed it on the warped end table next to his chair. She sat down and asked, "Now, young man, what can an old woman like me do for you?"

Robin could not wait to begin. "I'm here to find out all I can about JB. I saw the book that had been published about him at the state book festival in Topeka, and I drove straight to Gemini to discover more about him."

The infirm Rebecca, who looked as if she was over one hundred years old, replied, "I'm sorry to disappoint you, but nobody knows who JB was or what happened to him."

"Surely there must be someone who knows something. Is there anyone else in the town I can ask?"

"No, there is nobody else. I'm almost the last person living in Gemini. Ever since the oil refineries closed, the town started dying. After I go, there will be only a few other people left in

Gemini. I'm only able to stay here because I have a son who brings me groceries from the county seat once a week."

Robin felt like he wanted to cry. In a desperate tone, he pleaded, "What can you tell me about JB? Did you know him?"

As much as her toothless mouth would allow, Granny Rebecca made a little smile, and for a moment, her tiny blue eyes twinkled. "Like everyone else, I would see JB taking his early-morning walk at exactly the same time every day. Nobody could talk to JB because he was in his own world. He lived with his older brother and his wife, but they were discovered long dead in their house shortly after JB's mysterious disappearance. They were buried in the local cemetery."

Robin was scribbling rapidly in his notebook, only stopping to take small sips from his cup of tea. He asked next, "Did the initials JB stand for his real name?"

"No," replied Rebecca. "JB was a nickname given to him by the children who initially called him JB because he had a big pot belly that would shake like jelly with his every step. I guess JB stood for Jelly Belly." Upon saying these words, Rebecca belched up a curious little laugh that sounded more like a hiccup.

Robin was beside himself. It was beginning to look as if finding anything about JB was a dead-end street. The exasperated Robin asked again, "Granny, surely there is something more you can tell me about JB."

The ancient little woman cleared her voice and said, "All I can say are the rumors many were repeating about JB at the time. Some said that he was captured by aliens and then returned to Earth. Others said that he had been in a war and brainwashed by the enemy. A few thought he had been in Africa and lost his bearings there. None of this matters anymore. He was a good person and a great example for all of us, in his own peculiar way."

Robin was lost in thought for a few minutes. He was trying to think of what additional questions he could ask that would yield actionable information about JB. He broke his lengthy pause by saying, "You say his older brother was buried in the town's cemetery. Is there a name on his tombstone?"

Now it was Rebecca's turn to pause before replying. "I think initially his name was not known, but the mayor found his and his wife's names in some old property records kept by the town's deed manager. I believe it was discovered that his first name was Edgar. I can't remember his last name. Maybe it is on his tombstone. I know that he and his wife were found dead in 1984."

The prospect of finding Edgar's last name in the cemetery caused drops of perspiration to dribble down Robin's back. He could not wait to rush off to the cemetery and look for Edgar's grave. He quickly bid farewell to Granny, thanking her for taking the time for him and for the tea. He quickly petted the sleeping dog and rushed out the door to his car. He was in such a hurry that he forgot to ask Granny where the cemetery was. He did a prompt about-face and found unsteady Granny still standing hunched over her cane on her front porch.

Without his saying a word, she advised in a slow but more distinct voice, "If you keep your car headed in the same direction, you will find the cemetery after about a mile at the end of the road. Thank you for the visit. It has been many years since I have had a visitor. I doubt if I will ever have a visitor again, as my end is fast approaching."

Robin waved good-bye and saw something in Granny's eyes that told him she may also be worthy of a story of her own. As the last living resident of the former thriving town of Gemini, her case deserved to be documented. He made a mental note to return someday to do her story. But there was no time for this now. He needed to continue his pursuit of the mystery surrounding JB.

It was slow going to the cemetery because the road was full of potholes. When Robin finally arrived, he found the cemetery in a worse state than the town. Nature had taken over the cemetery, making it difficult to walk around and view the grave markers. Robin feared the day would end before he could locate Edgar's headstone. He moved quickly from stone to stone, looking for one that bore the name of Edgar and his wife. After almost two hours of panic-stricken searching and spooky stepping on old graves, Robin came upon a prominent gray granite headstone with the names of Edgar Peterson and his beloved wife, Gladys.

This was all Robin needed. He now knew that JB was a Peterson, and he was either from Gemini or one of the towns in the area. The next step was to go to the county courthouse in El Dorado and ask for records on any Petersons. Surely Edgar had some living relatives. There had to be some record of his younger brother. He would leave now for El Dorado, and first thing tomorrow morning, he would be making queries at the courthouse.

Robin barely slept a wink at a local motel located on the outskirts of El Dorado. He checked out early and went to a popular family restaurant on Main Street to grab some breakfast. From there, he headed a few blocks south on Central Avenue to the century-old, redbrick Romanesque county courthouse. He parked his car in the first empty space he found and marched up the steps into the grand old historic building. He asked the first person he saw where the county records were kept and was told to go to the county clerk's office on the second floor.

He walked briskly up the creaky old stairs. In front of him was a door with an antique glazed windowpane with a fading decal pasted on it indicating this was the county clerk's office. He slowly turned the shiny brass doorknob and opened the door to see a big open space with a counter at the far end of the barnlike room. The cavernous room was well lighted by sunlight pouring through the huge, curtainless windows that stretched from the floor almost to the high ceiling. Easily visible was a soiled, molded ceiling that had unsightly black stains caused by age and water damage. The dated environs and sparse decor made Robin feel as if he had stepped back in time. In his imagination, he saw generations of people walking on the same hard walnut floors that he was quietly tiptoeing across to see if there was anyone minding the counter.

Robin looked everywhere. He could not see or hear anyone. He leaned over the worn wooden counter as far as he could and looked both ways, but he could not spy the presence of anyone. At the far end of the counter, there was an old brass-plated bell with a button on top, the kind one would see on a motel reception counter. Robin gently tapped the bell, but it did not ring. He then slammed forcibly down on the bell with the open palm of his right hand. He expected to hear a loud ring, but his vigorous action only resulted in a soft, tinny clang. Obviously, the bell had been worn out from decades of use, but its puny sound was enough to incite a voice from somewhere in the back of the many rows of overloaded bookshelves. A high-pitched, screechy voice emanating from behind the mounds of documents simply said, "Coming!"

An elderly, well-kempt woman appeared from behind the stacks and promptly asked with a strong rural Kansas accent, "What can I do fer ya, young man?"

Robin hesitated as he sized up the prim, wiry old woman in front of him, "I'm looking for the records on Gemini, Kansas."

The rod-stiff woman lost no time replying in a steely voice, "Now, that's a tall order. Most of the records were burned when a good part of the town was destroyed by fire in 1986, and the town went belly up shortly thereafter. Any records remaining are stored at the state capital. I don't see how I can help you."

Robin asked in a pleading tone, "Are you sure there is nobody in this whole, big building who can help me?"

The spindly old woman responded in a softer, more sympathetic tone, "Why on earth do you want to see records for Gemini? It is not a town anymore."

Robin quickly blurted out his reasons for searching information about Gemini. The woman was familiar with the story about JB and became tinged with excitement when she learned that Robin was trying to discover who JB really was. She easily understood the link between Edgar Peterson and JB, and how revealing details on that link could lead to learning more about JB and his real name.

"Hmmm, that is interesting," exclaimed the skinny old woman. "There are a lot of Petersons around. Maybe you should start with Molly Peterson, who works in the driver's license office across the hallway. Tell Molly that Grandma Susie in Records sent you."

Robin hurriedly thanked Susie and said he would see Molly immediately. He rushed out the door and across the hall to find a similar cavernous room with a young, attractive, redheaded woman sitting on a high stool in a corner peering out the window at the old Carnegie Library across the side street. The sight of such a beautiful woman smiling at him stopped Robin in his tracks and had him trying to catch his breath and find the right words to say.

Before Robin could state his business, the voluptuous woman rose and said in a sweet, gentle voice, "Good morning. How can I help you?"

Robin cleared his voice and replied in a meek tone, "Grandma Susie from across the hall said I should pose my questions to a Molly Peterson who works in this office."

"Well, you came to the right place, because I am the one and only Molly Peterson."

Molly could not help but smile and giggle softly as she spoke. Robin was very charmed by her and felt immediately some chemistry at work between him and this well-shaped beauty. Her adorable presence made him nervous, but he managed to say, "Nice to meet you. I'm Robin Fletcher. I'm a journalist who is trying to do a story on the legendary JB of Gemini. I have some questions I would like to ask you."

Molly giggled again and smiled widely as she stepped closer to Robin. "Go right ahead and ask me all the questions you want. As you can see, I'm not busy at all."

Robin collected his wits and explained in rapid-fire fashion the chain of events that had brought him to her office. He ended his monologue by politely asking, "You are a Peterson, so I'm wondering if you can help me find a man named Edgar Peterson who died around 1984 in Gemini."

Molly wasted no time responding. "Wow. That is interesting, but what you ask is complicated, as there are hundreds of Petersons living in this part of Kansas. I would not know where to start. For sure, I have never known or heard of any Edgar Peterson. Can you give me an idea of how old Edgar was when he died?"

Robin reflected out loud, "I have no idea how old he was, but he must have been in his sixties."

The wheels were spinning in Molly's head. She really wanted to help Robin solve the JB mystery. "I'm really stumped as to how I can help you. Maybe my uncle can be of some help. He is seventy years old and has lived in this area all his life. Let me call him now."

Molly quickly walked a few steps to the counter and pushed the buttons on the beige-colored phone that looked as if it had been sitting in the same spot for years. Molly talked loudly into the phone, "Uncle, this is your niece Molly. I got a guy here in my office who is asking about an Edgar Peterson. Have you ever known anyone by that name?"

On the other end of the phone line, the old man paused before saying in a broken voice, "I went to high school in Lindsborg with an Edgar Peterson. Could that be the same person you are looking for?"

Smiling at Robin with a thumbs-up, Molly excitedly responded, "Yes, Grandpa, that could be the one. All we know is that he died and was buried in Gemini in 1984. Do you know if he had a younger brother?"

Robin was all smiles and delighted by the information Molly was learning over the phone. His spirits leaped, and he felt like doing a little jig.

It took Molly's uncle a long time to reply as he fought to get his feeble mind to remember things that had happened decades ago, in the 1950s. Finally, he shakily said, "I do recall Egg—we called him Egg—did mention a much younger brother he had been separated from. I can't remember any name. All I can remember is that the family had problems after the parents divorced, and the younger brother was placed in a foster home near Udall, Kansas."

"OK, uncle. That is very helpful. Please call me if you think of anything else. I need to get back to the man in my office. Have a good day. Love you."

Molly gently hung up the phone and gracefully turned to face Robin to tell him all she had learned from her grandpa. She could not contain her own excitement and happiness over helping find some pieces of information that could be the start of a process leading to the revelation of JB's true identity.

Robin was overjoyed. He wanted to depart immediately on the one-hour drive to Udall. Molly shared his desire to continue on his quest, but she also wanted to join him in the search for JB. She surprised Robin by boldly saying, "If you wait until tomorrow, I can go with you to Udall. I think I can be of some help. I have relatives living on a farm near the town. They might be able to tell us something."

Although Robin was in a hurry and had no time to lose, the thought of the vivacious Molly accompanying him to Udall was an offer he could not refuse. In a proper, mannerly way, Robin happily replied, "That is really nice of you. Of course I can wait until tomorrow. Anyway, I need to give my boss in Chicago a call. I'm really pleased that you can accompany me."

Robin continued by indicating the motel he was staying in and asking how they would meet up early the next morning. Molly made Robin's heart throb by proposing, "We should really meet tonight over dinner so we can discuss how we'll proceed once we have arrived in Udall. Can you meet me at Helen's Place on Main Street?"

"Yes, of course. Great idea! I know the place. I ate breakfast there this morning. I will see you there at six," Robin gushed as he walked toward the door. He was thanking his lucky stars. His head was in cloud nine and his feet barely touched the ground. He had not only found information that could lead him to JB's true identity, but one of the most beautiful women he had ever met was joining him in his search for JB. He told himself, "It doesn't get any better than this."

CHAPTER FOUR
LOSING GROUND

Chief Letivi was in a deep slump. He spent most of his days and nights camped out in front of the oldest grandfather's house hoping for some inspiration that would spark some new ideas for leading his people to new heights. The days turned into weeks, and Letivi remained unenlightened and more depressed. He felt as if he were in a dark tunnel searching for a light that would show him a new and better way forward for his village. He was wracking his brain for anything that would help him avoid total despair.

Apparently, the grandfathers were not capable of providing any advice on the challenges Letivi faced in this new age. Letivi felt very alone and abandoned by the other world. He feared he would have to face the challenges before him on his own. After a couple of years of leading his village to higher levels of prosperity, he found himself at a complicated crossroads, not knowing in which direction to turn. He knew that taking a wrong turn at this stage could result in losing ground, making it even harder to achieve long-term progress. Letivi was determined to do all he could to avoid any slippage backward.

He repeatedly examined the village's resources and capacities, looking for new innovations that could move the village further out of poverty to a higher level of self-sustaining development. One thing that was clear was that most of the villagers remained dependent on agriculture for their food and income. Almost all the cash every household generated was from the production and sale of cacao. Local soil and climate conditions were perfect for this cash crop. Everything had been done to improve cacao yields. Improved cacao tree varieties had been introduced, and the expensive, hard-to-obtain fertilizer needed for maximum yields was procured and correctly applied in a timely manner. Yet income derived from the sale of cacao was falling because world prices for cacao were in decline.

Increased competition from new cacao producers such as Malaysia was making it harder for cacao farmers in Africa to compete. Malaysia and other Asian countries had turned large sections of natural tropical forests into huge cacao plantations, achieving economies of scale that made it impossible for small farmers in Africa to compete. Most families in the village culti-vated less than two acres. The largest and most prosperous cacao farmer in the village had about four acres. These small farm sizes paled in comparison with the modern, state-owned, and highly subsidized cacao plantations in Malaysia and other countries, which were measured in hundreds of acres.

All these thoughts came into play in Letivi's head as he strug-gled with how to add value to the village's cacao crop. Alternative crops had been tested, but none were better suited to local con-ditions, nor could they earn more than cacao. Sesame and sun-flower had been tried, but these crops did not do well because of heavy rainfall. Cotton was planted once, but almost the entire harvest was washed away by the rains. The people also found cotton to be too labor intensive and harmful to the soil. People depended on corn and cowpea crops for their food and were always trying to increase the yields of these two crops. They wanted to produce more cowpeas, as there was also a good market for this protein-rich bean, but they were difficult to store without becoming infested by weevils. There were few tradeoffs in the relatively short annual agricultural season, which coincided with rainfall amounting to nearly sixty inches over five months. Also, available labor was not enough to properly cultivate these crops and tend to yam fields as well as oil palm and fruit trees. This labor bottleneck had increasingly become a problem as young people left the village, causing the average age of working farmers to increase every year.

It became obvious to Letivi that the only way to increase income was to process cacao beans into the powder used to make cocoa drink. As things stood now, all cacao beans were exported to Europe for processing. All the cocoa consumed locally was imported from Europe. People often joked that they did not get to enjoy cocoa and the chocolate from the cacao beans they produced until their beans had taken a round trip to Europe. The fact that the chocolate they consumed cost a multiple of the price for which they sold their cacao beans was not lost on the people.

For years, people had thought how wonderful it would be if they could grind and process their cacao beans in their own country so they could enjoy higher profits from the cacao they worked so hard to produce. Chief Letivi had come to the same conclusion after days of agonized thinking. He quickly convened an emergency session of elders and clan leaders. As usual, Letivi was seated in the front on the chief's royal chair, and Chief Gyasi sat next to him. When all were seated, Letivi rose and bluntly said to the dozen hushed men facing him, "Our progress is stymied unless we can add value to our production of cacao, and the only way to do this is to process our cacao at a site near us."

His words were met with immediate applause and cheers. People stood up and sang their praises of this wonderful idea. After a few minutes of jubilation, Chief Gyasi called for quiet and asked all the people to sit down on their benches. Gyasi stood and calmly said, "This is very good to hear and we're all pleased with what our chief has said, but how can we, a poor village, realize such an ambitious project?"

In a worried tone, Chief Letivi said in a muffled voice, "I don't know even where to begin to achieve this project. For sure, we'll need to find a technical expert who can advise us on the best way to proceed. I'm open to any suggestions on where we can obtain the expertise we need to make local cacao processing a reality."

There was a long silence. Nobody had a clue as to where advice on this important subject could be found. After a hushed interlude of over ten minutes, Chief Gyasi came to his feet and in a shaky voice asserted, "I'm afraid we have no choice but to ask for an audience with the president of our country, as this is an issue that concerns more than just our village, but all villages that produce cacao."

Chief Letivi quickly interjected, "Chief Gyasi is right. As much as we do not like to do so, we must see President Rafael Nasungu and ask for his advice and support. I will immediately send word to the president that I would like to meet with him to discuss a matter of great importance. Chief Gyasi will accompany me. In the meantime, I ask all of you to think hard about this matter and give me your ideas on what I should include in our discussion with the president. I will keep you up to date. Thanks for attending this important meeting on such short notice and for all the good work you continue to do to make our village a better place to live."

Chief Gyasi remained behind to discuss with Letivi how they would proceed to arrange a meeting with the president. They determined the best approach was to go to the not-too-distant regional capital, Kpolomo, and inform the provincial governor of their need to have an audience with the president. The governor was a presidential appointee and the top government official in the province. It would be correct protocol to go through him to request an appointment with the president. It was also the best way to ensure that such an appointment would take place in a timely manner, if at all.

Chief Letivi drafted a written message requesting a meeting with the president and carefully sealed it in a brown paper envelope. He gave the envelope to his most trusted palace guard, Askari, and instructed him to deliver it directly to the governor and wait until he had received a reply. Askari quickly began the ten-mile walk to Kpolomo along a little-used trail that led directly uphill to where the governor's office was located. After about eight miles, the trail turned into the old road built during colonial times.

On either side of the road were huge, old kapok trees. While such tree-lined country roads reminded Europeans of the bucolic countryside in their home countries, many Africans found bizarre the planting of trees in such a manner. For them, large trees should never be planted close to roads or buildings in order to avoid damage caused by falling trees. Also, the roots of the trees could undermine the stability of the soil and damage roads and buildings. Big trees along the road provided too much shade, making it harder for roads to stay dry and hard. There was also the problem of who owned the trees and who was allowed to harvest their fruits, leaves, and wood. Trees also harbored snakes and the feared chameleon. These scary creatures could fall from the trees onto people walking under them. The beauty of tree-lined lanes as perceived by the European eye was often beheld as a blemish by Africans.

Upon his arrival in the middle of the afternoon, Askari lost no time in handing the message over to the governor's secretary, who confirmed the presence of the governor. Once he had done that, he sat down stiffly and stared straight ahead at a wall that had been recently whitewashed. He was prepared to wait as long as it would take to receive a reply in spite of the burning thirst and hunger pangs from which he was suffering. He thought it very unkind of the secretary not to show traditional hospitality and offer him water to drink.

After about two hours, the governor broke the silence of the idle surroundings by summoning his secretary, who, in turn, told Askari to enter the governor's large office. Askari's attention was first captivated by the ceiling fan whirling overhead. This was his first time to see such an electric fan. He also marveled at the electric lights, as he had never experienced before the wonders of electricity. The governor noticed how Askari was eyeballing his surroundings as he loudly interrupted the distractions of what he considered a lowly "villager" by shouting at him a few sharp words. "Tell your chief I got his message, and I will pass it on to the president. When I hear from the president, I will inform your chief."

Askari quickly did a slight bow and said thank you, doing a robotic about-face as he rushed from the governor's richly adorned office. For him, the governor in his fancy suit and tie was a "black" replacement for the pre-independence "white" governor. As far as he was concerned, both governors were "foreigners" because neither came from his area or ethnic group. In some ways, he and others preferred the colonial governors, as they saw them as black and thus treated all blacks the same. The new black governors brought by independence based many of their judgments on one's ethnic group, family background, and home origins. The simple and straightforward white justice that treated all the same, wrongly or rightly, had been replaced by a variable justice that judged people more for whom they were connected than the merits of their case or the color of their skin.

The governor's house was built on the highest point of ground near the regional capital. The colonists always sought the cooler air that came with residing at higher altitudes. Also, with higher ground came fewer mosquitoes. The governor's office building and adjoining house were sturdily built vestiges of a distant colonial period. These old buildings had been remodeled, but their basic structure was well adapted to the tropical climate. The high foundation and ceiling, yard-wide adobe walls, and wraparound verandas made for comfortable insulation from the tropical heat. Of course, the colonialists had the advantage of using cheap or forced labor. As well adapted as the old buildings were to the local environs, it would be too costly to try to duplicate such buildings today.

Askari departed feeling that the governor had kept him waiting too long for no good reason and had spoken to him rudely. His tone of voice was impolite, and his manner suggested that he relished speaking harshly to a person of another ethnic group with no rank. The governor belonged to the president's distant northern ethnic group, and he and many others from his group delighted in being able to speak down to members of southern ethnic groups. Much of this delight stemmed from the fact that the southern groups had traditionally looked down on northern groups.

Historically, the southern groups were the first to have contact with whites and receive a Western education. This adoption of Western ways lent itself to the development of an air of superiority on the part of southern groups who liked flaunting their modernity over the perceived backwardness of northerners. The tables were turned on the southern groups when the current president's father took control of the country through a bloody military coup. A troubling uneasiness had existed for many years between these groups, and there persisted an explosive tension under an apparent calm surface of tolerance. The regime had built up over the years a well-armed military force dominated by northern troops to ensure its maintenance in power and suppress any dissidence, actual or perceived.

Askari announced his arrival at Chief Letivi's compound by clapping his hands in a manner that would communicate to all within that it was he and that he had returned with a message for the chief. Letivi heard the clapping. Before anyone else in the compound could react, he said loudly and in an eager tone, "I'm here. Come to me."

The breathless Askari approached his chief, who was sitting on a low bench under the shade of a neem tree. He stood silently at attention about three yards in front of the chief until he was told to deliver his report. Sweat was pouring off Askari's muscular body as words shot quickly from his mouth in a staccato fashion. "I saw the governor, and I gave him your message. He said he would deliver it to the president."

Chief Letivi was hoping for more than these few words. He gently asked Askari, "Is that all you have to say?"

Askari stood bolt straight and said, "Yes, my chief. That is all."

Chief Letivi thanked Askari for his service, wished him and his family well, and dismissed him. At the same time, he called another palace guard and instructed him to go and tell Chief Gyasi that he would like to talk with him.

Later in the day, Chief Gyasi found Letivi taking a nap on a grass mat under the same neem tree. He quietly waited for Letivi to awake. When he saw Letivi begin to stir, he whispered, "I'm here, my grandson and my chief."

Letivi sat up and welcomed his grandfather. He told him about what the returning guard had said and asked for his advice on what they should do next to prepare for their important audience with the president.

Chief Gyasi took his time in replying. After a long pause, he slowly emitted some words. "Yes, we could be called to see President Rafael at any time, so we must rehearse well what we will tell him. As much as he pretends to like us, he is not a man who puts up with any beating around the bush. We must polish the core of our message to him so that he quickly grasps why we believe we have good reason to see him."

Letivi responded without hesitation, "Yes, Grandfather, you are very right. I will first write a script, and we can practice it together, improving it as we repeat it. We need to impress the president at the very onset with our words and the seriousness with which we say them. He must be convinced of the high merits of our case."

Gyasi also noted, "We must carefully plan in advance all the logistics related to our trip to the capital city of Melomti. We'll wear our best traditional chief clothes and hire a nice taxi car to take us safely and without incident the one hundred miles to the capital. Most of the highway to the capital has now been blacktopped, so we should be able to make the trip in less than two hours. We should arrive the day before so we are sure to be there and rested before our appointment with the president. We must also take a gift to the president. We must budget for everything accordingly."

The more they discussed their meeting with the president, the more they worried about this momentous encounter with the supreme power of the country. They knew very well that much of the future of their village depended on the outcome of their meeting. If the president reacted poorly to what they proposed, the future of their village would indeed be bleak. If he reacted positively, there would be much work to do, but they would have hope for a better future. It was sad, but true, that the future of their village was held in the cruel hands of a poorly educated northerner who ruled their country with an iron grip.

CHAPTER FIVE
DISCOVERING DAVID

Molly pounded hard on the door of Robin's dingy motel room, hollering at the top of her voice, "Robin, wake up! It's Molly. It's time to go."

This racket interrupted the strange dream Robin was having in the quiet of this modest motel located just outside the El Dorado city limits. He was far away in a strange dreamland populated by black people and huge trees. Robin was in such a deep sleep that he did not hear his alarm clock. Molly's insistent knocking finally stirred him. In an instant, he was rudely awakened with the realization of the tasks he had to undertake today. He awkwardly yelled, "Molly, I'm coming. Give me a few minutes."

Robin moved as fast as he could. At first, he was going to quickly throw on his clothes and splash water on his face, but he slowed down a bit because he had to look halfway decent for Molly. He washed under his arms, wet his hair, and made sure it was combed nicely. He brushed his teeth vigorously and put on a clean shirt. He was about to take one more look at himself in the bathroom mirror when Molly started knocking on the door again, crying out, "Robin, what is the matter? Are you coming?"

Before Molly could finish her second barrage of knocks, a disheveled Robin opened the door, smiling sheepishly at Molly and saying, "Good morning. Sorry I'm late. Somehow, I overslept."

Robin was going to say more, but his breath was taken away by Molly's stunning beauty. The early-morning sunlight cast an angelic glow around Molly, who was dressed in tight jeans and an even tighter red sweater, revealing amply her well-formed cleavage. Robin knew that Molly was pretty, but the spectacular beauty his eyes beheld at this instant staggered him. He was speechless.

"Robin, what is the matter? Are you awake yet? Come on. Let's go." Molly could see that Robin was acting strangely, as if in some sort of trance.

"Molly, I'm sorry. I'm still trying to recover from a very odd but vivid dream I had. Yes, let's get going. Today, the Lord willing, we will discover what happened to David."

"First, let's have a big breakfast at Helen's place, as we agreed to do yesterday. We can talk about David over breakfast. Where's your car?"

Robin limply replied, "My car is right here in front of us." He was telling himself he should have cleaned his car and tidied up the stacks of books and papers inside it. He hoped that Molly would not get the wrong impression of him because his car was such a mess. He was thinking he should open the car door for Molly, but before he could do that, she got into the car on her own. Robin quickly got into the car on the driver's side.

"I can see that it has been a while since you cleaned your car," Molly said while emitting a hushed chuckle.

She could sense Robin's discomfort, so she tried to reassure him by giving him a big smile and saying sweetly, "You know I'm just teasing you. Just take it easy, and let's try to have some fun while we search for David."

Robin was surprised that Helen's diner was crowded at 6:30 a.m. Molly led the way through the busy restaurant, greeting people as she went by, simply introducing Robin as a visiting journalist from Chicago. Robin could see all the men eyeing Molly as she walked by. They found an empty table at the back of the crowded restaurant. Molly quickly told the teenage waitress that she would have her usual. When the spaced-out Robin was asked what he wanted, all he could manage to say was, "The same."

The acne-faced waitress laughed because she knew he did not know what he was ordering. She replied with a snicker, "You betcha."

Robin was surprised when he saw what food the waitress served. "The same" turned out to be French toast, which was his favorite breakfast. He was happy that both he and Molly had in common a liking of French toast. He grinned widely. "Molly, you know French toast is exactly what I wanted. I love it."

Molly beamed. "That's nice. I love French toast too. Now, let's get down to business. How do we go about our search for David in Udall?"

Robin took a big bite of French toast, which he had covered with butter and drenched in maple syrup, gulped, took a sip of coffee, and said, "I think we should go to the high school first and try to see if any David Peterson ever went to school there. If David was about ten years younger than his brother Edgar, he should have graduated from high school in the early 1960s. I suggest we look at school records, yearbooks, or something starting in 1960 and see what we find. What do you think?"

In his mind, Robin finished his sentence with "beautiful." He was working hard to act normal and not show any signs that he was involuntarily smitten by Molly and overcome by the chemistry he felt going on between them.

While Robin was trying to keep his cool, Molly easily replied, "Your plan sounds good to me. Let's finish up quickly here and hit the road. I can't wait. I'm so excited."

Robin paid the bill, leaving a good tip. Molly greeted some more people while he held the door open. As they went out the door and headed for the car, Molly said, "The people I just saw told me the best way to go to Udall is to go south to Augusta and take Highway 77 until we hit the County Road 15 turnoff, which goes directly to Udall. The whole trip is not more than seventy miles and should take us about an hour and a half. Let's get on the road."

Robin was eager to get to Udall, but he drove more slowly than usual. He wanted to be extra careful because of his gorgeous passenger. He was also distracted by every little move Molly made. He had a hard time not peering out of the corners of his eyes at her well-presented cleavage. Molly caught him sometimes glancing at her, and she smiled as if to acknowledge his admiration and to communicate that what he was doing was acceptable.

Time zipped by for Robin. Ninety minutes with Molly seemed like only a few minutes. They both jabbered nervously away, talking about their childhoods in different parts of Kansas. Robin was from a farm near Garden City in western Kansas, and Molly had spent her childhood in Lindsborg before moving to El Dorado. They were both happy to get to know each other better. They were so lost in the moment that Robin almost missed the turnoff to Udall.

Molly then pulled something from her purse that Robin had never seen before. Robin asked, "What is that gizmo?"

Molly laughingly said, "What is wrong with you? Have you never seen a mobile phone? My uncle works at AT&T, a company that is introducing cell phones, and he wanted me to be among the first to have this phone made by Motorola. I'm going to pull out the antenna and call my relatives who live in this area to ask them if they have heard of a David Peterson."

While Molly spoke to her relatives on her mobile phone, Robin marveled at this jewel of the latest technology. Molly finished her phone conversation, folded up her cell phone, and said, "No help there. Let's not lose time by visiting with my distant relatives."

It was about ten in the morning when they rolled slowly into Udall. They drove past a big billboard that welcomed them to "Udall - America's Safest City." Molly explained that Udall was called the "safest city" because after it was totally destroyed in 1955 by one of the deadliest tornadoes ever recorded, storm shelters were constructed everywhere when the town was rebuilt. Molly continued by saying in a most serious tone, "People here are still scared, and many sleep in their storm shelters during the May-to-June tornado season. There is not a single family who did not lose loved ones in that 1955 tornado, which killed 20 percent of the population and injured many more." Saying these words almost brought tears to Molly's eyes. She was also scared of tornadoes.

Robin was affected by Molly's emotion and, accordingly, tried to change the subject. He said, "Udall is a strange name for a town. How did it get this name?"

Molly brightened up and laughed as she replied, "Now, that is a controversial subject. My relatives tell me that the founders of the town named it at after an obscure English author, Cornelius Udall, but nobody can find any record of such a person. Other people say that the town is named after a cantankerous mule owned by one of the first settlers. They say the mule's name was Doll, and its owner would often argue with this stubborn mule, saying 'You, Doll.' The repeated saying of these words was transformed into Udall. Who really knows?"

A bemused Robin laughed and responded, "That is a funny story. Sounds like it was harder to find Cornelius than it has been for us to find David."

As the town was very small, fewer than eight hundred people, it was easy to find the high school at the end of a wide gravel road. They quietly parked their car in front of the school and entered through its main entrance. Before entering, they were confused by a sign that indicated this was the Udall middle school and high school. In spite of this double school denomination, they walked toward the school's main office to inquire about where they could find the names of those who graduated in the 1960s.

As soon as they entered the reception area, they were loudly greeted by a bespectacled middle-aged woman who acted as if she was overjoyed to have visitors. She immediately and loudly introduced herself. "Hello, I'm Marjorie Mayfield. Welcome to Udall's Middle and High Schools. How can I help you?"

Robin responded hesitantly, "Thank you. Actually, we were looking for the high school. Is it here?"

Marjorie gingerly replied, "I'm sorry for the confusion. In 1971, the middle school moved to join the high school in this same building. The middle school is in the east end of the building and the high school in the west end."

Molly interjected softly, "Oh, this is all news for us. What we are interested in is looking at anything that tells us who graduated from Udall High School in the early 1960s. Any suggestions on how we can do that? "

"Hmmm…That may be something of a challenge, as I'm not sure the records for those years are still kept at the school. We do keep here in our library the yearbooks for every graduating class. You are welcome to look at those."

Upon hearing about the yearbooks, Robin was ready to run to the library. But Molly gently held him back. She thanked Marjorie and asked, "How can we have access to the yearbooks? It would really be nice for us to look at them now, as we have driven all the way from El Dorado."

Sympathetically, Marjorie replied, "My dear, please don't worry your pretty self. You are welcome to go to our library now and look at all the yearbooks we have on our shelves. Let me escort you there and tell the librarian why you are here. This is a good time, as our students are busy elsewhere and our library is not being used."

Marjorie led the way out the door and down the wide hall to a door that was clearly marked 'Library.' She opened the door wide and politely asked Molly and Robin to enter. At the same time, she called out loudly, "Mable, are you there? We have some visitors who came all the way from El Dorado to see the year-books you have."

The very rotund and short Mable appeared from behind the far end of the book stacks and walked quickly up to Molly and Robin and greeted them energetically. Mable was bubbling with good humor and excitement as she welcomed Molly and Robin. "We don't get many visitors here. You are very much welcome. Why don't you take a seat at that table near the window? Which yearbooks would you like to see?"

Robin lost no time in blurting out, "To begin with, we would like to see all the yearbooks for the 1960s."

Marjorie simply said, "All righty. I'll be right back."

Molly and Robin thanked Marjorie, who said she had to return to her office. No sooner had they sat down than Mable returned carrying an armful of yearbooks. Robin immediately took them from her. After a quick thank-you, he gave half the books to Molly and took the other half for himself and breathlessly said, "Let's get going. I hope we find a David Peterson among the members of the graduating classes in these yearbooks."

A very nervous and agitated Robin flipped through the year-book pages as fast as he could manage, analyzing rapidly the names listed for every senior class. Molly remained relaxed and slowly leafed through the pages as if she were enjoying seeing the photos and reading the snippets about students who graduated many years ago. After some minutes, Molly exclaimed, "Robin, I think I got what you are looking for. It says right here, 'David Peterson, valedictorian of the class of 1963.'"

Robin let out a very loud "Whoopee." He quickly snatched the yearbook from Molly's hands and saw what she was talking about. He was beaming when he turned to Molly and said, "If this were not a school, I'd give you a big hug right now. You did it. You found David!"

Molly was feeling very good about herself when Mable came running to see what all the commotion was about. Robin wasted no time telling Mable, "We found him. We've found David Peterson."

Mable did not understand what all the celebrating was about, but she promptly said, "Well, that sounds like a good thing. I'm happy for the both of you."

Molly contained her happiness, sitting calmly in a nonplussed manner and asking herself whether or not they had indeed found David. She finally said in a polite, ladylike manner, "Robin, please settle down. What we have discovered is that a David Peterson graduated from Udall Rural High School in 1963. That tells us very little about him or what he did after high school. We still don't know what happened to David."

With the wind knocked gently out of his sails, Robin let out a big sigh, sat down, and told Molly, "You are right. We now need to find someone who knew David and can tell us what he did after high school."

They returned the yearbooks to the counter, where Mable was standing. Robin, in a soft voice, asked Mable, "Is there anyone around who can tell us about a student who graduated at the top of his class in 1963?"

Mable hesitated before replying, "That was twenty-seven years ago, and I don't know anyone who is still around who can recall people from such a long time ago. I have been working here ten years and have lived in the area all my life, but I have never heard of a David Peterson."

Mable's words had Molly and Robin worrying again that they would never find out what had happened to David. Robin could not accept that there was no way to find out where David went after graduating from high school. He pleaded, "Please, Mable, think hard. There must be somebody around who can remember students from 1963."

Suddenly a light went on in Mable's head. "Mr. Rankin might know. He is in his nineties and often incoherent, but sometimes he is clear as a bell about many things that happened in the distant past. He taught math at this school for over forty years, and he lives nearby. He is the only person still around who might be able to help you. I hope you find him on one of his good days."

The anxious and naturally nervous Robin was ready to race out of the school, but Molly grabbed his shirt sleeve and said,

"Can you wait a minute? We need to know where Rankin's house is located. Mable, please tell us how to find Rankin's house."

"That's easy. Just go straight back the way you came on the road leading from the school. It will be the third house on your right. If he is having a good day, Mr. Rankin will be sitting in front of his small white house in his rocking chair. If his day is really good, he will be wearing his old felt hat. He loves to receive visitors, so I'm sure he will like talking with you. Good luck, you two."

Molly and Robin quickly thanked Mable, saying good-bye as they rushed out of the library and down the school hall to the exit. Molly poked her head into Marjorie's office to thank her and say good-bye, but she was not there. Robin went ahead to turn his car around so that when Molly got into the car, he could speed the couple hundred yards to Mr. Rankin's house. Molly was giddy with excitement as she told Robin, as if giving him an order, "Let's go. I pray that we find him sitting in his rocking chair. This is a nice day, so he should be there."

Within minutes, they happily found themselves in front of a little house with a very old man sitting in a rocking chair and wearing oversized dark-brown wool felt fedora from the 1940s that hid most of his head. Robin and Molly were thanking their lucky stars for the fact that this must be one of the elderly Mr. Rankin's good days. They slowly walked across the weedy lawn. When they were within a few feet of Mr. Rankin, Robin cleared his throat loudly to make their presence known.

There was no sign of life from Mr. Rankin, so Robin cleared his throat a couple more times. Robin and Molly were beginning to think that their only hope in discovering David may already be dead. They were just about to get closer to Mr. Rankin when they heard a raspy, almost gasping, voice utter, "I hear you. I'm not dead yet, but I might as well be. Come in front of me so I can see you."

Molly and Robin took a few steps so they were directly in front of the skeletal and very weak old man. Mr. Rankin raised his head. He resembled an ancient tortoise protruding its head from its shell. He looked back and forth with his beady but weak eyes, examining Molly and Robin from top to bottom before struggling to say in an unstable voice, "Do I know you? Did I teach you?"

Molly glanced quickly at Robin in a way that conveyed she was the one who should respond first to Mr. Rankin. "Dear sir, it is very nice to see you. No, we did not have the pleasure of being your students. We are here because we were told you might be able to help us find one of your former students. We hope you can tell us something about David Peterson, who graduated in 1963."

A small smile appeared on Mr. Rankin's chunky lips, and his eyes seemed to brighten. He took his time to formulate a creaky reply. "I'm very happy to talk about David. He was the best student I ever had. He made straight A's, but he really deserved more, as he was so far ahead of all his classmates. He was also an outstanding athlete and a role model for all. I have wondered for years about what happened to him. I have not seen him since congratulating him on his superb valedictory speech. It would be nice if you could tell me something about David."

Speaking so many words appeared to exhaust Mr. Rankin. Molly and Robin were afraid he would tire out before they learned want they wanted to know.

Robin spoke next, as calmly and sparingly as he could. "Mr. Rankin, sir, we need to know where David went after high school. Can you tell us that?"

Mr. Rankin's reply surprised them as he cheerily asserted, "The butterfly of happiness cannot be chased and caught. You have to sit still, and it will land on your shoulder." Saying these words seemed to make Mr. Rankin very happy, but they made no sense to Molly and Robin.

Molly and Robin gave each other worried looks. They thought Mr. Rankin was drifting off into some dream world. Mr. Rankin had them both smiling again when he said, "Don't worry. I was just repeating the main theme of David's valedictory speech. I and many others who were there that night for his speech remember these words. I'm sure that wherever David is, a butterfly is sitting on his shoulder. He was wise beyond his years. Everyone liked David. I wish I could see him again."

"My dear sir, we would love to tell the world about David. That is why we are searching for information about him. To do that, we need to know where he went after high school," explained Molly with genuine passion.

Mr. Rankin skipped clearing his throat this time and clearly said, "That is easy to remember. He won a scholarship to go to Wichita State University (WSU) and left for the big city early in the morning in his old, green 1953 Mercury Monterey sedan. He had packed his car the day before, so he was all ready to go to Wichita early the next day. I heard he had already lined up a live-in job there in a mortuary. As far as I know, he has never been back."

Knowing where David went after high school was exciting news for Molly and Robin. They would have hugged Mr. Rankin if he were not so old and fragile. Almost in unison, they both blurted out, "Thank you, Mr. Rankin."

Molly continued by saying, "That is exactly what we needed to know to continue seeking what happened to David. Maybe we should also go and see the people David stayed with. They might have more information on David and what he did after high school."

Mr. Rankin made a moaning noise, as if he was in some sort of pain. Molly and Robin did not know how to interpret this noise. After a brief pause, Mr. Rankin licked his lips and began talking as if he were on his last breath. "No. Those people have died, and even before that, they stopped taking in juvenile delinquents for the state. David was the only decent boy they ever kept. He did not deserve living on that crummy little farm about four miles out of town."

Molly and Robin looked at each other in a way that indicated they had all the information they needed from Mr. Rankin. Molly spoke softly. "Mr. Rankin, thank you so much for talking to us about David. We will go next to WSU to see what more information we can find about David there. Our talk with you has been really helpful."

Molly and Robin were saying their good-byes to Mr. Rankin, who seemed thoroughly exhausted, when he asked in his hesitant, weak voice, "Can you please help me up and into my house?"

The more polite and diplomatic Molly immediately replied, "Of course, sir. It would be our pleasure."

Molly and Robin carefully helped Mr. Rankin out of his rocking chair and handed him his simple wooden cane. They helped steady him as he hobbled the six feet to his front door. Robin opened the door for him, and a silent Mr. Rankin disappeared into the darkness of his modest house. It was clear that his talk with Molly and Robin had drained him of the little energy he possessed at the ripe old age of ninety-two.

As Mr. Rankin disappeared into the darkness of his house, Molly and Robin walked back to their car in high spirits. Robin was all set to drive directly to Wichita, which was about thirty-five miles away, but Molly thought otherwise. After they entered the car, Molly looked straight at Robin and shared with him her logical thinking. "Robin, it is too late in the day to continue our search in Wichita. We have made much progress today. I know you are in a hurry, but I need to get back to El Dorado before dark; otherwise, my family will worry."

It was against Robin's nature to put off what he could do today until tomorrow; thus, he was about to object when Molly placed her hand on his and said to him in the sweetest tone, "Please, Robin. Let's head back to El Dorado now and strike out early tomorrow morning for Wichita."

Robin melted like soft butter on a hot plate and buried his natural urges, saying, "Of course, you are right. We'll need to hit Wichita early in the day. Anyway, I need to call my boss in Chicago and bring him up to date on how I have been spending my time. I only have a few more days before I have to return to my job in Chicago."

Molly smiled at Robin, suppressing an urge to kiss him on the cheek, saying only, "Good. Let's go and grab a hamburger at the takeout place I saw coming into town and eat while we drive back to El Dorado."

Molly and Robin ate their food while they had an enjoyable conversation that mainly involved getting to know each other much better. Robin was amazed at how fast time passed when he was with Molly. They were back at his motel in no time at all. They agreed to meet at the same time they had today and drive the thirty miles south to Wichita, going directly to WSU.

They were both exhausted from all they had done today, but their adrenalin levels were running high in anticipation of what they would discover in Wichita tomorrow. Robin walked with

Molly to her car. He said, "Good-bye. See you tomorrow at dawn's first light. Thanks for accompanying me and all your help."

Robin expected Molly to say something in return, but she remained silent as she stepped toward Robin and kissed him on the cheek. This surprise kiss put Robin in seventh heaven and sent him floating back to his room. As much as he tried to keep his mind on the quest for David and calling his boss, all he could think of was Molly and what her kiss meant.

CHAPTER SIX
NEW WORLD VS. OLD WORLD

Chief Letivi was in agony. He was a nervous wreck. The stress caused by the long wait for word from the president was tearing him apart. He had trouble sleeping and eating. He had lost much weight and was physically weak. The meeting he had requested to seek the aid of the president to establish a cacao-processing plant was of paramount importance to his village. He fretted repeatedly over every aspect of the meeting. He revised and practiced countless times with Chief Gyasi the script he had prepared. The stakes were high. Everything had to be perfect. The future of the village depended on gaining the approval and support of the president.

Two months had now elapsed since his request to meet the president had been transmitted. People were worrying about the health of their chief. He seldom left his compound and slept most nights on a grass mat in front of the eldest grandfather's house. He had neglected his usual fastidious personal hygiene.

His reddish-brown hair and beard had grown to lengths that nobody had observed before. His finger and toenails were too long, dirty, and jagged. He looked terrible.

The women in his compound frequently left shaving supplies for him near the neem tree where he usually shaved his face and head. These supplies consisted of two small bowls of water, a bar of imported soap, a mirror, a small towel, and a Bic razor stick. Normally, Letivi would shave his face and head once a week. He would apply the foamy soap to his head and face. He would then hang a little round mirror from a nail that had been driven into the tree's trunk, just at the right height. He would carefully shave his head and then his face. He would use the remaining water to rinse off any soap residue. After patting dry his head and face with a small towel, he would pour a few drops of cheap cologne into the palm of one hand and rub his hands together. He would then vigorously wipe his hands over his face and head. He liked the brief burning sensation the cologne caused.

Chief Letivi was very sensitive about his "whiteness," particularly as he was the chief of a village of about three thousand black inhabitants. Furthermore, he was the only half-caste person in his country to ever become chief. He did all he could to blend in and reduce the racial gap between him and his subjects. One way he did this was to keep his head shaven like the other men in the village. Letivi was the only person in the village who could grow long hair, but he did not do so because it would set him apart from all others in the village. He was also careful to keep the stubble on his face from growing too long. He did not want people to see that he had a color of facial hair that nobody else had. He would also strip down and take regular sunbaths in order to keep his skin complexion as dark as possible. He was happy that he had about the same short stature as most men in his village. He did his best to blend into the society in which he was born.

The compound women noticed Letivi's ragged nails when they brought him food and water. They were very disturbed about him not bathing often enough. They were upset because he often let the food they brought him go untouched. Many times the senior woman in the compound would approach Letivi respectfully and tell him softly that the man who cut fingernails and toenails was at the front gate. She would ask in a polite voice, "Should the nail-cutting man come to you?"

Most of the time, Letivi was lost in thought and only raised his right arm to make a motion that signaled the woman to go away. Previously, Letivi would have the nail-cutting man give him a manicure and pedicure once a week. When people saw this man leaving the chief's compound without having entered it, they knew their chief continued to worry over his all-important visit with the president. They were trying to be patient, but they were concerned that their chief was letting his health deteriorate too much. They knew Chief Gyasi, who visited Letivi almost every day, would inform them of anything really amiss about their chief. Many wished that their chief had a wife who could take care of him. This was another example of how awkward it was for people in the village to have a chief who was not married and childless.

The days and weeks passed, and Chief Letivi's pitiful situation remained unchanged. Chief Gyasi did not say so, but even he was worried about Letivi's weakened condition. Chief Gyasi was about to intervene more energetically to improve Letivi's condition when a messenger arrived with some words from his daughter, Atibona, who was Letivi's mother. Atibona was never seen by anyone. She was obliged to remain in her hidden forest enclave and serve her role as keeper of plants and trees and all their secrets. The village depended upon her for the production of their traditional medicines.

The verbal message was a simple one. Atibona had sent word that she wanted to see her son immediately. Chief Letivi usually visited his mother once a month, just after spending the night under a full moon at the ancient baobab tree. In this way, he could tell his mom if the baobab had any more to say about his father, Bobovovi, who had been buried over a year ago inside this giant tree. Letivi was also one of the few people welcome in Atibona's secluded forest domain. He cherished the memories of early years of his childhood that he had spent with his mother in this magical spot.

When Chief Gyasi told Letivi what his mother had said, Letivi thought for a moment and rose from his grass mat and called for the women to bring his shaving kit and ask the nail-cutting man to come. Letivi knew he could not see his mother the way he looked. He also could not be seen like this by any of the villagers. He grabbed a nearby towel and headed to his shower stall to take a long, overdue bath. The only words he muttered to Chief Gyasi were, "I will leave just before nightfall to go see my mother. I will return early in the morning. She would not ask me to come if it were not important."

There was some jubilation in the village as people heard their chief was up and about and making himself clean and neat, as was his usual habit. After eating his food and dressing himself in some clean clothes that his mother would appreciate, Letivi informed the senior woman in his compound that he would be spending the night with his mother. The senior woman did not need to know more. She knew who his real mother was. She and everyone in the compound were happy to see the chief up and on his way to see his mother.

While there was still some daylight left, Letivi took a rarely used path that passed behind the village. He wanted to avoid being seen and delayed by any need to engage in lengthy traditional greetings. He walked at a brisk pace, eager to join his mother just before it became too dark. It took him almost an hour to reach his mother's compound, which was located deep in a place where the virgin forest still existed. It was a place where thick forest cover made the night fall more quickly than anywhere else.

He was surprised not to hear the jabbering of the trees as he approached the compound. In the past, the trees would always become excited about his arrival and make a clamor to which he would respond by saying, "Yes, your Letivi has returned and is happy to be among you again."

Letivi had mastered "tree language" during the first few years of his life. He had been born in this compound, leaving when he was five years old to go to school in the capital city. This time was different. Letivi was eager to engage in his usual banter with the trees, but they were all silent. This made Letivi fear that something very bad had happened. He entered his mother's compound with some trepidation, calling out, "Mother. Your Letivi is here."

Atibona replied in a weak, sickly voice, "Letivi, my son, thank God you have come. I'm here next to the big iroko tree."

Letivi could barely hear Atibona, but the little he did hear was enough to guide his steps toward the base of the old iroko tree that dominated his mother's compound. He found his mother reclined on a thick grass mat next to the tree. He was astounded by her aged appearance. She looked as if she had aged ten years in only a couple of months. Her hair had turned white, and her face was a wad of wrinkles. He was not sure that the person lying in front of him was his mother.

Atibona could see on her son's face his surprise at the way she looked. She sat up and said, "My son, please wipe that expression of surprise off your face. It is your mother. I've wanted to talk to you about what has been happening to me for some time. Where have you been?"

Letivi knelt down so that he was eye level with his mother. "Mother, I am very sorry I have not visited you for some time, but I have been very distraught by my long wait for the president to respond to my request for a meeting with him."

Letivi wanted to embrace his mother as he usually did when they met, but this time, the way she looked gave him some pause. Atibona admonished Letivi, "Who is more important, me or the president? Now, come and give your rapidly aging mother a big hug."

Letivi reached out and held his mother close to him for a long time, whispering softly, "I am sorry, mother. I promise never to fail again to visit you as I did in the past after each full moon night."

After speaking those words, Letivi began to hear some muffled tree voices. This prompted him to exclaim, "Mother, I am now hearing the trees speak. I was surprised they did not greet me as usual upon my arrival."

"My son, the trees were feeling my emotions and were also upset with you for the long time you had been away. Now that they feel me brightening up, they too are ready to start talking with you again."

"Mother, what has happened to you? Tell me everything."

"Before I start, please fetch and light a kerosene lantern and bring it here so we can see each other in this dark place."

Letivi did as his mother asked and returned to sit next to her, prepared to talk all night, if necessary. "Mother, let's talk now. We have a lot of catching up to do. And, please, all you trees wait until morning to say anything to me. Anyway, it is night, and trees are supposed to be quiet while the sun does not shine."

Atibona began by saying in a hesitant manner, "My dear son, as you can see, I've aged considerably since the last time you saw me. I can now see that my unknown destiny is calling me much faster than I anticipated. It's evident that I'm not as strong as my ancient predecessor, Mama Atiwona."

Letivi became alarmed and with a high sense of urgency in his voice said, "Mother, what are you saying? You are scaring me! Just tell me in plain language what is happening to you."

"OK, my son. Here you have it as plain as I can make it. I'm slowly dying, and I don't believe I will live much longer."

When his mother said these words, tears swelled up in Letivi's eyes as he remonstrated, "Mother, how is this possible? You are not yet old."

"I don't know, my son. This job has taken a heavy toll on me. I feel as if I am changing into something else and the whole world is moving ahead more quickly in ways that we did not expect. I am not sure, but I feel much of the old world of our ancestors is giving way to a new and different world."

His mother's shocking words added to Letivi's already large load of worries. He could not believe what she was saying. It was as if his entire world was being turned upside down. He did not know what to say. The only words he could utter were, "Mother, your words shock me. Is there nothing I can do to make what you say otherwise?"

"No, my son, destiny cannot be changed. All was decided long ago by the grandfathers and the spirits. All we can do is make the best of what they have decided for this world."

"Please, Mother, tell me what I need to do to prepare myself for what is coming."

"My son, there is no turning back time, and there is no way we can be fully prepared for what may come our way in the future. All I know is that my time on this Earth is much shorter than I thought. I need to tell you what to do in the event of my death."

"Mother, you are not dying," Letivi firmly stated in a louder tone.

"Please calm down, son. For sure, I don't want to die, but I'm concerned that the rapid way I'm aging means my days are numbered. I want to tell you something now so that when the day comes, you will know what to do and what may happen."

"OK, Mother. Please go ahead and make me understand what I should do."

"First, if I die without a replacement, this place will die with me and the trees will stop talking. It is therefore most urgent that we find a replacement for me. It must be a woman. Given your knowledge of my work, it is unfortunate that you do not have a girl child to replace me. I fear that my death will mean the end of this place and all it has represented for generations to our people."

These were very heavy words for Letivi. He had no idea of what to say. He could not think of a single woman who would be a good candidate to replace his mother and the invaluable role she played. He wished he had a girl child of his own to give her. This wish prompted him to blurt out, "Mother, I will get married as soon as I can so my wife can have a girl child we can offer to replace you. I just hope you can hold on until this child is ready to join you. I will ask your father, Chief Gyasi, to select a village girl for me to marry. This will be good because people are complaining that I'm not married and I don't have any children."

Letivi's words made Atibona laugh. Letivi was surprised by his mother's laugh, but he was happy to see her in better spirits. The trees could also not resist, laughing with Atibona. After a few more giggles, Atibona cleared her throat and said, "Son, it is good and proper that you get married. The people are right. Their chief should be married and with children. If you have a girl child who can replace me, that is good. If you don't, it is because destiny has other plans."

There was a long pause in their conversation as they both lay down and looked up through the tree branches at the wondrous starlit night. Atibona turned on her side to look at her son and with a grin on her heavily wrinkled face said, "Son, you know how much I love you. I want you to have love in your life too. If you do not have love in your heart for the village girl you have to marry because of your position, you can always marry the woman you love later."

Now it was Letivi's turn to laugh, and when he laughed, his mother started laughing, and, in turn, all the trees joined in this hearty spell of laugher. All felt much better after laughing so much. This laughter was the tonic they needed to drift off into a deep sleep. Letivi thought he had only dozed for a few minutes when he was aroused by the booming voice of the old iroko tree he was sleeping under. "Wake up. Daylight has escaped the night."

Letivi threw off the cloth his mother had covered him with during the night and sprang up quickly. His mother was already up and about and heating a kettle of tea over a small campfire. When she saw her son standing near her, she poured him a large tin cup of tea, saying as she handed it to him, "Here, drink this special brew of mine. It will give you the energy you need for the walk back to the village."

Letivi grasped the cup in both hands and took a big sip. "Hey. This tastes good. What is it?"

Atibona's smile shined through her heavily wrinkled face as she said, "That is my secret. You should know better than to ask."

After Letivi had finishing drinking, Atibona handed him a damp towel to wipe off his face and told him, "Please do not tell my father or mother about anything we talked about. Don't even tell them how I look. Tell them I'm fine and that I summoned you only because I was missing you."

"I will do as you ask, my dear mother. And I promise to return soon. Next time, I will arrive earlier in the day so I can talk to my many tree friends. I must return now to the village to take care of important business."

"I know, my son. I, and all the trees and plants, wish you a safe return to the village. We hope to see you again very soon. And next time I will tell you what to do if no replacement can be found for me."

"Good-bye, Mother. I love you." With those brief but emotion-laden words, Letivi turned and began his fast-paced walk on the same path he had followed the day before. As the return was on a gradual downhill trajectory, it took him less time to reach the village. When he arrived in his compound, he found Chief Gyasi waiting for him in a lounge chair under the big neem tree.

Before Letivi could offer the usual morning greetings and tell him about his daughter, Chief Gyasi could not control himself and stood abruptly up and said outright, "We have our meeting with the president the day after tomorrow."

This long-awaited news trumped anything Letivi had on his mind to say. Both men looked intensely at each other before shaking hands firmly and shouting their praises to the gods and grandfathers. This was indeed something worth celebrating.

Letivi immediately called one of his guards and told him to inform the village messengers so they could fan out in the village and tell everyone about this great news.

Chief Gyasi could not know that Letivi was struggling with juggling how they would handle their meeting with the president as well as how he could help save his dying mother and the important part of the old world she served. Letivi's mind was overloaded with thoughts of his heavy responsibilities and of how to determine what he should do first. He could not help but decide that his first allegiance was to the future of the village, and this meant focusing on his visit with the president. Taking care of the old world would have to take a backseat while he was trying to make a better new world for his people.

CHAPTER SEVEN
WICHITA

This time Robin wanted to play a trick on Molly. He woke up early and got ready to go well before Molly's arrival. He left his motel room door slightly ajar and hid behind it. Molly arrived just after sunrise and rushed to Robin's door, prepared to knock loudly on it just as she had done the day before. She was thinking that Robin probably had overslept again. She was about to bang on the door when she noticed it was slightly open. This unexpected observation prompted her to call out quietly, "Robin. Good morning. It's Molly. Are you ready to go?"

Molly's words were met with silence. She paused for a couple minutes and then gently pushed the door open with the extended index finger of her right hand. The door swung fully open without making a sound. Molly could see that Robin's bed had been slept in, but Robin was nowhere in sight. She turned around and looked up and down the motel veranda and across the parking lot, but she could not see any sign of Robin. His car was parked directly in front of his room, but he was nowhere to be seen. Molly was deeply puzzled and a little afraid that some-thing had happened to Robin. She turned and stepped into the room to take a better look. She took a couple of steps inside the room and then was greeted with a loud shout from Robin, who jumped out from behind the door. "Molly. Good morning!"

The shock of Robin's sudden, noisy appearance scared Molly, catching her off guard. She fell onto the bed and remained still, as if she were in a coma. It was now Robin's turn to be afraid because he genuinely believed he had scared Molly out of her wits. He rushed over to see if she was OK, but he was stopped in his tracks for a fraction of a second by the way her radiant beauty was exposed on the bed. The top button on her tight white blouse had snapped, exposing an excess of her curvaceous breasts. Her short plaid skirt had twisted itself well above her knee, showing off the silky inside of her left thigh. Robin's concern for her well-being obliged him to drop immediately his lustful thoughts and run to the bathroom to dampen a washcloth with cold water for placing on her forehead. He hoped this would revive her. He was worrying already about how he might have damaged their friendship by pulling such a dumb stunt.

Robin quickly ran a stream of cold water on the washcloth and wrung it a bit before rushing back to Molly. "Yikes. What the hell!" cried Robin when he came out of the bathroom.

Molly was nowhere to be seen. The bed and the room were empty. He ran to the door and looked everywhere. It was as if Molly had disappeared into thin air. He saw her car in the park-ing lot, but he did not see her anywhere. He was at a loss about what to do. He turned around to go back into his room, and then whop! He was banged over the head with one of the bed pillows by a laughing Molly. "You're a nutty boy! You think I was born yesterday? I could never fall for such a stupid prank."

Robin was stunned. Molly had really turned the tables on him. He had been much more surprised than she had been. He could not believe she had faked so well fainting and collapsing on the bed. He turned toward Molly and raised his fist, acting as if he wanted to punch her in the face, but Molly's laugh and smile beguiled him sufficiently to cause him to laugh even louder. They both began laughing uncontrollably. The laughing stopped when Molly reached out and embraced Robin closely, holding him tightly against her body for a brief moment. She broke this unexpected hug with a small kiss on Robin's cheek, saying, "Well, let's get going. What are you waiting for?"

Molly's affectionate hug and kiss were the biggest surprises of all for Robin. He felt as if he was floating on air and his feet were not touching the ground as they headed to his car. Molly was humming a lullaby from her childhood as they both got into the car and Robin drove out of the motel parking lot. After an atypical spell of silence, Molly said, "I have an idea. Instead of going to Helen's again for breakfast, let's drive the thirty miles to Wichita and eat breakfast there. I know a diner called Stanley's that is a great place to eat breakfast. They make the most fabulous French toast. Anyway, we can't visit the WSU campus until after eight thirty, as all the offices will be closed until then. What do you say?"

Robin, who was slowly descending from the heavens and settling down on Earth, rolled his eyes and looked at Molly in the sweetest way he could manage, calmly saying, "Molly, whatever you say is more than fine with me."

They took Highway 254 straight east to Wichita, turning left near Kechi to head south into Wichita and the WSU campus. At the city limits, they were welcomed by a large billboard to the "Air Capital of the World." Robin asked Molly, "Why is Wichita called the Air Capital of the World?"

Molly replied with a cynical flair, "Robin, before we get too far into the city, let me give you a little history lesson." Molly then began a lengthy spiel, revealing all she knew about Wichita's history.

"With a population of over three hundred fifty thousand, Wichita is the largest city in Kansas. Wichita is called the Air Capital of the World because most of the companies that manufacture airplanes are located there. Also, a US Air Force base is located in Wichita. In the 1920s, famous aviation pioneers such as Walter Beech and Clyde Cessna began manufacturing small planes in Wichita. Their efforts, along with others like Boeing Aircraft, became prominent during World War II, when their companies produced large numbers of combat aircraft. Other aircraft firms were also attracted to Wichita because of the availability of skilled labor, its strategic location in the center of the country, and the large number of clear days during the year that permitted flying in good weather conditions."

Robin was impressed by Molly's knowledge of Kansas history. Molly was on a roll and continued, "With the advent of airplane manufacturing, Wichita's reputation as a Cowtown at the northern end of the old Chisholm Trail changed. An extension of the Santa Fe railway to Wichita in 1872 created something of an economic boom in Wichita, as tens of thousands of cattle were driven from Texas and shipped back east to consumers, who paid high prices for beef. By 1885, this wild-west boom ended, as rail lines were extended south into Texas and quarantine restrictions were placed on Texas longhorn cattle. Yet raising cattle locally and wheat farming remained important, and, in 1914, oil was discovered, creating another economic boom. Farming, cattle, and oil remain important mainstays of the state's economy, but Wichita's economic fortunes often rise and fall with the health of the aircraft industry."

Robin politely interrupted Molly. "How do you know all this stuff and I don't?"

Molly was really enjoying herself. She laughed and replied, "Well, I grew up closer to Wichita than you did, and I took a semester course in Kansas history when I was at WSU. Anyway, I'm not finished yet. I wanted to mention a few more things. I'll hurry, as we are almost at Stanley's."

Molly continued with her brief history lesson. "Wichita has come a long way since the first settlers met, around 1863, an American Indian tribe that called themselves the Wichitas, camped at the confluence of the Little and Big Arkansas Rivers. These Indians were the customers of a trading post established by the famous Jesse Chisholm, who was half-Indian and spoke fourteen Indian dialects. The historic Chisholm Trail was named after him. I wonder if there would be a Wichita today if he had not worked so hard to demarcate the Chisholm Trail.

"You know, Robin, early historians referred to most of the flat geographic area covered by the Kansas of today as the Great American Desert. Little did they know back then that today there would be a thriving city at the same place on these great Midwest plains where the Wichita Indians camped almost one hundred thirty years ago. Yet the place-name of Wichita was preserved over many generations, even though many have forgotten its origins."

Molly abruptly said, "That's it. End of my brief history lesson. There's Stanley's ahead. Turn into the parking lot on the right."

Stanley's was located in a small shopping center. Molly explained to Robin that this was a new location for this family restaurant; it had operated for decades in an old building in downtown Wichita. They entered the restaurant, and a middle-aged Hispanic waitress promptly showed them to one of the few empty tables. Robin was digesting the surroundings. He saw many old black-and-white photos from bygone days hanging on the walls. Most of the people in the diner were older, retired people, who Robin thought must be regular customers.

The waitress returned to take their orders. Robin impressed Molly by greeting the waitress in Spanish. Robin and the waitress had some good laughs, speaking for several moments. Molly was ill at ease, as she felt left out because she could not understand what was being said. It was evident that the waitress was noting on her little pad the order for food that Robin was placing. The waitress closed her pad and extended her hand to shake Molly's hand. Before going, she muttered some words in Spanish that Molly did not understand.

As she turned to leave, Molly was very impatient to ask Robin some questions. "Robin, I did not know you could speak Spanish. How is that possible? And what were you two talking about?"

Robin cleared his throat and with a little smile said, "I spent an enriching junior year abroad from my journalism studies at Emporia State at the University of Honduras in Tegucigalpa. We were just exchanging greetings, and I explained to her where I learned my Spanish. Angela was born in Wichita, and so were her parents. But her grandfather came from Mexico as a young man to work on building of the railroads. I also placed our order. Someday, I will have to tell you about my exciting drive to and from Honduras through Mexico and Guatemala."

Molly, who was a little peeved, blurted out, "Was that all? It sounded to me that much more was said than that. What did she say to me before leaving?"

Robin hesitated, but knowing full well that Molly would not stop until she had more details, he explained, "She congratulated you on your beauty and for having such a handsome boyfriend."

Molly exclaimed, "What? Who said you are my boyfriend?"

Robin was clearly on the defensive. "In Spanish, this is the kind of respectful language you use. It does not translate well into English."

"OK, but you better not be getting any wrong ideas in your head about us," Molly asserted firmly.

"By the way, what did you order?" inquired Molly in a calmer voice.

A confused Robin meekly replied, "The same as we ate last time at Helen's. You did indicate you wanted the fabulous French toast."

Molly was about to say something more when Angela returned with their food. Again, Robin and Angela jabbered away in Spanish. Molly listened intently, trying to capture the meaning of their words. She noticed that one word was often repeated. That word was *novia*.

Angela smiled at Molly, saying in plain Kansas English, "Darling…you beautiful thing. I hope you enjoy your breakfast."

As Angela departed, Molly continued her assault on Robin. "Tell me. I heard the word *novia* repeated several times. What does it mean?"

With a sheepish grin on his face, Robin gently replied, "The best translation into English of that word is girlfriend, but maybe it also means a girl who is a friend. I would not worry about this. This is just how people talk in Spanish."

"OK, Señor Robin, just make sure you got this novia business straight in your own mind. Let's eat and think about what we came to Wichita to do."

The French toast was fabulous, and they ate in silence as each reflected on their next move. Finally, Robin inquired, "Where do we start at WSU?"

Molly quickly replied, "I'm a Wichita State graduate in business management. In recent years, I've been to the campus many times to visit friends and to take in some exciting Shocker basketball games. They are really one of the nation's best college teams. I think we should start at the registrar's office in Fiske Hall to see when David graduated from WSU."

Robin nodded in the affirmative as he paid the bill, leaving Angela a nice tip. Angela was profuse in thanking Robin and telling him how lucky he was to have such a beautiful woman. Robin also thanked Angela. Robin told himself to be sure not to tell Molly what Angela had said about his luck.

They headed for Robin's car as Molly gave him directions to WSU, which was less than a mile away.

They arrived at the sprawling campus, but it took some time for them to find a visitor parking space that was free. They set out on foot to find Fiske Hall. It was a warm, sunny autumn day. The foliage on the trees was beginning to produce a spectacular variety of orange, yellow, and brown colors. It was one of those days when it felt good to be alive and out and about. As they walked, Robin admitted, "I don't get what WSU's mascot, Shocker, means."

Molly scolded politely, "Robin, have you forgotten what state you are from? This is the wheat state, and in the old days, they harvested wheat and gathered it into bundles called *shocks*. The people who made these bundles were called *wheat shockers*. In general, anyone who harvested wheat was called a *shocker*. Today, WSU students and athletic teams refer to themselves as Shockers. Anyway, that is how I think the name Shocker came about."

They walked a couple hundred yards and arrived at the main entrance of Fiske Hall, which was built in the same colonial style and red brick as were most of the older buildings on campus.

They entered and stopped to read a bronze plaque on the wall which provided some of the building's history. It was built in 1904 with a generous donation from Charlotte M. Fiske, and it was one of the main buildings of a predecessor institution of higher learning, Fairmount College, which was founded in 1895.

Molly explained some of the history of the university to Robin. She told him how Fairmount College became a municipal university in 1926 and one of the main state universities in 1964. It was in that year it changed its name from Municipal University of Wichita to WSU. They reasoned, therefore, that WSU was a municipal university when David began his studies in 1963 and a state university when he should have completed four years of college in 1967. They needed confirmation from the registrar's office that he did indeed graduate from WSU in 1967.

Next to the plaque conveying the building's history was an enclosed black directory board with removable white plastic letters. Robin and Molly could see that there were professors of history, philosophy, and geography. The fact that any mention of the Registrar's Office was absent from the directory prompted Molly to stop a passing student. She asked the young woman where the Registrar's Office was located. She replied, "The Registrar's Office is located in Jardine Hall. You need to go out the way you came in, turn right, and keep walking on the sidewalk for about one hundred yards. The building is clearly marked and located in front of the student union, which is called the Campus Activities Center, or CAC."

Molly and Robin trudged along the sidewalk as directed. Molly apologized for the mistake she had made in thinking Fiske Hall housed the Registrar's Office. They passed other buildings along their way, as well as many students who were hustling to get to their classes. They entered Jardine Hall and found just inside the entrance a similar plaque that provided some details on the building. The construction of the original building was completed in 1930, and it was named after William M. Jardine, US Secretary of Agriculture under President Coolidge in the late 1920s and WSU president in the 1930s. There was also the mention that he died in 1955.

There was no problem in finding the Registrar's Office. There were a number of signs that clearly pointed the way to it. Molly and Robin walked through the office's open door. Molly inclined toward Robin and whispered, "Please let me do the talking."

Molly smiled at the redheaded young woman working the counter and cheerfully said, "Hello. My name is Molly Peterson. I wonder if you can confirm to me if my cousin, David Peterson, graduated from WSU in 1967."

The woman rapidly responded, "That's easy. Let me show you the list of graduates for that year."

The woman rustled through a stack of papers on a shelf behind her and returned to the counter with an alphabetical listing of 1967 graduates. She handed it to Molly, who immediately began looking at all the last names that started with *P*. She saw three Petersons, but there was not any David Peterson. She passed the list to Robin, who also could not find any David Peterson. They both thought that maybe David graduated late, so they asked to see the list for 1968. Again, there was no mention of any David Peterson. Molly and Robin were greatly disappointed and agonized over what to do next.

Molly returned the lists to the woman, soberly telling her, "Thank you, but we can't find the name of the David Peterson we are looking for. Is there any way you can graduate from WSU without having your name cited on one of these lists?"

The woman emphatically replied, "Nope. If your name is not on one of these lists, you did not graduate from WSU."

Molly responded, "Thanks. I thought so. Tell me. Is there any record of students who attended WSU but did not graduate?"

The woman, who was becoming impatient because a line of people was forming behind Molly and Robin, said firmly, "No, we don't keep those kinds of records. Perhaps if you know the major course of study of the person, you can consult records at the department level. Now, please, I must tend to the next person in the line."

Molly and Robin walked out of the Registrar's Office with their heads hanging low. They were at a loss as to what to do next. Molly looked up and saw a sign pointing the way to the CAC, so she said, "Let's take a little break and have a cup of coffee at the CAC snack bar."

All Robin could manage to say was, "Good idea."

They exited the back entrance of Jardine Hall and walked the short distance to the CAC. Once inside, they followed the signs and went upstairs to the snack bar. They found themselves an empty booth, and Molly volunteered to go to the self-service bar and buy two cups of coffee. Robin was beside himself trying to think of what to do next. Surely, he thought, there must be a way to find some trace of David at WSU. When Molly returned with their coffee tray, Robin proposed, "Let's go to the university library and look through yearbooks like we did in Udall."

Molly replied, "Well, if that is all we can think of, that is what we will do. But I'm worried that even if we find something about David in a yearbook, that will not provide us with any leads on what happened to him. I'm really getting discouraged."

They finished their coffee. In a somber mood, they walked slowly down the stairs to the main lobby. As they prepared to exit the building, Robin spied a wooden plaque on the wall that had attached to it individual bronze tags with the names of all the students who had served as night managers of the CAC and the dates of their service. As they walked nearer the plaque, he thought he could make out the name of a David, so he moved within an arm's-length distance from the plaque, and, lo and behold, there was clearly stamped in a bronze tag the following: "David Peterson, 1965–66."

Robin moved aside and pointed at the plaque. "Molly, here's the proof we need to indicate that David was indeed here."

Molly let out a gleeful shout when she saw David's name. She was so happy that she was about to give Robin a hug but decided it was better to dance a little two-step jig instead. Molly's words flew out of her mouth. "This means that there must be someone in this building who knew David. Let's go to the CAC management office and see what we can find out."

They hustled up a nearby stairway that had a small sign pointing up to the management office. They rushed through the open door to the office. Molly again took charge when they encountered an elderly receptionist. Molly conjured up all her charm to sweetly say, "Hello. My name is Molly Peterson. This is my friend Robin. We have come from El Dorado to visit the WSU campus. We were just walking around downstairs when we noticed a plaque with all the names of CAC night managers. We see that one of those names is David Peterson, who worked here in 1965 and 66. As this may be my cousin whom I have not heard from in years, I was wondering if anyone here could tell us how to contact him."

The receptionist had a smirk on her face, but Molly was not sure if she was making some kind grimace or if it was a permanent facial feature. In a nasal voice, the old woman said, "Why, young lady, that was almost twenty-four years ago. I have been working here for about ten years. I don't think anyone who is still around was here in 1966. Please give me a minute while I go ask my director."

The woman quickly darted off through a side door. A few minutes later, she returned and said, "Well, as I said, nobody working here now was here back in 1966, but we do have a man who retired a couple of years ago who may have known David. His name is Jasper, and he was the chief custodian when he retired. I can give you his phone number. He is very kindhearted. I'm sure he would like to help you out."

Molly exclaimed, "That is great! We appreciate so much all the help you are giving us. Thanks so much."

The woman quickly jotted down Jasper's phone number on a piece of paper and handed it to Molly, who grabbed Robin by the arm and led him outside. "Robin, we need to call this number immediately, but I did not bring my mobile phone. We need to find a pay phone. Do you have some quarters?"

Robin dug deeply into his pants pockets and came up with two quarters. He held them out in his open palm to show Molly, saying, "This should be enough to call. I saw some pay phones in the hallway next to the main lobby downstairs. Let's go there now."

They rushed downstairs and walked at a brisk pace to the row of phones at the end of the hall. Robin took charge this time. Molly handed him the piece of paper with Jasper's number on it. He carefully pushed the number buttons and deposited one quarter as requested by the automatic recording. They both felt the tension as the phone rang at the other end. It rang five times before Robin heard a raspy but kind voice saying, "Hello, this is Jasper. How can I help you?"

A nervous Robin tried to keep a measured tone of voice as he said, "Jasper, sir. Hello, my name is Robin Fletcher, and I'm trying to track down an old friend of mine. The receptionist here at the CAC thought you may be able to tell us something about the whereabouts of David Peterson. Did you know him? He was the CAC night manager in 1965 and 1966."

The talkative Jasper lost no time in replying. "Oh, yes. I knew David very well. He was a fine young man and one of the kindest and most intelligent people I ever met. He did not have to help me, but sometimes he would sweep and mop floors with me. He was always talking about going on a big adventure one day and making a positive difference in the world. Then one day he abruptly resigned, dropped out of school one semester before his graduation, and said he was going to Africa with the Peace Corps. As you can imagine, we were all shocked by his leaving like this. But he said he had to go. I said my good-byes to him and wished him the best of luck. Nobody has seen or heard from him since he left WSU early in 1967."

Molly had her ear next to Robin's on the handset, so they both were hearing every word Jasper said. They were elated to hear some news about David and talk to someone who had actually known him. Robin could not wait to ask Jasper his next question. "Jasper, do you know which country in Africa David went to?"

In an apologetic tone, Jasper replied, "No, I don't. I should know, but I don't. But I recall the *Sunflower* published an article on him. It was quite a story at the time. If you can get your hands on that article, it probably tells you all you want to know."

Robin and Molly gasped simultaneously. Robin asked, "Jasper, can you recall when that article was published?"

Jasper asked for a minute to think and then said, "It must have been in the same month he left. I believe that was in February 1967."

Robin rushed to say good-bye. "Jasper, thanks so much. You have been a real lifesaver. You have given us the information we needed."

Jasper politely said, "It has been a pleasure helping you folks. I wish you the best of luck. Good-bye."

Both Robin and Molly knew what they had to do next. They had to go to the *Sunflower*'s office and search its archives for its February 1967 issues. They asked the next passing student where the office was located. Once they had this information, they rushed out and across campus in the direction of the *Sunflower*, which, even Robin knew was named after Kansas's state flower.

They arrived out of breath in the *Sunflower*'s main office in the basement of Wilner Auditorium, one of the oldest buildings on campus. It was mainly used for plays and drama classes. While Robin was trying to catch his breath, Molly asked the first person she encountered where they could find the student newspaper's archives. They were told to see the person in the next office. There, they found themselves among almost unending rows of shelves that were as high as the ceiling. It appeared that old copies of the *Sunflower* were kept in oversized cardboard folders that were stacked in chronological order. They turned to a disheveled young man sitting at a small desk in the corner of the room who had his face close to a book he was reading. It seemed that the young man did not notice their presence. It was only after Robin made a loud sound by clearing his throat that the solitary man looked up and said, "How can I help you?"

Molly stepped up closer to the poorly dressed man and said as clearly as she could, "Is there any way we can see your newspaper issues from February 1967?"

The unkempt man stood up and said in a grumpy tone, "Please sign the form on the clipboard lying on my desk while I go look for our February folder for that year."

Robin commented, "Sure glad he does not want to be bothered and is going to get what we came for. This is starting to look too easy."

Almost before Robin finished his comment, the man was back toting a hefty folder in both hands. He slammed it on a sturdy old table jammed against the opposite wall, saying, "Here it is." He then went back to his desk and became engrossed again in his book.

There it was on the table before them—a blackened folder stained with ink, as big as an open newspaper. Clearly marked on its cover in heavy black paint was a notice that it contained all the *Sunflower* editions for January, February, and March 1967. Molly and Robin held their breaths as they began to leaf slowly through each folder. They both began to sneeze and get the sniffles, as the old folder seemed to exude some musty odors and invisible particles that irritated their nasal passages.

They both held their hankies to their noses as they flipped and scanned quickly through the pages of the moldy old newspapers. The *Sunflower* came out weekly, and one issue consisted of twelve to fourteen pages. They found the first February issue and began scrutinizing every inch of each page. Some of the pages were smudged, so they had to look closely to make sure they did not miss any mention of David. Their job was made more difficult by the dim lighting in the room. They were both squinting as they ran their eyes up and down and back and forth across each page. When one was done with a page, he or she would say, "Check," to indicate they were done and ready to move on to the next page. They continued this tense process for over thirty minutes.

They had made their way through the first two issues of February 1967 and were starting the first page of the third when there it was—smack dab in the middle of the front page. It was so clear. It was as if it jumped off the page and hit them squarely in the eyes. Under a genial photo of a young man, they read the caption, "David Peterson drops out of school one semester before graduation to join the Peace Corps. See page 2."

They turned the page so fast they almost ripped it. They found on the next page a short article that quoted David as saying, "I 'm thrilled to join the Peace Corps and go to the Republic of Kotoku, a small country in Africa. I can always come back to finish school."

They felt a great sense of achievement. They now knew what had happened to David. He had gone to Africa with the Peace Corps. They thought that the Peace Corps would surely have some record of David and his service in Kotoku. Robin knew immediately that he would have to call the Peace Corps' headquarters in Washington, D.C. to see if it had any records on David.

Molly was thinking differently. She said in all seriousness, "Let's go to Africa. If you really want to know what happened to David, you need to go and see where he lived. This would make a great story."

Robin was taken aback at first by Molly's idea, but deep down, he knew she was right. He turned and looked at her, saying, "I know you're right. We need to go to Africa. But how can we do that?"

"I don't know, Robin, but we must find a way." She did not understand why, but a small voice buried inside her was telling her to go to Africa.

Robin marked the place in the folder and asked the man if they could photocopy a couple of pages. Without looking up, he pointed toward the back and said, "Ten cents a page."

Robin and Molly carried the folder to the photocopy machine and made ten copies. They returned the folder to the man's desk and left a dollar bill. Molly said, "Thank you for your help."

The man did not say anything and did not look up from his book. Robin and Molly rushed out the door with the copies clutched in their hands. They continued on their way until they were out of the building. They were happy to breathe some fresh air. Molly turned to Robin and with her most beguiling smile said, "Robin, we are going to Africa."

Again, Robin could not help but reply, "How can we do that, Molly? A trip like that would cost a mint. I would like to go, but I cannot see how we can afford it."

Molly smiled again and said, "I know that it sounds impossible, but we must go. I don't know how either, but my mom always said that where there is a will there is a way."

They walked to their car without saying another word. They drove in silence back to El Dorado. They arrived at Robin's motel. Molly walked Robin to his door. He expected another hug and kiss, but this time Molly said a simple good-bye and joyfully sang loudly out, "I'm so thrilled. I'm going to Africa!"

Robin was speechless. As he watched the attractive way Molly moved as she walked to her car, he could not help but think how nice it would be to travel to Africa with her.

CHAPTER EIGHT
PRESIDENTIAL PACT

Chiefs Letivi and Gyasi nervously adjusted the cascading layers of their best traditional clothes before stepping out among their people. The entire population of Ataku had assembled to see them depart on their journey to Melomti. Such a visit was unprecedented in the annals of village history. Everyone knew that the future of the village depended on this crucial meeting with the country's president. In many ways, their lives were in the hands of their two chiefs. The possible risks involved with dealing with an authoritarian president were high, but so were the potential gains.

Nobody could predict the outcome of this propitious meeting with President Rafael. He was a taciturn, moody man who could easily and quickly come to the wrong conclusions. A simple gesture or word could have unintended consequences, as the egotistical president could easily misinterpret them. It was excruciatingly difficult to find a way to behave to avoid falling on the wrong side of the president. Sometimes the harder you tried to conform to what you thought the president wanted, the more he suspected you. This unschooled man worked according to his natural instincts and the way he felt on a given day. The chiefs had prayed at length to God, the ancestors, and key spirits for the president to be on one of his better days when they saw him.

The chiefs felt well prepared. Letivi had made numerous drafts of their presentation to the president, and they had rehearsed it many times. Letivi had also produced a general script of what they would say and how they would act. They had gone over every detail of their planned visit, trying to anticipate every possible contingency. They believed they were ready for both the foreseeable and the unforeseen. They were confident of the compelling nature of their case and their ability to gain the president's support. Their main fear was that the president would ask for too big a cut. They knew the president would never do anything unless there was some personal gain in it for him.

The chiefs shook the hands of the elders and clan heads and began weaving their way through the many well-wishers. They slowly descended the wide path from Letivi's compound to the taxi waiting for them at the base of the mountain on the road leading to the national highway. All along the way, praises were sung in their honor and prayers were shouted for the success of their mission. When they arrived near the waiting taxi, the chief fetish priest slit the throat of a white rooster and poured its blood on the ground in a pattern that favored the success of their mission. Surrounding the car was the church choir, which sang a hymn to bless their mission, followed by a loud prayer delivered by their Christian pastor. The chiefs both thought that with these kinds of blessings, the success of their mission was assured. Moreover, Letivi's hopes ran high, as he was convinced that the power of tomorrow's full moon would give him the upper hand.

They were helped into the backseat of the small blue Toyota sedan. Great care was taken to make sure their ample traditional robes did not touch the ground and were fully tucked inside the car before shutting the doors. At this point, drummers and buglers began playing in a frantic manner. A multicolored banner was tied to the car antenna to indicate that important personages were aboard. Both the fetish priests and Christian pastor prayed over the driver. They both asked that the driver receive a special blessing to help him ensure a safe trip to and from Melomti. Everyone gathered around the car and waved goodbye as the shiny but old car inched its way forward to begin this historic trip.

The chiefs remained silent for the two miles between the village and the main highway. The only talking came from the driver, who introduced himself shortly after their departure from the village, saying it was a great honor for him to drive them to and from Melomti. Of course, the village had raised funds to rent this chauffeured car from a wealthy man in the regional capital of Kpolomo. The cost of this trip would put a big dent in the village treasury. Besides the cost of the rented vehicle, there were hotel and food expenses, and, most importantly, the cost of the gift they would give the president.

This gift was a large, hand-woven *kente* cloth that had taken local weavers years to complete. This colorful cloth was the kind that only superior chiefs would wear or display in their homes. This was the best gift they could offer. It was nicely packaged in an embroidered case. It was something they believed the president would well appreciate, especially as the weavers in their village had the reputation of being the best in the country. The giving of such a royal cloth would also indicate to the president the high esteem they had for him. It also played into the president's huge ego—that he was the supreme chief of all and, thus, everyone else should act subservient to him, particularly if they were in his presence. It was indeed a unique, high-value gift that should help gain the favor of the mercurial president.

The chiefs remained mostly quiet because they did not want to say anything that the driver could overhear. They dared not utter any word they would not want him to pass along. Their conversation was therefore about mundane topics such as the weather and their observations of what they saw along the sides of the road. Chief Gyasi had the most to say, as it had been many years since he had been to the capital. The last time he had been in the capital was over twenty years ago, and he had fallen very ill during that trip. He told Letivi, "I hope the coastal air and heat does not make me sick again. I have not traveled to the capital for a very long time because I fear the sea-level climate will make me sick. I really do not like leaving our home area."

Letivi replied, "Well, you know that I spent many years in the capital pursuing my studies, and I was never ill. By the way, if we have time, I would like to pass by my school to greet some of my teachers."

Gyasi yawned and said, "That's a good idea. We'll see if we have time for that. One thing I am looking forward to is eating some deep-fried turkey tails. I hope the women cooking food at the side of the roads in the capital are still able to get turkey tails from America to cook."

Letivi was amused by his grandfather's remarks. "I'm sure that we can easily find some succulent turkey tails to eat. I would not mind eating some myself."

Letivi was amazed by how quickly they were passing towns. He found that the newly paved road permitted passing places that previously had taken much more time to reach. He wanted to say something about some places, but they had already passed them before he realized where they were on the road. Before they knew it, they were out of their forest-covered district and on a long but very gradual descent through tall savannah land to the capital. Their trip was also faster than usual because they were not stopped at any of the numerous police or customs road-blocks. Either the officials could see they were important chiefs, or the president had sent out the word that they were not to be bothered. In any event, a trip that could take all day on the old unpaved road was now taking them much less than two hours.

They whizzed along in an unhindered, almost magical way. Chief Letivi commented that he felt he was flying through the air on a magical carpet. The closer they came to the capital city, the shorter the savannah grass became and the more the air smelled of the salty sea. They could not believe how little time it took them to arrive. As they entered the riotous traffic of Melomti, Chief Gyasi instructed the driver to take them to the President Hotel, located on the Boulevard Nasungu, a road recently renamed after the long-serving former president, the deceased father of the current president. This was the three-star hotel often used by traditional chiefs coming from upcountry to visit government officials.

They arrived in front of the unimposing three-story President Hotel, and a young man quickly exited the hotel to help them with their baggage. They instructed the driver to return to this same spot the following day at 6:00 a.m., as their meeting at the nearby presidency was at 6:30 a.m. It was President Rafael's custom to receive visitors early in the morning. Many thought he slept very little. There were rumors that he was addicted to pornographic videos and spent much of the night watching them with scantily clad coterie of young women he lodged in his presidential suites. His gluttonous appetite for women, fine whis-key, large sums of money, and African rumba music was widely known but rarely mentioned by anyone because of fear of ret-ribution. He also liked eating too much. His physiognomy had transformed over the years from an emaciated, underfed misfit to an obese, malevolent, stodgy despot.

Chief Gyasi's first question for the porter was about where he could find some turkey tails. The porter told him that he could buy some from a woman who fried them on her charcoal cooker at a nearby street stand. Chief Gyasi immediately dug into his deep gown pockets and gave him enough money to buy a couple dozen turkey tails. He told the porter that he wanted to eat some turkey tails as soon as he was settled into his room.

They completed the hotel check-in formalities with a petite, middle-aged woman at the reception counter, and the porter led them to their spacious room on the ground floor. The room fur-nishings were basic. There was one double bed and a table with two upright wooden chairs. A small, threadbare rug was lying in the middle of the room. Equally threadbare beige curtains hung from two windows that faced an unfinished concrete-block wall of a neighboring building about four feet away. A tiny bathroom with a shower stall, toilet, and sink was located on one side of the room. In the bathroom, there were two stiff towels, two min-iature bars of soap, and several galvanized buckets filled with water.

This extra water was needed because the city water often ceased to flow. The porter also showed them a supply of candles and matches in the drawer of the nightstand next to the bed that they were to use during one of the frequent electrical power out-ages. There was one florescent tube light on the plywood ceiling. The porter explained, "We have city electricity most of the time and water about half the time. I am sorry to tell you that our generator is broken down, and without electricity, we can't operate the pressure pump needed to make water run in the hotel. Anyway, I am very pleased to welcome you. I am happy that you have this special room, which we reserve for high dignitaries."

When the porter exited, Chiefs Letivi and Gyasi had a hearty laugh. Chief Letivi said, "If this is their best room, I would not like to see their worst room."

They both laughed again, and Chief Gyasi replied, "I don't care. For one night, I can stay anywhere. I just want to finish our business here in the capital and go back to our village."

They helped each other remove their colorful royal chief gowns and took from their small handbags their everyday wraparound cloths. They carefully hung their gowns from the tops of the doors of an old mahogany armoire in the room, as they would wear the same clothes tomorrow for their audience with the president. They placed their valuable gift for the president on a small side table. They took turns using the bathroom to wrap their waistcloths around themselves. Chief Gyasi did not wear any kind of shirt, while Letivi kept on his white jersey undershirt. In preparation for eating some deep-fried turkey tails, both used the tiny white porcelain bathroom sink to wash their hands with soap, using water from the buckets sitting on the floor.

They sat at the small table waiting for the porter to return with their turkey tails. They made ample use of the two palm-frond hand fans lying on the table. It was much hotter and more humid than they were used to, and there was not any air circulating in their room. They agreed that the turkey tails would be their evening meal, and after eating, they would go over once more how they would meet the president and convey to him what they needed.

Chief Gyasi was having trouble concentrating because he kept thinking about munching on turkey tails. He was almost drooling when they heard the porter knock on the door. Letivi opened the door, and in came the very animated porter carrying a plastic bag, two glasses, and a pitcher of cool, clear filtered water. He placed these items on the table and dug into his pocket for the change. In his eagerness to begin devouring turkey tails, Chief Gyasi told the porter to keep the change and that his services were no longer needed.

They carefully removed the brown paper wrapping that contained the turkey tails. They knew that the greasy brown paper came from the interior lining of cement bags. Chief Gyasi placed one brown package in front of Letivi and the other in front of himself. Each carefully unfolded the grease-stained paper wraps, exposing the oily turkey tails. Chief Gyasi said a brief prayer and poured a few drops of water on the floor in honor of the grandfathers. As soon as the last drop of water hit the floor, Chief Gyasi snatched a turkey tail with his right hand and thrust it into his mouth. He chewed with a slurping, smacking sound. Letivi quickly followed suit. They were both enjoying the taste of the juicy fat turkey tails in their mouths. They rapidly ate and became stuffed by such an abundant feast of fat.

They toasted each other with glasses of water and asked God, all the spirits, and the grandfathers to bless their visit with the president. They reviewed again the approach they would use tomorrow with the president. They knew that they must act very subservient in front of the president, showing him as much deference as possible because he was the supreme power in the country and they were only simple village chiefs. They also knew they had to keep their spiel simple and to the point so as not to waste his time and make it easy for him to grasp why they needed his support. There was no margin for error. They had to get their message convincingly across during the first five minutes of their meeting. They were trying to remain calm and chiefly, but in the knotted pits of their stomachs, they were deeply stressed and fearful.

Chief Gyasi said he was tired and would do as he did in the village and sleep on one of the grass mats rolled up and stacked in the corner of the room. Letivi said that he was looking forward to sleeping in a bed. In reality, it was a long and sleepless night for each man, as neither could stop thinking about their meeting with the president. The pressure was becoming unbearable. They worried about being so ill at ease that they would choke and blow completely this unique opportunity. They both trembled at the thought of going home with bad news.

Well before sunrise, with the first crow of a rooster in a neighboring compound, the chiefs wished each other good morning and began readying themselves for the big encounter with the president. There was no electricity, so they lit candles and stuck them upright in their own wax at several places in the room and the bathroom. They took turns using the bathroom. Neither took a full bath. They dunked their stiff towels in their buckets of water and wiped their bodies down from head to toe. They rubbed their eyes and mouths vigorously, making sure their faces were shiny clean. Each took a mouthful of water and swished it around several times inside his mouth. They vigorously stroked their heads with a brush made for shining shoes.

They were now ready to help each other put on their elaborate royal gowns. They would both wear today their ornamental chief hats they had brought with them. Once each had approved of the other, they slipped on their flat but fancy red goat leather sandals and sat down to wait for their taxi driver. They began once more to rehearse their pitch. These last preparations were interrupted by an odd knock at the door. Letivi slowly unlocked and opened the door to see a young girl carrying a large tray that had obliged her to knock with her elbow.

The girl entered the room and placed on the table a thermos full of hot water, a bowl of sugar cubes, a cup of powdered milk, and a can of Nescafé. She also set on the table a small basket filled with balls of deep-fried bean bread. The chiefs thanked her for her service, but they really did not have any appetite for breakfast. They each drank a glass of water from the container brought to them the night before. They wanted to stay focused on their meeting with the president and make sure nothing they ingested would cause any stomach problems that could interfere with this all-important meeting.

Chief Gyasi looked at his watch, and it was exactly 6:00 a.m. This was the time the driver was supposed to fetch them. They fought the urge to leave their room and go out front to search for the driver. It would be dishonorable for a chief to behave in that fashion. After a few minutes, their rising anxiety was relieved with the arrival of their driver, who quickly picked up their two handbags and the gift case and then escorted them to his car parked just in front of the hotel. He was bubbling over with excitement as he said, "I was a little late because I was explaining to the hotel manager that you had come to Melomti to see the president. When he heard this, he told me that you did not have to pay for your stay. He is a good man."

The taxi sped off with its emergency lights blinking and the driver honking the horn at short intervals as he knifed through traffic at a high speed. Everyone knew that when a car was per-forming like this, it was carrying important people on a visit to see the president or some high government official. It did not take more than ten minutes before the car slowed down and came to a halt on the broad paved street that separated the presidential palace from the ocean. A pair of palace guards who were dressed in a style known only in association with royal palaces in Europe quickly marched out to open the car doors for the chiefs, while two other guards opened the front gates. It was obvious they had been forewarned of the early-morning arrival of two traditional chiefs.

The driver was told to park his car on the ocean side of the broad way and wait there until he was summoned. Two guards walked with the chiefs along a wide sidewalk that cut through a well-manicured lawn for about forty yards in the direction of the main entrance of the palace. When they were about twenty yards from the entrance, they stopped at a barrier made of concertina wire. The palace guards left them when two soldiers popped out from behind adjoining bunkers made from sandbags to assure they were indeed the expected visitors. The soldiers opened a passageway through the concertina wire. The chiefs slowly walked past the razor wire, making sure that their ample gowns did not catch on any of the barbs.

After they had made it safely past this barrier, they were only five yards from the glass door. They were preparing to enter when suddenly they were stopped in their tracks by a fetish priest who jumped out from behind a partition at the side of the walkway. The fetish priest was dressed in a messy assortment of animal skins with small bones and pieces of iron sewn into them. He made grunting sounds, and his every step made the dangling iron fragments pinned on him jangle. With his blood-shot eyes and dilated pupils, he looked intensely into the eyes of each chief. He then crouched down and began waddling slowly around them as he waved up and down with his right hand a cow-hair fly whisk and shook a small pod rattle in his left hand. The chiefs knew the job of this powerful fetish priest was to detect any signs of bad intent against the president.

In a flash, the fetish priest disappeared, and the one-way, bulletproof glass door in front of them was opened wide by a man in a black suit with dark sunglasses. From the obvious bulge under his vest, the chiefs knew this was one of the president's armed personal bodyguards. The man did not say a word but indicated with his hand that they should follow him. They followed the quick-stepping bodyguard up a wide marble stairway that curved continuously to the right. At the end of this stairway was a richly decorated and furnished waiting room. The man pointed to the nearest sofa, and the nervous chiefs sat down.

They wanted to ask the stone-faced bodyguard how long they would have to wait, but he darted away to take up his position near the entrance to the president's office. Heavy, well-varnished, thick mahogany doors displaying the president's official seal carved in an elaborate fashion presented an intimidating last obstacle to entering the president's inner sanctum. On the doors were huge brass door handles that had been polished in such a way as to resemble shiny gold. Just to the right of the doors were red and green lights embedded into the wall. The red light was currently illuminated. This indicated that nobody was to enter. The chiefs knew that when the green light lit up, it would be their turn to go inside the president's inner sanctum.

They expected their waiting time would be short, but it was about forty-five minutes before the red light was turned off and the green light switched on. The sudden appearance of the green light sent a shiver up their spines, and they immediately sprang to their feet. At the same time, the guard motioned them to approach the door. As they stood before the door, they began to tremble. Doubts about succeeding in their mission swelled within them. Before they had time to think about their plight, the guard threw the hefty door open and pushed them gently forward with his outstretched arm.

As the door quietly latched itself behind them, their senses were being overwhelmed by the layout of the cavernous hall in which they now found themselves. It was as if they had entered a different and very cold world. The room temperature was lower than anything they had previously experienced. They knew the president liked his air conditioning, but they had not been aware of the super frosty condition of his office. There was so much light in the room that they could not distinguish the president sitting behind a huge table at the other end of the hall. They were blinded by all the light pouring in from the seaside, floor-to-ceiling, oversized series of windows. This early-morning sunlight combined with the light cast by the countless bulbs of the huge crystal chandelier hanging from the middle of the ceiling.

They looked down to shade their eyes from the brilliant light and saw stretched out before them a rare, handwoven Persian carpet with intricate designs that so dazzled them they felt dizzy. This very expensive carpet stretched from one end of the forty-yard-long hall to the other. They instinctively knew to take off their sandals before stepping on this antique carpet. They were thrown off balance by the wonders that surrounded them. Walking over the swirling designs of the carpet proved to be another distraction. On the opposite wall of the grand hall was hanging a gigantic tapestry that depicted in colorful detail an old English fox-hunting scene from the sixteenth century. The entire room was furnished with genuine Louis XIV and XV furniture. They had heard the president had hired top French interior decorators to design and furnish his office, but they had never imagined such extraordinary ostentatiousness.

It was as if the president's intent was to re-create an office like those that existed in palaces and the offices of top government officials in Europe. The chiefs knew that this lavish layout was the president's way of conveying that he was special too and deserved the same respect as the top leaders in the world. The president was prepared to spare no expense to elevate his status. He wanted all to see that he was a capable and well-endowed leader who was as good, or better, than any other leader in the world. He wallowed in self-delusion and damned anyone who questioned him or did anything to stir up his paranoia. He was born to be a tyrant.

The chiefs slowly plodded ahead on the soft carpet toward the expansive table at the end of the hall. Letivi held their gift for the president tightly, as if it were some kind of stabilizing anchor. As they progressed, they could begin to make out the image of the president sitting across the table. They were both taken aback when they could see that the president was staring directly at them. They tried to avoid eye contact with the president by keeping their heads slightly bowed. As their eyes began to adjust to their bright foreign environs, they could see the rotund but diminutive president sitting on the other side of the table, tapping the fingers of his right hand softly against the well-lacquered burgundy surface of the highly polished Parisian table. There was nothing on the table, not even one scrap of paper. There were some matching side tables displaying assorted gifts and mementos the president had received from various dignitaries and wealthy businessmen. Next to his ornate chair was a smaller table holding four different telephones. So far, they had not observed anything in the president's office that was from Africa.

The president appeared taller than his five-foot, two-inch height because his chair had been elevated. He was dressed in the latest European fashion. It was known that a Chinese tailor came regularly from Singapore to make suits for the president. He also had special elevated shoes made in Italy. He did everything he could to look taller, but he often bragged that he was the same height as Napoleon. It was probable that he was as round as he was tall.

There were two stuffed chairs on their side of the table. The president raised his right hand and pointed at the two chairs. They interpreted this sign as meaning that they should sit down. Contrary to local custom, there were not any greetings or the shaking of hands. Before sitting down, Chief Letivi wanted to hand the president the gift they had brought for him, but before he could do so, the president pointed at a side table, indicating that the gift should be placed on it. Two very disoriented and anxious chiefs sat down and waited for the president to speak.

President Rafael did not waste any time in saying in a rough, booming voice, "So, you are here. What do you want from me?"

Chief Letivi squirmed in his chair as he tried to stop his head from spinning. At this moment, all their prior preparations seemed irrelevant. Letivi knew he should not show any hesitation, so he quickly blurted out, "Your Excellency, we need your help to build a cacao-processing plant."

The president grinned as he said, "So, this is why you have come to see me. Is that all?"

Chief Gyasi felt obliged to say something. "Yes, Mr. President. That is why we are here."

In an uncharacteristic jovial manner, the president smiled and said, "Very well. I am happy to receive you because just the other day I was speaking with the country director of the US development program about this very same topic. I will put him in touch with you so he and his staff can work with you to elaborate a feasibility study."

The chiefs glanced at each other in a way in which mutual consent was evident. Chief Letivi quickly exhorted, "Mr. President, thank you for such wise and much welcome help."

While Letivi was talking, the president was pulling something out of a side drawer. In a rapid movement, he sent sliding across the polished tabletop a small white box, saying, "Here, take this. It is a mobile phone. On the back, you will see pasted my private number and the number of this phone. Always keep this phone charged and with you. I will call you on this phone. Never call me unless I tell you to do so or it is an emergency."

Both chiefs tried to hide their puzzlement. They had never seen a mobile phone and were worried they would not know how to operate it. They also did not know how they would keep it charged, as there was not any electricity in the village. Being given this phone by a strangely buoyant president was a wrinkle they could not have anticipated. While they were not sure what having this phone represented, Letivi could only say, "Mr. President, thank you so much. We are very encouraged by this gesture on the part of Your Excellency, and we assure you that we will do as you have instructed."

The president dryly said, "Very well. I will summon the guard to escort you out. I hope we can do business together. I will be calling you."

The president pushed a button under his table, and the guard came almost running to see them out. They rose from their chairs prepared to say good-bye to the president, but he was lost in his thoughts and acted as if they were not there as he gazed out the window. The guard gave them no time to tarry and encouraged them with hand gestures to walk quickly out of the hall grabbing their sandals as they went. The chiefs had the impression that the guards were prohibited from talking. Before they knew it, they had been hustled back to their waiting taxi in front of the president's palace. It felt good to be in the warm sun after the nearly twenty minutes they had spent in the president's refrigerated office. As soon as they were seated in the taxi, the driver stepped on the accelerator, and they moved away with a jolt. The driver asked, "Where do we go now?"

The chiefs looked at each other, and Letivi knew that responding to the driver was his responsibility. He replied emphatically, "Take us home!"

They were both eager to hurry home to report to the elders and the clan heads what had transpired. They also needed time alone to discuss all the ramifications of their surreal meeting with the president. Their many concerns weighed heavily on them. Their biggest worry was the little box Letivi was holding in his hands. They did not know whether the mobile phone was some kind of Machiavellian trap or a real help in pursuing their cacao-plant project. They were frightened at the prospect of being at the beck and call of the president. This piece of new technology was a double-edged sword that would reduce their independence and freedom. They now felt like slaves to the president's phone. They feared the little white box contained the seeds of the ruination of their way of life.

CHAPTER NINE
AFRICA BOUND

Robin slammed shut the trunk of his car. He was startled when he looked up because a smiling Molly had magically appeared. The rays of the rising sun shrouded her, making her look like a glowing angelic apparition. Robin had to move around the car to gain a clear view of her. He saw a Molly he had not seen before. This time he saw an informal Molly who was dressed in ragged jeans and a simple white T-shirt. Her hair was tied up in a bun, and she did not wear any makeup. He did not know why, but there was something very appealing about the unvarnished Molly he was seeing. He suppressed the urge to embrace her.

He was expecting Molly to come and see him depart, but the way she appeared out of nowhere caught him off guard. His car was all packed, and he had checked out of his motel. He needed to leave soon on his long drive back to Chicago. He had spoken with his boss last night on the phone, and it was made imminently clear to him that he had to return to work. Feeling the way he did about Molly made his departure much more difficult than anticipated, but he knew he must leave. He was thinking of how to say good-bye to Molly when she told him again in a very determined voice, "We are going to Africa."

Robin had heard all this from Molly the day before, and he repeated what he had told her then: "Molly, there is no way we can afford a trip to Africa, even if I could get off work."

Molly laughed as she said, "Robin, you don't understand. This is our destiny. We have no other choice. We must go to Africa and see what happened to David. Please, Robin, believe what I say."

Robin hesitated. He found that he was unable to argue with a vivacious woman to whom he was so strongly attracted. He simply said, "OK. How do you propose we go to Africa?"

He did not know Molly had a plan, so he was surprised when she said, "Please don't worry about how much our trip to Africa will cost because I will pay for everything. I will have my twenty-second birthday next week, making me eligible to receive the trust funds my maternal grandfather left me in his will when he died many years ago. At that time, I will have more than enough money to pay for our trip."

With the money issue out of the way, Robin was lost for words. He could see that the main hurdle to going to Africa had been removed, but he could not bring himself to accept completely Molly's bold plan. He kept thinking of reasons why he should not go to Africa instead of why he should go. He did not want to rain on Molly's parade, so he tried to share her excitement and choose his words carefully. "Molly, wow! So you'll be rich. That's wonderful news. But how can I leave my job? How long will we be gone?"

Molly was adamant. "You must persuade your boss to release you for work purposes or give you an unpaid sabbatical leave to do research on David's case. If this does not work, give notice and quit. This is an once-in-a-lifetime opportunity that you cannot miss! You can always find another job."

Molly's words were almost too much for Robin to digest. He was speechless. He felt as if he were totally under her control. All he could meekly say was, "Molly, I will do my best to do as you propose. It would be a very good and great thing for us to travel to Africa together. You are right. This is not something we should miss doing."

Upon hearing Robin's words, Molly stepped briskly forward and tightly embraced him with a long and ever-so-sweet kiss on the lips. Robin could not resist such a loving gesture and wished the kiss would never end. He was indeed like putty in Molly's affectionate hands. Molly released her lips from Robin's and looked deeply into his dark-brown eyes.

Sensing her control over Robin, she made a muffled little laugh, smiled, and gave him another quick peck on the cheek before stepping away. They both felt their body temperatures rising but knew very well that this was not the time or the place for any sexual arousal.

Robin found himself asking why Molly just did what she did. Was it because she was beginning to feel love for him, or was it because she wanted to show him how happy she was with his agreement to go to Africa with her? Either way, Robin was now thinking he was prepared to sacrifice everything to be with Molly. He could feel surging within his innards the undeniable pull of adventure and love. He could not suppress the growing passion he felt for being fully immersed in the exciting pursuit of this captivating combination. He softly whispered to himself, "Adventure and love. To hell with everything else; I'm going to Africa with Molly."

Molly brought Robin almost down to earth by saying, "I know you have to go now. Don't worry about anything. I'll work with a travel agent on all our trip details. We both need to apply for passports and get visas and our shots. I will collect as much info as I can on the country of Kotoku. I think that we should be ready to travel in about a month. Of course, I will quit my boring, little job at the courthouse."

A much more agitated Robin reaffirmed, "If my boss will not give me leave, I will also quit my job. In that way, I can get my severance pay and use it for our trip. I will also contact the Peace Corps' office in Washington to see if they have any information on David. Oh, Molly. I'm getting so wired! I can't wait to go with you to Africa."

Molly was tempted to hug and kiss Robin again, but she restrained her natural affectionate self and opened the car door for him, saying, "Robin, we will be in frequent contact. You have my phone numbers and address, and I have yours. Please drive safely and call me as soon as you are settled in Chicago. And, Robin, thank you for making my life so much more interesting than it was."

Molly wanted to add, "I love you," but the words stuck in her mouth. She did stand and watch him pull his car out of the motel parking lot, waving as he drove away. She stood there a long while as she thought about how much she liked Robin and how thankful she was for his coming into her life. She believed without any doubt that God had brought Robin into her life for a purpose. As she walked to her own car, she tried to focus on all she had to do to inform her family and friends that she was going to Africa with Robin Fletcher. She was sure her shocking news would hit the small town of El Dorado like a bombshell.

Robin drove the almost two hundred miles to Kansas City before his feet were fully back on terra firma. His mind was over-whelmed by thoughts of Molly, Africa, and unraveling the mystery of David's disappearance. He stopped only for gas and some snacks he could eat while he drove. He drove all day and part of the night to reach Chicago. On the last leg of the trip, he began practicing out loud what he would tell his boss about his trip to Africa. He knew his news would be a huge jolt to his office. People would question his sanity, but he was already beyond the point of turning back.

The next day, Robin confidently strolled into his cantanker-ous old boss's office and told him all about why he was going to Africa. His boss lost no time in telling him that there was no way he could give him any time off for such a nutty adventure. Robin had no choice but to give a thirty-day notice. He was surprised that his boss quietly accepted his resignation without further dis-cussion. While disappointed, Robin felt relieved to get this tense meeting with his boss behind him. He also felt exhilarated by the knowledge that he would soon be free from work. He liked the way he felt. It was as if he had a new lease on his life.

Molly had no qualms about quitting her low-paid, mundane job at the courthouse. She informed everyone she encountered about her upcoming trip to Africa. Most people laughed when they heard her say this because they thought she was joking. In general, people did not know anything about Africa, and nobody had ever heard of the country of Kotoku. For most, Africa was a distant, dark continent where Tarzan roamed in a jungle full of ferocious wild animals and primitive black people. Nobody in El Dorado or the entire county had ever been to Africa.

The hard part for Molly was informing her family, especially her mother, of her plans. She knew they would not understand

and they would prefer for her not to spend part of her trust funds on such an unproductive adventure. The most difficult part of all for her was leaving her secret treasure: an adorable two-year old daughter, Elisa. This daughter was the fruit of a brief relationship she had had with a young man she had met while in college. While she regretted deeply having ever met this young man, she loved her daughter more than life itself.

Molly's mother knew her daughter well enough to know that she should not interfere with anything Molly set her mind on. It was an easy matter for her to take care of little Elisa because they had always lived together and she had been her main caregiver since her birth. Molly's great love for her mother was only exceeded by her love for her daughter. She would leave all the explaining to her father for her mother to do, as she knew her father would never agree with her going to Africa, showing his grumpy disagreement by staying distant.

Robin called Peace Corps Washington several times to find someone who could provide him information on David. He found that the records for the period in the late 1960s, when David had served as a Peace Corps volunteer, had long ago been sent to a government warehouse for storage and ultimate destruction. The Peace Corps headquarters kept records for only five years and then sent them off for storage. As the Peace Corps had a rule that nobody could work there for more than five years, it was impossible to find anyone who could remember anything about what had happened to David over twenty years ago. The Peace Corps bureaucracy simply did not have any institutional memory.

Robin and Molly were running up huge phone bills as they called each other almost every other day. Robin explained how he had struck out with Peace Corps Washington. They agreed that any available information on David would probably be located at the Peace Corps office in Melomti, the capital city of Kotoku. Molly had already contacted a travel agent and photo-copied material from the library about Kotoku. She told Robin that he would have plenty of time on the long plane ride to read this material. She would fly to Chicago to join him at O'Hare Airport, and from there, they would fly to JFK Airport in New York to catch their direct Pan Am flight to Dakar, Senegal. After a brief stopover in Dakar, they would fly on to Melomti.

They both had applied for their passports. The travel agent told Molly they could get their one-month entry visas for Kotoku when they arrived at the airport in Melomti. If they stayed longer, they could go to the immigration office in Melomti to extend their visas. In any event, Molly did not think they would be in Kotoku for more than a month. They both had also gone to their local offices of the US Public Health Service to obtain their required World Health Organization yellow cards, which certi-fied they had received all of the vaccinations needed for inter-national travel. They were also working with local physicians and drug stores to obtain the medicine they must take to help protect them from malaria. Molly was waiting to be certain of the date her trust funds would be available before reserving the dates for their travel and obtaining their tickets.

They were both worried about what kind of clothes they should take. Molly shared with Robin the information she had found on the climate in Kotoku. They both knew that Kotoku's hot and humid tropical climate would require light summer clothing. They decided to buy new suitcases and carry-on bags with strong padlocks. They would take as much as the airline would allow. If there was any room in their luggage, they would be taking sur-vival items such as their favorite snack food.

Molly would be taking lots of sunscreen and insect repellent, and a good supply of what she considered essential beauty products. Robin made sure he had enough of the deodorant and hair cream that he regularly used. They were also considering taking iodine tablets to purify their drinking water. Molly had read enough about health conditions in Kotoku to be worried about how they would avoid being sick while they were in this low-income country. She was concerned about the absence of hospitals with international standards.

The big day finally arrived when Molly's lawyer confirmed the date that several hundred thousand dollars in her trust fund would be transferred to her bank account. Based on this information, she made their airline and Melomti hotel reservations with her travel agent. She wrote a check for the whole amount, using the date her trust funds were to be deposited. She had already informed her bank of her trip and her need for several thousand dollars' worth of traveler's checks. She had also obtained a couple of credit cards in case they would need them. She was constantly reflecting on all they would need on their trip. She bought a leather-bound notebook to use as a journal to record every detail of their trip. She estimated the cost of the entire trip would be about $15,000.

Robin worried about what to do with his apartment and car. He decided to put his car in long-term parking at the O'Hare Airport and lock his apartment. He informed his landlord of his upcoming trip and advised the post office and the newspaper company to stop all deliveries to his house. He paid all his bills in advance. He pasted a note on his refrigerator door to remind himself to make sure all the water faucets and gas burners on his stove were tightly shut. He emptied his refrigerator and unplugged it. He left a key to his front door with a trusted neighbor so that he could enter his apartment in the event of an emergency. Robin was also constantly reflecting on all that he needed to do before taking off for unknown parts in Africa.

The long-awaited day finally arrived when Molly was able to inform Robin of their travel dates. Molly would leave from Wichita Mid-Continent Airport on an American Airlines flight early in the morning on Thursday, November 8, to join Robin on the same day in the outer departure lounge of O'Hare Airport. They would take an afternoon flight to JFK Airport and lay over there for several hours before boarding their over nine-hour night flight with Pan Am to Dakar. They would arrive in Melomti late on the following day. Molly noted that she was leaving the return dates of their nonrefundable round-trip tickets open. She also noted that Melomti time was six hours later than Kansas time. Molly repeatedly told Robin (and herself) not to forget anything.

Molly said her tearful good-byes to family and friends at home in El Dorado. Her best friend from high school drove her the thirty-five miles to the airport on the west side of Wichita. Tears were streaming down their cheeks as Molly checked in and headed for the departure lounge. Deep down, Molly was very scared and beginning to have doubts about why she was traveling to Africa. It seemed so unreal for her. Why was she leaving the place she had grown up in and going to a small, underdeveloped country in a vast, unknown continent that was on the other side of the world? It really made no sense. She kept telling herself that no matter what, she had to go. She was committed to pursuing this madcap trip to Africa in spite of any of the possible consequences. Such determination, right or wrong, is never easy, especially for someone who has never been out of her home state.

Everything went smoothly for Molly, and she arrived at O'Hare Airport as planned. She felt so lost and lonely that when she spotted Robin in the crowded airport, she could not restrain herself. She sprinted toward him, and, when Robin saw her, he ran toward her. They dropped their handbags and collided in a passionate embrace while hundreds looked on. They kissed each other numerous times. Those watching them could only assume that this was an amorous young couple who had been happily reunited after a lengthy separation. They held hands and looked into each other's eyes. At that moment, they knew it was them against the world.

These were dizzying moments for Molly and Robin. It took them a while to get their bearings and head for their departure gate. After a long walk through chaotic crowds of people hustling to and fro, they arrived at their gate to learn that their flight to JFK had been delayed for a couple of hours because of an oncoming winter storm. Robin went ahead and checked in. As Molly had done in Wichita, he checked his suitcase all the way to Melomti. They passed through the final formalities and began a long wait in the outer boarding area for their flight to JFK. They were afraid they would arrive too late in New York to catch their flight to Dakar.

They breathed more easily when it was announced over the public address system that their flight to JFK had finally arrived and boarding would start in about thirty minutes. For almost this entire time, Molly and Robin were holding hands and sitting close to each other, ignoring those around them. It was as if they were involuntarily giving each other the courage they needed to stay on the course that would take them to Africa. They knew they were beyond the point of turning back, and they needed each other to keep moving forward. They knew they could make it to Africa only if they stayed closely together and supported each other. The force of events was forging a strong bond between them. They were obliged to stop caring about anything else except themselves and their trip to Africa.

Molly took her window seat, and Robin sat next to her. Molly snuggled up close to Robin, and, when it came time for takeoff, she squeezed his hand tightly. Once they reached cruising altitude and the pilot turned off the fasten-your-seat-belt sign, she released Robin's hand and sat up straight and said softly, "Robin, I need to admit something to you. Today is the first time I have ever flown in a plane."

Her words provoked a deep, hearty laugh in Robin, who happily replied, "Molly, I 'm so glad you told me that because I wanted to tell you the same thing. This is also my first time to fly."

On that jovial note, they both had a good laugh and began talking about the trip they had ahead of them. They were so engrossed in their conversation that they did not notice the plane starting to descend as it approached New York. It was only when the stewardess announced over the plane's PA system to buckle their seat belts and prepare for arrival that they realized they were almost at JFK. They enjoyed a smooth landing and joined in the hustle-bustle of transferring terminals at JFK. It took them some time to get to the Pan Am terminal desk and obtain their boarding passes for Flight 186 to Dakar. Once they arrived in the boarding zone, they had only a short wait before passengers were called to board the plane, a Boeing 707.

They were starkly reminded that they were indeed headed for Africa by the fact that most of their fellow passengers were Africans. Their eyes were darting from one person to another as they tried to take in all there was to see in this very animated group. They saw people dressed in colorful clothes they had not seen before, and they heard a number of different languages. In front and in back of them were Africans of all shades of black and brown, jostling for places in line with huge quantities of carry-on baggage. It was obvious that most of these people were carrying back to Africa as many goods as they could for reselling. Fitting all these people and their diverse bundles into the plane was an almost impossible chore for the flight attendants.

They overheard one stewardess complaining about the excess luggage people had brought with them. Molly and Robin felt lucky to find the two seats they had reserved together still available for them. All the overhead compartments were chock full, so Molly and Robin had to cram their relatively small handbags under the seats in front of them. It took more time than normal to get all the people seated and all their excessive and unusual carry-on bags stuffed into all the empty spaces available in the plane. There was much bantering and laughter among the polyglot group of Africans. The lively, motley group created a festive environment. Molly and Robin were acutely aware that this was the beginning of their exposure to a world very different from their own. They feared that the plane was so overloaded that it would not be able to take off. Molly was already making notes in her journal.

One of the American stewardesses noticed the worried looks on Molly's and Robin's faces and stopped to reassure these two innocent and naïve kids from Kansas. She said in a very pronounced Southern drawl, "Please don't worry. We do this flight every day, and we have never had a major problem. This old plane has been doing this haul almost daily for many years. In fact, I think this is the oldest plane Pan Am has in its large fleet."

Molly and Robin were not reassured by these words. They had the impression that Pan Am employed its oldest plane on the

African route because of the unwieldy nature of the clientele and their cumbersome assortment of luggage. When the captain flashed on the seat belt indicator and announced over the PA system that they were taxiing to a takeoff point, the rambunctious group of passengers quickly became silent. All of them began to pray in their own ways for the safety of the flight. There were Christian and Muslim prayers, and some prayed as well to their ancestors and African spirits for protection. Molly looked at Robin and said, "Well, at least we have one thing in common with these people. Let's also pray."

CHAPTER TEN
LIFE CHANGES

hiefs Letivi and Gyasi sped out of Melomti as fast as they could. They were anxious to return to Ataku to inform the village elders and clan heads about their meeting with the president. They kept urging their driver to go at top speed. At every checkpoint, they were quickly waved through by highway police and customs agents. It was as if the whole country knew they had been to see the president and were, therefore, special elites who should not be hindered in any way. Of course, the entire country had heard of Ataku's white chief, and seeing him was a novel delight for all those along the roadside who caught sight of him as his car whizzed by.

The chiefs were an unusual pair. Chief Letivi looked white, and his boyish face betrayed his status as a chief. Indeed, he was the youngest chief in the entire country, although he was the most educated. Chief Gyasi was nearly seventy years old and had a deep-black complexion; he very much fit the traditional image of a chief. And he had indeed been a chief for almost his entire adult life. People who saw them go by would often remark,

"There goes the baby white chief and the old grandpa chief." Never before had anyone seen such an incomparable pair of chiefs. Nobody knew that they were actually seeing an elderly grandfather with his half-caste grandson.

When they reached the turnoff to the road that led to Ataku, Chief Letivi glanced at the little white box lying on the seat between him and Gyasi. Seeing this box rudely reminded him that they had to keep the mobile phone it contained charged so the president could call them. Just as the driver was about to turn to go to Ataku, Letivi firmly instructed him to keep going to Kpolomo, the regional capital, which was located fifteen miles farther down the highway. Letivi turned to Gyasi and explained, "We must go to Kpolomo first to buy a small generator so we can charge the president's phone." Gyasi nodded and grunted his understanding of this last-minute change in plans.

Letivi continued, "We will go to the Lebanese store. If we do not have enough money, I know the owner will sell it to us on credit."

They arrived at Aziz and Son's store and were well received by the young Aziz. Letivi could not know that the father of this man had supplied his father with construction materials for his various projects. And, of course, the young Aziz could not know that his deceased father had been of much help years ago to Letivi's father, Bobovovi, who mysteriously disappeared months before Letivi was born. Neither knew that they both looked very much like their fathers. Aziz, the younger, served Letivi in the same gracious and helpful manner that his father had done with Bobovovi.

Aziz was delighted to see the chiefs. "Welcome, my chiefs. I am very happy to see you. How can I help you?"

Letivi replied, "Thank you, Aziz. We do not have much time. We need a small generator that can charge our new mobile phone."

Aziz smiled and said, "Of course, I can help you. I am very impressed that you are among the first to acquire a mobile phone. Let me show you a small Honda generator that can keep your phone charged."

Aziz escorted them inside his shop and pointed to a small, bright-red Honda generator, explaining, "This generator can fully charge your phone after only thirty minutes of operation. You should charge your phone every day. Although the gasoline tank looks small, a full tank can run for about eight hours. It is easy to start...you just pull once or twice on this rope. I am selling this little generator for about four hundred dollars, or two hundred thousand gadis in local money. It is the smallest and cheapest generator I have."

The chiefs gulped in unison when they heard the price. This amount was a colossal sum for them. Paying for the generator would put a big hole in their village's treasury. But they had no choice. They must buy the generator to stay in touch with the president and respect their end of the deal they had struck with him. Letivi reacted to Aziz's sale pitch by saying, "This is exactly what we need, but we cannot pay you all at once. We can pay you a down payment now and the rest over the next three months."

Aziz lost no time in replying, "No problem, my chiefs. I know I can trust you, and I am happy to be of service to you. I will have my assistant load the generator into your car. I will provide you free a jerry can for the gasoline. You will always need to keep a supply of fuel. If you like, I can show you how the generator works."

The chiefs were in a hurry, but they thought it best that Aziz show them how to operate the generator. Aziz sent one of the young African men working for him to fetch some fuel while his other assistant carried the generator to an area outside in front of his shop. Aziz poured some fuel into the generator's reservoir, adjusted the choke, and pulled on the starter rope. The generator started with one pull. He then showed them how to turn it off.

Aziz then told Letivi, "Now, you try it."

Letivi adjusted and tightened his robes before repeating what he had observed Aziz do. He was easily able to start the generator. While the generator was running, Aziz said, "Bring your phone so we can see if it charges."

The driver brought the phone, and Aziz showed the chiefs how to hook up the charger and turn on the phone. He plugged it into the generator and noted to them the blinking light that indicated it needed charging. He explained that when the little red light stopped blinking, the phone was fully charged and useable for at least twenty-four hours. He also showed Letivi how to set the loudest ring tone.

Letivi was thankful for this demonstration and all the information Aziz had provided, but deep down, his uneasiness about the care and maintenance of this phone was growing. The obligatory link this phone caused him to maintain with the president troubled him greatly. He was beginning to see this troublesome phone as a necessary evil. He was also disturbed that he could not even tell Aziz who had given him the phone. He thanked Aziz and asked Gyasi to pay him some money. They loaded everything into the taxi and bid farewell to Aziz and his helpers.

The driver quickly told the chiefs that he would need to purchase gas before going to Ataku, so they would need to pay him.

They gave the driver the money due him and his boss, the owner of the car, adding a little so he could also fill the plastic jerry can. They stopped briefly at a Mobil service station on the way out of Kpolomo before heading to their beloved Ataku.

The first person to see the chiefs arriving shouted out the news, and word spread like a super sonic boom to every corner of the village. Everyone dropped what they were doing and ran to cheer the return of their chiefs. The drums rolled, and the people sang the praises of their chiefs. The excitement rose as the crowd gathered. Everyone was eager to hear about the results of their meeting. Chief Letivi raised his right hand to quiet those assembled around him and Gyasi. In a loud voice he announced, "We are very glad to be home. In one hour, I ask that all our elders and clan leaders meet with me and Chief Gyasi in my compound meeting room. Thank all of you for giving us such a warm welcome."

As the chiefs began the uphill walk to the royal compound, the people sang louder their praises, and the drummers pounded harder their goatskin-covered tambours. Following them were some young men carrying the generator and gasoline container. The sight of these items was the cause of much speculative comment. Most people had never seen a generator before, and they were wondering what it was and how the chief would use it. Many assumed that it was something the president had given them.

The spontaneous joyous outburst demonstrated by the villagers was sincere and heartfelt. It would take some hours before this fervent outpouring of thankfulness for the safe return of their chiefs would dissipate. Meanwhile, elders and clan leaders were preparing themselves to go to Chief Letivi's compound to receive the news on the unprecedented visit with the highest authority in the land. Hearts were beating faster than usual in anticipation. Everyone knew this could be a historical turning point for their village.

Chiefs Letivi and Gyasi quickly ate some white corn bread and sardines that the women in Letivi's compound had prepared for their arrival and laid out on a small, low table under the shade of a big neem tree. Once they had their fill of this much-welcome snack and drank some cool, clear water, they walked to an adjoining compound to await the senior leaders of their village. As they walked through the compound, Letivi noticed a new and very pretty young woman, or teenage girl, standing alone under another neem tree. He could see she was watching him closely. He asked Gyasi, "Who is that new young woman? Do you know who she is and what she is doing here?"

Gyasi replied with a wry grin on his aged face, "Don't worry about her. I will tell you about her later."

They took their places in front of the rows of benches to be occupied by village leaders and had a brief exchange about how they would present their meeting with the president. They waited quietly as they asked in whispers for the grandfathers and a number of key spirits to join and bless their meeting. These moments of devout meditation were interrupted by the top compound guard, who came to the doorway and announced that village leaders had arrived and were grouped in the passageway just outside the main compound entrance. Chief Letivi signaled to the guard to tell the leaders to enter.

The elders filed in first, in order of their ages, beginning with the oldest. Then, clan heads followed in order of the rank and age of their respective clans. They all stood in their places until everyone had entered and Chief Letivi asked them to be seated. A few moments passed as the two chiefs looked into the eyes of every man there. Chief Gyasi spoke first, saying, "This is an important day in the life of our village. We did meet with the president to ask his help in establishing a cacao-processing plant. Chief Letivi will tell you about our meeting. Please listen carefully to his words and be prepared to comment after he has finished speaking. Thank you."

It was not customary for Letivi to stand when addressing the leaders, but this time, he did. By his standing, the leaders knew what he had to say would be exceptionally important. All eyes were on Letivi. The thirty or so men assembled were ready to weigh each word he uttered. Their lives were at a standstill until they knew what Letivi and Gyasi already knew.

Letivi followed custom and greeted everyone in the traditional manner, calling also on the grandfathers to bless and join this meeting. The leaders reacted with loud applause and 'amen's.' Letivi had decided to focus only on the results of their meeting with the president and not say a word about his impressions of the president and his office, or anything that could be interpreted negatively with regard to the person of the president. Everything must be done to please the president and to avoid doing anything that could provoke his wrath.

Letivi looked around the room before saying in a loud and affirmative voice, "My fellow brothers, I will limit my words to the essential. This will make for a dry presentation, but I find it best this way. I will start by saying I am pleased to inform you that our mission was a success. The president has agreed to help us."

Before he could continue, his first sentences were met with loud cheering and applause. Letivi raised both arms to quiet the men. He went on to say in a factual-as-possible way, "We saw the president, and he agreed to help us. He will contact one of the foreign embassies in Melomti and ask it to provide a technical expert who can assist us. He gave us a mobile phone so he can stay in contact with us on this matter."

Letivi reached into a deep pocket of his traditional gown, fished out the mobile phone, and held it high so all could see and marvel at this heretofore unknown technological advancement. Holding the phone high above his head, he exclaimed, "Behold what the president will use to talk to me. I must now keep this phone charged and with me at all times. As we know, our president never sleeps, and he can call me at any time."

The men could hardly believe what they were hearing and what they saw. They had never heard of or seen a cell phone before and could not imagine how it was possible for one to talk on such a small apparatus. This was indeed some powerful magic that surpassed anything they had previously experienced. They were spellbound and speechless as they tried to comprehend the unimaginable.

Letivi continued his presentation. "This phone comes with one major complication. It requires some electricity daily to stay charged, and this has obliged us to purchase at our expense a small generator." He signaled to the guard at the door to bring in the generator so all could see.

The generator represented another marvel they had heard of but not seen before. Letivi asked all to gather around as he demonstrated how the generator operated and how he would use it to charge his phone. Seeing the phone and the generator made many of the men believe the village had already taken a decisive step into the future. Some of the older elders worried about how these new technical inventions would interfere with the spirit world and the village's traditions. Letivi said nothing about his own fears of staying connected with a self-centered president who was capable of the most treacherous acts.

Letivi finished his demonstration and asked the men to take their seats. He then asked, "Do any of you have any questions or comments?"

The group fell silent. Not one hand was raised. Nobody knew what to say. Many in the group were thinking only of returning to their families to recount the wonders they had just observed. After waiting a few minutes to see if anyone had anything to say, Letivi said, "It appears that nobody has anything to add at this time. Therefore, all we can do now is to wait for the president's call. I wish all of you a safe return to your respective households. May the grandfathers bless your paths home."

After the last man shook the hands of the chiefs with the usual resounding snapping of fingers and exited the royal meeting room, Gyasi asked Letivi to sit down so he could tell him something. Gyasi cleared his throat and said, "That young lady you saw outside is the one we have selected as a potential wife for you."

Letivi abruptly interrupted his grandfather. "What? That is not possible! She is too young. She does not look like she has the legal age of eighteen that the government now requires for marriage. How can this be?"

"My dear son, please be calm. Age has nothing to do with this. She is old enough, and that is all that counts. She can read and write. She is intelligent, has a good heart, and is of the highest character. She comes from a prominent family. She is also very beautiful and wants to be your wife. She is ready and capable of taking care of your every need. She possesses all the qualities sought in a chief's wife. You can't do better."

Letivi was beginning to see that he could not argue with this choice. He understood that as chief, he must be married and father children in order to maintain the respect of all his subjects. He did not know what to say. He finally said in a doubt-ful tone, "OK. I will try my best to make our relationship work. I just hope this works and she is as good as you say."

Gyasi replied in a compassionate manner, "I do not want you to feel you are pressured to marry this girl. She will stay here with you for a few nights so that you can be your own judge as to her desirability as a wife. If you find you are not compatible with her, she will leave gracefully and we will look for another candidate. Please do not forget that having a wife is in your best interests, and that means it is in the best interests of Ataku. Furthermore, your mother would highly approve of this girl."

Letivi quietly acceded to what his grandfather said and simply replied, "So be it. Tell her she is welcome to join me."

Gyasi embraced his grandson, saying, "I am very tired. Today has been too much for this old man. I will tell the girl on my way out that you have accepted. From this point on, she will have the lead in caring for you. By the way, her name is Delalia."

Letivi was also very tired. He walked across the compound to his sleeping room. Although it was only late in the afternoon, he wanted to change clothes, take a bath, and go to bed. He also needed time to reflect on all that had happened today and what he would say when the president called. He made sure his mobile phone was sufficiently charged. He told one of his guards to put the generator and its fuel container in the small shed next to his sleeping room.

He did not notice, but while he strode across the compound to his sleeping quarters, Delalia was watching him quietly from the shadows of the neem tree. Once he had entered his sleeping room, she advanced and stationed herself at the entrance to his room. Meanwhile, Letivi was in his room wrestling with taking off his layers of royal robes. He stepped out of his room to call for help to remove his robes, and there he found the attractive Delalia acting coy and smiling.

The shy Letivi was put in an awkward position and found himself lost for words. In reality, he did not have to say anything. Gracefully, Delalia swung into action, reaching behind Letivi and untying his robes. Once she had finished unfastening his robes, she stepped back with her head slightly bowed to show her respect and subservience. Letivi was barely able to thank her before returning to his room to remove his clothes and wrap himself in a towel.

He exited his room to walk the short distance to his shower stall. He found Delalia waiting there for him with a large galvanized bucket of warm water, a soap dish, and an akuja pod sponge. She placed these items inside the stall and stepped away so Letivi could enter. Once Letivi was inside the stall, she covered the entrance with a cloth so he could have his privacy. When Letivi finished bathing, she was waiting for him just outside the shower stall, ready to assist him in any way. She took his bucket, soap dish, and sponge and followed him back to his room. When Letivi entered his room, he was surprised to find that his royal robes had been hung neatly in their place in his large mahogany armoire.

So far, Delalia had not said a word, and he could not see one thing to complain about. Her presence made him nervous. He was certainly not accustomed to this kind of female attention, but he had no good reason to object to it. He did not want to admit it, but a big part of his reluctance to be with Delalia was that he had never been with a woman before. His best-kept secret was that he was still a virgin. He knew if people knew that he had never had sex, it would be the end of his chieftaincy. Nobody had ever heard of a man his age who was a virgin. A chief could never be a virgin because to become a chief, you had to prove your virility. In this and so many other things, Letivi was indeed the exception to the rules governing the selection of a chief.

Letivi changed into his sleeping clothes. He cleaned his teeth with some small sticks he kept for that purpose. He lay down on his simple double bed, which was covered with a thin foam-rubber mattress topped by a sheet and some blankets folded and placed at the foot of the bed. His intention was to think over the day's events and to visit the grandfather's houses at nightfall. But his fatigue was more than he thought, and he fell into a deep sleep.

Later in the night, Delalia quietly entered Letivi's room with a lit candle that was stuck upright on a small tin dish. She waited until her eyes adjusted to the light and set the candle down on the floor. She could see Letivi sleeping on one side of the bed, so she went to the opposite side. She unwrapped and dropped to the floor the blue cotton cloth that covered her shapely, nude body. She lay down gently next to Letivi and waited to see if he had noted her presence. She would lie awake all night. She did not want to miss any opportunity to satisfy Letivi's manhood.

The night wore on, and hours passed before Letivi stirred. The cool night air prompted him to reach down to pull one of the covers over him. Delalia saw his hand groping for a cover. She quickly grabbed one cover and placed it carefully over Letivi, who fell back to sleep without realizing that it was someone else who had covered him. Later on, Letivi's eyes suddenly popped wide open. There was a little red light blinking incessantly. It was that infernal mobile phone he had left on a chair next to his bed. It irritated him to know that the light meant the phone needed charging. He certainly was not going to get up and charge the phone at this time of night.

He turned over so he would not be facing the phone's blinking light. It was then that he saw lying next to him his wife-to-be, the lovely Delalia. As much as the flickering candlelight would allow, his eyes timidly scanned her very feminine and well-developed body from head to toe. His eyes stopped at her angelic face. He could see she was wide awake and smiling happily. At that instant, Delalia knew that Letivi would be hers that night. As for Letivi, he felt trapped between a marriage with a presidential mobile phone and a marriage with a girl not of his choosing. He did not know which way to turn. At the moment, it seemed much easier to succumb to Delalia's charms than to deal with the bête noire that the president's mobile phone represented.

CHAPTER ELEVEN
HELTER-SWELTER

The flight from New York to Dakar seemed to take forever. Molly and Robin had overlooked the fact that there was a five-hour time difference between the US East Coast and West Africa. Molly saw it getting light outside, and she woke Robin to tell him that they must be getting close to Dakar. Robin looked at his watch and told Molly, "Lower the window blind and go back to sleep. We are only a couple of hours into a nine-hour flight. Our night was short because we are flying east into the rising sun."

Molly sighed and snuggled up against Robin's shoulder again to try to sleep. The anticipation of their arrival in Africa and the stomach rumblings caused by their almost inedible in-flight meal made it hard for her to rest. She knew she needed to conserve her energy and get as much rest as possible for the rigors of tomorrow (which had already arrived). As much as she tried, she could not sleep, although it appeared that everyone else on the plane was dead asleep. It was hard for her to believe that such a loud and boisterous group of African passengers could be so quiet and sleeping. She wondered if they knew something she did not know. All she could think of was arriving in Kotoku and finding some clues about what had happened to David in that small African country.

She did enjoy cuddling up next to Robin under the airplane covers, especially when the plane was rocked by some rough air turbulence. The hours ground on, and Molly's impatience with arriving in Dakar was growing. She was convinced the plane was going too slow, as it seemed as if it was just taking too long to arrive. She wanted to talk with Robin, but like most of the other passengers, he was fast asleep. Having Molly next to him made him feel very good and relaxed. He knew he needed all the rest he could get and was trying his best to sleep.

In an attempt to make the time pass faster, Molly turned on her reading light and began going over again all the information on Kotoku that she had collected. She had perused all this material many times, but as she neared the continent and actual firsthand contact with Africa, the information grew in importance and relevance. It was something of a relief for her when the stewardess turned on the cabin lights and the plane's captain announced that breakfast would be served and they would soon begin their descending flight pattern into Dakar. She shook Robin and said, "Wake up. We are almost there. I'm so excited about arriving in Africa!"

Robin slowly stirred. Once he was fully awake, he wanted to make a dash for one of the plane's mini-restrooms before the captain turned on the illuminated fasten-your-seat-belt indicator. Molly also wanted to go to the restroom to relieve herself and freshen up. They got up from their seats in the middle of the plane and fetched their small toiletry cases from their hand luggage stowed under the seats. Then they headed to the back of the plane, where the restrooms were located. There was already a long line, so they had to wait for over twenty minutes before gaining access to the restroom cubicles.

Robin finished his restroom business quickly and returned to his seat. He thought breakfast would be served shortly, and he wanted to be in his seat before it arrived. Molly did not return quickly, and Robin became worried that something was wrong. He was almost ready to go search for her when she returned smiling and chuckling to herself. Robin asked Molly, "What happened? I was becoming worried about you."

Molly laughed and said, "Well, it took me some time to figure out how to work the restroom door lock."

Now it was Robin's turn to laugh. "I didn't have that problem because I was afraid to lock the latch on my door." His words had them both laughing and feeling better in spite of the lengthy flight and their growing jet lag.

Small trays, each with a tiny croissant and a large tablespoon of cold scrambled eggs on the side, were rapidly served. Other stewardesses came swiftly by to offer coffee or tea. Robin and Molly ate the croissants, spreading on them the orange marmalade from the little plastic containers that had been provided. They both had coffee with milk and a large dose of sugar. The plane was beginning its descent to Dakar. The stewardesses were hustling to and fro to collect all the breakfast trays and trash. The captain turned on the fasten-your-seat-belt sign and announced over the PA system that they should be arriving at the Dakar Yoff International Airport in about thirty minutes. Molly and Robin braced themselves for their first contact with Africa.

Everyone was praying out loud for a safe landing. It was after 3:00 p.m. local time when the old 707 workhorse of the Pan Am fleet landed smoothly on the tarmac. Molly grasped tightly

Robin's hand, and they joined in the prayers. The plane turned around at the end of the airstrip and taxied slowly to its indicated parking place a good distance from the terminal. Departing passengers were instructed to prepare to deboard and take a bus to the terminal. As the deboarding passengers passed Molly and Robin, they politely said good-bye and wished them safe travels. Molly and Robin were sincerely impressed by these polite farewell gestures.

The few transit passengers, such as Molly and Robin, were instructed to remain in their seats. The temperature in the plane rose because the engines were turned off and the doors were left open. For the first time, Molly and Robin were able to get a full whiff of Africa's different smell. They were eager to get up and walk to the door to look out upon Senegal. Just when they were about to stand up, an announcement over the PA system asked all transit passengers to deboard with their hand baggage and wait for a while on the tarmac next to the plane before re-boarding. They were told that this would give them an opportunity to stretch their legs and breathe some fresh air.

The outside air was indeed refreshing, and it was not hot, as Molly and Robin had expected. Evidently, Dakar's location on a peninsula surrounded by the Atlantic Ocean gave it a mild, cool climate. They thought they had been asked to get off the plane in order to allow for its cleaning. That was true, but something else very unusual was happening before their eyes. Men were climbing all over the plane to stick huge decals over all of Pan Am's markings. On the decals they were placing were the words, "Air Afrique." It was apparent that from here on, the plane would be considered part of this West African airline. This all came as a huge surprise for transit passengers. Molly and Robin did not really care as long as they arrived in Melomti as scheduled. They did, however, have some concerns about the change from a Pan Am to an Air Afrique crew.

It was almost dark before the plane was ready to take off for Melomti. During this two-and-one-half-hour last leg of their trip, Molly and Robin chatted constantly about what they would do following their arrival in Melomti. As they would be arriving after 9:00 p.m. local time, they wanted to go straight to their hotel after obtaining an entry visa, clearing customs, and collecting their baggage at the airport. Their travel agent had made them a reservation at Melo Hotel, the highest-rated hotel in Melomti. They had a few hundred dollars that they would change into local currency at the airport. They would look for the hotel shuttle at the airport, and if one was not available, they would take a taxi to Melo Hotel. Most of their money was in traveler's checks that Molly kept in a money-pouch belt with their passports and tickets. This belt was always strapped tightly around her waist. They would change these checks progressively at a local bank as they needed cash. They firmly believed they had everything under control and were ready for any unanticipated contingencies Kotoku would pose.

The Air Afrique plane made a smooth landing in spite of the rough runway. Molly and Robin both vied to look out the small airplane window to catch a first glance of Melomti. They had seen, as they flew over this coastal city that it did not have much electricity, and now that they were on the ground, they could not see many lights. The plane came to a halt, and all Melomti passengers were asked not to forget their hand luggage and to deboard. Molly and Robin were very roused and eagerly looking forward to getting off the plane. They had been in travel status for almost twenty-four hours and were eager to get on with their search for information about David in Kotoku.

As they carefully stepped down the airplane stairs, they were not prepared for the blast of the hot and humid weather that enveloped them. They quickly became drenched in their own perspiration. Molly's makeup ran down her face, and her hair hung in wet strands around her head. They were both feeling very uncomfortable in a sultry climate they had not known before. Robin exclaimed, "Damn, it's hot! I'm soaked by the high humidity. I can't wait to take a shower and put on my shorts and tropical shirt."

Molly replied, "Ditto here. All I want to do is get through this airport to our hotel for a cold shower and a good night's sleep in a bed."

Not only was Melomti's climate very different from Dakar's, they both could see already that the country was not as developed. Weeds were growing up through the cracks of the crumbling asphalt runway, and the airport terminal was a shabby building that resembled a large warehouse. An old man carrying a flashlight led them to the terminal entrance door which was covered with a tattered and very soiled gray curtain. An armed security guard dressed in dirty green military fatigues would hold the curtain open and signal the next passenger in the line to enter. All the passengers were required to enter alone and separately from those traveling with them. Robin was concerned about being separated from Molly, especially as it was dark and hard to see. Robin, therefore, told Molly, "I will go first, and if there is any problem, I will yell out a warning at the top of my voice."

Molly agreed with this idea but became afraid when Robin disappeared behind the filthy curtain. She listened intently for Robin's voice and any message he might try to yell out to her. The guard then held back the curtain and beckoned Molly forward. She passed through the curtain and was relieved when she saw Robin on the other side of a rope barrier giving her two thumbs up. Her body and her hand luggage were thoroughly searched by two other guards tending a makeshift wood counter. Later, they were told that this kind of intense searching was required because the country's president feared the opposition would try to import guns to assassinate him.

Molly and Robin were happily united behind the rope barrier, but their sweaty, smelly bodies discouraged them from embracing. They looked around and did not see any other tourists like them. The few other expatriates looked like people who worked for foreign embassies based in Melomti or for missionary groups. Certainly, the dismal arrival conditions in the airport did nothing to encourage tourism. In fact, if you wanted to discourage tourism, you would have an unwelcoming, seedy airport just like this one.

They struggled through a swarming mass of guys with an unusual fetid body odor who offered their services as baggage handlers. There were also numerous policemen and others who did not seem to have any role. They arrived at a desk that had a hand-drawn sign on it boldly stating 'Visas.' They showed the official sitting at the desk their two American passports. He scrutinized them carefully, looking at each page for a long time, even if the page was blank. All the while this overfed man was inspecting their passports, he kept making grunting sounds. After he finished, he looked at both of them closely and then took from a desk drawer some forms printed on flimsy yellow paper. He shoved the forms at both of them and barked out in a rough voice an instruction to complete them and return them to him as quickly as possible.

Robin found that he had lost his ballpoint pen, and he asked Molly if she had one. It took her some time to fish one out of her bulging large purse. She gave it to Robin and said, "You complete your form first, and then I will use yours to complete mine."

They could not use the visa desk to write on, and, as there was no other place on which to write, Robin used Molly's back. The difficulties of completing these visa forms were exacerbated by the lack of lighting. It was hard to see anything in the dimly lighted airport terminal warehouse. There were only a few low-wattage light bulbs dangling from the ceiling. Robin also had trouble writing because of his sweaty hands. The pen slipped in his hands, and perspiration soiled parts of the form.

Completing the forms was further complicated by the information they required. For example, they asked for the full names, birth dates, and professions of their parents. In the blank that asked for length of stay, Robin told Molly he would put down one month. He finished filling in his form and signed and dated it at the bottom as required. He then had Molly turn around and review his form so that she could complete hers in the same way.

Robin was embarrassed by one piece of information required by the form. It asked for marital status. He thought it best to put down that he was married to Molly. When they arrived at that line on the form, Robin explained, "Molly, as you can see here, I put down that I'm married. I think that it is in our interest that everyone thinks we are married. I hope you agree."

In spite of her physical misery, Molly was able to laugh while saying, "No problem, my dear husband. I understand."

Robin turned around so Molly could use his back to fill out the form. She had the same difficulties that he had experienced, plus an additional one—mosquitoes kept landing on her forearms and hands, and she would have to stop to swat at them. The entire airport terminal was full of mosquitoes. Molly was afraid of contracting malaria. It seemed that the mosquitoes were particularly attracted to her. Robin had less of a problem with the mosquitoes and said, "The mosquitoes seem to love your soft, tender skin and your smell. I once heard that mosquitoes are attracted to the 'fresh meat' of people who are arriving for the first time in the humid tropics."

Molly said, as she shooed away another mosquito, "That is not funny. I have never seen so many mosquitoes. I wonder which ones carry the parasite that infects you with malaria." Molly was undoubtedly being caused much stress by her new, strange, and uncomfortable surroundings. She was beginning to ask herself again why she had ever left the comfort of her own home in Kansas to come to such an obviously backward place that offered few of the amenities to which she was accustomed.

Molly completed her form, and Robin took their forms and passports back to the visa desk and handed them to the obese official in charge. The impolite official examined carefully the two forms and stamped them and the passports with his crudely made rubber stamp. He then said, "That will be twenty US dollars each."

Robin turned to Molly and asked for money. She handed him a hundred-dollar bill, and he in turn handed it to the official. The grumpy official grabbed the bill out of Robin's hand, saying, "I cannot give you change."

Robin was about to protest, but he was abruptly cut short when the man handed him the passports and got up and left. At that point, Molly and Robin were left with no choice but to head toward the baggage claim area at the far end of the terminal. There, they found men pulling and pushing large flatbed wagons heaped with a wide assortment of luggage. They unloaded the luggage in long rows, and passengers pushed forward to search for their suitcases. Young boys were hanging around to assist for a fee with the recovery of luggage.

Molly and Robin entered this chaotic scene, pushing their way forward through the mob of people to search the long lines of baggage for their two suitcases. At one point, a surge in the crowd forced Molly to be separated from Robin, and they struggled for a while to rejoin each other. They were both keeping a tight hold on their handbags and the jackets they had removed. The crowd eventually thinned as people located their suitcases. Molly and Robin spent over an hour looking for their suitcases without success. Their first thought was that they had been stolen in the melee.

They were fretting over the loss of all their stuff when they were approached by a man in an Air Afrique uniform who was holding a clipboard. He asked if they had found their luggage. They both replied in unison a loud 'no.'

He asked for their baggage tickets and compared the numbers on the tickets with a list of numbers on a paper on his clipboard. He then said, "Aha. I can see that your suitcases did not arrive. I suspect they were off-loaded in Dakar by mistake. In that case, they should arrive on tomorrow's flight. Please come back tomorrow at this time to claim your suitcases. See you tomorrow." He abruptly did an about-face and walked away, leaving Molly and Robin alone in the vast airport warehouse.

The non-arrival of their suitcases was a huge blow to Molly and Robin. They worried about what they would do for clothes, as the clothes they were wearing were already soiled from the long flight and the almost two hours they had spent perspiring profusely in the grimy airport warehouse. They had no choice but to go to their hotel. They had missed the hotel shuttle, but a number of taxi men came up to them asking if they needed a ride. They wanted to change money at the airport, but the taxi men told them there was no place to change money there, and all the illegal money changers had left. They assured them that they could change money at the hotel. They finally chose a taxi driver who promised them they could pay him from the money they changed at the hotel.

On their way out of the airport terminal, Robin spotted an unusual, brightly lit spot on a wall next to the exit. He approached this incongruent spot to see a spiffy new tourist promotion poster showing an attractive photo of people enjoying themselves on a white-sand beach along a sparkling blue ocean shaded by a coconut grove. The photo

was framed by an outline of the continent of Africa. Written across the poster in large letters were the words, "If you do not know Kotoku, you do not know Africa." Robin thought that it would take much more than this nice poster and these catchy words to attract tourists to this country. He believed that as soon as the word got out about the conditions at the airport, nobody would come to Kotoku. He was convinced it would take more than airplane decals and isolated fancy posters to prompt a tourist boom in this part of Africa.

They followed the taxi driver to the parking lot and were taken aback when they saw the pitiful condition of his old, junky car. The little car looked as if it had been through a brutal accident and put together from different colored scraps of cars collected randomly at several salvage yards. There was no way to tell what kind of car this had been. Its current mongrel structure conveyed doubts about its being able to start and operate. Molly and Robin sat closely together on the springy backseat. They held hands tightly and began praying as they had done for their plane's safe landing.

The car's interior was stripped of any comfort, and in most places, there was not any vinyl covering, exposing unpleasantly its rusty springs inside. The doors would not shut properly, and the driver had to tie them shut with wire before sitting down behind the small, well-worn steering wheel. He reached under the steering wheel for two bare-ended wires, which he pressed together to start the car's engine. The car started with a number of backfires that belched out black clouds of exhaust that invaded the car and caused Molly and Robin to cover their faces and cough. The smoke cleared after a few minutes, and the driver forced the gearshift into position, making a noisy screeching sound. In starts and fits, the car started to roll forward, jerking Molly and Robin back and forth. Once the car picked up speed, it moved right along, but not without making a crazy assortment of noises that gave the impression it could fall apart at any moment. Molly and Robin wondered if they could safely travel the two miles to their hotel.

Thus far, all they had experienced in their first few hours in Kotoku was unlike anything they had ever known before or imagined in their wildest dreams. They were both afraid that adjusting to the demands of this very different planet would be more than they could manage. The drive into the city accentuated the nightmarish dream they believed they were living. The city was dimly lit, and the layers of ocean fog rolling in made it look surreal. Visibility was very low, and it was rare that they saw any other people. All they could think of was taking refuge in their hotel room.

Arriving at their hotel was something like a miracle. The hotel was well lit and set in beautifully manicured lawns bordered by well-trimmed bushes. It appeared like a lovely mirage in the mist. The driver accompanied them into the hotel and showed them how to change their money at the reception desk. He patiently waited for them to change $100 into the local currency, the gadi, so he could get what was owed him. Robin paid the driver, adding a slight tip because he wanted to show their appreciation for arriving in this welcoming oasis (he had no idea that he was being grossly overcharged by the taxi driver). The hotel looked so much better than anything else they had seen thus far in Melomti, thereby helping improve their initial impressions of the country.

They were correctly and competently received at the reception desk by another young man dressed in a neat and appealing uniform. He had their reservation and was expecting them. He asked Robin, as the husband, to complete a hotel identity card and called a porter to escort them to their room on the second floor. He told them he was giving them the best double room they had, on the ocean side of the hotel.

The elevator was out of order, so they took the stairs up to their floor. Not far from the stairs was their room, number 201. The porter opened the room and showed them how to work the small TV, the lights, and ceiling fan. He also showed them how to turn on the electric hot water heater bolted to the wall in the small bathroom. Before exiting the room, he handed them two keys and expressed regret over the hotel's electrical problems, which prevented the operation of the air-conditioner wall unit. The porter hesitated until Robin handed him a small tip.

As soon as the porter left the room and Robin locked the door, they felt like rejoicing over the fact that they had actually made it this far. But their happiness was restrained by the heat in their rather drab, simply appointed room. Even with the ceiling fan swirling overhead, they were too hot and continued to perspire. They pulled back the heavy curtains and tried to open the windows but found them bolted shut. They spied a few mosquitoes in their room and surmised that the windows were shut to prevent the entry of mosquitoes. They knew they had to take a bath, but they did not know what to wear afterward. The only clothes they had were those they were wearing, and they were filthy.

They both felt very uncomfortable about being alone together in the same room and sharing the same bed, but those problems paled in comparison with not having clothes. Robin finally said, "I have to take a bath. I will wrap myself in a towel and sleep like that. I really need to sleep!"

Molly replied, "That is a good idea. I will do the same and wrap myself with the top sheet, as I don't think that we will need it in this heat. It is important we get a good night's sleep so we will have the energy we need to face tomorrow's challenges."

Robin entered the smallish bathroom, which had the same blue tiles on the walls as it had on the floor, and shut the wood door behind him. He found there was not any bathtub but only a simple shower stall with a soiled plastic curtain that was fastened to a galvanized pipe whose ends were buried in the concrete walls. He turned on the water heater, but apparently it took a long time to heat the water. The lack of hot water did not deter him because he was thinking that a cold-water shower would be refreshing and help lower his body temperature. Nonetheless, he found the cold water pouring straight down to be something of a shock, especially as he had never before in his life taken a cold shower.

He found it hard to stay in the shower, as the water was too cold. Once his body was wet, he stepped out of the shower and took one of the two small pieces of hotel soap and washed his entire body before quickly rinsing off in the shower. He did feel refreshed, clean, and cooler. Luckily, there were two large towels and two small ones. He used one of the small ones to dry off and wrapped one of the larger ones around his waist. He then got the idea to soak all his clothes in the shower and wring them out to dry under the ceiling fan. He thought this would be better than nothing and would make his clothes less smelly and more wearable tomorrow.

Robin exited the bathroom with a big grin on his face, telling Molly, "I feel much better. There is no bathtub, but you can take a cold shower. As you can see, I also rinsed my clothes in the shower. I suggest that you do the same. We can hang them over the chairs and place them under the ceiling fan. They should be dry by the morning. Hey, can you loan me a comb? And, by the way, the water has a heavy salt content that makes your skin feel sticky."

Molly nodded but expressed her disappointment over the "sticky" water and not being able to use a bathtub as she would do daily at her home in Kansas. She grabbed the sheet and entered the bathroom, closing and locking the door tightly behind her. She then proceeded to go through the same bathing and clothes-washing experience that Robin had. She could see that she would have to get used to not wearing makeup in this humid climate and allow her hair and nails to take on a natural look.

While Molly was in the bathroom, Robin could see that she had rolled up a cover and placed it in the middle of the bed to demarcate clearly a division into two sides—his and hers. He placed the two wooden armchairs as close as he could under the ceiling fan and hung his clothes over one of these chairs, leaving the other one for Molly's clothes. He kept tying and retying the towel around his waist to make sure it would not come loose.

Molly came out of the bathroom looking like a sensual Greek goddess. Robin had a hard time keeping his eyes off her, especially as he could almost see through the thin wet sheet wrapped around her curvy body. The dampness exposed a clear outline of her heavy breasts beneath the flimsy sheet. He was titillated by the sight of her pointed nipples poking against the sheet. Her every move aroused him, but he worked hard to suppress his natural feelings because he knew Molly would not want any of that from him, especially now. This was not the time for any thoughts about sexual shenanigans. He steered his mind elsewhere. He did not want to think or do anything that would cause him to have an embarrassing erection.

Molly was feeling better and hummed a little ditty while she hung her clothes on the chair next to Robin's. She thought how odd it looked to see her pink panties hanging next to his white underwear. She quietly thanked God that she was not on her period. She told Robin, "I can't wait to get into bed and sleep. I'll take the left side, near the bathroom, and you take the right side. We must try to get some sleep."

Robin was trying to be as nonchalant as possible about his first experience of being alone in a hotel room all night with a desirable woman. He calmly said, "OK," and headed to his side of the bed.

Molly switched off the room lights but left the bathroom light on. She climbed into bed and let out a loud sigh, saying, "We made it, Robin. Thanks for being with me. Let's sleep now, as we have many adventures ahead of us."

Their high state of exhaustion overcame all their discomforts and worries to send them both into a deep sleep. They had been sleeping for about two hours when a noise on top of the plywood ceiling boards awakened Molly. She listened quietly to this scary noise for a while before calling out to Robin. He struggled to wake up, but it did not take him long to be wide awake, as he also heard the disturbing noise. Robin quickly arose, adjusted his towel around his waist, and went over to the wall to turn on the room lights. Once the lights were on, the noised ceased. Molly agreed with Robin that this noise was probably caused by rats running around on top of the ceiling boards, and, if the lights kept them from doing that, they would leave the room lights on.

Robin returned to his side of the bed and was trying to go back to sleep when Molly let out a startling scream and reached over to grab him, pulling them together. Robin could see that she was very frightened, but he did not know why. While holding Robin close to her, she blurted out, "Robin, do you see the white lizards over there on the wall near the florescent tube? I've never seen a lizard before. What are they doing in our room? How can I sleep with lizards running around on the walls?"

Robin could easily see the white lizards—geckos—on the walls. He did not like them any more than Molly, but he tried to play the role of the male protector and soothe Molly by telling her, "Don't be afraid. They will not bother us. If they get close to us, I will chase them away. Please try to sleep."

Molly was already dozing off. In spite of herself, she found being close to Robin very comforting. She whispered politely to him, "Thank you. If you don't mind, I will stay close to you until it is daylight outside." With those words, Molly fell fast asleep.

Robin felt as if he were now in heaven. For him, there was nothing better than being in bed and having Molly snuggled up close to him, particularly as they were both naked under their improvised coverings. He was intent on being a gentleman and avoiding anything that would mess up Molly's trust in him and the beauty of this precious moment. In his mind, Robin was thanking the geckos on the wall and God for bringing him to Kotoku with Molly. For him, this precious moment alone with Molly in his arms was worth all the trials of arriving in this small country on the west coast of Africa.

CHAPTER TWELVE
NEW BEGINNINGS

Chief Letivi had never slept so late. A combination of travel fatigue and the pleasant sensation of sharing his bed with Delalia had worked together to keep him in bed much longer than usual. His thoughts about the intimate physical contact he had with the beautiful Delalia during the night would not leave his mind. His first sexual encounter with a woman had left him feeling whole and relaxed. He felt like a new man who was now capable of surmounting any obstacle placed in his way. He could have dwelled more on his amorous night and what it meant for him and his future, but when he turned over, there it was, staring unmercifully at him, directly into his face. There it was. The accursed cell phone's little blinking red light silently screaming, "Charge me!"

The sight of the president's mobile phone caused Letivi to bolt out of bed and throw on his nearest home gown and rush outside. He ran out of his sleeping room so fast that he nearly knocked over Delalia, who had been waiting patiently for him to rise to eat breakfast and take a bath. He rushed to the small shed where the generator had been placed and started it immediately. Then he walked briskly back to his sleeping room to fetch his watch so he would be sure not to charge the phone more than thirty minutes. All this time, Delalia was watching him closely, wondering if he would say anything to her while she tried to decide how she could help him.

When the thirty minutes was up, Letivi shut the generator off, put the phone in his pocket, and safely placed the charger in his room. He knew that from now on, he would have to make charging the phone part of his early-morning routine. Delalia was now standing with a towel draped over her left forearm while holding Letivi's soap and shaving dish in her right hand. He approached her to receive these items, saying his first words to her: "Thank you."

Delalia smiled and slightly bowed her head. She maintained her calm exterior, but her heart was singing loudly. She was so very happy because Letivi had thanked her and did not send her away. In the distant corners of the compound, some small children were also watching to see what Letivi would do with Delalia. When they saw that Delalia would be staying, they raced to the adjoining compound to inform all the women (mostly deceased wives of Chief Yofu) sitting in a group that the chief was keeping Delalia. The women became very agitated. They began clapping their hands and loudly praising God for putting a woman in Letivi's life.

The village grapevine worked at its usual lightning speed. An hour later, there was not a living soul within a ten-mile radius who did not know that Letivi was keeping Delalia. Everyone, except perhaps Letivi, was looking forward to the feast that would be provided to mark the chief's marriage to Delalia. Everyone was proud to announce that their chief was getting married.

Chief Gyasi was pleased to be among those hearing that Letivi had accepted Delalia. He completed his morning meditation and toilet before heading to Letivi's compound to confirm directly with him this good news. As he walked toward Letivi's royal compound, people shouted out their happy comments. Everyone was all smiles and full of good cheer. The news of Letivi and Delalia's marriage was considered a good omen and a blessing for the village. Their chief would finally be a fully acceptable chief with a wife and, eventually, children. They were satisfied that these customary prerequisites to being a chief would finally be met. They breathed more easily knowing their beloved and much-respected young chief would now be above all criticism.

Chief Gyasi found Letivi munching his breakfast of cassava flour mixed with groundnuts, water, and sugar. After completing their morning greetings, Chief Gyasi sat down on a small stool on the opposite side of the low wooden table. As soon as Chief Gyasi had sat down, Delalia quickly came forth to serve him the same food that Letivi was eating and then retreated to a distant spot from where she would keep a watchful eye on the chiefs in case they needed something. Chief Gyasi could not wait to tell Letivi, "All of us in the village are praising God for your acceptance of Delalia."

Letivi responded quickly, "Who said I accepted her?"

Gyasi laughed and said, "Well, she is still here, and we have heard no complaints about her from you."

"That is true," replied Letivi. "There is nothing about her I can complain about, but she has only been here one night."

Gyasi interjected, "One good night with a woman is usually enough to know if you like her and you are compatible. As I said before, this beautiful young woman has impeccable credentials, and it would be foolish and harmful for you and the village to reject her."

Letivi took some minutes before saying any more. "You are right, Grandfather. She is here to stay. Please go ahead and make all the marriage arrangements."

Gyasi smiled and said, "Thank you, my son. Please do not worry. All will be well, and your life and our lives will be much better because of this union between you and Delalia."

Trying to change the subject, Gyasi noted, "I see you like the same breakfast your father liked. The old women, Aba and Assi, who cooked for him, told me once that he ate every morning the same cereal mixture you are presently eating. They are now deceased, so maybe it is only me, my wife, and my daughter, your mother, who know this. Do you know this?"

"Yes, Grandfather. My mother told me this a long time ago. Maybe Kontor also knows. Speaking of Kontor, I have not seen him in some time. We should really involve him and his powers with the aftermath of our visit with the president. Maybe you can tell him to come and see us."

A dark shadow fell over Gyasi's face as he was obliged to say, "My chief. I am sorry to tell you that the great Kontor has traveled. He has been gone for several weeks."

Letivi was quite upset to hear this startling news. He knew this meant that the formidable Kontor had died and been buried secretly so nobody would easily know of his passing. He was devastated by this terrible news and could no longer eat. He bellowed like a wounded animal, "What? How can this be? Why wasn't I told? Kontor was very important to me, particularly as he knew my father and was with him when he entered the old baobab."

Gyasi tried hard to console Letivi, telling him, "We did not tell you because Kontor's dying instruction was for us not to tell you.

He did not want to do anything to disturb the good work you were doing, especially the preparations you were making to see the president. He asked us not to hurry in breaking to you the news of his departure to the other world."

Letivi lamented, "There is now a huge empty space in my life. It will be extra hard managing without Kontor's wise counsel and his many powers. Who do we have to replace this great fetish priest and sorcerer?"

Gyasi simply responded, "Nobody can replace Kontor. He was one of a kind, and none of the remaining fetish priests in the village can begin to compare with this man, whose lifetime spanned over one hundred years. He looked young, but, in reality, he was very old. He possessed magical powers that nobody else knows. He tried to stay in this world because of you, but his time to join the other world was overdue and he was finally obliged to move on. There is nothing we can do. His passing is also a great personal loss to me."

Letivi continued to lament Kontor's passing. "His departure represents a huge loss to our village. He was an invaluable resource, and it will be much harder to face the future without him. Without Kontor around, we are not the same village. His passing marks a real turning point in the village's history. At the appropriate time, let's make sure his lifetime is well recorded in our oral history. We must make a point of calling on him to help us from where he sits now with the grandfathers."

After these solemn words, both Letivi and Gyasi hung their heads in silence as they prayed to Kontor and his memory. They were in deep meditation when a strange sound kept repeating itself. Over and over, there was a soft, incessant ding-dong sound that would not stop. They looked around to see if they could detect the origins of this mysterious sound. Could it be that Kontor was answering their prayers in this way? Finally, it dawned on Letivi that it was the bugbear phone in his pocket that was making this monotonous musical chime. He blurted out, "Grandfather, it's the president's phone ringing!"

Frantically, Letivi reached into his pocket to grab the phone. He pushed the reception button and held the phone near his mouth to say, "Chief Letivi."

A raspy voice on the phone said pointedly, "USAID will send a cacao specialist to visit you next Monday in your village. Be ready to receive him. I will call you to learn about the meeting results."

The president abruptly hung up. He gave no time for Letivi to say a word. There was no greeting or any good-bye. It would take time to adjust to the president's rude and imperial ways. Letivi turned to Gyasi and told him what the president had said. Gyasi commented, "We have only three days to prepare for this important meeting. We must meet with our elders, clan heads, and cacao association leaders. We can use the old church for this meeting."

Letivi immediately decided, "I will call a meeting for early tomorrow morning."

Gyasi nodded his agreement and was about to say more when he saw Leon approaching them, the young man who assisted his daughter, Atibona, in her medicinal enclave in the mountainous forest. Leon arrived breathless with a quickened pace, saying, "Mama Atibona sent me to tell Chief Letivi to come now to see her."

Letivi sprung to his feet and went into his sleeping room to change clothes. He exited his room fully prepared to walk directly to his mother's encampment. Before speeding away, he said, "Grandfather, please make the arrangements for tomorrow's meeting. I must go now to see my mother. I will return as soon as I can."

Gyasi rapidly said, "I also wanted to talk to you about the Chinaman in our village and the new complaints about our youth scholarship program, but that can wait until you return. Go now quickly. Give your mother my greetings. I hope all is well with her."

Without a word to anyone else, Letivi exited the compound and set off on a back path that would lead him up the mountain to another path that led to his mother's location deep in the forest.

It took Letivi about an hour of walking as fast as he could to reach his mom's leafy domain. As usual, the trees greeted him and advised his mom of his impending arrival. He asked the trees to guide him to her. He found her in the center of her compound lying against an old tree stump. He noted that her clothes were filthy, and the entire encampment had not been tended as it had been when he lived there as a child. Everything seemed to be aging quickly and falling apart. He called out to his mother, "I am here. Your son is here."

When hearing her son's voice, Atibona turned her head to face him, saying in a soft, barely audible voice, "Welcome, my dear son. Thanks for coming so quickly."

Letivi could not believe how old and wrinkled his mom's face had become. She was not an old woman and it had been only a few weeks since he had last seen her, but it looked as if decades had been added to her age. He did not know how her once beautiful face could now look like a fruit that had been left too long in the sun. Her high cheekbones had sagged, and her once smooth face had become a series of overlapping wrinkles. Her nicely shaped lips had been pushed into a pucker, and her aquiline nose was now sunk into her face, exposing prominently her nostrils. Her face had become unrecognizable, and Letivi had to wonder whether this was indeed his mother or some spirit being occupying her body.

He was reassured that it was his mom when she said in a weak voice, "Son, come to me. I am your mother, and I want to hold your hand and tell you some things."

Letivi knelt beside his mother and held her hand. The trees stopped talking so that there would be no interference with what Atibona would tell her son. Atibona gazed into her son's eyes and squeezed his hand slightly, saying slowly, "Please, my son. You need to be strong, as what I am about to tell you is very sad news. My world is coming to an end. My time in this domain on Earth is drawing quickly to a close. Son, there will soon be nothing more left of me or this place. We will all fade away, and tree talk will no longer be heard in this land."

Letivi could not believe what his mother was saying. In a strong, vehement tone, he remonstrated, "Mother, what are you saying? That is not possible. This world cannot go on without you and your domain! I cannot accept what you are saying."

Atibona increased her grip on Letivi's hand and whispered more words in a low voice. "I am sorry, son, but you must accept what I say and prepare yourself for a future without us. There is no other way. It has been written since the beginning of time, and now the end has come."

Letivi cried out, "Mother, why is this happening?"

Atibona did not have the strength to talk much, but she managed to convey, "It is happening now because the younger generation no longer cares about any of this. The old world cannot stay where it no longer has a place. For better or worse, it is time for the new world to prevail."

Letivi lifted his mother and held her close to him. Tears welled up in his eyes. He did not know what to say or do. The trees remained silent. They knew that any talk at this point was pointless. Their final destiny was at hand, and there was no changing that. Soon they and all the plants in this domain would wither and die. The lucky ones would remain as ordinary features of this mountainside redoubt. After over two hundred years of magical life on Earth serving humans, their time was coming to an ordained end. There was no fighting a destiny set by the gods hundreds of years ago. Nothing lasts forever, and everything has its time to come and to go.

Atibona gently said, "My son, please release me. I need you to go tell my mother to come and see me. You must also know that the old baobab has communicated to my trees that you should not fail to visit him at the next full moon. Please, my son, accept that the world is changing at a fast pace, and nothing will remain as it was in the past. Prepare yourself to deal with a new, more modern world."

"My dearest mother, thank you for your good advice and wise words. I will do as you say. I will also visit you more often. Please do not leave this Earth without seeing me again. Also, Mother, I hope you are pleased to know that I now have a woman in my life. I am working so that you will be a grandmother as soon as possible."

As much as her deformed, scrunched-up face would permit, Atibona smiled and said, "Son, you make me happy. I love you so much."

Letivi carefully placed his mother on the ground and told her, "Mother, I love you more than words can describe. I will go now to tell your mother to come to you. Good-bye, Mother. Good-bye to all my friends in the plant and tree world."

The plants and trees had the last word. In a calamitous and confusing spiel, they bid farewell to Letivi. The oldest tree called in a deep voice, using his odd dialect to halt all the noise, saying, "Letivi. You are our child too. We all love you, and we will miss you for an eternity. We wish you well. May you have much success in the life that lies before you. Good-bye."

Letivi limped out of this sacred place of botanical magic with tears streaming down his face. He was having difficulty coping with the demise of his birthplace and where he had lived the first five years of his life. His world was crumbling into pieces, and he did not think he would like the new world that would replace it. With Kontor gone and his mother and her domain about to vanish, things were indeed falling apart. And he was disconcerted by the summons of the old baobab tree for him to come at the next full moon. He was afraid that the old baobab would have additional bad news for him. He did not know whether he could take any more trauma in his life. Dealing with the president's mobile phone already involved more changes in his life than he wanted. He did not want life as he knew it to end because he was afraid he was not capable of coping well with a new beginning.

CHAPTER THIRTEEN
FIRST DAY IN AFRICA

Molly and Robin had overslept. Their sleep was so deep they almost forgot where they were. Robin opened his eyes first. He was pleasantly petrified by the luscious sight of a half-naked Molly lying next to him. The sheet wrapped around her had fallen aside during the night, exposing her plump but very symmetrical breasts. His breathing became uneven when he saw that her left breast was lightly touching his rib cage. He dared not move. He did not want to do anything that would wake Molly. He wanted to prolong this precious moment as long as he could. He could not get enough of devouring with his eyes Molly's natural feminine beauty. He was happy that he had been the perfect gentleman, providing comfort to Molly all night long. He was sorry his good behavior with Molly had not been shared by his mindless male organ, which had involuntarily soiled the thin towel he had wrapped around his waist.

He found that the intimacy of their physical closeness was accentuated by the mingling of their perspiration. Their joint perspiration had saturated their mattress. Robin tried to ignore the uncomfortable moisture soaking the backside of his body. But he could not ignore the bright sunshine flooding through the windows. He could hear in the distance the honking of car horns and the muffled roar of the unending succession of crashing ocean waves that dissolved into watery foam as they slid deftly onto the sandy shore. He began to worry about the time. Judging by the strength of the sunlight coming through the windows, it must be late in the morning. They had forgotten to set their watches. He was disturbed that he had no idea what the local time was.

Molly began to stir. After stretching, she quickly jumped out of bed and headed for the bathroom, saying, "I got to pee!"

Robin marveled at the beautiful movement of her bouncy buttocks as she rushed from her bed fully naked. In a hurry to pee, she had left on the bed the sheet in which she had wrapped herself. Robin eagerly anticipated seeing her return naked, but this dream was busted when Molly called to him, "Robin, can you please hand me the sheet I'm using to wrap myself?"

Robin rose from the bed, adjusted his towel around his bony hips so the semen spots were not visible, and picked up the sheet to hand to Molly through the narrowly opened bathroom door. Molly thanked him, and he sighed to himself because he knew that the sheer delight and sexual stimulation of having a skimpily clad Molly close to his semi-nude body had come to an end. He was asking himself if all of Molly's uninhibited nudity had been exhibited intentionally to excite him, or was it just Molly being Molly? In any event, he had no time to dwell on the pros and cons of this delectable subject, as Molly yelled through the bathroom door, "Robin. I'm taking a shower. Can you call the hotel reception desk to see what time it is? We have big things to do today."

Robin dutifully manipulated the in-room phone, dialing 0 for the reception desk. The front desk promptly answered. "Good morning, room 201. How can I help you?"

Robin timidly asked, "What time is it?"

The reception clerk replied with a chuckle, "It is ten ten a.m. local time. We are sorry, but we stopped serving breakfast in our restaurant at ten. But, if you like, we can deliver to your room a continental breakfast for two."

Robin was not quite sure what a 'continental breakfast' was, but he knew they had to eat something, so he said, "Yes, breakfast for us would be good."

The man on the other end of the phone replied, "Excellent. You should have your breakfast delivered to your room in about thirty minutes."

Robin set his watch to local time and checked to see if their clothes had dried under the ceiling fan. He was pleased to see that they were dry and did not smell as badly as they did before they washed them in the hotel's gummy water. At that moment, the more modest Molly opened the door a crack to request, "Robin, please hand me my clothes so I can get dressed. Also, bring me my toiletry kit."

Robin gingerly picked up Molly clothes, deriving a wee pleasure as he grasped in his hand her panties, and handed them all in a bunch through the door to her. He tried to get one last look at Molly through the small door opening, but she stood in such a way that he could not see her. He sighed again. He knew that for the rest of the day, he would only see a fully clothed Molly and would have to wait until night to have any hopes of being close to her again. He was saddened that the arrival of their suitcases would provide Molly with clothes to wear.

An animated Molly flew from the bathroom full of vim and vigor, saying. "Hurry, take a shower and get dressed. We need to go to the Peace Corps office to see if we can find any information on David."

Robin picked up his clothes and his own toiletry kit and toddled to the bathroom. Before closing the bathroom door behind him, he said, "Good morning, Molly. Glad to see you are so fit and raring for action. They should be bringing our breakfast shortly. By the way, it is about ten thirty a.m. local time."

Robin turned on the cold shower and fully immersed himself this time. When his body was amply wet, he turned off the shower and slid the small, shrinking bar of soap over his entire body, paying special attention to his genital area, armpits, and intergluteal cleft. He turned the shower back on, but the water had stopped flowing. The shower pipe noisily rattled and spurts of water coughed out of the shower head, but there was not enough water to rinse the soap off his body. He now understood why there was a plastic bucket full of water sitting in the corner of the bathroom. He picked up the bucket, returned to the shower stall, and lifted the bucket over his head and poured it over his body.

He moved over to the adjoining white porcelain sink to shave, comb his hair, and brush his teeth. He twisted on both cold and hot faucets, but only a trickle of brown, muddy water flowed from them. He quickly dismissed the idea of shaving and brushing his teeth and settled for combing his long, wavy black hair while looking closely at his face in the mirror over the sink. He wondered how Molly had managed so well while she was in the bathroom. She certainly looked clean, and her shoulder-length red hair was nicely brushed.

Robin stepped out of the bathroom to find Molly arranging their breakfast on the round glass table placed at the side of their room, near the windows. He asked Molly, "Did you have water for your shower?"

Molly happily replied, "Of course, Robin. Why do you ask?"

"Well, no water was coming out when I took my shower, and only a small amount of muddy water came out of the sink faucets. I could not shave or brush my teeth."

Molly laughed at hearing Robin complain about water in the bathroom and said, "You look fine, Robin. And you should not brush your teeth with that water. Don't you remember what the tourist guidebook said about using only bottled water for drinking and brushing your teeth? Anyway, come and eat your breakfast."

Robin looked down at the table and immediately grasped what a continental breakfast was. Spread before him was an assortment of bread and jam accompanied by coffee and tea. Molly made them coffee by pouring hot water from a thermos into their cups and mixing granules from a Nescafé tin can with the water. She then added two lumps of cube sugar to each cup and mixed a spoonful of Nido powdered milk into the coffee. Although this simple breakfast offering was nothing like the sumptuous American breakfasts they had enjoyed at Helen's in Molly's hometown, their ravishing hunger had them devouring every piece of bread. The jam was quickly used up, but that did not discourage them from eating all the remaining bread. Actually, they found the French croissants, and chocolate and raisin breads to be quite tasty.

They only thing missing was bottled water to drink. They both agreed they should buy water at the hotel bar before going into town. For sure, they needed water to take their daily doses of malaria pills. Molly lifted her cup of coffee to make a toast with Robin. As their cups clinked together, Molly said, "Our first day in Africa. I'm so thrilled! I cannot wait to go out into the town to see what this place is like."

Robin could not disagree, but deep down, he was feeling a bit of homesickness and a desire to be back in more familiar and comfortable surroundings. This was not a trip he would have ever attempted alone. He had to say something, so he said, "I guess we find a taxi and ask the driver to take us to the Peace Corps office. Right?"

"That's right, Robin. Let's go," replied Molly as she rose and made sure all she needed was in her large purse before pushing open the room door.

Robin quickly joined her, asking, "Molly, are you sure you have our passports, yellow cards, and tickets in your purse? We need to make sure we don't lose these. Also, I think you should keep all our important documents and traveler's checks in the hotel safe. As I know you recall, the tourist guide said to be wary of pickpockets when walking about the city."

"You are right, Robin. We should put everything except the money we need for the day in the hotel safe. Let's do that now."

They exited their room, making sure they both had their keys and the door was properly locked behind them. They descended the same barren stairwell they had used the previous night and walked over to the reception desk to leave their keys and to ask to use the hotel safe. The dapper young man at the desk responded to their request with a form to complete and a plastic bag in which to place their valuables. They filled out the simple form and placed their passports, yellow cards, tickets, and traveler's checks into the bag. Molly told Robin, "I have already written down in my notebook the serial numbers of all the checks in case I have to report them lost or stolen."

The reception clerk told them, "You need to keep your passports in case you are stopped by the police at one of the many checkpoints in town. They will want to see what nationality you are and if you entered the country legally. Please keep them in your purse, and always hold tightly onto your purse. Never let your purse out of your sight. There are many thieves everywhere, and they like to prey on rich foreigners like you."

Robin looked at Molly and said in an inquisitive manner, "I did not know we are rich, but maybe we are compared to most people in this poor country. And, for sure, we are not in Kansas anymore."

Molly asked the reception clerk if he could help them find a taxi to take them to the American Peace Corps office. The clerk whistled and made a hand gesture to the front doorman, who, in turn, beckoned Molly and Robin to come to where he was standing just inside the front door. They thanked the clerk and approached the doorman, who politely said, "Wait here. I will call one of our hotel taxis."

They could see through the plate-glass door a car parked in front of the hotel and the doorman signaling to them to come. They stepped outside and were rudely reminded how hot and humid it was. They were shaded from the sun by the hotel portico, but they began to perspire profusely. The high humidity caused Molly's long hair to sag and curl. Robin looked as if he had just stepped out of a steam bath. They took their place in the little green Renault taxi and asked the driver how much it would cost to take them to the Peace Corps office. The driver quoted his price and it sounded very reasonable, so they said OK. Little did they know that he was giving them an exorbitant "white person" price. Local people could have made the same trip for less than half the cost.

The taxi was old but clean. They were hoping it would be air-conditioned, but the driver announced as he started the car that his AC was not working. They slowly headed for the hotel's exit gate. They could see the hotel was surrounded by high walls and was well protected. The taxi positioned itself outside the exit, waiting for an opening in the wild and congested assortment of rowdy traffic that rumbled by. Nobody slowed down to allow the taxi access onto the road. Molly and Robin had never before seen such a riotous traffic scene. Cars and trucks of every type vied with motorbikes, bicycles, donkey carts, push wagons, and mobs of pedestrians to move along this narrow asphalt road. All vehicles appeared to drive recklessly as they tried to avoid pedestrians and potholes.

The taxi driver knew he had to be aggressive if he was to ever turn onto the road. He inched the car ever closer into the street until the traffic was obliged to slow down enough to allow him to enter. The driver noted that traffic was bad right now because many people were going home for lunch and rest during the hottest part of the day. He expressed surprise that his passengers had waited until this time to come out of the hotel because most tourists go out very early in the morning to avoid the midday heat. Molly and Robin looked at each other, telling themselves that henceforth they too would be early risers.

They traveled only a couple of blocks before encountering the main seaside road. The driver said that after he turned left at the next corner, the traffic would not be so bad. Maneuvering around this corner was made easier by the policemen who were directing traffic. While they waited for the policeman to signal to them to move ahead, their car was surrounded on all sides by beggars of all ages and physical condition. They were all saying they were hungry and needed some small coin to buy food. Molly and Robin were horrified. They coped with this awful moment by lowering their heads to avoid looking at the beggars. They were appalled that at every traffic stop, the beggary scene was much the same.

The taxi moved onto the wider paved road running parallel with the wide beach and ocean. The breeze coming off the ocean was quite brisk, and Molly's and Robin's hair was blowing around wildly. Robin wanted to roll up his car window to reduce the wind, but he found that the lever was absent. He wanted to complain about this to the driver, but he refrained from doing so because the driver was humming a happy tune, and he could see that the wind was no problem for his short-cropped African hair. Robin looked at Molly with her messy, wind-blown hair and said, "Wow. You look like Sheila the jungle woman."

Molly somehow was able to keep her sense of humor, saying, "No, I'm Jane, and you are Tarzan. But where's the jungle and all the wild animals? This Africa looks very different from the one I imagined."

As they looked to their right at the broad expanse of ocean and felt the salty sea air blast their bodies, they knew they were far from any jungle. They could see large ships lined up far out to sea, waiting for a berth at the port. They could also see small pirogues full of local fisherman bobbing up and down in the ocean. It was hard to look across the wide beach because the sun's reflection on the sand was blinding. Neither of them wanted to admit to the other that this was their first time to see an ocean.

The driver slowed down as he prepared to make a sharp left turn. He said, "We are very near the Peace Corps office. Please be ready to get out of my car quickly, as I'll be obliged to stop in traffic in front of the front gate."

It was only a matter of a couple of minutes before they found themselves at the Peace Corps office. They hurriedly exited the taxi on the side facing the Peace Corps and handed the driver his money. The pressing onslaught of traffic obliged the driver to depart immediately. They found before them another high wall topped with broken glass. Next to the closed green door was a small sign that noted this was indeed the Peace Corps office. The sign also provided the daily office hours.

Robin knocked hard on the wooden gate. They could hear the gate being unlatched. It was opened halfway, and a uniformed watchman appeared, saying, "The office is closed for the midday lunch break. It will reopen at two thirty p.m. Come back then." He then banged shut the gate and locked it.

Molly and Robin were very disappointed. They did not know what they would do until 2:30. Robin looked at his watch, and it was only 12:45. They had a lot of time to kill and were at a loss as to what to do. They knew they needed to go somewhere cooler. But where was that?

At that moment, they heard someone whistling from across the street. They looked up and could see that the taxi man had returned and was waving at them. He signaled that he would turn around to pick them up. It took some time, but the taxi was finally able to stop in front of them. They quickly jumped in. The driver took them a short way down the road to a place where he could pull off so they could talk. He said, "I came back because I knew you would need a ride, and I thought the Peace Corps office would be closed. You know, you should really hire me for the day so that you are sure to have transport and a guide."

Molly wasted no time in saying, "You are right. How much for the day? And we need to go to the airport tonight to get our lost luggage. By the way, what is your name?" Robin was nodding his agreement the entire time she spoke.

The driver quoted his daily fee, and it was readily accepted. He added, "My name is Cyprien." Again, Molly and Robin did not know that the fee quoted was quite exorbitant.

Molly said, "Cyprien, where can we go until the Peace Corps office reopens at two thirty?"

Cyprien said, "I would like to show you around town, but it is too hot and there is too much traffic. There is a nice German restaurant nearby that many foreigners frequent. Would you like to go there?"

Molly and Robin consulted with each other before replying, "Yes, take us there."

Within a few minutes, they arrived at a place with a big sign in front informing them this was the Markus Restaurant and Store. They were looking forward to some inside air-conditioned comfort, but they found the inside part of this place consisted of a small butchery and store. The restaurant part was located outside under a lattice covered by the rich growth of various types of vines. There were potted plants growing everywhere and cages of parrots hanging along the sides, and in the front were a small curio stall and fruit stand. It was still hot and humid, but less so than outside this tropical cover. Molly and Robin were shown a bench along one of the picnic tables in the back. They were in a totally different world. Trying to keep a stiff upper lip, Molly commented, "Robin, looks like we have found our jungle."

The waitress provided them with two menus. They could see that all the main dishes were varieties of meats and chicken. Obviously, this place was serving produce that came from a private farm upcountry. They were not yet hungry, but they ordered food anyway. They both ordered well-cooked beefsteak and fries and asked for Cokes to drink. They looked around, and all they could see were other white people. This appeared to be a family restaurant, as a number of tables included children. Nobody seemed to be bothered by the heat and humidity. Molly and Robin hoped they would get used to the steamy climate.

Their food actually proved to be quite good. And it was accompanied by the same Heinz ketchup they knew in Kansas. They took their time, as they had lots of time to kill before the Peace Corps office opened. They slowly sipped their Cokes just as they would do in Kansas, except no ice had been provided. Drinking their Cokes reminded them that they had forgotten to buy the bottled water they needed to take their malaria pills. Molly quickly called the waitress over and asked her if they could have two bottles of water.

The waitress immediately asked, "Still or gas?"

Molly and Robin did not understand what she meant. Molly said, "What do you mean? Is there more than one kind of bottled water?"

The young, very dark-skinned and thin waitress explained, "Yes, there are two kinds of water. There is the natural still one, and there is the one with bubbles."

Molly said, "Oh. I guess we want two bottles of the one without bubbles."

The waitress returned with two large, quart-size plastic bottles of pure drinking water. She also brought the check. They paid their bill, adding a nice tip. Molly removed from her purse the packet of malaria pills and gave Robin two, and she took two. The instructions said they should take these bitter pills with food, so their timing was late but good. They still had some time before the Peace Corps office opened and were thinking of what they could do to make the time pass by more quickly. Robin said, "One thing we should do before leaving here is to go to the toilet. I did not see anywhere else to go to the toilet, so let's not miss this opportunity. I see a sign with an arrow indicating that the toilets, or WCs, are in the back. Do you want to go first?"

Molly said, "Yes. I need to pee and freshen up a bit." She got up and quickly walked toward the toilet. She was surprised to see in the restroom two types of toilets. One was the usual sit-down type she was familiar with, and the one in the other stall was a squat-type toilet embedded in the ground, which she had never seen before. She did her business and dampened some toilet tissue with water from the sink and used it to wipe her face and the back of her neck. Although the water was brinish, this made her feel better. She also benefitted from the mirror hanging above the sink to try to put her hair in some kind of decent order. She did feel a bit refreshed when she exited the WC but found that "bit" was indeed fleeting.

She found Robin tapping on the cage of a gray parrot located near their table, trying to see if it could talk. When he saw Molly arrive, he excused himself and headed to the WC. When he returned to join Molly at their table, it was almost 2:00 p.m. Robin suggested, "Let's return to the Peace Corps office. We will arrive before it is open, but maybe someone will come early. Anyway, we want to be there when it opens."

Molly agreed, and they returned with their water bottles in hand to join Cyprien, who was sitting in his car listening to the radio. They returned to the Peace Corps office, arriving fifteen minutes ahead of its afternoon opening time. They had to get out of the car because they could not park and block traffic in front of the office. Cyprien said he would find a place on the opposite side of the road to park and wait for them.

Molly and Robin hoped somebody would come soon to open the office because they could not take standing in the sun too long. Neither of them had a hat or sunglasses. Their hats were in their lost suitcases, and they had neglected to buy sunglasses. They were relieved when a middle-aged African man arrived and unlocked the front gate and began to enter the office grounds. Molly quickly greeted the man and said, "We have come from the States to talk to someone in the Peace Corps Kotoku office. This matter is very important for us, and we have been waiting for a long time for your office to open."

The man replied in a helpful tone, "Please follow me in. It will be much nicer for you to wait in our air-conditioned office. My name is Jacob, and I have worked for the Peace Corps for many years. I'm currently the office receptionist. Tell me, which state are you from?"

Molly and Robin gave him a hearty thanks before Molly said, "We are from Kansas. My name is Molly, and his name is Robin."

"Kansas. I have seen volunteers from every state, but it is rare that we receive volunteers from Kansas. I only know Kansas is located in the very center of the United States."

They entered the main reception area, which was really no more than a small house. Jacob asked them to sit down on the cushioned chairs while he prepared the office for its opening. They were enjoying more familiar surroundings, with a big map of the United States pasted on the wall. Of course, the coolness of the office made them feel much better. After a while, Jacob returned to his small desk near the entrance.

Once Jacob was sitting comfortably at his workstation, he looked at Molly and Robin and said, "I am curious. Why have you come from so far to Kotoku?"

Molly began to explain the reason for their visit, and Jacob listened intently. The more Molly talked, the more Jacob's interest rose. When she mentioned the name David Peterson, his face tightened, and it was obvious that this name caused him some distress. He bluntly interrupted her. "Please, did you say David Peterson?"

"Yes, I did. I may be related to him. I'm Molly Peterson. We are trying to find out what happened to him many years ago in this country. Did you know him?"

The unsettled Jacob was finding it difficult to reply. After much hesitation, he slowly said, "I am the only one remaining in this office who knew David. He was a super, much-loved volunteer who kept to himself. He finished an exceptional third year as a volunteer and remained for a long time afterward in his village. For some years, nobody knew where David was until our embassy was contacted about him and was obliged to evacuate him back to his home state of Kansas. He remains a legend in the area of the country that he worked in."

Jacob's words moved Molly and Robin to the edge of their seats. They were ready to jump for joy. Jacob could see they were ecstatic, but he was reluctant to say any more about David's sensitive case, which had been classified confidential in his office and at the embassy. He continued by saying, "There is not much more that I can tell you, and I should not tell you more. You will need to go to his village, Ataku, to find out more. Ataku is located about one hundred miles northwest of Melomti, just off the national highway. In a rented taxi, you can easily get there in less than two hours."

Molly and Robin wanted to hear more from Jacob about David, but they could see that he was reluctant to say more. Also, they knew he was right about the need for them to go to Ataku and get the full story about David for themselves. They rose to shake Jabob's hand, thanking him repeatedly for all his invaluable help and advice. Jacob bid them good-bye, saying, "Be careful in your travel up-country. I hope you find all you want to know about David. He was a very special person to all of us, especially to the people of Ataku. If you can, please come see me again after your visit to Ataku."

Molly and Robin hustled out of the Peace Corps office yard to find their taxi waiting on the opposite side of the street. Cyprien warned them not to take any risks by trying to cross the street, so he drove to a place that would allow him to turn around and then return to fetch them where they stood. While they waited for Cyprien to appear with his car, Molly's and Robin's minds were engaged in the highest gear as they tried to see clearly their next move. They felt they had achieved much by learning that David had been a Peace Corps volunteer in Kotoku, serving in the village of Ataku. Their hearts and minds could not be at peace until they were able to continue their investigation in Ataku.

They wanted to leave for Ataku immediately, but they knew that was not possible. They had to get their missing luggage that night. They also needed more time to think through what they would do when they arrived in Ataku. The first question they had for Cyprien when he picked them up was, "Do you know where the village of Ataku is?"

Cyprien fired back, "Of course. Everyone knows where Ataku is because it's a famous village with a white chief. Do you want me to take you there?"

Molly spontaneously replied, "Yes, we must go there early tomorrow morning!"

Cyprien's mention of a white chief had suspended Molly's and Robin's thinking in midair. They both wondered if the white chief could be David. With this tantalizing thought, their excitement soared to new heights. Nothing could stop them now. It was Ataku or bust.

CHAPTER FOURTEEN
WORLD UNHINGED

Letivi's heavy heart slowed his feverish race to his grandmother's house in Aniko. He ran as fast as he could to inform his grandmother, Evelyne, that she was urgently needed by her daughter, Atibona, his mother, whom he had just left in her dying botanical world. His deep sadness over the gradual disintegration of his mother and her magical forest enclave made him want to sit down and cry. He fought this impulse because his mother had told him to quickly inform her mother. He was digging deeply within himself to find the courage and strength he needed to carry on. He could not let his mother down, but the thought of her imminent departure from this world was tearing him apart.

He was in a wretched state when he reached his grandmother's house. His grandmother could not help but be alarmed when she saw Letivi's troubled condition. With a fearful quiver in her voice, she pleaded, "Letivi, what's the matter? What could possibly make you so distraught?"

Letivi was lost for words, and his exhaustion made it difficult to say anything. All he could mutter was, "Grandmother, your daughter needs to see you. Please go to her now!"

Evelyne could see that asking Letivi for any more information would be futile. Letivi sat down as if in a trance to rest. Within a few minutes, Evelyne was ready to rush to her daughter's side, saying in a rapid, staccato voice to Letivi, "My grandson, I am leaving now. Please tell my husband, Gyasi, where I have gone."

Letivi remained seated for a long time. His sorrow was growing steadily, and he did not feel like doing anything. After a long while, he slowly stood up and began ambling unsteadily toward his home compound in Ataku. He took a series of back paths because he did not want anyone to see him in such a dreadful state. He stumbled into the back gate of his compound and fell into a reclining chair under the shady neem tree. All he wanted was to be left alone so he could try to deal with his grief over his mother's pitiful situation.

In the adjoining compound, Chief Gyasi had been waiting for Letivi to return. It was only after about an hour that Delalia informed Gyasi that Letivi had arrived and was resting under the old neem tree. Gyasi found it unusual that Letivi would return by the back gate instead of the front one and that he did not send word to him about his return. Gyasi quickly rose and strode over to where Letivi was located. He found Letivi with his eyes closed and very still, as if he were in deep meditation. He sat down beside him and waited for him to open his eyes. Gyasi waited for more than an hour for Letivi to show some sign of life. When Letivi opened his eyes, he whispered, "Letivi. It's your grandfather. Are you OK? I am here to help you."

After several minutes, Letivi slowly turned his head to face Gyasi. He looked at his grandfather a long time before forcing some words out of his mouth. "Grandfather, the world as we know it will be coming to an end. I cannot tell you more now. You first need to see your wife, who is now with your daughter."

The aged Gyasi was quite alarmed by Letivi's words and his overall demeanor. He did not learn more from Letivi, and he could feel this was not the time to pressure Letivi for any more information. He did feel compelled to say, "Are you able to listen now? As I mentioned before your departure, I have some matters to bring to your attention."

Out of a sense of duty, Letivi felt obliged to say, "Grandfather, I can listen to you now, but my depressed mood and state of exhaustion does not allow me to talk much."

Gyasi said, "OK. I want to convey to you for reflection some concerns about the Chinaman and our scholarship program."

Gyasi went into a lengthy recounting of what the Chinaman had been doing since he had arrived in Ataku a couple of years ago. When the Chinaman arrived, he asked for some land to plant rice. He was given irrigable land next to a creek that had been abandoned since colonial days. To the surprise of everyone, he was able to rehabilitate the land and produce several crops each year of high-value long-grain rice. Several local farmers were inspired by his example and tried to replicate growing rice as he did but failed in their efforts. They said they could not work as hard as the Chinaman, and he knew much more about rice than they did.

The Chinaman was doing well with his rice production until the arrival of an aquatic hyacinth plant that never had been seen before. This waterweed quickly multiplied and congested the creek, making it impossible to pump water for irrigating the several acres of the Chinaman's rice fields. The Chinaman was therefore forced to abandon rice cultivation and invest his hard-earned money elsewhere. He decided to go into business, and he managed to buy Chez André's, the main store, bar, and restaurant in Ataku. Many people in Ataku did not like seeing this old local establishment fall into the hands of an aloof foreigner.

People tried to persuade the elderly André not to sell his store to the Chinaman, but André said he was old and wanted to retire. He also said that if he did not sell his place to the Chinaman, the Asian foreigner would set up his own store, and he knew he could not compete against the Chinaman. Furthermore, somehow the Chinaman had developed a relationship with one of his daughters. It was therefore in the best interest of his daughter for him to sell out to the Chinaman. The idea of the Chinaman having a baby with a local woman did not sit well with many people. People did not like the Chinaman because he kept to himself, did most of his work himself, and was not able to speak clearly with them in a language they understood. They also thought he was mean and stingy, as the few times he hired local people, he treated them badly and paid them low wages.

Gyasi concluded by saying, "There, you have some background on the Chinaman's case to think about. Personally, I do not know if this is a good thing or not. I hear there are Chinese people residing everywhere now in our country doing all kinds of things. I fear the babies they produce with our local women will be a force to contend with in the future. Now, give me a few minutes to relate to you some grumblings about our scholarship program."

Gyasi continued, "Some families think they are being treated unfairly because none of their children have been selected for scholarships. Now, those families who have benefitted for a long time from the scholarship program are complaining that their children working abroad no longer send them remittances, as they did before. Many of their children married Europeans, and their spouses do not look favorably on sending money to their African families. They were having children in Europe and elsewhere who did not care about Ataku and its people. Many were saving money for their own children's education abroad. People complained that when the foreign spouses of their children visit Ataku, they treat them like 'primitive children.'"

"Despite all these growing shortcomings with our scholarship program, its benefits remain in high demand by our young people. It has become increasingly apparent that all our young people want in life is the opportunity to leave the country. For them, the best they can hope for is to leave the country and obtain a job in Europe, Canada, or the US. Those young people who successfully obtain employment outside Africa are idolized. Those who cannot achieve the same success consider themselves failures and are condemned to living a poor life. If all the young people get their wish and leave the country, we will become a village of poor old people. Is there not something else our young people can aspire to, to be happy? Is leaving the country the best our young people can do? How can our country develop if the best and brightest of our youth have gone away?"

Gyasi's long presentation on these two subjects added to Letivi's fatigue and preoccupation with how his world was crumbling under his feet. He did not think he could take any more and feebly said, "Grandfather. That is quite enough. You have really given me much to consider. We will need to revisit these subjects in more depth when I am up to it and we both have the time. Thanks for all the information you have provided me."

Gyasi thanked Letivi and reminded him, "I have alerted all those concerned about our meeting early tomorrow morning on the visit to our village by the foreign technical expert to discuss the installation of a cacao-processing plant in our district."

Letivi acknowledged what his grandfather had told him and thanked him for arranging the meeting, saying, "I look very much forward to this meeting. We need to be ready to answer the expert's questions and to ask relevant questions of him. Above all, we must show him that we are serious and prepared to do all we can to have a processing plant of our own."

Letivi added, "One more thing: please remember that I will be spending tomorrow night with the old baobab tree. I must rest now."

As Gyasi exited the compound, Delalia entered and asked Letivi, "Is there anything I can help you with? I will prepare now your evening bath and meal."

Letivi replied, "Thank you, Delalia. That will be nice."

Delalia's heart was singing again because this was the first time Letivi had said her name. She quickly busied herself with warming water for Letivi's bath and fixing his evening meal of yam fufu with a meat sauce.

Letivi was too tired to eat all his well-prepared food. As soon as he finished his bath, he passed by the oldest grandfather's cabin to call upon him and his father, Bobovovi, to give him the extra strength and guidance he needed to cope with all the profound changes occurring in his world. He then headed for his sleeping room to find the rest and peace he needed so much.

Delalia could see that Letivi was tired and preoccupied, so she tried not to disturb him as she slept next to him, listening to his every heartbeat and attuned to his every move. She watched him sleeping and examined closely the scars he had received as part of his chief initiation ceremonies. She was intent on being the perfect mate and supportive companion. Her job was to be the dutiful wife required by a chief. Being totally committed to Letivi's well-being was all that mattered. Any notions about

Western-type love and romance were alien to her and the important role for which she had been chosen.

The first light of the next day reminded Letivi that he needed to rise and make himself ready for his important meeting with elders, clan heads, and key cocoa association members. He also needed to charge that irksome mobile phone. He found his clothes already placed on a chair in his room by Delalia, who was dutifully waiting for him outside next to his breakfast table.

Letivi was finishing his breakfast when Gyasi appeared at the entrance to his compound. He could tell by the long face Gyasi was wearing that he had talked to his wife about his mother's critical condition. Gyasi approached Letivi and said in a somber tone. "I spoke with my wife, and I know now why you were so down in the dumps yesterday. This is a terrible event of huge significance, but we must try to put all this aside for now so we can focus on our meeting."

Letivi nodded his agreement and rose to clasp his grandfather's hand and walk with him to the circular meeting room. They sat together and discussed briefly the points they wanted to be sure to make in today's meeting. The men and women invited to this meeting began filing into the room. When the appointed time arrived, Letivi rose to welcome and greet all those in attendance. He tried to keep his introductory words to an essential minimum. "We have summoned you here today because the president called to advise that a foreign cacao-processing specialist will visit us on Monday."

Upon hearing these words, everyone present applauded and sang a few praises to the gods and ancestors. When the assembly settled down, Letivi continued. "Today we must make sure we are well prepared for this important visit. We must be ready to provide all the information possible on our cacao production and have in hand good ideas for its local processing. I trust that a small group of our cacao-association members will work over the weekend to have all this information available. We will need to be able to answer completely any questions posed by the specialist and to ask intelligently our own questions. Above all, we need to convey to the specialist that we are very serious and capable of operating a cacao-processing plant. That is all I have to say."

Letivi sat down, and, as customary, the group waited for Chief Gyasi to speak. Gyasi stood up, balancing part of his weight on his well-worn ebony cane, to greet the group and state, "I really have nothing to add to what Chief Letivi said. We count on key members of our cacao association to make this meeting with the specialist a success. We believe that only I, Chief Letivi, and a small number of cacao association members should be in this technical meeting with the specialist. If anyone else thinks they need to be in this meeting, please contact me. One more thing: we must have at least one woman in this meeting. As you know, foreigners want to see women participating in such things. Are there any questions?"

Heads turned toward Gregoire, the manager of the cacao association and the one in the room most knowledgeable about cacao cultivation. Gregoire rose and said in his booming voice, "Thank you, my chiefs. I assure you that I and a few other association leaders will be fully prepared for this meeting. As far as we are concerned, nobody in the whole country knows more about cacao than we do. We look eagerly forward to meeting here on Monday with the specialist."

The chiefs looked around to see if anyone else wanted to speak. As nobody was asking for the floor, Letivi said, "I can see that this meeting has come to an end. If nobody objects, I hereby adjourn this meeting. I ask that those participating in the meeting on Monday arrive early so we can make, as necessary, any last-minute preparations. Until Monday...safe return to your homes."

After the last person departed, Gyasi turned to Letivi and asked, "Do you want to talk now about your mother's dire situation?"

Letivi tearfully retorted, "Grandfather, we need very much to talk about that, but I feel I must first complete my visit with the old baobab. I need to learn why he summoned me. I will spend this full-moon night with the old tree and return tomorrow morning to discuss all with you. I will spend the rest of the day praying before the grandfathers' cabins and leave late in the afternoon to be with the baobab."

Gyasi replied, "I understand, my son. We do need more time to reflect on the gravity of this unprecedented tragedy. I wish you success with the old baobab, and I look forward to seeing you upon your return. Now, I must go to be with my wife, who is beside herself with grief over the demise of our daughter and all her work on this Earth."

Letivi remained alone for a long while in the meeting room. When he left the room, he found Delalia waiting to see if he needed anything. He quietly told her of his plans for the day and night. She simply said, "I understand. I will prepare for you food and water to take with you and a special fufu plate to offer the old baobab. Please let me know if you need anything else."

As planned, Letivi spent the day praying to the grandfathers. He also called upon the spirit of his father to assist him with his mission to the old baobab. He hoped for a sign to help him with his task, but none was revealed. He felt all alone in heeding this summons from the ancient tree.

Letivi picked up the bundle Delalia had prepared for him and told her he would return the next morning. He set out on a circular route, taking a number of back paths that passed well behind the village before leaving the mountain slope for the tall savannah land where the old baobab dominated. As he left the wooded mountain slope and entered the grassy plain, he noted that land that had not been previously cultivated was now being farmed. The growing population had obliged the extension of farmland into the territory where the old baobab reigned. Indeed, from the last cultivated field, he could see in the distance the gigantic old baobab. He did not know why, but he was troubled by the fact that the old baobab was no longer located alone in what had once been a vast, empty plain. He was sad to see the baobab's domain encroached upon by human activity.

It was late in the afternoon when he arrived at the base of the huge baobab. He immediately placed his offering of fufu at the foot of the tree and knelt to say some respectful greetings and prayers to the old tree. He placed his hands on the tree's rough trunk to confirm to it his presence and see if the tree was ready to say anything to him. He was met with only silence. Everything around him was quiet and still. There was no wind and not a bird was chirping. Letivi found the profound silence surrounding him annoying.

Nothing stirred as Letivi began to encircle the tree five times as tradition required. When he finished his fifth turn around the enormous circumference of the tree, the sun was setting on the western horizon like a big fat fiery orange. As he stopped to appreciate the fabulous sunset, he heard a loud and very strange noise. He could see the tree shaking. It sounded as if it were ripping itself apart. With a final snap that sounded like the breaking of a branch, the timber-splitting noise stopped. Letivi controlled his fright and walked around the tree again to see what could have possibly made that ear-shattering racket. He could not believe what he saw on the other side of the tree.

There before him was a large opening in the tree's trunk. The aperture in the trunk rose from the ground like an upside-down V. The opening was large enough for a man to easily walk through it. Letivi did not hesitate. He instantly knew that the reason the tree had opened was for him to enter. He passed through the opening just as his father had done many years ago. There was barely enough light to see, but he could not miss the huge hole in the ground in the middle of the spacious tree hollow. He peered into the hole, expecting to see the remains of his dead father whose body he had left at this same spot some years earlier. There was no sign of any human remains or the cloth with which he had covered his father. Instead, he saw something shiny at the bottom of the hole. He quickly jumped into the five-foot-deep hole to see what was emitting such a golden glow. He cast all his fears aside, knowing instinctively that he was doing what the old baobab had summoned him to do.

At the bottom of the hole, he found a bronze chest that was the size of a large child's coffin. He reached down and worked to get his hands under the chest so he could pull it upward. The chest was very heavy. He had to use all his strength to lift it. After much effort and maneuvering, he was able to pull the chest up. He knew he had to get it out of the hole and the tree to open it to see what it was inside. With all his might, he lifted the chest above his head and shoved it onto solid ground. He climbed out of the hole and dragged the chest outside of the trunk hollow.

He moved rapidly to brush off with his hands the dirt covering the chest, revealing an intricate relief pattern that portrayed many different kinds of animals. The chest was tightly shut, but he found a button protruding from the top of one of its sides.

He pushed the button, and the top of the chest sprang partially open. He carefully raised the chest top until it was fully open. His eyes were dazzled by what he saw in the red, felt-lined interior of the chest. There, tightly fitted into the chest, was a golden chief's stool. It was then that he knew this gold stool was the tree's big secret—a secret that had been lost by his people generations ago. There was no doubt in his mind that this was indeed the five-leaf secret so many had sought over many years.

He tried to lift the stool out of the chest, but it was very heavy. Its weight told him that it was made of pure gold. He knew this antique artifact was worth a huge fortune, both for its gold as well as for its historical and artistic qualities. This village treasure was certainly worth more money than anyone in his country had ever possessed. At first he was very happy about this miraculous finding, but then he began to worry about the consequences of revealing such a rich treasure to his fellow villagers. He asked himself what would happen when the people knew they possessed the immense wealth this golden stool represents.

Letivi feared his people would quarrel over what to do with the stool, and there would never be peace again in the village. He knew that such a rare stool from long-forgotten days should be kept in a special place in a well-protected museum. But there was no such museum in his country. The best thing that could be done for the safekeeping of the stool would be to sell it to a museum in Europe, but this would mean the loss of this treasure to his people and Africa. And what would become of the millions of dollars paid for the stool? For sure, as soon as the president learned about the stool, he would confiscate it and do with it as he pleased.

There was no end to the insupportable complications and problems the revelation of the stool would cause. Letivi could now see that the unearthing of the stool would be more of a curse than a blessing. He sat down for a long time and thought over what he should do with the golden stool. As nightfall descended all around him and the full moon flooded the Earth with its brilliant light, Letivi decided that it was best to put the stool back into the hole from which he had extracted it and keep its secret to himself. He was convinced that any other option would have bad results for his people.

He brought out his kerosene lantern and lit it. He placed the lantern inside the tree next to the hole. He closed the chest and pulled it back inside the tree hollow, working hard to place it as it had been when he had first seen it at the bottom of the hole. He then used his hands to push all the loose earth he could find over the stool. When the stool was covered and the hole filled, he walked on top of it to tamp down the soil. He picked up his lamp and exited the tree.

As the light of the full moon made the night almost into day, he blew out the wick in his lamp. He then placed his hands on the old baobab and asked it in multiple tree languages to close its trunk up and keep with it the secret of the golden stool. He exhorted, "Please, ancient one, keep this secret with you. I am flattered that you demonstrated your trust in me by revealing this precious secret, but the time has not yet come for any human to know this secret."

Letivi continued his exhortations until there occurred near him a loud crashing sound. About five yards from where he knelt, a huge branch from the old baobab had fallen to the ground. As he stepped forward to examine the tree-size branch that had landed near him, he heard another loud crashing sound made by another falling branch. At that moment, he knew this could mean only one thing: the ancient baobab was dying. It, too, was following his mother and her botanical domain into the past. Before his eyes, the old world was giving way to make room for the new world. For better or worse, there was no stopping the wheels of time. Humans had no say about a destiny that had been set for their world at the beginning of time.

All that remained for Letivi was the full moon and his affiliation with it. He turned to ask for the moon's empathy and support. He had nowhere else to turn. He worried that with the death of the old baobab, someone would find the golden stool. He was at a loss as to what to do. It then hit him hard in the gut that if the old baobab was dying, so was his mother. He quickly gathered his things and began running through the spooky night to join her before it was too late. The growing void in his life made him weak and unable to cope with his fast-changing world.

For the first time, he began to see that the new world had little use for a moonchild. He also began to realize that the passing of the baobab meant the link between it and the full moon would be broken. The dissolution of this magical connection between the baobab and the moon would make it impossible for his father to return again in any form. The demise of the baobab and his mother's domain would leave him fully dependent on his special relationship with the moon. He was not sure the moon alone would provide him with all the strength and magic he needed to succeed.

CHAPTER FIFTEEN
STALLED IN MELOMTI

The last thing they wanted to do was to go to Melomti's seedy airport. But Molly and Robin had no choice. If they wanted to recover their lost luggage, they must return to the airport and its anarchic disorder. As the sun was setting, they asked their driver to take them to the airport and help them locate their two suitcases.

They arrived at the airport and forced themselves to adopt the aggressive attitude they needed to push their way through the rowdy crowd of well-wishers, beggars, hawkers, and hustlers. The police prevented them from entering the baggage collection area. Only after a lengthy explanation and showing their tickets and baggage tags were they allowed to venture into the tightly packed mob of frantic people and a vast assortment of lost, misplaced, and recently arrived baggage. This was a mad place that could be handled successfully only by the most patient, courageous, and determined.

Molly and Robin looked desperately around for the airline agent with the clipboard with whom they had talked after arriving the previous night. After much shoving and looking in all directions, they spotted the man and shoved their way toward him. When they managed to reach the man, Molly said in a loud, demanding voice, "Remember us?"

The tall, skinny man with a cocoa-butter complexion slowly turned to see who was yelling at him above the noisy crowd. When he saw Molly next to him, he said, "Of course I remember you. How could I forget you? I know you are here for your two suitcases that did not arrive with you last night. Let us go look in our storeroom for lost luggage."

The agent forced his way through the crowd. Molly and Robin followed him across the vast warehouse-like area to a locked room that jutted out from an exterior wall. He pulled from his belt a ring full of keys and fumbled with them until he found the key that would open the metal door to the storeroom. He unlocked the door and flung it open. He groped for the light switch on the wall next to the inside of the door to turn on a dim, low-wattage light bulb that dangled from a high rafter. The large room was piled high with suitcases. He instructed Molly and Robin, "Please look for your suitcases."

Robin took the lead in searching for their bags in the dusty room. He was required to lift and move many bags. It was apparent to Robin that most of the bags had been in storage for a long time. After over thirty minutes of searching up and down and everywhere in the room, he could not find their suitcases. In disgust, he turned to the airline agent and firmly said, "Our suitcases are not here!"

The agent replied in a sympathetic tone, "That's too bad, because they should be here. Past experience has shown that if bags do not show up the day after they are supposed to arrive, they usually never come."

Molly and Robin were having a difficult time accepting what the man's words meant. Furiously, Molly spouted, "You mean to tell us that our suitcases are permanently lost? How can that be?"

As calmly as he could, the man simply said, "Probably. Bags are frequently stolen before a plane arrives here. Your case is not unusual. I'm sorry, but I have some forms you can complete for a limited monetary reimbursement from the airline."

An infuriated Molly shouted, "How much can we get and when?"

Defensively, the man said, "There is a maximum of one hundred dollars per suitcase, and it takes about two weeks for our office in town to process the paper work and issue you a check drawn on a local bank."

In Molly's mind, there was no way she was going to fill out any forms and wait for a measly reimbursement. All she wanted to do was to get out of Melomti and go to Ataku, the village where David had done his Peace Corps service. Defiantly, she turned to the man and told him bluntly, "Forget it! We must leave town tomorrow, and we have no time for this kind of nonsense."

She then turned to Robin and commanded, "Let's get out of here now!"

They quickly turned their backs on the man and headed for the exit and their waiting taxi driver. If they had looked back at the airline agent, they would have seen a triumphant smile on his face. He was happy that he had been able to work again another scam on white tourists. He was in the habit of systematically stealing the tourists' suitcases and selling their contents so he could support his large extended family. Stealing in his society was a real bad 'no-no,' but he believed it was all right to steal from whites, as they were rich and could easily replace all their losses. He was also grinning because Molly and Robin had forgotten all about the two jackets they had been wearing when they arrived. He was able to sell their nifty jackets for a tidy sum.

The mound of suitcases in the storeroom was for show only. They were suitcases that he had previously stolen and stuffed with old papers. All this was for misleading his hapless victims by a show of his good intentions. Of course, he had to split his profits with airport police and customs officials who also participated in this routine rip-off. Africa can be a tough place at times for the gullible and naïve well-off foreigner who is ignorant of local ways.

Molly and Robin jumped into their taxi with only one question pounding in their heads: What would they do for clothes?

They explained to the driver about the loss of their suitcases with all their clothes. The driver listened intently, seeing an opportunity to make a few gadis as well as to help his two passengers satisfy their need for clothes. He said, "I know just what to do. I have a friend who is a tailor, and I am sure he and his apprentices would be happy to work all night to make you some clothes, especially if you pay them a little extra. Do you want to go to his place now?"

Without hesitation, Molly said, "Yes, let's go there now. What kind of clothes can he make for us?"

The driver nonchalantly replied, "The same kind of clothes we wear. This will be good because it will make you fit better into the local scene."

Robin said, "Molly, I think he had a good point. I have noticed that nobody is dressed like us. For sure, in spite of the heat, I have not yet seen any man wearing shorts, and most of what I had in my suitcase was shorts. I also like the colorful tropical shirts they make here."

Molly said, "I would also not mind wearing a long, colorful skirt and matching blouse in the same way I see most women dressed here. I really like the multicolored African print cloth."

All of a sudden, they were both eager to go to the tailor's and have some local clothes made. The driver speeded up, and before long, they were bumping over rough dirt roads in a dark neighborhood where few lights shone. They stopped in front of a completely dark and closed workshop room. The driver called out, and a man appeared from the shadows. The driver said, "We are lucky. The tailor is here."

After speaking a few minutes to the man through his car window, the driver said, "He will do it. Give him a few minutes to get organized so he can measure you, and you can pick out the cloth for your clothes. He says his team can produce overnight two outfits for each of you. Of course, you will have to pay a premium price."

Molly said contently, "We don't care what it costs as long as the clothes are nicely made and fit us well."

Within minutes, a Petromax lamp was lit, and the darkness of the place disappeared. There was some commotion as the tailor called for his apprentices and opened his small shop, which consisted of one tiny room and a front veranda. Following their driver's suggestion, Molly and Robin got out of the car and approached the tailor, who immediately took out his tape and measured them, noting all the details with a stubby pencil in his worn notebook. After recording their measurements, he said, "I will make a nice two-piece ensemble for her and two pants and two shirts for you. I have a limited supply of cloth here that you can choose from."

The tailor brought out some stacks of cloth and sat them on a solid wooden table. He placed the Petromax lamp next to the cloth so they could easily see the material under its bright light.

Molly chose two colorful African wraps, and Robin chose the same cloth for his shirts, as well as picking from another stack khaki and gray cloths for his two pairs of pants. They both were delighted at the prospect of having tailor-made clothes for the first time in their lives. They could see that the practice of having clothes made by a tailor instead of buying ready-made clothes in a shop was an attractive alternative.

The tailor talked to the driver, who in turn said to Molly and Robin, "He will need an advance of some money to buy some thread, needles, and kerosene for his lamp. They will also be munching on a lot of kola nuts and drinking coffee to stay awake through the night."

Molly replied, "That is understandable. How much do they want, and how much will everything cost? Also, when can we pick up our clothes?"

The driver hesitated and said, "The advance is fifty percent of the total cost of sixty dollars. You clothes will be ready when you wake up tomorrow. If you like, I can bring them to you when I come to fetch you at your hotel."

Molly and Robin looked at each other. For them, this was a super bargain. They did not know that a local person would pay almost half this total price. They also could not know that the driver would receive a 10 percent finder's fee. This was an ideal situation in which everyone involved considered himself or herself a winner.

Molly tried to look as if all was under control, saying, "We find these conditions agreeable, and we like the idea of your bringing our finished clothes to us at the hotel. Of course, if our clothes don't fit well, we will come back here to have them adjusted. We will not pay the rest of the money until we are satisfied with our clothes."

They handed money over to a very happy tailor, who immediately began ordering his three sleepy-eyed apprentices around while he started to measure and cut pieces of cloth. Molly wondered if they would do all the sewing by hand or if they had sewing machines. She thought it must be the former, as they did not have any electricity. As she said good-bye, she wished them, "Good luck. I hope your hands don't get tired from all the sewing."

The tailor quickly replied, "No, Ma'am. Thanks to Mr. Singer and Mrs. Butterfly, we do most of the work on our two sewing machines." Upon saying these words, he lifted the lamp over to the other side of the veranda to expose two very old treadle sewing machines carrying the brand names of the people he had mentioned.

Molly and Robin were astounded to see that people still used sewing machines not seen in Kansas since their great grandparents' time. They were both pleased and disappointed to see such museum pieces still in use. They were slowly waking up to the fact that the country they were in was at a very different stage of development and outlook. They did wonder how a country could progress if it did not have an affordable and reliable source of electricity.

The driver hummed a happy tune as he drove Molly and Robin to their hotel. He was thanking God for his good luck in making so much money in one day. He was looking forward to returning to his family with the good news, paying off some debts, and buying some of the essentials his wife and children needed. He was also happy because he could see more money coming to him from Molly and Robin in the days ahead. It had been years since he had enjoyed such fantastic good fortune.

Robin was worried about some other clothing articles that the tailor could not provide. What about socks and underwear? When he mentioned this problem to Molly, the driver overheard him and said, "Excuse me. What you just said is not a problem. Tomorrow morning, we will stop at some roadside market stalls where you can buy those items. You may also want to buy some local leather sandals and some rubber flip-flops."

When they arrived at their hotel's entrance, Molly and Robin were also feeling much better, as it appeared their clothing problems had been resolved. They bid farewell to their taxi driver until his return early the next morning. They knew they had to focus on what they had to do tomorrow. They very much wanted to go to Ataku as early as possible in the morning, and they needed to make sure they were thoroughly prepared. They—particularly Molly—were bound and determined to complete their mission.

They entered their hotel room prepared to repeat a night like the one they had yesterday. It was only after they entered their room that they realized they were hungry and needed bottled water. Robin called the front desk to ask for food and drink. He was told that a man would come to their room to take their order. Within minutes, there was a loud knock on the door, and Robin opened it slowly to see who it was. There before him was a uniformed bellboy with a pad and pencil in hand. The man said, "Good evening, sir. I am here to take your order."

Robin replied, "What do you have on your menu?"

The man said in rapid fashion, "This time of night, we have only ham or ham and cheese sandwiches on a French baguette."

Molly yelled from across the room, "Robin, get one of each, and we'll decide later who gets what."

Robin passed the order on to the man at the door and added, "Besides the two sandwiches, bring us two Cokes and two bottles of still water."

The bellboy dashed away, and Robin latched the door. He turned to Molly, who looked radiant to him in spite of the trials they had been through and the clammy condition of their bodies, which were covered with a filthy film of sweat and grime. Molly was in a good mood, so Robin tried to be cheerful and said, "Look on the bright side. We only have to rinse our underwear and socks tonight. Now, that's real progress."

Molly laughed and walked over to give Robin a warm embrace of appreciation, saying softly in Robin's ear, "Thank you, dear, for hanging in there with me and being such a good trooper. I owe you."

Robin was delighted and sexually aroused. He had been embraced and kissed by Molly before, but now it seemed different, especially as it was only the two of them in the intimate confines of their hotel room. It was becoming much harder for him to keep his hands off of her. He was afraid of making any wrong moves. He did not want to ruin the good relationship they already had. He knew the time was approaching when it would be impossible for him to control himself. His only hope was for Molly to make the first move.

Robin's unseemly thoughts were stopped by another loud knock on the door. While Molly escaped into the bathroom with her sheet, Robin opened the door to let the bellboy place a tray with the sandwiches and beverages on the table in their room. He told the bellboy to add the cost on their room bill and he would tip him tomorrow, as they did not have any change now. The bellboy thanked him and departed. Robin then locked all three of the latches on the door and turned the ceiling fan up to its highest speed.

He then knocked on the bathroom door, telling Molly, "Dinner has been served." He could hear by the splish-splash of water that Molly was already bathing. This knowledge caused him to begin preparing himself for seeing again a naked Molly though a thin, damp sheet. He told himself that he needed to stop these kinds of perverted thoughts. He needed to recognize Molly as his good friend and not as a sex object.

Molly yelled through the door, "OK. I will be out in a jiffy."

While waiting for Molly, Robin examined the sandwiches which had been nicely wrapped in large white paper napkins. He was surprised to see that they actually looked pretty good. He was also impressed that there were tiny ceramic bowls with mustard and mayonnaise on the side, as well as small pickles. Both the water and Cokes were well chilled. Looking at the sandwiches made him hungrier, and thus it was harder for him to wait for Molly before taking a bite.

Molly swung the bathroom door wide open, singing and dancing a popular tune from the States. This was the happiest Robin had seen her since they had found evidence about David at WSU. All her gyrations had loosened the sheet wrapped around her, and for a brief moment, one of her plump breasts emerged from beneath the sheet. Robin politely acted as if he had not seen anything, but his body temperature hiked up a notch. He had seen many African women during the day with their breasts exposed to feed their infants, and that did not cause him a moment's pause. So why did seeing Molly's lone breast for a second almost throw him for a loop?

Molly adjusted her sheet wrap and surprised Robin with an affectionate peck on the cheek. In one hand, she was swinging around her panties in time with the song she was singing. Robin had never seen her act so crazily. She hung her panties on the back of one of the chairs and sat across from Robin, saying, "Let's do scissors, paper, and stones to see who gets which sandwich. The winner gets the ham and cheese."

It was Robin's turn to laugh and say, "OK." He was really trying hard to keep his cool around the sensual feminine form in front of him. He was thinking that he was just too horny. He was also finding it hard to not be affected by Molly's panties swaying in the breeze made by the fan.

Molly quickly won rights to the ham-and-cheese sandwich. Robin handed her the sandwich, and they both began chomping down on their big baguettes, finding them very tasty. They reached for their Cokes, only to find the caps were still on them. The bellboy had forgotten to open them, and neither Molly nor Robin had a bottle opener.

It was Molly who came to rescue, saying, "I know how to open bottles using the bathroom doorjamb." She gingerly rose and strode quickly the few paces to the bathroom door. She held the Coke bottle in a horizontal position and stuck its top in the door slot. The inner edge of the bottle cap was wedged tightly against the metal edge of the door slot while Molly forced the bottle toward herself. The bottle easily opened, spilling a bit on the floor before Molly could put it in an upright position.

She was beginning to work on opening the second bottle in the same way when the sheet wrapped around her loosened itself and fell to the floor. Robin wanted to avert his eyes from seeing a fully naked Molly, but he could not do so. His vision was unwillingly riveted on the beautifully unclothed Molly just a couple of yards in front of him. Molly laughed and said, "Whoops."

She then reached down and grabbed her sheet and wrapped it around her shapely body while smiling at Robin. She did not seem bothered at all. She could see that the brief apparition of her nudity almost caused Robin to gasp. She wagged her forefinger at him, saying jokingly in a scolding tone, "You naughty boy."

They both enjoyed their sandwiches and Cokes. Robin was trying to recover a sense of normalcy, but the way Molly nibbled around the end of her hard baguette bread kept him in an agitated state. For him, Molly's every move now had a sexual connotation. He now had strong, almost uncontrollable feelings for Molly. He was afraid that he was developing an itch for which there was only one remedy, and he knew his chances of obtaining such a remedy were remote.

They finished their sandwiches and took their antimalarial pills. Molly sensed Robin's discomfort and suspected the reason for it. She was also having feelings for Robin, but she was much better at not showing her true feelings. For a while, she just looked at Robin with a little smile on her face. She was feeling pity for him—as she would for a lost little puppy dog. She did not want to see him like this. She needed him to be a strong, happy, and supportive companion. Molly finally opened her mouth and said in a sweet tone, "My dear Robin, why don't you go take your bath? It is getting late. We need a good night's sleep if we are going to make it to Ataku tomorrow."

Robin quickly agreed and headed for the bathroom. He was hoping the geckos would be out again tonight so that Molly would be so afraid that she would want to sleep in his arms as she had done the night before. The thought of having Molly again in his arms all night long made him hurry through his bathing ritual, wrap the remaining dry towel around himself, and exit the bathroom to join Molly in bed.

He found all the room ceiling lights turned off and Molly already asleep. As he turned off the light next to his side of the bed, a depressing chill crept over him. He felt alone and neglected. He regretted that Molly was already asleep and that there were no geckos crawling on the walls and ceiling to scare her into his arms. He reluctantly lay down on his back, knowing that under these conditions, it would be a very long and sleepless night for him. The minutes passed slowly, and he was resigning himself to his lonely status when he felt a hand touch his body. He was transfixed as Molly's hand gently caressed in a slow, tender but deliberate fashion his chest.

He became immediately aroused, and he could feel his male hormones surging. He automatically reached over to caress Molly in the same way and was pleasantly surprised to find that she had removed her sheet. His heart skipped a beat, and his breath was taken away. His body trembled at the thought of what was now possible. There was no way their mutual caresses would not lead to the ultimate act of intimacy. Whether the act would be done out of pity, a need for comfort, love, or lust did not matter. The only thing that mattered now was the moment at hand and satisfying the undeniable laws of nature.

CHAPTER SIXTEEN
CACAO CUM COCOA

"He's coming!" These words were shouted out loudly by the first sentinel posted at the junction of the village road with the main highway, and they were rapidly passed on from one sentinel to another. In only a few minutes, the news reached the village. The drummers and gong-gong men swung into action, adding to the noisy spread of the news of the arrival of the USAID cocoa-processing specialist. In less than ten minutes, the village welcoming committee was assembled at the entrance of the village to warmly welcome this specialist and escort him to Chief Letivi's compound. The excitement in the air was so thick that it could be cut with a knife. The people acted as if they were welcoming a hero who would rescue them from their poverty.

The people were impressed by the large size of the car carrying the American specialist. They had never before seen a big US Chevrolet Suburban. When the car stopped in the village commons, it was immediately surrounded by drummers and dancers who did their best to demonstrate how happy the people were to see their very important visitors. They were glad to see that there were two white men instead of the one expected. The leader of the welcoming committee signaled to the elated crowd that they should make way for the visitors so they could pass and be properly greeted.

As the visitors approached those assigned to welcome them, a fetish priest stopped their forward progress in order to offer a blessing by asking the grandfathers to make their visit a productive one. He finished his words by pouring a libation for the grandfathers on the ground in front of the two visitors. At that point, two young girls elaborately dressed in the traditional way and with heavy makeup stepped up to the visitors to offer them a calabash of frothy-white, fresh palm wine. The visitors politely took turns taking small sips of the palm wine and handed the calabash to the girls.

The leader of the group then formed a line of the dozen people in the welcoming committee so the two men could pass in front of them to shake hands and exchange greetings. After this initial welcome, the two men were asked to follow them to their chief's house. As they slowly made their way up the gradual slope to Letivi's compound, people lined each side of the wide path and waved and cheered. The men were very impressed with the lively reception they were receiving from hundreds of villagers. They felt like celebrities. If the intention was to imprint on them a first good impression, the village had already succeeded in making their visit a success.

Chiefs Letivi and Gyasi were dressed in their best traditional clothes. They stood in a chiefly manner in front of the royal compound to receive and greet their distinguished visitors. The chiefs vigorously welcomed the two white men and shook their hands with a tight grip, as they knew was done in Europe. They invited the men to follow them inside the compound to the meeting room. As they entered, the twenty or so people stood and began clapping. The chiefs showed the men their two comfortable armchairs in front of the group, and they took similar seats next to them. After they were seated, Letivi signaled to the group to sit down.

Nobody knew it, but Chief Letivi was struggling to stay poised and focused on the subject at hand. His mother's dire situation and his discovery of the golden stool under the old baobab tree were weighing heavily on him. Letivi fought to clear his mind of these two serious concerns as he stood to welcome formally the two white men and commence the meeting with them. He first asked everyone in the room to stand individually and introduce themselves. When everyone had finished with their introductions, he presented himself and asked Chief Gyasi to do the same. He then asked the two men to introduce themselves.

The first white man to talk was very tall and slightly bald with a protruding potbelly. He had a reddish complexion like other white men previously seen in the village. This reddish skin made people think that white men were not really white, but that they were red. He wore a long-sleeve white shirt with shiny snap buttons and Levi jeans. His leather belt was bigger than any ever seen before, and it had a large buckle with designs engraved on it. The boots he wore were also unlike any seen before. The people could not possibly know that his dress was considered "old western" in the United States.

This tall man stood up and bent his head to the left to avoid touching one of the lower crossbeams in the rafters. The local people, who were generally short in stature, had never seen a person so tall. The man appeared to them as a being from another world. This alien being spoke in an accent they had never heard before. With a pronounced twang in his voice, he said, "Thank you very much for your warm and much-appreciated welcome. This is my first time to come to Africa, and I have never been so warmly welcomed before. My name is Phil Mason. I have spent most of my life working in the cocoa-processing industry. I'm very happy to be here with you today. I hope that I can be of some help to you."

Phil sat down, and his very different-looking colleague rose to introduce himself. This was a much younger, shorter, and whiter man who looked like a teenager. He had long brown hair and a nervous tic that shook his hands about every two minutes. This odd-looking man spoke in a low voice. "My name is Steve Morgan. I work at the US Embassy in Melomti. I came today to accompany Mr. Mason and take notes on the substance of your meeting. Your president has requested that we give priority to assisting you with the establishment of a cocoa-processing plant. Therefore, this is an important component of the excellent bilateral relations we maintain with your country. In this first meeting, we need to take full advantage of Mr. Mason's expertise, particularly as he will be in the country only for a few weeks. Thank you for the welcome and your attention."

Letivi's mind was dwelling on his problems, so he missed most of what Phil and Steve said. Gyasi nudged him slightly so he could know that it was now time again for him to intervene. Letivi stood and thanked the two men for their words and said, "Everyone here knows that the cultivation of cacao is the mainstay of our local economy and the source of most of our income. We have done all we know to increase cacao production, but this has not resulted in a sufficient increase in our incomes. We concluded that the only way to increase our incomes is to add value to our cacao production by processing our cacao beans here instead of having them shipped to Europe for processing. We are therefore counting on your help to set up a cacao-bean-processing plant so we can produce cocoa powder. We are eager to hear what Mr. Mason has to say about all this. Mr. Mason, please enlighten us."

Letivi sat down, and the towering Phil stood up. He cleared his voice before saying, "I want very much to help you, but you need to know that what you are asking is very complicated. I understand very well why you want a cacao-processing plant, but establishing one is fraught with many challenges. I don't want to discourage you. All I want is that you accept that what you are asking requires resolving monumental issues."

Hearing these words caused all present to fall into a deep silence. You could hear a pin drop. Every person in the group believed that their high hopes for establishing a processing plant had been dashed even before they understood why this had to be so. They waited for Phil to say more. They wanted to know why it would be so difficult to set up a modest processing plant. For them, this should not be so complicated.

Phil continued, "I'm sure you know how many acres of cacao trees you collectively have and that the cacao beans you produce are of the high quality needed for processing. One thing I fear is that your combined production of cacao beans will not be enough to operate the processing plant continuously throughout the year. This is one thing we will need to study carefully."

At that moment, Gregoire, the manager of the cacao planters association, raised his hand. He stood up and said, "Thank you, Mr. Mason. I assure you that we have all the details about cacao beans harvested annually from our members and that they produce top-quality beans. The average family farm size is about two acres, and we have about four hundred families cultivating cacao trees. Our overall annual cacao bean production is nearly three hundred tons. Our beans are carefully fermented and dried before being placed in one-hundred-pound jute bags for sale to traders who represent European companies."

Phil said, "That is all good information to have. I look forward to visiting some of your cacao fields. I assume that your average yields per acre on these small family farms are about three hundred and fifty pounds. I note that more efficient large-scale cacao plantations using the latest hybrid trees and modern inputs can obtain yields of over one thousand pounds per acre of top-quality beans."

This latter comment had heads spinning, and some were asking themselves how they could also increase the yields of their cacao farms. The information they were receiving today was almost more than they could digest.

Phil continued. "One fear I have is that the processing of your total annual production of cacao beans would produce more cocoa powder than the national market could absorb. Even the smallest processing plant can probably produce in a few weeks more cocoa powder than is consumed in a few years in Kotoku. And I'm only talking about the production of Ataku and not the rest of the district. Moreover, the quality of the cocoa powder you produce would not be as good as the powder imported from Europe."

These were very disquieting words for those assembled. They were having difficulty registering all the implications of what the specialist had just said. Before they could fully digest these words, Phil added, "But we can't be certain about this until we have analyzed the market for cocoa powder. I 'm sure there must be much competition from imported cocoa powder."

Those present believed they had thought of everything, but they had not given the slightest attention to the marketing of their cocoa powder. This was a new wrinkle for them. Already they could see that producing cocoa powder was much more complicated than they had first believed.

Steve and Letivi were furiously jotting down notes in their respective notebooks. Steve knew he would have to draft and submit a full report to his ambassador after his return to his office in Melomti. Letivi knew he needed a good record of the meeting so he could call in his report to the president.

While they were scribbling away, Phil continued. "I don't think that in this first meeting I should burden you with too many details. Please let me outline a few key facts about what is entailed in setting up a cacao-processing plant and keeping it functioning smoothly. I will try to focus on the main requirements, as these must be satisfied before working on the myriad of other details that are needed to complete a comprehensive feasibility study and a convincing business case."

Everyone in the room mechanically nodded their heads in agreement. They were eager to hear what else Phil had to say. They could see that he was a real expert and possessed all the knowledge they needed. Phil continued his presentation at a quicker pace, saying, "I think it would be good if I walked you through the major steps required in processing cacao beans so you have a good idea of what is involved."

Phil lost no time in reciting the processing basics: "The beans must arrive at the plant dried and in good condition. They will be roasted at a high temperature, winnowed, and broken into nib pieces before being rolled hydraulically into cocoa butter and press cake. The former is used to make chocolate, and the latter is crushed into cocoa powder. Before the press cake is crushed, it should be treated with an alkali chemical such as potassium carbonate. The powder is then sealed inside attractive packages and marketed through a pre-established distribution system."

Most in attendance were struggling to understand what Phil was saying. Many were turning to those next to them to ask for the meaning of Phil's words. Even the well-educated and super intelligent Letivi was having trouble grasping all of Phil's points. Phil's brief exposé raised more questions than it answered.

At this point, Letivi felt compelled to intervene so that Phil could provide needed clarifications. "Thank you, Mr. Mason, for your instructive presentation. I know that many of us are in need of some clarifications before continuing our discussions. In this regard, I have a couple of questions. One question I have is, how do you roast the beans? One other question I have for now is, what do we do with the cocoa butter?"

Phil thanked Letivi and said, "The mechanical roaster requires lots of natural gas to function. You would need to store on site a large quantity of propane gas. As for the cocoa butter, the best thing would be to collect it in metal barrels and export it to Europe."

Letivi was beginning to see that there was much more to cacao processing than he or anyone else in the room could know. He was afraid that before Phil finished what he had to say to them, there would be more revelations of unanticipated challenges. He felt a knot of worry growing in his gut that they might be biting off more than they could chew. Before turning things back to Phil, he asked if anyone else had any questions.

One of the big producers of cacao raised his hand and asked, "Where will we acquire the material for packaging our cocoa powder?"

Phil quickly replied, "Very good question. I have found that in other countries where I have worked, packaging was what we call a showstopper. Unless you can obtain within your country the good-quality small containers needed to package your powder, it will be too expensive to import such packaging material. This is something that needs to be investigated immediately."

Perhaps the oldest man in attendance asked, "How do you run the plant? Doesn't it require electricity? As you can see, we don't have any electricity in our village."

Phil said, "Of course. It is all powered by electricity. You must have a big generator with a good and reliable fuel supply or have access to the national electrical grid. Either way, access to dependable electricity is essential, and this will be a major operational cost."

Letivi and Gyasi quietly conferred. They did not think there was a supplier of suitable packaging in the country, and they knew the cost of electricity was prohibitive. In their own minds, they were already looking for solutions to these seemingly insurmountable problems.

One of the two women in the group asked in a timid voice, "There seems to be a lot of machinery involved. How do we obtain such machines and learn to maintain and operate them?"

Phil said, "Another very good question. Everything will have to be ordered from Europe, and those who will be operating the plant will have to be trained in Europe. You will need all the required tools and a good stock of spare parts. As I said before, setting up and operating a processing plant is a complicated business, and it can take two years or more before the first batch of cocoa powder is produced."

There was almost a collective gulp. Every person seated in the room looked left and right to see the reactions of those around them. Everyone was really discouraged now, not by all the unforeseen complications, but by the length of time it would take to begin processing cacao. These were people who lived for the day at hand. It was the quick satisfaction of their present needs that interested them. It was difficult for them to think about or work for something that would not occur for over two years. It was a challenge for them to put such distant objectives on their daily survival agenda.

The other woman, who had held her hand in the air for a long time, was called on to ask her question. In a forceful and no-nonsense voice, she asked, "The main thing we need to know is how all this will make more money for us. After all, this is why we are doing this. We need more money so that we are less poor."

Phil smiled and thanked this courageous lady for her pertinent query. He replied in uncertain words, "Yes, that is the crux of the matter. And the truth is that you will have more headaches than you have now, and you may make very little more money, if any at all. Much depends on the demand for your cocoa powder and how much people are willing to pay for it. I have to do my analysis, but I'm almost certain that you will not be able to sell you cacao beans for a higher price. How much you can profit from producing cocoa powder will depend greatly on the management structure you put in place and the investment and operational costs."

Phil's words deflated the group's elation and brought them back to reality's ground with a heavy and depressing thud. Nobody made a sound. Their spirits had dropped so low that even the geckos on the walls stopped croaking. Letivi took some time before standing and then took a couple more minutes before saying, "We thank Mr. Mason for opening our eyes to a number of things we had not thought about. As Mr. Mason does not have much time, I ask him to tell us what additional information he needs from us and what he needs to do here today so he can complete his report on our processing plant."

Phil stood again and said, "I think I have most of the information I need. It would be good if I could work awhile with your technical team to elaborate a rough sketch of where cacao is cultivated around your village and in your district. It would also be good if I could visit a few cacao fields and the location where you would like to build the plant. One thing I'm concerned about is how cacao beans will be collected and transported to the plant. I also have some questions about land ownership and banking facilities."

Phil's last remarks added to Letivi's increasing worries about the feasibility of this cocoa-powder project. He tried to stay composed as he said, "Very well. I think it would be a good idea if you could sit down for an hour or so with our core team to draw up a map showing in an illustrative manner where cacao is grown around our village. After that, the same team can show you some nearby cacao fields. We can also assemble here again for lunch and our final discussion. I hope this is agreeable to everyone."

Most of the people in the room exited. Those remaining included Gregoire and the officers of the cacao growers association. Letivi turned to the two white men and said, "Please excuse me and my fellow chief. We'll leave you until lunch in the good hands of those who know the most about the cultivation of cacao by our village. We'll discuss more later."

As soon as Letivi and Gyasi stepped outside, Letivi dug into a deep pocket of his gown to retrieve his mobile phone. He turned to Gyasi and said, "Let's find a quiet place so I can try to call the president. I need to tell him about the meeting and obtain his opinions on a number of topics."

Letivi and Gyasi walked to a distant corner of his vast compound. With a trembling hand, Letivi punched in the president's number. He could hear the phone ringing at the other end. It rang a long time before the president answered in a gruff tone, "Letivi, what do you want? I am very busy!"

Letivi quickly replied, "Mr. President, I need to talk to you about the meeting we are having now with the USAID expert."

The president immediately said, "OK. Go ahead, but don't waste my time."

As rapidly as he could, Letivi responded, saying, "Mr. President, the expert says we need electricity and packaging for our cocoa powder. He also says it will be hard for us to compete against imported cocoa powder. What do you advise?"

The president put Letivi on hold for several minutes before barking out advice. "Don't worry about electricity. We are extending high-tension lines from Melomti to Kpolomo, and we can run a short branch line into your village at a subsidized rate. We are also planning to build a packaging manufacturing plant. So don't worry about that either. If need be, I will raise tariffs on imported cocoa powder so it will not be able to compete with our cocoa powder. I have to go."

Letivi held the silent phone next to his ear for a minute before turning to his grandfather to tell him what the president had said. They both thought long and hard over the president's words. They were impressed that the president seemed to have answers to all their concerns. But, somehow, they worried about such close involvement with the president and the dependence of their cacao-processing plant on him. The last thing they wanted was to be hostage to the president's whims.

***

In distant Melomti, the president had a very different set of ideas running through his mind. The president's major concern on this matter and everything else was how he could make the most money. He was making a lot of money from kickbacks from the companies selected to install the power line to Kpolomo. This donor-funded project cost his country nothing, and a second phase was already planned to offer electricity to the villages near the power line. The president also planned to collect a percentage of the money paid by the villages for the supply of electricity.

The president would also gain a percentage of the value of the contract signed for the building of a plant to manufacture packaging material. It would be easy for him to apply higher tariffs on imported cocoa powder or prohibit altogether the importation of foreign-made powder. He was thinking that maybe the foreign firms would give him a lucrative payment to permit the entry into the country of their cocoa powder. Everywhere the president looked, he saw opportunities to rake off money. And, on top of making handsome sums of money, he would be building up his prestige. He would be given the credit for creating the first cacao-processing and packaging plant in the country, as well as for being the one who made rural electrification possible. He could visualize cutting a big red ribbon to inaugurate the plant with the American ambassador. He would definitely bestow upon the ambassador his country's highest award, the gold medal of the Order of Kotoku. There was nothing sweeter for him than gaining more glory and padding his large offshore bank accounts at the same time.

The president was delighted by all the possibilities the establishment of a cacao-processing plant presented him. His head was spinning over all the schemes he could use to make money. Of course, he would handpick the people who would operate the plant, and they would therefore be beholden to him and pay him part of their salaries. He could keep the people of Ataku happy by paying them a premium price for the cocoa powder, even if he were to sell it for a lower price on the open market. If the foreign cocoa-producing companies offered him high enough bribes to sell their cocoa powder on the local market, he would have no qualms about throwing into the ocean the cocoa powder produced by the Ataku plant. He saw that the most lucrative part of these corrupt practices would be in the money foreign firms paid for tariffs or in bribes. And, in any deal with foreign firms, he would insist they pay him a good price for the cocoa butter produced by the Ataku plant.

***

Lunch had been served in the small, straw-covered banquet hangar in another corner of the chief's compound by a number of hardworking village women who had done their best to prepare the finest meal possible. Chez André's had provided bottled water and soft drinks. Just in case it would be needed, a large clay jar of fresh palm wine was kept on the side. Letivi and Gyasi took their seats at the head of the nicely decorated banquet tables which had been arranged in a big rectangle. Despite their hunger, they patiently waited for the two white men to return from their walk to visit nearby cacao fields.

They did not have to wait long. The white men and the core technical group sat down at their designated places along the banquet tables. The two white men sat at the head table between Letivi and Gyasi. Letivi tapped his spoon on a drinking glass to gain the attention of the others. When there was quiet and all eyes were focused on Letivi, he said, "First, let us fill our glasses so we can toast our honored guests. Second, let us eat our fill, and while we eat, we can talk. I am interested to hear more of what Mr. Mason has to say."

They all raised their glasses in praise of the two white men. They drank and loudly clinked their glasses together with those on their right and left. There was some boisterousness and much laughing. In spite of all the obstacles to establishing the cacao-processing plant that had been revealed, there was still some optimism about making cocoa powder locally. Food of every kind was piled high on huge platters, which were passed around until everyone had on their plates all the food they wanted.

Phil took a little of everything, and his plate was stacked high. He ate a few bites and asked for the chiefs' permission to speak. Letivi tapped on his glass again, asking for everyone to give Mr. Mason their full attention. Phil started by saying, "Please keep eating. I would normally not talk while I eat, but in the interest of time, I will do so today. Dear chiefs and everyone, I would like to say again how happy I'm with the fabulous reception you have given us and all the information you provided me today. I could have not have asked for better."

Everyone applauded loudly Phil's words. They were eager to hear what else he had to say. Phil continued by saying, "It is possible to set up a cacao-processing plant as you desire, but there are a good number of conditions that must be met first. I will not be able to be clear on these conditions and other details until I complete my feasibility study. It will take about two weeks for me to finish the first draft of my study. Then I will need your comments on it before moving to a final version. Mr. Morgan will be in touch with you on this, and I will return to visit with you as needed and indicated by USAID."

Phil was interrupted by another round of applause and the passing of calabashes full of palm wine for those wishing to partake. All of those from the village, except the two chiefs, were not going to miss this free opportunity to drink their fill of palm wine, as well as stuff themselves with food. Phil and Steve were impressed by how much more the people around the table could eat than they could. As Phil watched the members of the technical committee gorge themselves, he continued speaking. "In conclusion, I want to say that the site chosen for the plant is good, but I want to underscore my main concerns. These concerns fall under the following four main headings: electricity, packaging, competition, and land tenure. We have discussed the first three points, but not the last. Please let me say something about land tenure."

Letivi said, "By all means, Mr. Mason, talk to us about land tenure."

Phil said, "I will try to be brief and not too blunt. I'm sorry to say that as long as you don't have deeds for your land and your family cacao fields are widely scattered into small plots hither and thither, you can't move to the higher level of cacao production achieved by modern cacao plantations."

Gregoire's hand immediately flew into the air, and he pleaded to be permitted to speak. Letivi signaled that his interruption of Phil was OK and he could speak. Gregoire spoke loudly. "Why do we need deeds? Nobody has deeds here. Our farming land stays with the families that have cultivated it for generations. Everyone knows who has the rights to cultivate each plot of land. If there is any problem, it is quickly settled in village court."

Phil quickly replied, "I'm very familiar with the traditional land practices you have in your village. I will just say that to achieve economies of scale and the highest level of productivity, all the land should be one large farm. I will also add that to obtain loans from a bank, you need land deeds to provide as collateral. Furthermore, for the operations of your cacao-processing plant, it would be good to persuade one of the banks in the regional capital of Kpolomo to open a branch in your village. Someday, all of you will need bank accounts."

Phil's final words were sobering ones for all those present. Instead of smiles and applause, feelings had again taken a downturn. The degree of residual optimism that had existed at the start of this luncheon was now reduced to the very minimum. Letivi sensed deeply the depressive mood caused by Phil's words and tried to pick up everyone's sprits by conveying the news he had learned from his phone call with the president. Letivi stood and said forthrightly, "Please do not let yourselves be down in the dumps because of all the daunting challenges we face. My recent talk with the president gives us new hope. The president will make a special effort to run a branch line to our village when the approaching new power line to Kpolomo is completed. He will also provide our village and our planned processing plant with electricity at a subsidized rate. In addition, he is supporting the building of a factory in Melomti to manufacture packaging materials. Finally, he says he will restrict the imports of cocoa powder in order to reduce or eliminate competition for our cocoa powder."

The news was met with loud applause. Smiles reappeared on the faces of all in attendance. Letivi asked for quiet to say some final words. "I want to thank again Mr. Mason and Mr. Morgan for taking time out of their busy schedules to meet with us today. Mr. Mason has provided us with very useful information, and we will be discussing all he said for some days to come. We look forward to collaborating with you as we pursue the next steps in the establishment of our cacao-processing plant. We wish both of you a safe return to Melomti."

There was another loud applause, and then the chief escorted the white men to the compound exit, where the welcoming committee was waiting to escort them to their car, which was parked at the bottom of the hill. Again, the wide pathway was packed with villagers singing the praises of the white men and wishing them safe travel. The white men bade farewell to all as they stepped up into their big car, which immediately sped off. As the driver headed toward the junction with the main national highway, Steve turned to Phil and asked, "What do you really think?"

Phil said, "I wish there were another way to raise their incomes, because I don't believe a cacao-processing plant will do that. Even if a cacao plant is set up, it will be more of a politicized showcase project than a profitable entity. In any event, let's go through the motions so we have the details to back up any arguments we wish to put forth."

Steve responded, "Thanks. I thought as much. In the end, it will be our ambassador and how this project relates to our bilateral relations with this country that will determine whether we provide assistance or not. I do know that we are nervous about supporting any project with which the president is involved. I also note that it is against our policies to support projects that benefit from subsidies and trade protection. You know the US government's stand on subsidization and free trade, even though we often don't practice at home what we preach abroad."

CHAPTER SEVENTEEN
ATAKU BOUND

T he loud knocking on their hotel room door could not wake Molly and Robin from their deep slumber. Robin was the first to be stirred by the reverberating racket being made by the taxi driver, who continuously pounded his fist on the simple wooden door. Robin did not want to move a muscle because he wanted to prolong his joy of lying in bed with Molly. Their two naked bodies were intertwined, and Robin wanted their physical contact to endure as long as possible. He wished there was a way to stop the knocking so he could remain immersed in his high state of ecstasy.

Cyprien, the driver, continued his assault of the door, adding in a booming voice, "Wake up! I have your clothes."

Molly had not made the slightest sign that she was aware of any noise emanating from the door. Her eyes were shut tight, but in a soft voice, she spoke first. "Robin, go to the door. It's the taxi driver with our new clothes."

Against his every desire, Robin gently untangled his body from the luscious Molly and searched for a towel to wrap around himself. He was upset about this brash interruption of his lovely interlude with Molly. He felt like going to the door, grabbing the clothes from the driver, and telling him to come back tomorrow. All he wanted was to jump back in bed with Molly. As far as he was concerned, they did not have to go to Ataku today. He needed more time with Molly now. Not later. He was willing to do anything to keep this moment with Molly alive.

Robin wrapped tightly around his stocky frame a white bathroom towel and stomped involuntarily toward the clamor at the door. He unlocked the door and opened it a crack to see if it indeed was their taxi driver. Upon seeing the smiling driver holding two blue plastic bags, he grumpily said, "What is it? Why wake us up so early?"

For some reason, Robin's questions and demeanor made the wide-eyed driver laugh and say, "Good morning, sir. It's Cyprien, your driver. Your lady told me to come early with the clothes so you can try them on. Here are the clothes."

Robin opened the door a bit wider and reached to grab the two plastic bags, saying, "OK. Now, please go wait in your taxi for us."

Robin turned around to find that Molly was already in the bathroom. His heart sank, as he knew this meant their amorous night was over. His heart sank further when he heard the sound of splashing water coming from the bathroom. He knew this meant Molly was not coming back to bed and was preparing for the day. While he waited for Molly to exit the bathroom, he took their newly made clothes from the plastic bags. He was very impressed that such colorful clothes could be made overnight by a local tailor. He laid Molly's clothes on one chair and began trying on his clothes. He put on first the shirt that most appealed to him. He was surprised that it fit very well. He liked the feel of the African print cotton cloth next to his skin.

As he was admiring his first African shirt, Molly stepped out of the bathroom with a white towel wrapped tightly around her body just above her breasts. When she saw Robin in his new shirt, she could not contain herself. She laughed in a high-pitched manner Robin had never heard before and said, "Wow! You look so much different. I like your new look. I can't wait to try my clothes on. Go take your bath while I try on my new clothes."

Robin removed his shirt and headed for the bathroom like a docile little puppy, but, in his heart, he had so many things to say about his love for Molly and the passion they had enjoyed during the night. He wanted to give her a kiss as he passed by her on his way to the bathroom, but he discerned that her changed mood would make such a move on his part untimely. He did feel compelled to say something after such a lovely night and nervously looked into Molly's eyes and simply said, "Thank you for such a good night."

Molly returned his words with a smile that might be interpreted as a grimace. Robin sensed that she preferred at this minute for him not to mention anything about what had happened between them last night. He knew it was best not say anything about it until she did. He told himself to keep his cool and wait for Molly to speak first about the sweet bonding that had occurred between them.

Robin quickly did his usual morning bathroom routine and stepped outside to fetch his underwear and clothes but was stopped in his tracks by a beautiful sight. There was Molly showing off like a model in her new African print clothes. It was as if Robin were seeing a whole different person in front of him. The colorful clothes made her more attractive than ever. Her matching blouse and long, tight skirt looked as if they had been made just for her. She had a big smile on her face when she looked at Robin and said, "I love these clothes. They are a perfect fit. They will take some time to get used to, but I feel very comfortable in them."

Robin shared in her excitement and responded, "You do look good. You almost look like you were born to wear such clothes. I'm sure that you will turn many an eye."

Robin grabbed one set of his clothes and underwear and retreated into the bathroom to make a quick change. He donned his new African duds and made a big deal of his new look as he exited the bathroom and swaggered around the room. He made Molly laugh. Their erotic joining during the night, their new clothes, and Molly's laughter had elevated their relationship to a new level where nothing was the same, including themselves. Kansas now seemed like a distant and very different planet. They were beginning to become caught in a web of adventure they could not have possibly anticipated.

Molly broke this fun-filled moment by saying, "Mr. Fletcher, let's stop our nonsense and get serious. We need to make our plans for the day. Let's have our breakfast and discuss what we have to do to make it to Ataku today."

Robin immediately picked up the phone and asked the front desk to deliver their breakfast to their room. He turned to Molly and with a chuckle said, "Well, Miss Molly, how do you see our day going?"

Molly told Robin, "Sit down so we can talk about what we need to do." She then listed all the things they must do before leaving Melomti and going to Ataku.

"Robin, we need to check out of the hotel and pay our bill. We need to decide how many traveler's checks to change at a bank before leaving town. We have to pay the rest of the money for our new clothes. We have to buy socks, underwear, and flip-flops. Maybe we need to advance money to our taxi driver."

Robin was busy noting in his spiral notebook all that Molly was saying. When Molly paused, he asked her, "Is that all? Are you sure you haven't missed something?"

"There is one more thing. We need to buy a camera. I foolishly packed my Kodak and all the film I had purchased in my suitcase. We cannot go to Ataku and not take any photographs. We must buy a camera and some rolls of film."

Robin made a quick note and dryly asked again, "Is that all?"

Pensively, Molly said, "Yes, I think that is it."

"Well, when we eat our breakfast, there is one thing that we should never forget. What I mean to say is that we need to take our daily dose of antimalarial pills. We also need to take bottled water with us. No telling what kind of food and water are waiting for us in Ataku."

They were both thinking of all they needed to do to prepare for their trip to Ataku, the village where David Peterson had served many years ago as a Peace Corp volunteer. The thought of finding the truth about David kept driving them forward, making them willing to make sacrifices. Their thoughts were rudely interrupted by a loud rap on the door.

They knew that this rap could only mean that their breakfast had been delivered. Robin hustled to unlatch the door. Following the usual exchanges of morning greetings, the smiling waiter gently set down their breakfast tray and wished them a hearty appetite. Robin asked Molly for a few gadis to tip the waiter. The dapper waiter left no doubt about his happy reaction to receiving an unexpected tip.

They devoured their breakfast and gulped their malaria pills. Then they began quickly arranging to depart from the hotel.

They stuffed their old clothes into the empty plastic bags used for delivering their new clothes. Molly remarked, "I'm not even sure we should keep these old clothes. I want to get more African clothes made and only wear them. It will really be neat when I return to Kansas dressed in such authentic clothing."

Robin nodded his agreement but expressed his concerns on this subject. "Yes, the clothes are nice, but Kansans would find it weird to see white people dressed in such outfits. They may think that I forgot to take off my pajamas."

Molly checked her purse to make sure its contents were safe. They looked carefully around their room to make sure they had not forgotten anything. They were in a hurry, but at the same time, there was a growing tightness in their stomachs because they knew that today, they would be on a real adventure and possibly unravel the mystery surrounding David Peterson. Robin wanted to hug Molly one more time before they left the privacy of their room, but before he could act on that wish, Molly was unlatching the door and beckoning Robin to follow her, saying, "Mr. Fletcher, I presume it is time for us to hit the road."

They quickly settled their bill at the front desk, saying they would return, but they did not know when. Molly took the final hotel invoice and stuck it in a large yellow envelope she was keeping for all the bills they incurred on the trip. They bid their farewells to the hotel staff and headed for the front door exit and their waiting taxi. Cyprien, all smiles as usual, was there holding open the rear door of the car for them. They slid onto the backseat, and Cyprien took his place in the front seat behind the wheel. Cyprien turned his head to face them, exposing his very white and large teeth with a big gap between his two front teeth, saying, "Good morning again. Cyprien at your service. Where do we go?"

Molly tried to keep her instructions to Cyprien as simple as possible. "We need to go to a bank. We need to pay the balance owed the tailor for our clothes. We need to buy a camera, underwear, and socks. Most of all, we need to arrive in Ataku today."

Cyprien was happy to hear that he would be earning money for a whole day. Visions of paying off his overdue debts and buying all the things he and his family needed danced in his head. He started his old car and gunned the engine twice before saying, "Yes, ma'am. We go to bank now."

They arrived in front of an old bank building that was obviously part of the country's colonial legacy. Cyprien found a space along the road to park his car and insisted on accompanying Molly and Robin into the bank. They struggled to enter the bank. The entire reception area was tightly packed, and people were jostling with one another as they tried to approach the four teller's windows. A watchman at the door gave them a metal token with a number engraved on it and told them their number would be called. They waited in the jammed and sweltering reception area for over forty-five minutes, but they were no closer to a teller than they had been when they began. People were pushing and shoving, but they stopped short of doing the same to Molly and Robin after seeing their whiteness. They were concerned because people who entered after them were much closer to the tellers than they were. They could hear those entering saying things like: "My brother, or, my sister." Then the people uttering these words moved ahead to join whomever they were referring to.

A frustrated and perspiring Molly finally asked Cyprien, "What can we do to get through this unruly crowd?"

Cyprien could sense that his precious cargo was becoming irritated. He saw this irritation as a threat to his current goal in life, which was to keep his clients happy so they would keep him as their driver. He calmly told Molly, "Ma'am, please be patient. I am looking for someone I know so that we can advance. I am sure we will be at the teller window very soon."

Molly and Robin looked at each other in disbelief, as neither could understand how they could bust through the very animated crowd to do their business with a teller. They were thinking that maybe they should try another bank. Just when they were about to give up hope of moving forward, Cyprien said, "Follow me."

Cyprien aggressively forced his way through the crowd until they were very near one teller window. He asked Molly to give him the token and raised it high over his head, waving his arm while he said, "My sister, I have a token and white patrons who need your help. Please serve us."

Molly and Robin were perplexed by Cyprien's behavior. They could not understand why the bank did not place more priority on customer service and organizing the people into obedient lines. They were surprised when the crowd allowed them to approach the teller's window after Cyprien spouted out his words. It was apparent to them that once people knew you had a family member working a window, you would automatically be given preference. It was easy for Molly and Robin to see that they were lucky that Cyprien had a family relation working at the bank.

After Cyprien and the young woman working behind the teller bars exchanged some lengthy greetings in the local language, Cyprien asked Molly, "How much in travelers' checks do you want to change?"

Molly quietly whispered, "One thousand dollars."

Cyprien said, "My niece says there is a ten percent fee, so you will only receive the equivalent of nine hundred dollars. Please sign in front of her the checks you wish to exchange and show her your passport."

Molly took one booklet of her American Express traveler's checks out of her purse. Each booklet contained ten checks of one hundred dollars each. She carefully signed each check on the counter and then slid the checks and her passport through the small opening in the bars. All this time, a nervous Robin was on the lookout. He was very concerned there were robbers and purse snatchers in the motley crowd. He feared they would be robbed as soon as they stepped outside the bank. It was clear to him that everyone already knew they were carrying a large sum of money. He felt very vulnerable.

The teller shoved the big stack of local money and a receipt through the window opening to Molly. The gadi was trading at the bank at eight hundred to one US dollar, so the stack of gadis Molly received was almost too big to fit into her purse. The gadis also had a moldy smell and were faded and ragged. On each bill was either an imprint of the current Kotoku president or his father, the past president. It looked as if the bills would fall apart if handled roughly. The rumor was that the president had hired an unknown firm in Eastern Europe to print the country's money, and they did a cheap job on purpose so the president could get a fat kickback.

Molly was extremely careful when putting the money into her purse because she was afraid that some bills would break into pieces. Both she and Robin were amazed that a living president's image could figure so prominently on the newer bills. Robin feared that her bulging purse would attract even more attention. He told Molly to put her purse strap over her head and hold on to it tightly. Cyprien overheard what Robin said and told them, "You do not need to fear anything as long as you stay close to me, so that people can see that you have hired me. People here usually do not want to mess with the livelihood of one of their own."

People behind Molly and Robin began to complain about how much time they were taking at the teller's window. Cyprien said his good-bye greetings to his "niece," and they threaded their way through an even larger and more tightly packed crowd to the exit. Once they were outside the bank, they found even more people than before milling about. Cyprien escorted them to his car. He paid a small sum to a young man who had been watching his car and jumped in behind the wheel, saying, "Good thing we came to the bank early in the morning because it becomes more crowded as the day goes on. You know you can change money in the street and get twice the bank rate, but that is illegal, even though everyone does it. Also, I know an old American man who changes money at any time in his house at a very low commission rate. That is illegal too, but he has hundreds of clients."

One thing Cyprien did not tell them was that the bank rate for changing traveler's checks was less than 10 percent. It was 5 percent. He had made a deal with the teller to split the difference. Cyprien was looking forward to making money coming and going by helping his precious cargo achieve their objectives. For him, no harm was being done. His hustling was not like stealing, and it was an acceptable practice in his country to engage in the reasonable ripping off of wealthy foreigners. This was considered a "right" of poor people who survived on a miniscule percentage of what the foreigners possessed. This was a happy solution. He got his fair share, and the foreigners never complained because they believed they were getting a good deal.

Molly commented, "Cyprien, thanks for all your help. It was really lucky that you had a niece working as a teller. We could have never been able to change money without you. But, tell me, was that woman really your niece?"

Cyprien was delighted because happy white customers always gave a big tip. He knew now that these two customers would make him a relatively well-off man. He replied, "Well, she is my older brother's wife's niece on her husband's side. I have only seen her once or twice before. But that was enough. Where do we go next?"

Molly quickly replied, "Let's go to where I can buy a camera and film."

With a chuckle and visions of making more money, Cyprien wasted no time in saying, "No problem, ma'am. I know a camera shop located just a few blocks from here."

The main problem was that the riotous, over congested inner-city traffic had built up. This made it difficult for Cyprien to get on the road and on their way. A short drive of a few blocks took twenty minutes, and then there was no place to park. Cyprien looked about until he spied a group of four or five young men and motioned to them that he wanted to park. These men signaled their OK and began to lift from one parking spot an old car body that evidently was empty of its engine and other mechanical parts. They moved the hollow car body out of the way and motioned to Cyprien to park in the nice, shady spot previously occupied by the hollow car. He knew this would cost a little bit extra, but he would pass all costs, and then some, on to his highly valued passengers.

Molly and Robin were amazed by what they had just observed, but they were happy to have such a nice parking space just across the narrow street from the camera shop, which was unmistakable with its big yellow Kodak sign. They found that the sign was almost bigger than the shop, which was very small but chock full of cameras in every shape and condition. Molly knew exactly what kind of camera she wanted. She was determined to buy the same camera she had foolishly put in her lost luggage. She said to the short, balding man behind the old glass showcase counter, "I want a Kodak 2000 with twenty rolls of four-hundred speed, thirty-five-millimeter color film with forty photos in each roll."

The shop owner tried to hide his pleasure at receiving such an exceptionally big order from clients who would pay cash. He immediately began placing on the glass counter all the Kodak cameras he had like the model Molly had requested. After he had finished displaying about a dozen cameras on the counter, he said, "This is what I have in the model you are looking for. Some are used, some are almost new, and two are new and, as you see, still in their original packaging. Of course, the prices vary widely."

Molly and Robin did not know that most of these cameras had been stolen, either from tourists or from shipments arriving at the seaport or airport by unscrupulous agents. The parallel and informal markets were larger than the formal sector market. They also could not know that among the cameras was the very one that Molly had lost in her suitcase. The entire city was bursting with petty commercial activity that in many instances involved goods obtained illegally. It seemed that everyone had a scheme with a connection who was able to obtain merchandise at a cut rate through clandestine channels. All the small merchants were dead set against paying any taxes or customs fees and working hard to stay far away from any government controls.

Petty traders and small businesses depended on an elaborate scheme of payoffs and kickbacks. Every service had two prices: the official one and the informal one. Nothing would be done if the latter was not paid. In other parts of the world, these deeply ingrained practices would be referred to as corruption. Here it was business as usual. Everyone was out to increase his or her profit margin, and that margin had to be very large. It was not unusual to find business people who regularly achieved a 100 percent profit margin. Such business people were highly regarded and considered local role models to be emulated.

Any efforts to reform such long-standing commercial practices would result in much suffering and popular revolt. The cost of threatening vested interests and meddling with widespread business practices would be so economically devastating as to be unthinkable. The entire survival system depended on maintaining the corrupt status quo. This was a can of worms that should not be tampered with unless one wanted the social order to fall apart and violent upheaval to ensue. For sure, nothing should be done that would raise the cost of living for the poor masses. Keeping prices low for major food staples and essential goods was critical to maintaining political stability. Nothing would bring thousands of protesters into the streets faster that a hike in the cost of living. Political survival in Kotoku depended heavily on preserving the purchasing power of the poor masses.

The elite class was acutely aware of the need to keep the masses sufficiently content. This class was composed of top government officials, a few rich entrepreneurs, and a well-entrenched group of wealthy foreign businessmen. As these people enriched themselves, they made sure they did not step too hard on the toes of the large class of petty traders and small and medium-sized entrepreneurs. Quite the contrary, they were the main suppliers of this lower but powerful class, and much of their wealth depended on keeping the businesses of this class thriving. They saw the moneymaking trough as a huge, multilayered one where everyone had his or her place and an opportunity to make a buck or a few cents.

While Molly and Robin were looking over the cameras displayed on the glass counter, Cyprien was huddled just outside with the shop owner. He wanted to make sure Molly got the best camera and he got his rightful cut for bringing a lucrative customer to the shop. He learned from the owner that one of the used cameras was the best, as it had been recently lifted from a European tourist. He was informed that the so-called new cameras in their original boxes were actually fakes expertly assembled by specialized con artists in a neighboring country. When they entered the tiny shop, he quickly indicated to Cyprien the best camera. They had already decided the higher "white" price for this camera and what percentage of a kickback Cyprien would receive.

Molly was all set to buy one of the new cameras when Cyprien intervened by saying, "I have just had a heart-to-heart talk with the owner, and he admitted to me that the new cameras are counterfeit, and all the other cameras except one did not work correctly."

Cyprien picked up the one good camera and told Molly that he was asking the equivalent of two hundred US dollars for it. Molly incredulously said, "That is too expensive. It is used, and I can buy a new camera for that price in the States."

Molly's remarks told Cyprien that he had a selling job on his hands if he was to protect his own interests in this deal. He said to Molly, "Yes, you are right, but these cameras are made in the States, and it is difficult and expensive to import them into our country. I will speak to the owner to see if he can reduce his price."

Cyprien talked briefly to the owner and turned to Molly to say, "He says his last price is one hundred eighty US dollars, and he will give you at no cost two rolls of film." Molly and Robin had no way of knowing what was really going on behind the scenes. They did not know that the camera recommended by Cyprien had been stolen and the owner possessed a huge inventory of genuine film that an airport baggage handler had consigned to him. Molly and Robin were in that class of much-welcomed customers that the local business community referred to as "easy pickings."

Molly asked Robin for his advice. He said, "Looks like we have no choice, and we are in a hurry to get to Ataku before sundown. Pay the man, and let's go."

As Molly began to dig out of her purse the sum she needed to pay the owner in gadis, the owner sheepishly suggested, "Please, ma'am. Pay me in dollars. If you do that, I can sell you the camera and all the film you want for two hundred US dollars."

Molly asked Cyprien for his advice. Of course, he said it was a good deal. Molly then asked the owner if traveler's checks were OK. He nodded his head. Molly tore out two one-hundred-dollar checks, signed them, and handed them to the smiling owner as she said, "It's a deal, but I want to see the film and test the camera with film in it."

The owner grabbed from a box sitting in the corner of his shop twenty rolls of film and placed them on the counter in front of Molly. She took one roll and loaded it into the camera. She then asked Cyprien, the owner, and Robin to step outside to the front of the shop so she could take their photo. She snapped a photo of this unlikely trio. The camera seemed to operate correctly. Molly smiled and said excitedly to Robin, "Our first photo in Kotoku, and you are in it. I hope we will always treasure this photo and the many others to come."

The happy shop owner offered for free to Molly a locally sewn, cloth shoulder bag to carry her camera and film. For all concerned, it was a win-win bargain, particularly for the owner, who would negotiate the travelers' checks in the parallel market for twice the rate that Molly had been given in the bank.

Cyprien waved to the young men across the street to indicate to them that they were returning to his car. The road was jammed with all kinds of two-wheeled vehicles, push carts, and pedestrians, including throngs of women carrying all sorts of things on their heads. The parking boys had to stop traffic and clear a path so they could cross the street. This was all part of the service they offered for using the parking spot they managed. Cyprien paid them handsomely for this service. Once they were seated in the car and ready to depart, the parking men stopped traffic again to allow them to back onto the road. As soon as they departed, they could see the parking men lifting the shell of the old car into its original space in order to preserve the space for their next customer.

The road was so clogged with traffic that they could only inch ahead. Molly and Robin were totally fixated on the fascinating movement of people and vehicles surrounding them. They had never seen such an unimaginable sight before. The slowness of their movement was so frustrating for Cyprien that he could not resist saying, "There are just too many motorbikes now. There were not that many motorbikes before. The population is growing quickly, but the roads stay the same. Soon, it will be impossible to drive into the center of town."

The car was tightly surrounded by motorbikes driven by people who did not seem to care how their actions might harm others or themselves. Cyprien said, "You see all these Yamaha motorbikes? They are fake. In the bush in a neighboring country, they are assembled using Chinese parts and made to look like genuine Yamahas, but they are not. The Japanese government has brought suit against our government in international court because nothing is being done to stop the import of these counterfeit motorbikes. Yet more and more of these motorbikes are entering the country every year. The demand for them is very strong. If it were not for these fake motorbikes, there would be less traffic congestion."

They crept slowly ahead as Cyprien did his best to guide his car through impossible traffic without hitting another car or person or being hit by another vehicle. They had already observed several bloody accidents. Navigating the rumble of unruly traffic was scary to Molly and Robin. They did not think they or anyone else they knew in the States could drive here. It was certainly very different from Kansas's wide, well-paved, and clean streets, which were often empty of traffic. They also noted that they had yet to see a stoplight that worked. At a few intersections, uniformed policemen tried to direct traffic, but their efforts appeared to be futile.

A reflective Cyprien said, "It is best we get away from the center of town to buy the other things you want. It would be very hard at this hour for me to drive across town to the tailor's workshop, but that is OK. You can give me the money you owe him when we return to Melomti, and I will pay him. We really need to get on the road to Ataku if you want to arrive there before dark."

Molly and Robin looked at each other, and Robin said to Cyprien, "You are right. Let's buy the other things we need at a roadside market stand near the edge of town on the way to Ataku."

It took an hour to escape traffic jams and reach the edge of town. Cyprien stopped at the first suite of outdoor market stalls he saw that he thought would have the items Molly and Robin sought. Before they got out of the car, Cyprien told them, "When you see something you want to buy, tell me, and I will buy it like it is for myself. In that way, I will get the much lower African price."

Molly and Robin both said in unison, "OK, Cyprien."

They began looking at all the items displayed in tiered rows, hanging on wooden slats that were lashed or nailed to posts made from small trees. Some items were in clear plastic to protect them from dust kicked up by passing vehicles. All the stalls were mostly tended by young girls. Sometimes their mothers or aunts could be seen sitting in the background watching carefully, ready to swing into action if the young girl attendants made any wrong moves. Small children and animals were running around everywhere. There was a festive air about this small market that reminded Molly and Robin of when the carnival came to town in Kansas.

Everything they needed was lined up in various sections. It was hard to tell which size was theirs, but there were socks, underwear, panties, bras, flip-flops, and handkerchiefs. Cyprien followed them, and, when he saw them look at something, he unhooked the item and carried it in his arms. Molly and Robin could see that all the items were of a quality inferior to what they were used to, but they had no choice but to take what was available. They noted that many of the items had been manufactured in China or Thailand.

Cyprien took all the items and placed them on a nearby rickety old wood table. Various market women gathered around the table, and Cyprien began haggling with them over the price of each item. Sometimes they laughed. Other times they appeared to be having heated disagreements. After about fifteen minutes, Cyprien joined Molly and Robin and said, "For the whole lot, they want fifty thousand gadis."

Molly exploded, "No way! That is over one hundred dollars. I'm not paying that much for such cheap stuff. Come on, Robin, let's go somewhere else."

As Molly and Robin headed for the car, one of the more senior market women quickly approached Cyprien, and they had a bitter but quick exchange. Cyprien called out to Molly and Robin, "Wait. They have now dropped their price to forty thousand gadis. Also, don't forget that the dollar value of gadis is much less on the parallel market."

Molly turned and started walking toward Cyprien. "OK. It's a deal."

She turned her back so that nobody could see her fishing in her purse to remove the exact amount of money for this purchase. While she was doing this, the women were carefully placing the items in flimsy black plastic bags. Molly handed the money to Cyprien, who in turn handed it to the head market woman. Of course, before giving them the money, he took a five-thousand-gadi finder's fee for himself. He was lamenting that Molly had refused the first price offered because he stood to gain ten thousand gadi if that higher, initial price had been accepted.

They got back into the car with their things, waving good-bye to the happy market women. As there were no other customers around, Molly and Robin thought they might be the only customers they would see that day. It was difficult to imagine how these women and their families could survive on what little they earned, if anything, each day. There were dozens of market stalls, and all the women were selling the same things. In view of all the competition, they wondered how any single market woman could make any money.

Molly and Robin were finding Cyprien to be quite a talker and the source of much knowledge about his country and fellow countrymen. This time he said, "It is good that you see how most poor people buy their clothes. Poor people have their clothes made or buy cheap clothing items from the stalls you just saw. Many poor people buy much of their clothing from the bundles of used clothes imported from America. But please remember that the rich people do not buy their clothes in such places. There are a few exclusive shops in Melomti that cater to the clothing needs of the rich. These shops carry the latest styles from America and Europe. But many rich buy most of their clothes when they travel abroad."

What Cyprien was saying was of interest to Molly and Robin, but their thoughts were now focused on what lay ahead on the road to Ataku. They knew that Ataku was about one hundred miles away. They were becoming elated that today they would see the village David Peterson had worked in as a Peace Corps Volunteer. They welcomed leaving the bustling city of Melomti and heading into unknown frontiers of rural Africa. They could not wait to arrive in Ataku and discover the truth about David. Little did they know that the truth was much different from the reality David had experienced many years ago in Ataku.

CHAPTER EIGHTEEN
WIFE MAKING IN CHANGING TIMES

Delalia's big day was fast approaching. Soon she would publicly be recognized as the chief's official wife. She had been staying with Chief Letivi for some weeks, and he neither complained nor chased her away. It was time to confirm his union with Delalia as an accepted marriage. Village leaders needed to proclaim them a couple to the people, ancestors, and gods. Letivi had some misgivings, but he did not want to lose the helpful company of Delalia. He needed to solidify the worthiness of his chieftaincy by being married and fathering children.

The responsibility for preparing Letivi for the traditional wedding ceremonies fell to his maternal grandfather and mentor, Chief Gyasi. In the days leading up to the joyous ceremonies that would make Delalia Letivi's wife in the eyes of the people, Gyasi met with Letivi daily to discuss all the events that would occur on the wedding day. Gyasi wanted to make sure Letivi understood well all that would occur so he would not be caught off guard or do anything unbecoming as a chief. Letivi listened intently to all that Gyasi had to tell him, but he raised many questions.

Letivi told Gyasi, "I like Delalia very much and I want to keep her close to me, but I am not sure marrying me is the best thing for her."

Gyasi smiled and replied, "Son, this young and attractive woman wants you to be her husband, and so does her family and the entire village. You should not be talking like this at this point."

"But she is so young, and she needs more schooling," interjected Letivi.

Gyasi laughed before saying, "Most married women in the village were younger than she is when they got married. She is old enough. That's all that counts. Age is just a number, and most of us do not have a true birth certificate to confirm accurately that number."

Letivi still possessed doubts about marrying a teenage girl. He told Gyasi, "I feel uncomfortable because when I was in school in Melomti, I joined a campaign that spoke out against early marriage and premature pregnancies. I worked with a group to have the government pass a law fixing the legal marrying age for a woman at eighteen."

"That is very well and good, my son. If you want, I will arrange to obtain a birth certificate for her that states she is eighteen. You can get a new birth certificate too. How old do you want to be?"

In spite of himself, Letivi laughed and said, "Grandfather, you are making light of a serious matter that needs to be addressed well if our country is to advance."

"All this is not worth discussing because you are getting married to Delalia tomorrow, and I have news for you: you have already made her pregnant."

Letivi was not ready to hear about Delalia being pregnant and quickly asked Gyasi, "How do you know that? How can that be?"

"Well, her mother told me, and she has been sleeping with you every night for weeks. I assume that you do know how babies are made."

Letivi was now getting excited as he thought of all the things he would do as a father. He told Gyasi, "OK. I accept this as good news, and I look forward to being a model father. I will accompany Delalia in every step of her pregnancy, making sure she gets the best care and the baby is delivered in a decent clinic."

"I understand you, my son, and all you say is good, but what you propose is different from what we do in our culture. Pregnancies, having and caring for babies, are women's business. It is best that the man keep his distance and not interfere with the role of women. It would be embarrassing for Delalia and the village if you do as you propose."

Letivi changed the subject. His thoughts drifted toward his mother and her tragic plight. He wished his mom could come to his wedding ceremony and know about his unborn baby. He told Gyasi, "Before the wedding, I must go and check on my mother and inform her of my wedding and Delalia's pregnancy."

"I understand, my son, but I warn you that the sight you will see will sicken your heart. My wife, Evelyne, has been going almost daily to see our daughter, your mother, and she reports that your mom and her world could vanish at any time."

Upon hearing these words, Letivi impatiently told Gyasi, "In spite of everything else, I must leave immediately and stay the night with my mother. I do not want to miss seeing her on this Earth one last time."

Gyasi wanted to tell Letivi to wait until after his wedding, but he knew that once Letivi had made up his mind, there was no stopping him. All he could do was say, "You have my blessing, my son. However, my wife, Evelyne, told me that your mother said you should not come to see her until she summons you."

Letivi became agitated, and drops of perspiration rolled down his childlike face as he began to think of all the serious changes occurring in his world. He could not restrain himself and vented his fears and frustrations on Gyasi. "What is happening? My mother's world is dissolving into nothingness, and the old baobab is dying. How can such important parts of our life that have existed for hundreds of years leave us so quickly? Why does all this have to happen now, when our village is on the threshold of achieving lasting progress? It's not fair!"

Gyasi shared deeply Letivi's bitter anguish, but he tried not to show it. He tried to soothe Letivi by saying softly, "You are right to feel as you do, but there is nothing we can do. The world as we know it is evolving into a different world, and we have to work to adapt to it, whether we like it or not. Nothing is forever, and everything has its time. Don't fret so much. Life will go on, and we will go on with it until our time has ended."

Gyasi's words calmed Letivi a bit, but nobody could really appreciate how profoundly unhappy he was with the changes in his world. As he had been born and raised for the first five years of his life in his mom's domain, he was doubly grieved at the loss of his mom and her enchanted domain. Losing the old baobab at the same time pushed him to the breaking point. He knew the demise of the old baobab meant he would never see his father again in any form. He feared that the loss of these two key components in his world could lead to his total collapse.

Gyasi commented, "My son, I really see only one major problem that we need to worry about. The water table is dropping rapidly, and it appears the mountain is drying up. If this continues, we will soon have a serious problem with sourcing enough water for our essential needs."

Letivi moaned out loud, "Please, Grandfather, I do not need any more bad news now. I feel I am on the verge of a nervous breakdown. It is as if my whole world is collapsing around me."

Adding to Letivi's stress was the secret about the golden stool buried under the old baobab. Letivi was beginning to think this was a good time to tell Gyasi about the stool, but at the last minute, he reversed his thinking, deciding that this potential curse should stay with him. He was haunted day and night by the heavy burden of his secret knowledge of the existence of the golden stool. The thought of this stool and what to do with it was clouding his mind. He believed he was already cursed for all eternity by the damned stool. For the first time, he thought the option of going to the Vatican could have been better than becoming chief at the exceptionally young age of eighteen.

Letivi was very depressed. Looking closely at his aging grandfather added to the growing burdens of being a chief during a time when big chunks of his world were falling apart. At this moment, he saw clearly that advanced age was catching up to Gyasi. He did not know why, but he had not paid much attention to Gyasi's age. For the first time, he could see that the elderly man sitting next to him was growing old fast.

Gyasi's eyes seemed to be retreating more deeply into his head, and his cheekbones appeared more prominent as his face shrank, creating rows of wrinkles. He seemed shorter, he was slightly stooped, and his gait was more hesitant than before. Suddenly, it dawned on Letivi that he may lose Gyasi too. The thought of losing Gyasi made him quiver inside and out. His very core shuddered at the thought of losing Gyasi. He did not think he could survive such a great loss, particularly as it would come on top of other important losses in his life.

Letivi looked at Gyasi with much more love and sympathy for him in his heart. He said calmly, "Grandfather. You are right. I will wait until my mother calls me before going to see her. I agree that I must now focus on my wedding."

Gyasi smiled widely, showing big teeth that had been tarnished brown by years of partaking of tobacco snuff. Energized, he said, "Good decision, my son. By the way, did you remember to charge your mobile phone? I expect that the president will call us soon about our cacao-processing project."

"Yes, Grandfather. The phone is charged, and I keep it in a special-made cloth pouch that you see hanging from a soft cord around my neck. I always keep my phone with me, and Delalia is very good at reminding me to keep it charged and with me."

Gyasi was prepared to say a few more words about the wedding and bid farewell to his grandson for the day, but a foreign and dreaded noise rudely interrupted their conversation. It was the bugbear cell phone making a noise like a sick frog. The last thing Letivi wanted right now was to answer the phone and talk to the megalomaniac president, but he had no choice. He reached into his phone pouch as he found the courage to answer the phone.

Letivi pushed the answer button on the phone and said as firmly as he could, "Mr. President, Letivi at your service."

The president spoke forcefully as soon as the phone connection was established. As was his habit, he dismissed any sort of customary greeting and dove directly into the heart of what he had called to say. "Listen well. I have arranged everything, and USAID will support our cacao-processing project. USAID should soon begin working on plans to establish the plant. Be ready to cooperate. We'll talk more later."

Without Letivi having said a word, the connection was cut. He held the phone to his ear for another minute to make sure his one-way conversation with the president was over. With a grimace on his face, he told his grandfather, "Of course, it was the president. What he said is good news, but my gut tells me we are in for trouble. He says USAID approved our cacao-processing project and will start soon working on implementation plans."

Gyasi slammed his right fist into his left hand and excitedly said, "My son, that is good news. How could you feel any other way?"

With some hesitation and mixed feelings, a worried Letivi replied, "Grandfather, I'm sorry, but I do not like being at the beck and call of our unpredictable and corrupt president. I feel enslaved to the mobile phone he gave me, and I know the only reason he is helping us with the cacao-processing plant is to make money for himself. Quite frankly, I do not see such a plant as being financially viable, and I doubt that it will help reduce poverty in our village. The president is only using us and the plant to make money and glorify his own image."

"I hear what you are saying, my son, but you could be wrong. In any event, at this stage we have no choice but to go along with this unprecedented attempt to process our cacao beans instead of sending them to Europe. Even if we fail to increase our incomes as desired, it is worth a try. Please try to raise your spirits. The entire village is counting on your unfailing and enthusiastic leadership in this and many other endeavors. You will need to inform the village, but that can wait until after your wedding."

Letivi thanked his grandfather for his words and encouragement. He asked, "Grandfather, do you have anything else to tell me about what will take place at my wedding the day after tomorrow?"

Gyasi was becoming tired of talking and told Letivi, "If I say anything more about your wedding day, I will only repeat myself. Don't worry about anything. You need to be relaxed and happy on your wedding day. I will be there next to you every step of the way on the day and night of your wedding. Please try to enjoy yourself and put on a happy face for all our brothers and sisters. Now, get some rest."

In spite of his depressed mood, Letivi forced his small mouth into a crooked little smile. He knew instinctively this would be a good night to sleep in front of the grandfathers' house and see if they had anything to signal to him. He told Gyasi of his intention to seek any counsel the grandfathers might want to provide him. Gyasi clapped his hands and said, "Amen."

The starlit night was a peaceful one. Letivi lay alone on a thick grass mat on his back looking at the endless, clear, star-filled sky as he watched whiffs of thin clouds float slowly over-head. He was on the lookout for any signs the grandfathers might make. He found the awesome view offered by the heav-ens to be therapeutic and soothing to his tormented soul. A wave of tranquility passed over him. He began to feel comfort-able again with his place in life, in spite of all the turmoil he was experiencing. He felt uplifted and inspired to redouble his efforts to tackle to the best of his ability any obstacle strewn in his path.

When the sun's first rays peeked over the mountain, Letivi awoke, feeling renewed and wiser. He stood up ready to take on all adversaries, known and unknown, and to overcome his fears and worries so he could be the chief his people needed to achieve progress and escape from the poverty trap in which they were mired. There had been a total reversal in his outlook. He felt invigorated and able to succeed at anything he wished to do.

He surprised himself by seeing that what had been impossible yesterday was possible today.

Letivi was perplexed by this seismic turnaround in his mood and perspective on all the challenges he was facing. He felt content and did not know why he was feeling so very happy. Then he remembered his vivid dream. That night, a beautiful white angel from his father's tribe had visited him. He recalled her tender caresses, her long red hair, and her captivating smile. Most of all, he recalled her words, "Letivi, do not worry. Better days are ahead. All will be well, and you will be eternally rewarded. Your father is watching over you, and some of his people are coming to see you."

The thought of these words and his enchanting encounter with a surreal angel boosted his strength and happiness levels. He was very excited about the prospect that some people from his father's country would be coming. This was really something he looked forward to. He told himself he needed to be in top form when he met these important visitors. He put all his cares aside and whistled a little ditty about fried or boiled yams that his mom had sung to him in his childhood. All of sudden, he looked eagerly forward to having his bond with Delalia publicly recognized.

Custom called for Delalia to stop sleeping with Letivi some days before the wedding. During that time, Delalia would be confined to her parents' compound and instructed by older women on how to serve her husband and be a good wife. She would also be washed and cleaned several times a day. Every part of her body, including every orifice, would be scrubbed with a special herbal soap. Every hair under her arms and pubic area would be plucked. It would take several days to braid her hair into a complicated weave reserved only for brides. Her fingernails and toenails would be carefully cut and burned along with any of her body hair.

Early on the day of the wedding, a specialist would apply to her face, eyebrows, and eyelashes heavy dark makeup. Prior to her wedding night, her vagina would be swabbed with an herbal liquid that would constrict the vaginal muscles, making it tighter. Many prayers and secret ceremonies would be uttered by elderly women who were tasked with safeguarding such occult traditions. As she was to become a chief's wife, extraordinary and lengthy ceremonies were an integral part of the obligatory marriage process.

Delalia slept little during these pre-wedding days. She was fed sumptuous meals almost every hour. There was a strong belief that a married woman must be corpulent to be pleasing to her husband, and Delalia was far from having any body fat. She was obliged to eat many plates of starchy food and drink lots of milk. The women believed that men preferred big women, and they feared that Delalia, with her slim, boyish figure, would fail at wife making and keeping her husband satisfied.

Several dressmakers brought their treadle sewing machines to Delalia's compound to work nonstop on the clothes she would need on her wedding day, ensuring all her clothes fit perfectly. There were clothes for meeting her husband, clothes for receiving gifts from her husband, clothes for partying, and clothes for sleeping with her husband. There was also a special cape to cover Delalia's head for when she was playfully kidnapped by her brothers and taken to her husband-to-be's compound as a "prisoner" to be wed. In this way, all could pretend they did not know who was to be the chief's new bride.

On the day before the wedding, Letivi was also given a similar special treatment. The same men who had accompanied him during his initiation to become a chief approached him with hair-cutting and nail specialists. Letivi wrapped a white cloth made from hand-spun cotton around his waist. He sat with his legs crossed on a colorful old cloth laid on the ground in the grandfathers' compound under the shade of the old neem tree. His head and face were closely shaved, and every hair on his body was shaved or plucked. His fingernails and toenails were carefully trimmed. Everything cut off his body was carefully burned so as to avoid any wicked use of his body parts by evil fetish priests.

His entire body was scrubbed with akudja pod sponges that had been dipped in a clay jug of herbal water that had been blessed by all the top fetish priests. His body was rinsed by clean water that had been collected from a mountaintop spring. When his body had dried naturally in the gentle breeze flowing down the mountain slope, it was wiped softly with cotton pads that had been soaked in perfumed lotion made from the nuts harvested from the oldest shea butter trees. His body was rubbed and patted vigorously. Letivi's golden-brown body glistened in the sunlight, and all those in attendance nodded and grunted their approval. He was told to go to his room and stay there without talking to anyone until he was called early the next morning to begin his joyous wedding day.

Letivi did as instructed. He found that food and water had been placed on a tray on the floor just inside the door of his room. For the first time in his life, Letivi felt isolated and alone. He used this solitary condition to reflect in depth on his life, the challenges he faced, and what he wanted to achieve over the next five to ten years as chief. He told himself that he really wanted to make a lasting and positive difference for his village. He was determined to set his village on a path that would lead to ever-higher levels of prosperity. He could not bear to witness any longer the deprivations his people suffered because of poverty, ignorance, and negative thinking and practices. He would not rest until his people and their surroundings were transformed into a better and more hopeful place.

As the first rays of the rising sun peeked over the mountain summit, the same men who had overseen Letivi's cleansing ceremonies the day before gathered in front of Letivi's sleeping room. They carried with them the special robes that generations of chiefs had worn on their wedding days. The oldest elder approached the door of Letivi's room and clapped his hands to waken Letivi and alert him to their presence. Letivi acknowledged his hearing of the clapping by saying he was present. He slowly got up. Wrapped around his waist was the same white cloth. He opened his door and pulled back the curtain hanging in front of the door. He greeted everyone as tradition required and stepped outside his room.

One man stepped forward with a bucket of the same clear spring water and used a sponge to wipe Letivi's body and clean carefully his eyes and face. Once his body was dry, the men began to dress Letivi. First, a pair of white cotton long underpants with a drawstring at the waist was put on him. After that, a similar white long-sleeve shirt was placed over his head and neatly layered over his torso.

After he was dressed in these under garments, several men lifted the heavy royal wedding gown and carefully lowered it over the chief's head and helped him put his arms into the wide, ample sleeves. This gown was made of the finest kente cloth strips. At its edges was a wide strip of white cloth that had been elaborately embroidered with expensive, colorful thread to depict many meaningful traditional symbols. One could spend a lifetime trying to decipher the meaning of these symbols. Few people still knew what these symbols meant. Everyone knew they were important, but almost nobody could say exactly why, as that knowledge was almost totally lost. Everyone did know and appreciate that tailoring such a royal gown today would cost the equivalent of a multiple of the average annual income.

Letivi was acutely aware of the cost of the gown and the festivities that would follow and that his predecessor, Chief Yofu, had spoken against the wastefulness of this kind of ostentatious wedding. But he could clearly see that he should not do anything to thwart the joyful insistence of his people to make his wedding day a big and expensive affair. For the people, the prestige of the village and their young white chief was at stake, and, therefore, they had to go overboard to make his traditional wedding day a spectacular event that would be noticed by the whole country and talked about for years to come. Even if they had to exhaust all their resources and borrow money, they believed that ensuring the prestige of their village and chief was worth it. Nothing was more important at this moment than making the chief's wedding one that would live forever in their oral history and the memory of the people.

After Letivi was fully dressed and his specially made royal leather sandals were placed on his feet, he was escorted to a neighboring compound where a round structure had been built and covered with a straw roof. The pillars of the hangar were decorated with flowers. Clay pots containing exotic tropical plants encircled a huge chief's chair that had been covered with the most luxurious hand-woven cloth. Letivi was impressed by what he saw. He wanted to comment and also note how hot, heavy, and awkward his gown was, but he continued to obey the instruction to remain silent and stone faced.

Letivi was helped to sit down in the chair. His gown was neatly arranged around him. Chief Gyasi stood behind Letivi. Incense was lit at several locations, and cheap perfume was splattered here and there by the women of his compound. Head fetish priests paced to and fro, saying magical words and blessing the ground with libations of fresh palm wine. Abruptly, the silence of this scene was loudly interrupted by a huge crowd standing outside the compound gate. The boisterous songs and chants of this crowd were suddenly pierced by the frantic screams of women. These screams made everyone in Letivi's compound stop what they were doing and huddle quietly along the exterior walls.

A rowdy group of young men burst nosily through the compound gate like thieves intent on plundering the chief's riches. These men ran about wildly, wearing only the skimpiest of loincloths. Sheep blood was smeared on their bodies, and their hair and faces were covered in white ashes. Each man carried a spear and threatened all those in the compound except the chief, who was wide-eyed and awed but silent. An old bugler near the gate sounded several loud blasts on his World War I brass horn. All the wild men shouted in unison and fell prostrate to the ground at the outer perimeter of the chief's round hangar.

At that moment, a smaller group of men marched into the compound holding tightly a person who was covered by a large sack and dressed in ragged clothes. Closely behind these men was a group of women who were screaming at the top of their voices a high-pitched ululating sound that was traditionally used to indicate immediate danger. Incongruently, these men and women were nicely dressed, as if they were going to a party.

The men approached Letivi in uneven steps as they struggled to hold on to the unruly person hidden under the white cape. As they neared where Letivi was sitting, people flowed into the compound until it was tightly packed. Everyone in the village was there. An older man stepped forth to stand in front of the young men holding the unwilling "prisoner" they had captured. This man said in a high voice, "Most exalted chief, we have found this woman sneaking around our compound, and we bring her to you for your most wise judgment."

The prisoner was forced on her knees in front of the chief, and the old man said, "Most honored chief, I now reveal the identity of this unwanted trespasser."

The man swiftly unknotted and removed the cape hiding the head of the prisoner. The man and the other men with him took several steps back so that Letivi could see well the person they had brought for him to judge. Letivi looked intently at the person kneeling before him, but her head was bowed, so he could not see her face. The older man noted Letivi's hesitation. He stepped forward and placed his hand under the chin of what was clearly a female prisoner, forcing her head upward so the chief could see clearly her face.

Letivi raised his staff in the air, and the man immediately let the prisoner's head fall. The crowd became quiet, listening intently for what Letivi would say. Letivi stood up and looked around at the crowd and then down at the woman kneeling before him. He smiled and cheerfully said, "Thanks to all who did this good deed and brought this wayward person to me. I'm not sure yet what punishment I should mete out to this person. As nobody wants this woman, I will keep her here until I can decide what to do with her. Does her family agree?"

The older man came forth again and dryly said, "Thank you, my chief. I am the head of the family from whence this woman originates, and I can assure you that we do not want her, and we would be very happy if you would keep her."

After these words were pronounced, the people cheered loudly, and dancers and drummers pushed their way forward to animate and entertain the crowd. While all this enjoyable distraction was going on, the women from Letivi's compound came before him and dragged the prisoner away. People laughed and clapped loudly at seeing this hysterical scene.

Another group of women entered the compound with huge clay pots full of fresh palm wine balanced on their heads. They ordered the young wild men to get up so they could place their pots on the ground. Behind the women were young girls carrying large stacks of hundreds of small calabashes. Palm wine was poured into one calabash and offered to the chief, who let a few drops fall to the ground for the grandfathers before heartily drinking the rest. The chief's action was a signal to the rest of the people to line up to be served the first of many calabashes of palm wine they would drink that day and night.

While the festive mood of the crowd was growing, a small group of men entered carrying a huge trunk that was covered with red goat leather inscribed with important traditional symbols relating to the union of a man and woman. All eyes were focused on the trunk when Letivi stood up again and spoke as he had been instructed by Gyasi. "I see the prisoner is a beautiful woman, and I have decided to keep her for myself. To demonstrate to you that I am serious about my desires for this woman, I want to show you what I will give her. Please bring the woman back so that she can also see how serious I am about her staying with me."

Delalia was most radiant in her natural beauty and all the finery she wore as she was escorted through the crowd to stand next to Letivi and the trunk. She looked so stunningly different that nobody recognized her as the young woman who had already consorted with the chief. The chief commanded Delalia to open the trunk and share with the crowd all he was willing to give her to stay with him. She took two short, lady-like steps forward, unlatched the trunk, and slowly opened it to expose all the treasures it contained. It was filled with African print cloth, many necklaces and bracelets made of traditional Venetian beads, and a special little box with gold jewelry that all properly wed women had received for generations.

Daintily, Delalia slowly lifted each item out of the trunk to show off to the public. Every time she lifted an item out of the trunk and held it high above her head, the crowd and musicians made a loud and joyous noise. The last item to be displayed was the gold jewelry, which Delalia put on while the crowd cheered and clapped wildly. This wedding gift display took over an hour to complete, and by the time the final gift was displayed, the sun was already indicating it was late afternoon. When everything was placed neatly back into the trunk, a group of women came to carry the trunk away and escort Delalia to another hiding place in the compound.

There was another round of palm-wine drinking, and then the head of Delalia's family stepped forth again, with much fanfare being provided by the drummers and bugler. Letivi raised his staff so the crowd would become silent. Delalia's senior elder then said, "Dear chief, may you always be blessed by the gods, spirits, and grandfathers. I can see by your many gifts that you indeed want this woman to stay with you. We have also received a generous gift of money and livestock from you, and this makes us even more certain about the purity of your desires for this woman. My family wishes you the best of luck with this woman. From this day forward, she is yours to do with as you please."

Another round of palm-wine drinking ensued as people lined up to shake the hand of Letivi and wish him luck with his new woman and encourage him to have many children with her. At this point, the music, dancing, and singing became much more animated and widespread. This was going to be a party that nobody would ever forget. As dusk began to descend on the chief's compound, kerosene lanterns and powerful Aladdin and Petromax lamps were set about the compound. There had never before been so much light at night in the village.

The loud sound of women pounding yams into fufu could be heard throughout the village, and the smell of the large batches of spicy palm-oil sauce that would accompany it permeated the air. Taste buds were also tantalized by the smell of roasted meat. Several steers and dozens of goats and sheep had been slaughtered and grilled over an open fire for this extraordinary wedding feast. Cases of bottled beer were delivered by the Chinaman who now owned Chez André's. Everyone would overeat and drink and sleep little that night. It would be days before the village could sober up and return to its normal routines.

Letivi sat with the elders and clan leaders, who were served first. They ate and drank and laughed until they were exhausted by an excess of food and friendly pleasure. They knew that the spirit world was also celebrating with them. The ground was soaked by the many libations they offered in honor of the grandfathers. It was about midnight when Gyasi hinted to Letivi that it may be time for him to excuse himself and retire to his sleeping room. Letivi knew that this was a signal that Delalia had finished partying with the women and was now waiting for him in his room. Letivi bid farewell to the group of men he was sitting with and, keeping as low a profile as possible, walked out of the compound to an adjoining one where his sleeping room was located.

He found the door of his sleeping room ajar and Delalia inside, waiting for him in the skimpiest of sleepwear. Without saying a word, Delalia tenderly helped to remove his robes and undergarments. Letivi had drunk too much and complained of a headache and dizziness. Delalia asked him to lie down so she could give him a massage. Letivi lay on his stomach. She then mounted nude on top of him and began to give him a full body massage that made his headache go away and his whole body relax. Delalia's magic fingers had unwittingly put Letivi into a deep sleep. Delalia emitted a muffled laugh when she observed that Letivi was fast asleep. As she expected to be with Letivi for a lifetime, his sleeping now was not a problem for her. She snuggled close to him and pulled the thin cover over them. She could not be happier.

Morning arrived more quickly than usual, and Delalia could hear the crowing of the compound roosters. Letivi remained asleep next to her. She did not want to do anything to disturb him. Later, someone began clapping loudly at the door. Delalia knew that this meant that the old women had come to collect the white sheet with spots of blood on it that would prove she had been a virgin and had had sex for the first time with Letivi last night. Everyone knew that no young girl in the village remained a virgin for long anymore, but this ancient custom persisted and was important for the reputation of the bride and her family.

Delalia was obliged to wake Letivi, as it was the man who must throw out the door to the waiting women the soiled sheet. Delalia had brought a white sheet stained with spots of sheep's blood for this purpose. She handed the sheet to Letivi and told him to open the door only wide enough to toss the sheet outside. The groggy and very hungover Letivi did as Delalia said. As soon as the sheet landed outside, they could hear the old women cackling with happiness. They would walk through the village displaying the sheet to all before handing it over to Delalia's family. Everyone who saw the sheet would applaud and say a loud amen.

The sheet ceremony was the last act of a customary process that now made Letivi and Delalia recognized by all as a couple. While the sheet and so much else about the wedding customs were unreal, the people were now satisfied that their chief was a man who met all the criteria for being a chief. There was no longer any reason to doubt their chief, and everyone was proud of the man their chief had become. They had enjoyed immensely the costly wedding day, and they were happy that it had boosted the prestige of their village. The happiest people of all were Letivi and Delalia. They were now smiling at each other as they embraced and started doing what they were supposed to have done during the night to soil the white sheet.

CHAPTER NINETEEN
NOT IN KANSAS ANYMORE

Molly and Robin stared blankly at the passing countryside as their taxi zoomed along the narrow tarmac road leading to Mount Ataku. They sat at opposite ends of the car's shabby backseat, looking out their respective side windows, trying to make sense of what they saw. They paid no mind to the sweltering heat and the strong breeze blowing through the windows of the un-air-conditioned car. They appeared not to care that the wind and high humidity had made a mess of their hair. Molly kept her eyes glued to the scene that was passing quickly in front of her as she tied her long hair behind her head. They did not speak. Their minds were pressed to the limit to understand the unfamiliar world they were observing.

Not one thing they saw had anything in common with their home state of Kansas. The ground, the air, and everything in between was new to them. Nothing was the same, not even the smell and taste of the air. The national highway they sped along reminded them of a country road in Kansas, but it was not as well maintained and constructed. There were frequent potholes and many bumps in the road where potholes had been hand filled. The sides of the tarmac road had crumbled to one degree or another, and there was no shoulder on which to pull off. And, at many places along the road, they observed much litter. It was difficult to believe that this was one of the main national highways. Molly could not help but ask Cyprien, the driver, "Are you sure this is the road to Ataku?"

Cyprien let out a loud, one-syllable, harping laugh and said, "Yes, of course. This road heads straight toward Mount Ataku, and the village of Ataku lies at the foot of its western slope. You'll see that we will slowly be climbing in altitude until we reach the mountain."

Then, Molly blurted out what she really wanted to say. "But the road seems in such poor condition to be a national highway."

Cyprien clacked his teeth together and licked his thick lips twice, relishing the opportunity to say, "The road is in poor condition because of our corrupt government. Every few years they rebuild this road, but they purposely cover it with a thin coat of asphalt so they can charge for a thick coat of tar and pocket the difference. They really worked a big scam on donor countries, which are often all too willing to help repave this important national artery. This road and others are real 'cash cows' for the president and his cronies."

Molly and Robin were struggling to cope with the profound gravity of what Cyprien had just told them. In their world, such blatant corruption would create a major scandal and be the object of much publicity and widespread protests. The guilty parties would be brought to trial and punished to the limit of the law. Molly could not understand. In a very patronizing manner, she asked Cyprien, "How can that be true? Why are the guilty not arrested and punished? Are there no jails and courts in this country? Surely your newspapers would report on such criminal acts."

Cyprien heard well what Molly said, but he did not know how to reply. He could see that she was right in what she was saying, but none of what she said was applicable in his country, where the rule of law was a remote concept. He took a deep breath before belting out in rapid fashion, "Madame, I am sorry that our country is not like your country. There is no such thing here as applying the law equally to everyone. Here, a small group of rich and politically powerful elites do as they please, and the ones punished are those who cross them. All that the elites think about is enriching themselves and their families. They really care little for their country and have no sense of nation building. Anyone who wants to get ahead must pay tribute in one form or another to these elites. For sure, no matter how high the crime, no important person has ever gone to jail unless he or she has crossed the president."

Molly and Robin were impressed by Cyprien's ability to provide them with this summary analysis of governance in his country and how the local power dynamics worked. They were learning much more than they had expected from their very smart driver. They had on the tip of their tongues a number of follow-up questions when Cyprien interjected in a pleading tone, "Please, can we not talk about politics? I can get into a lot of trouble for what I just told you. Please do not tell anyone what I said. Let's talk about something else."

Molly and Robin fully understood the point Cyprien was trying to make. They both had plenty of safer questions. Robin changed the subject and lightened the conversation by asking,

"Where are the monkeys? I've been watching in the bushes and trees along the roadside, but I have yet to see any monkeys or, for that matter, any other wild animal."

This time Cyprien laughed loud and long before saying, "Excuse me, but that is just too funny. In all my life, I have never seen a monkey or any other wild animal, other than snakes, mice, bats, a few birds, and agouti cane rats. I don't think my parents ever saw any wild animals. Maybe my grandparents saw some. Anyway, there have not been any wild animals in this area for generations, and maybe there were never any."

After this explanation, Robin turned to Molly and said, "This is nothing like the Africa we learned about growing up in Kansas. All we knew then was about the Africa of Tarzan and Jane depicted in movies, and what our fellow and late Kansans, Osa and Martin Johnson, recorded in the 1920s and 1930s on film. Maybe all that happened somewhere else in Africa. We really should visit the Johnsons' museum in Chanute, Kansas, Osa's hometown. They and their work are really quite famous. Maybe I will do like Osa and write a book about our trip. Her book, *I Married Adventure*, was a best seller in 1940. Maybe we are modern-day versions of Osa and Martin."

All this made Molly laugh and smile at Robin. "Well, times have changed since the Johnsons came to Africa. I'm sure that few, if any, roads existed back then, and for sure there were a lot fewer people and no corrupt governments. I do admire the Johnsons. I don't know how they managed. We're having more challenges than we can handle. Imagine how things were in Africa seventy years ago."

Robin was closely watching Molly as she spoke. His tender heart began to glow as he thought of the intimacy they had shared the previous night. Those delicious thoughts prompted his hand to move toward Molly's hand, but Molly quickly removed her hand from the car seat to her lap. This coldly shattered the raptured attachment Robin felt for Molly, and he could not help but feel hurt.

Molly sensed Robin's hurt feelings and in a sympathetic tone softly said, "My dear Robin, you know I have strong feelings for you, but please don't rush things or read too much into what happened between us last night. What happened last night may happen again, but it may also not happen. What I'm saying is don't count on me, at least not yet. Give me some time and room. I'm not yet ready for a serious relationship. And, I beg you, please don't be hurt by anything I say or do. I can't bear seeing you acting like a hurt little puppy dog."

Robin knew what Molly was saying was right, but he was having trouble keeping on a happy face. Deep down, he felt as if his love parade for Molly had just been canceled by an unexpected heavy rain. He paused for a moment and looked straight forward so as to avoid Molly's face and said with tight lips, "I understand. Don't worry. I get it. For sure, I don't want to do anything that would damage our friendship."

Molly reached over and quickly squeezed and released Robin's hand, saying sweetly, "Thanks for your understanding and for being such a good friend."

At that moment, Cyprien dangerously swerved the car to the right, knocking Molly and Robin together. Cyprien immediately righted the car and said loudly, "Missed it!"

"Missed what?" inquired a scared Molly.

"A black snake that was crawling across the road. We hate snakes, and we do everything we can to kill them when we see them."

No sooner had Cyprien said these words when he pressed down forcefully on the brake pedal, throwing Molly and Robin violently forward. This time they could see he was trying to avoid hitting two sheep that had suddenly decided to scamper across the road in front of the car. He barely missed hitting the trailing sheep.

Molly thought she needed to encourage Cyprien and said, "Way to go, Cyprien. Great driving in missing those sheep."

Cyprien chuckled in his usual joyful manner and said, "Thank you, but they were a pair of goats. They are usually smarter than sheep and do not dart out in front of oncoming vehicles."

Molly and Robin had seen many times along the roadsides what they thought were sheep. But now they looked more closely and could see there were two distinct types of "sheep." They had never before seen animals like these being raised in Kansas and were surprised to see them running free to graze. They did not want to reveal their ignorance, so they refrained from asking Cyprien how to tell the difference between a goat and a sheep. While they were trying to determine on their own the difference between these two very distinct small ruminant species, Cyprien rolled slowly to a stop, saying with disgust, "Our first roadblock."

Tied firmly to two wooden posts on each side of the road was a barely visible locally made sisal rope stretching across the road in front of them. Cyprien had no choice but to stop. On each side of the road was a uniformed policeman. Molly and Robin were scared when one of the policemen approached their car and walked slowly around it, peering menacingly through every window. The burly policeman asked Cyprien to get out of the car and open the trunk. Before doing as instructed, Cyprien reassured his passengers by saying, "Don't worry. There is no problem."

Following a quick inspection of the contents of the almost empty car trunk, Cyprien returned behind the wheel and started the car. A small boy lowered the rope blocking the road, and Cyprien waved happily, putting on a false smile as he drove forward and passed this makeshift roadblock. Once they were a safe distance past the roadblock, Molly could not wait to demand, "Why did they stop us? What did the policemen want?"

Cyprien replied in a matter-of-fact tone, "They were not policeman. They were customs agents faking their interest in finding contraband. All they really wanted was the payment of a bribe. We were lucky because they let us go without paying anything."

A perturbed Molly continued, "I'm surprised. We have barely gone twenty miles, and we are stopped. Does this happen frequently?"

"All the time. We have all kinds of roadblocks. We have roadblocks set by the national police, the local police, and customs. Sometimes we have roadblocks set by local chiefs trying to earn an extra gadi. We will see many more roadblocks before we arrive in Ataku. I know this is confusing to you, particularly as they all wear the same faded olive green army uniforms."

"Why didn't we have to pay anything this time?"

"The thing that helped us get by this time was my telling the agents that you are two special visitors going to see the White Chief. Usually, if they see white people, they think that they can ask for a bigger bribe, as everyone knows white people are rich. They know the White Chief has contact with the president, so they were afraid to ask for anything. I will say the same thing at every roadblock we encounter."

Molly and Robin returned to staring out their windows, trying their best to comprehend their new and very different surroundings. They could feel the road was gradually climbing upward.

They could see they were slowly leaving a countryside covered by tall grass to one dominated by small trees and bushes. The grass reminded them of the bluestem grass on the Kansas prairie, but it really was nothing like the grass they knew. None of the bushes were anything they had seen before. The trees were all different. They kept looking for trees they knew—elm, oak, ash, cottonwood, maple—but there were none to be seen. They did recognize banana trees, although they had never seen one before, but they were not able to distinguish one kind of banana from another. Robin commented, "It is clear to me that being in the tropics and closer to the equator changes everything."

They were absorbed by what they observed in the numerous villages they passed. Naked, or almost naked, children would run up to the sides of the road to wave and yell excitedly at the passing white people. Some of the boys pushed well-worn bicycle rims with sticks or rolled old car tires before them. Others maneuvered small toy cars they had fabricated from sardine and other small tin cans. A few boys had assembled from the barest of scrap materials wooden scooters. Everywhere boys were playing soccer, often times with a ball made from a bundle of rags and banana leaves. It was easy for Molly and Robin to comprehend that if they ever wanted to make a gift to children, a real soccer ball would be more than welcome. They were also impressed that in spite of their obvious poverty and grubby bodies, the children seemed happy and full of laughter.

They saw many chickens scavenging everywhere for anything they could eat. They knew that they were chickens, but they had never seen scrawny chickens like these. They had also never seen donkeys or guinea fowl, but they knew what they were from photos they had seen in books or on TV. It was their first time to see a donkey pulling a cart. They saw many palm trees, assuming they were all coconut trees, although what they were seeing consisted of a wide variety of different kinds of palm trees. They did recognize cornfields but had no idea what the nearby cassava plants were or why there were yam mounds in some fields. They could not tell the difference between corn, sorghum, or millet stalks. They kept looking for wheat, for which Kansas is known, but they saw no sign of any, either the actual plant or stubble left in the fields.

They did not see a single tractor. This prompted Robin to ask Cyprien, "How do they cultivate their fields without tractors?"

Robin's innocent question gave Cyprien a good laugh. "Nobody can afford a tractor, and even if they could, it would be hard to maintain. Also, the fields are too small and dispersed to justify the use of a tractor. The major instruments of farm work here are the daba, a short-handled hoe, and the long machete knife. Haven't you seen some women working with their dabas?"

"Yes, I have seen many women working in their fields, and some were carrying babies wrapped tightly against their backs. I have also seen many women and girls carrying water, firewood, and many other items on their heads. That is indeed very remarkable, but it makes me wonder even more what kinds of work men do. I did see some men sitting in groups in the villages talking and drinking something from fibrous yellowish bowls."

Cyprien cleared his throat as he contemplated how to reply to Robin's astute but complicated observations. "Sir, these are very good questions you are asking, and they are not easy to respond to. Please keep in mind that we have a very different culture here, and it assigns the roles and tasks normally reserved for women and men. What you are observing is how our culture works. True, the women work very hard, but the men also have their work and must take responsibility for the management of village affairs."

Robin was not satisfied with this answer, but he knew that it would be too much to ask Cyprien to explain more about gender dynamics in his society. He did want to know what the men were drinking, so he said, "Thank you. You have given me much to think about. Can you tell me what the men are drinking?"

"They are drinking various locally made, low-alcoholic fermented beverages made by women. They drink from calabash gourds that grow on a local tree. The beverages could be palm wine made from the sap of the oil palm tree, sorghum or millet beer, or liquor that is distilled from a corn mash. Many men in the rural areas sometimes drink these beverages instead of eating. In any event, they consume many calories in this way. I note that you are seeing many men drinking now, as it is the dry season and there is not any fieldwork to do. Also, you should know that many young men leave the village during this season to find work in neighboring countries."

It was Molly's turn to chime in. "What season is this? It looks like autumn because the leaves on many trees are turning yellow and falling to the ground."

Cyprien quickly responded, "We only have two seasons here: wet and dry. We are now starting our dry season. The leaves are falling because it is dry."

Molly whispered to Robin, "I don't think I could live in a place that does not have four seasons. Having only two seasons and about the same temperature year around seems so boring."

The men overseeing the next two roadblocks waved them by. It seemed that word about their visit with the White Chief had traveled ahead of them. Cyprien pointed to the far horizon, where the outline of Mount Ataku was barely discernible in the smoky sky. Just as they were beginning to wonder why there was so much smoke, flames roared up to both sides of the road, almost engulfing their vehicle. Cyprien stepped on the gas as he tried to move rapidly beyond the burning fields. Molly and Robin were very frightened, choking on the smoke and brushing ash off their clothes. A frightened Robin was infuriated. Once their car was safely beyond the fires, he belted out, "What in the hell was that?"

Cyprien calmly replied, "That was hunters burning off the fields so they can hunt agouti cane rats. They burn the fields, the agoutis run out, and they shoot them with their homemade rifles or club them to death. Everybody is happy with what they are doing because agouti meat is our favorite. Also, farmers like it because the burning clears their fields and kills snakes and insects."

Molly and Robin debated between themselves whether burning was good or detrimental for the land. They could see that all vegetal matter had been removed from the fields, and they wondered how needed organic matter would build up in the soil. They doubted that the ashes left on the burned fields would be much compensation for the loss of organic matter. And the red, hard soil that prevailed in many fields looked as if it became harder by the burning and long exposure to the hot sun. There were red soils in Kansas, but the red soil they saw now seemed much different and less fertile, especially as they could see no sign of any kind of fertilizer being used.

As they reached a slightly higher altitude, the temperature cooled a few degrees, and the vegetation became increasingly lush as they entered a higher rainfall zone. Mount Ataku was now clearly visible in the far distance, rising prominently over three thousand feet above the plain. Cyprien abruptly announced, "It is time to eat and relieve ourselves."

Molly understood what Cyprien meant by "relieving" one-self. They had seen everywhere since their arrival in the country men and women peeing at the side of the road. Men pissed anywhere, not minding who was watching them. Women were more discreet, finding a bit of cover before squatting down and relieving themselves. Robin was eager to pee and was ready to go behind the nearest bush. Molly needed to pee badly, but she did not know what to do. She had never previously peed outside.

Cyprien said, "Let me find a place where there are not any people and good bush cover."

He then came to a slow stop near a dense teak tree plantation and exclaimed, "This is a good place to relieve ourselves. The men should go to the right side of the road, and the woman to the left. Please be careful, as sometimes black spitting cobras like to lie under the heavy layer of teak tree leaves that have fallen to the ground."

Both Molly and Robin wished that Cyprien had not said anything about cobras. This snake factor kept Robin near the edge of the road as he tried his best to empty his bladder. Molly tip-toed carefully through the tall grass and plentiful dry teak leaves covering the ground until she found a spot where she was sure no one would see her. She unzipped her African skirt, pulled it down below her knees, and followed quickly with her panties. She then did a full squat and passed urine the best she could under those unusual circumstances. The thought of someone seeing her and a snake biting her butt made her hurry, preventing the full emptying of her bladder. As she pulled up her skirt, she noticed that she had wet part of her shoes. She told herself she hoped to never have to pee in the bush again.

When they were back in the car, Molly could see Robin looking at her shoes. She gave him a stern look and warned him, "You better not say a word."

Cyprien said, "Now that that is over with, I know a little place just around the next bend that serves some nice plates of rice and sauce. We'll stop there for lunch."

Molly said to Robin, "I have not eaten much rice in my life. Have you?"

Robin replied, "No. When I was a boy, my mother would sometimes make some hot rice porridge with sugar and butter for breakfast. After I moved to Chicago for work, I would sometimes eat rice at a Chinese restaurant. I'm definitely not a rice eater, but I think that today I'm so hungry I could eat anything."

Molly said blankly, "I'm also not a rice eater. I have eaten very little rice in my life. But when in Rome, do like the Romans, except if it makes you sick."

Cyprien pulled up to a roadside stand that was composed of a small shed and a few tables under a tree. An obese woman ran the place with two of her young nieces. They were cooking food in two big aluminum pots set precariously on three stones over a crackling wood fire. Robin, Molly, and Cyprien sat down on the tiny stools placed around one of the low, small tables. The women quickly brought out three tin plates heaped with steamy, overcooked rice along with three tablespoons. The corpulent woman returned with a metal pot full of hot palm oil with guinea fowl meat sauce.

A very hungry Cyprien quickly showed Molly and Robin what to do. He poured some of the orange sauce with pieces of guinea fowl over his pile of rice while he mixed it with his spoon. Molly and Robin followed suit. Cyprien devoured the rice as if it were his last meal. He placed spoonful after spoonful of rice into his mouth until it could hold no more. He called for water, and clay jugs of clear water were brought. He began washing his food down after almost every bite. Molly and Robin were awed by Cyprien's ability to eat so much so fast.

Molly and Robin mixed some of the sauce with rice on one side of their plates. They both were being cautious in spite of their hunger pangs, taking only a partial spoonful for their first bite. No sooner had the spoon touched their lips than they immediately dropped their spoons and yelled in unison. "Wow, that is too hot and spicy!"

Robin ran to the car to fetch their water bottles. They both drank and swished water around in their mouths and said to Cyprien, "Too much hot pepper in that sauce for us."

Cyprien ate every rice grain and piece of guinea fowl. Molly and Robin could not believe he could eat such a large serving of food. Even if the sauce had not been too spicy, they did not think they could have eaten half the food on their plates. As the situation was, they were nibbling around the sides of their plates to eat plain rice that had not been touched by the super-hot sauce. Compared to Cyprien they ate very little, but they had had enough.

Robin really wanted to taste what he perceived as chicken pieces in the sauce, but they were too covered with the spicy oil. He asked Cyprien, "How's that local chicken taste?"

In between bites, Cyprien laughed and said, "That is not chicken. It is Guinea fowl."

Robin exclaimed, "But it looks like chicken."

"Yes, but it is tastier," retorted Cyprien.

Molly and Robin then realized that many of the chickens they saw running around were not chickens but guinea fowl, something neither of them had seen live before.

One thing that discouraged Molly and Robin from eating more was the countless number of flies that hovered everywhere and infested their food. They constantly shooed the flies away, but they were too many and too insistent on contaminating their food. Robin exclaimed quietly to Molly, "Maybe Cyprien eats fast in order to minimize the time flies have to land on his food."

Molly retorted, "I'm sure our leftovers will be re-served to the next customers. If not, look at all the scrawny sparrows and weird-looking lizards darting back and forth, ready to pounce on any food that falls to the ground. Also, look at those skinny dogs lying in the shade at the edge of the road. I'm sure they would devour all our food, hot sauce and all."

As Molly was talking, Robin looked straight up to see sitting in the top branches of a nearby tree what he thought was a vulture. This sight prompted Robin to say, "Well, if there is anything dead around, I'm sure that big bird up there will clean it up, just like a Kansas buzzard."

Molly looked up to see what Robin was talking about. The instant she saw the vulture, she said, "Ekes! That does it for me. I'm going to the car."

They paid an unbelievably small sum to the big woman and kept straight faces as they thanked her for such good food. They got into the car as Cyprien started the motor for the last leg of their trip to Ataku. Soon they found themselves staring right at the mountain, observing villages located at various levels on the mountainside. Cyprien drove slowly because the area was increasingly more populated with people and marauding animals. He did not want to miss the turnoff to Ataku, which was located about three miles off the main highway.

They soon arrived at a rather large, attractive sign that presented Ataku as a model village and pointed the direction with a big red arrow. Molly insisted on stopping so Cyprien could take a photo of her and Robin next to the sign. After that brief interlude, Cyprien started the engine and turned slowly onto the road. They drove only a short distance before being stopped at the Ataku road toll-booth. Payment of a toll was not obligatory, but the young couple managing the booth said all contributions to the village's development fund were welcome. They explained that this road to their village was maintained with money contributed to this fund.

Molly happily handed a wad of gadis out the window to one of the attendants, saying, "We are coming to see the White Chief. Is Ataku his village?"

The man at the booth responded with a smile, "Yes, our chief is often referred to as the White Chief. Please enjoy your stay in our village."

The man was intrigued as to why they were so interested in seeing Chief Letivi. If he had a way to do so, he would have sent a messenger to Letivi's compound to let him know that two white people were coming his way.

It did not take long before they were rolling slowly into the village's main public center. On the left side of the road were some market women sitting behind the vegetables, fruits, and other items they were trying to sell. On the right side of the road were a huge kapok tree and the beginning of the wide path that led up the mountainside to Chief Letivi's compound.

Next to the road where the women were displaying their wares was Chez André's, the local general store, bar, and restaurant. Cyprien stopped the car in front of Chez André's and said, "This is a good place for you to ask about seeing the chief. I see that like many villages these days, they have a Chinaman."

Molly and Robin got out of the car and headed for the steps leading up to Chez André's. Sitting on the steps was a strange

Asian man. He was the first nonblack man they had seen and the first man they had seen wearing shorts. Their eyes locked for a moment, and the unintimidated Molly asked, "Can you please tell us where we can find the chief?"

The man yelled in Chinese to someone inside the store. A young woman appeared and asked politely, "How can I help you?"

Molly and Robin repeated their wish to see the chief. The woman beckoned them to come up to the terrace. They walked by the Chinaman, who acted as if he did not care about the strange white people entering his establishment. Once on the terrace, the woman said, "Please sit down and have a nice, cool drink while I send someone to see if the chief can receive you. Who should I tell the chief wants to see him?"

Molly thanked the woman and said with equal politeness, "Thank you. Please communicate to the chief that Molly and Robin have come all the way from Kansas in America in search of the village where David Peterson lived years ago."

The woman immediately called to a young man sitting nearby and repeated to him why these two white visitors wanted to see the chief. Before she could finish talking, the young man took off at a fast pace. The woman turned to Molly and Robin and asked them what they would like to drink. They both played it safe and ordered Cokes for themselves and Cyprien. While they waited for their drinks, they looked out at the village and at their surroundings. They did not see anything special about Ataku except the backdrop of the mountain. It looked similar to the many other simple villages they had passed on the road. They did hear some strange sounds coming from rooms that had been improvised at one end of Chez André's. When the woman returned with their drinks, Robin had the gumption to ask, "What is that noise coming from those big rooms?"

The woman grinned and chuckled softly as she explained, "In one room, there is a television, and in the other is a movie projector. We put up a television antenna and installed a small generator to provide electrical power. Thanks to our efforts, many people are seeing TV and moving pictures for the first time."

Robin was curious. "Do you charge a viewing fee?"

The woman quickly replied, "For the TV, we ask only that our patrons buy at least one drink. For the movie, we charge a small entrance amount."

"You said movie. Surely you meant to say movies," insisted Robin.

"I am sorry, but so far, we have only one black-and-white moving picture. We show it several times a day to an overflowing crowd—a beautiful Hindu movie. Many people have seen this movie so many times that they can repeat by memory in Hindi the dialog. Some people are able to communicate to each other in Hindi. People enjoy this movie very much and want to visit India and speak Hindi."

Molly and Robin were becoming confused. They could not fully digest the different world they were in, and now they were sitting at a bar owned by a Chinaman who showed old Hindu movies. Cyprien was sitting nearby and following their conversation. After the woman left, he came over and sat down with Molly and Robin, saying quietly, "I need to tell you some things. Nobody likes these Chinamen, but we tolerate them because they sell stuff for cheap prices and bring things like TV and movies to us. But, on the other hand, these TV programs and movies have damaged the traditional social fabric and diverted limited time and resources away from more productive activities. People no longer take time to visit with their friends and relatives because of the damned TV and movies. These changes are like a curse!"

Molly and Robin were taken aback by the passionate manner in which Cyprien expressed himself. Molly could only say, "Thanks, Cyprien, for your views. You have given us much to think about."

Molly had no sooner finished her words when the young man who had been sent to advise the chief of their presence returned, out of breath. Once the man could catch his breath, he calmly said, "I delivered your message to the chief's compound. I was told to tell you to stay here until the chief sends a message as to when you can meet him."

Molly and Robin thanked the young man and offered him a small tip for his services. They were prepared to wait as long as it would take to gain an audience with the chief.

One of Letivi's bodyguards approached him as he was sitting alone in the shade under the old neem tree in his compound. The bodyguard said, "My chief, I have two messages for you. Both arrived at the same time. The first one is written on this piece of paper. The second one was given to me verbally, and it is about two white people from America at Chez André's who want to see you about someone named David Peterson."

When the guard uttered the name of David, Letivi's body trembled and his stomach tightened. He thought that was the name his mother once told him his father had when he first arrived in the village. He tried to conceal the impact of hearing that name had on him as he read what was scribbled on the small piece of paper. There were only two words, "Come quickly," on the scrap of paper, but that was enough to communicate to Letivi that he needed to go immediately to see his mother.

Letivi tried to keep his calm as he turned to the guard and gave him instructions. "Tell the two white people that they must stay the night because I cannot receive them until tomorrow. Find Chief Gyasi for me and tell him I need to see him now."

The guard said, "Yes, sir," and did an abrupt about-face and ran off to do the chief's bidding.

In less than ten minutes, Gyasi marched briskly into Letivi's compound to see what urgency required his presence. Letivi lost no time in telling his grandfather, "I received a note from my mother. I must go see her now. I fear that the last days of my mother, your daughter, are upon us. Also, there are two white people at Chez André's asking to see me to inquire about a David Peterson. If my mother can still talk, I will ask her to remind me of the real name of my father. It could very well be David Peterson. Please take care of the president's cell phone in case he calls while I am away. I hope to be back tomorrow. I will see our white visitors then."

The pressure on Letivi was enormous. Deep in his heart, he knew he was going to see his mother and her vanishing magical forest domain for the last time. He was eager to see what information the white people might possibly have about his long-departed and mysterious father, but before knowing more about his father, he had to say his final good-bye to what was left of his mother. He was saddened by the fact that he would soon be an orphan and on his own in a changing world that he liked less and less.

CHAPTER TWENTY
COLLISION COURSE

Letivi lost no time in making his way to his mother's forest domain. It was late afternoon by the time he arrived at the entrance of what had once been a mystical place where miracles often occurred. He could not believe how bad his birthplace looked. He cherished his childhood memories of this once-happy camp. In the past, he would have been already engaged in a lively conversation with the trees and felt uplifted by the wonders possessed by this traditional stronghold of botanical secrets. Now, there was only ruin, decay, and deafening silence. He was made heartsick by what he saw and felt.

The trees and plants which had once been his close friends were dead, or almost so. It was as if they could not talk now, as they were too busy self-destructing as they prepared to leave this world. Letivi was deeply troubled to see the glorious multi-century reign of this sacred domain was expiring quickly, with not even the slightest notice of the uncaring outside world. This place of legendary acts and the source of many cures would soon be no different from anywhere else. The demise of such an integral part of his people's traditional way of life was more than Letivi could bear. This harsh confrontation with life's unfairness and unpredictability made him ill and queasy.

Gone were the hundreds of enchanting birds and their sweet melodies. The ground was strewn with rotting tree branches and fallen leaves. It was as if the place had been saturated with a powerful herbicide that was killing every living plant. The freshwater spring was no longer spouting from the rocks and trickling along its ancient track. Multitudes of ants and termites had invaded this holy sanctuary and were busy consuming and carrying off everything in their paths. Letivi searched frantically in this awful mess for any sign of his mother. As he had done since he could talk, he yelled, "Mother, I am here. Your Letivi is here."

He called out repeatedly for his mother, but he heard not a sound in reply. He grasped energetically large armfuls of fallen brush and threw them aside to clear all the places where his mother might be. He rushed from one spot to another like a madman as he tried to find any remains of his mother. His clothes were drenched with sweat. He cried out to the gods and the ancestors for help. Suddenly, he spied part of his mother's soiled color-patch gown protruding from under a pile of small tree limbs. He quickly but carefully removed the limbs so he could see if his mother lay beneath them.

He found, lying limply on the ground before him, his mother's gown. He doubted there could be a body inside the flattened garment. He also did not see any feet, hands, or head poking out from the gown. Tears rolled down his cheeks as he realized he had arrived too late. His mother had already passed on to the other world. He knelt down beside the empty cloth and sobbed uncontrollably. Once he was able to stabilize himself, he reached down to collect his mother's old gown. He was profoundly startled when he saw below the gown the shriveled remains of his mother. It was a ghastly sight. His once-beautiful mother looked like a long-dead, shrunken mummy. It was as if his mother's intent was to return her remains to the earth at that very spot. He thought the only thing for him to do was to cover what was left of her with the dirt and debris surrounding the low depression in which she lay.

He avoided looking at his mother's remains because he preferred to remember her as she had been when he was a child. As he slowly peeled the gown from the sticky earth, he heard a barely audible mumbling that gave him a scary start. He lowered his head so he could hear better the odd sounds coming from his mother's remains. He was shocked. He could hear a feeble, crackling voice struggling to form a few broken words. He knew it was his mother when he heard ever so faintly, "My son. I love you. I am sorry I am not here for you, and I have to go now."

Letivi could not restrain himself and bluntly replied, "Mother, please do not go yet. I need to know if David Peterson is the name of my father."

He moved his ears closer to the ground and listened as intently as he could. After a long and agonizing pause, he was able to hear, "Yes, that was his name. Good-bye, my son. I will always look over you."

As the last, almost-inaudible word rose from the ground, his mother's physical remains instantly vaporized, transforming into a sparkling mist that floated rapidly upward, disappearing in a flash into the darkening sky. Letivi gathered up his mother's gown and looked around at a bewildering sight. All living things around him were crashing noisily to the ground and sizzling as if they were in a steam bath. The ground began to heave and shake. Letivi ran for safety to a spot just outside the perimeter of his mother's former domain.

In his hurry to seek safety, he dropped his mother's gown. In a split second, the ground in the middle of the old domain opened up, and an invisible force pulled everything lying around it into this yawning crevice in the earth's surface. The ground was like a carpet that was being dragged deep into the crevice, taking everything on it. In less than a minute, the ground was swept clean, and nothing remained of his mother's domain. The very existence of this revered place was being erased forever. Letivi was stunned by the sudden transformation of his wondrous childhood home into a common bare spot in the forest. The only thing remaining on the ground was his mother's old gown. He stepped forward to retrieve the gown, but it too became a glowing nebula of mist and flew skyward at the speed of light. Now, all was gone, and the place of generations of wonders was no more.

Letivi was on the verge of collapse. Nightfall was approaching fast, and he did not know what to do. He felt lost in his own home, and there was nowhere he wanted to go. All he knew was that he wanted to go far away from this place and never return. He forced himself to move one foot in front of the other and began stumbling along a path that would lead him to his village. He wobbled like a drunk as he made his way slowly down the path. A moonless night descended quickly like a black blindfold. He could not see one foot in front of him. He scraped his feet on the ground so he could hear if he was on the path or not. Many times he got off the path and ran into bushes and trees. Sometimes he tripped and fell to the ground. His body was scratched and bruised in many places. He tasted blood coming from one deep scratch on his face. He feared the most the snakes that came out at night to seek warmth and prey. He beseeched the grandfathers to guide his feet home.

It was near midnight before Letivi hobbled into his compound and headed straight to his sleeping room. He found the faithful Delalia sitting in front of the bedroom door with a small kerosene lamp lit at her feet. When she saw Letivi arrive, she quickly jumped to her feet to see if he was all right. She had agonized over Letivi's sudden departure. His long absence had almost made her sick with worry. She held the lamp up high so she could see Letivi. She was horrified by his appearance. He had cuts and scratches all over his body, and his clothes had been ripped in many places. It looked as if he had taken a rough tumble down the mountainside. It was not for her to ask any questions but only to care for her husband the best way she knew how.

In a gentle voice, she asked Letivi to sit down on a nearby stool. She brought a basin of water and a ball of soap and fetched from within the room a small clay jar full of a special cream made by Letivi's mother. She tenderly removed his clothes so that he was left wearing only his undergarment. She lovingly washed carefully every sore on his body and dried his skin by blowing softly on it. She then applied a thin layer of the special medicinal ointment on each sore and bruise. The cream smelled like stink bait, but its formidable medicinal powers were well known. By sunrise, all the sores should be well on the way to healing and Letivi should not feel any pain. Sadly, he would be one of the last persons to benefit from this miracle ointment.

Letivi genuinely appreciated all that Delalia did for him. He did not know how he could survive without the devout attentiveness she showed him. Her level of commitment to him and his well-being astounded him. He knew now that he needed all her tender care more than ever, as he was truly an orphan in this changing and increasingly unfriendly world. It was easy for him to submit to her desires, as all she ever asked was in his own best interest. She took his hand and helped him into the sleeping room. She assisted him to lie down on a clean cloth she had placed on the bed and covered him with another cloth. She sang softly a sweet melody to help soothe Letivi's wounds and put his exhausted body to sleep. While she sang, she was undressing and preparing to lie next to Letivi. The last thing Letivi remembered before falling into a deep slumber was Delalia's ample, pendulous breasts swaying exquisitely in the flickering lantern light in time with her enchanting song. He also noted how round her stomach was becoming.

***

While Letivi was dealing with the dramatic demise of his mother and her domain, Molly and Robin were facing challenges of a different kind and dimension. While they waited to learn when Letivi could receive them, they stepped out of Chez André's to observe what the women were selling along the roadside. Avoiding the redheaded fence lizards that were running around everywhere, they observed the items the women had spread before them on mats placed on the ground or on small bare wood tables. There was an assortment of items, but many women sold the same items. Wrapped in miniature plastic packages were matches, salt, sugar, cooking oil, and cigarettes. Thus, a customer with the smallest coin could purchase a tiny quantity of what he or she needed for that day. Molly and Robin also saw large, live land snails, dead smoked bats and rats being sold.

Molly found most interesting the colorful cloths the women were wearing and how they sat so easily on tiny wooden stools. She also observed that most of the women were either nursing infants or holding on their laps small children. They did not appear to allow child rearing to interfere with their activities. Molly was disturbed to see so many flies landing on the children's faces and babies with runny noses. One baby had snot running from his nose all the way down to his chin. Seeing this prompted Molly to reach into her purse and pull out a couple of Kleenex tissues to hand to the baby's mother. When the mother saw what Molly was offering her, she shook her head and quickly wiped the baby's nose with the palm of her hand. She then shocked Molly by placing her mouth over the baby's nose and sucking out any remaining snot in the baby's nasal passages and spitting it on the ground. Molly was disgusted and was eager to tell Robin about how the women cleaned their babies' noses, but she was interrupted by another troubling encounter.

Suddenly, a totally naked man ran up to Molly in a crazed fashion to examine her closely. This disheveled and filth-laden man with shaggy hair stood within six inches of Molly and stared at her with an intensity that doubled her fright. The man was much taller than she was, and he ground his teeth while he studied her from head to toe. Robin could see the man was mentally ill and was prepared to step in between him and Molly, but before he could make his move, Molly quickly turned around and headed back to the safety of the terrace at Chez André. Everyone could easily see that Molly was quite shaken by this ugly encounter with one of the village fools.

The naked man followed Molly, and just before she was about to step into Chez André's entranceway, he smacked her forcefully with his open right hand on her exposed left shoulder. This slap terrorized Molly, causing her to scream and run quickly into Chez André's. Robin was ready to pounce on the naked man and beat him, but he was restrained by a couple of bystanders.

The naked man slowly turned around, gleefully saying repeatedly, "Tsétsé."

When hearing this word, it was obvious to those who had observed this strange encounter that the harmless fool was only trying to do a good deed. Evidently, he had spied a tsétsé fly on Molly's shoulder and he wanted to kill it before its potentially infectious bite transmitted sleeping sickness through Molly's delicate skin. As the naked man wandered away saying, "Tsétsé," with a big grin on his face, he was applauded by the people standing around, who were also smiling and laughing. Cyprien explained everything to Robin, who was now becoming upset by the apparently joyful way the people were accepting what he perceived as a violent act on the part of the naked man. Once Robin heard Cyprien's explanation, he settled down and rushed to check on Molly and tell her why she had been "attacked" by the naked man.

Only the Chinaman, who was still sitting on his front steps, acted as if he did not care about the commotion caused by Molly's unsavory meeting with a town fool. He looked straight ahead as he had done when Molly and Robin passed him on the steps when they first arrived. Nonetheless, Molly was much happier to see him this time. She found it reassuring to see another foreigner of any racial type. At that moment, she was feeling hurt and very lost in a sea of black people. She felt a tinge of homesickness as she recalled that, even in Kansas with its mostly white population, there was some racial diversity. There were also all kinds of skin tones and hair colors. She missed the rich human diversity and the almost 'flyless' environment of her home in Kansas.

Just as they were taking refuge on Chez André's terrace, the young man who had gone to inform the chief of their arrival and desire to meet with him returned. The man, ignorant of the ordeal Molly had just experienced, politely informed them, "Chief Letivi is away and will not return until tomorrow. Therefore, he will not be able to receive you until tomorrow. I have instructions to show you some accommodations that we maintain for the many visitors coming to our village."

Molly was still in recovery from her shocking encounter, so Robin replied, "Thank you. Let's collect our things from the car and inform our taxi driver of our plans."

The young man quickly responded, "I have already informed your driver, and he is aware that all of you will be staying the night. As you can see, he is waiting with your things to accompany us to your nearby room in a family compound."

Robin turned to Molly, who was sitting with her head buried in her arms, which were placed on the table. She did not want anyone to see that a few tears were rolling down her high cheekbones. She was searching for inner strength to compose herself so that she could go with Robin to see their room. For the first time, she was beginning to have self-doubts about her decision to go on an African adventure. She slowly arose from her chair, saying, "Let's go."

Molly tried to act as if nothing were going on, but Robin could clearly sense that she was not all right. They quietly trotted behind the young man and Cyprien. As they crossed the wide public place, children gathered around them to gawk and sing a little ditty that expressed their delight at seeing white people as well as plead for a small gift of five gadis. The young man shouted at the children, telling them to go home to their mothers or he would find a stick and beat them all.

They walked a short distance up the mountainside along the main village pathway before turning off into an expansive family compound. As soon as the many women in the compound saw them, they dropped what they were doing and began singing and dancing a huge welcome. The young man bid them farewell. "You will be well taken care of here. Please enjoy our legendary African hospitality and learn all you can about our way of life. I will return tomorrow morning to tell you when you can meet the chief."

Molly and Robin thanked the man and took their things from Cyprien, who said, "Please do not worry about anything. You are in good and safe hands here. I will be staying with another family. If you need me, send someone for me. I go now." Actually, Cyprien was very happy, as circumstances had played into his hands. He could now see that he would be earning extra money because of Molly and Robin's need to stay longer in the village than they had planned.

Several women took the small plastic bags with Molly's and Robin's things and escorted them across the busy compound grounds to a newly made circular, thatched-roof, spacious mud-brick room. They opened the door and pulled a thin curtain aside to reveal a pleasantly adorned room with a glossy cement floor. They opened two windows to allow more light and air into the room. Molly and Robin were pleased to see that the windows were covered by screens and the beds were equipped with mosquito nets. There were two nicely made-up twin beds, and the walls were decorated with various African curios. In the middle of the floor was a circular goat-leather rug that had been topped with patched, hairy cowhide that had been sewn tightly together. The room had an aseptic smell, as it had been recently swept with a dousing of lemongrass water.

Molly and Robin were quite content, as their room was much nicer than they had expected. Molly did not say a word, but she was happy to see there were twin beds and not one double bed as in the hotel in Melomti. She certainly was not in the mood for any more intimacy with Robin. Right now her mind was focused on getting their business done in Ataku and heading back to Kansas as quickly as possible. She was surprised that she was quickly getting her fill of Africa and its lack of modern conveniences and amenities.

Robin expressed their appreciation for the room by saying, "This is indeed a very nice and clean room. We thank you for this. Can you also please show us the toilet and where we can bathe?"

A couple of women quickly said, "Follow us." They walked together to a place well behind their room to find a shower stall and an adjoining stall with a covered squat latrine hole. Molly and Robin were happy that both stalls looked clean and did not smell. They were also made happy by seeing a roll of toilet paper stuck on a peg in the latrine stall. Robin again thanked the women.

One woman said, "Just before dark, we will place two galvanized buckets of water with calabashes and local soap in front of your shower stall. We will also light two kerosene lamps and set them inside the door of your room. When we see that you have finished your baths, we will bring your food and place it on a small table located just outside your room. We wish you a pleasant stay with us, and please do not hesitate to call on us if you need anything."

Molly and Robin thanked the women and returned to their room. It was late in the afternoon, and nightfall was rapidly approaching. Molly wanted to talk to Robin about what they would say when they met the chief. She sat on the edge of her bed and asked Robin to sit on his bed, which was located about six feet away. She began by saying, "Robin, I'm not feeling well. We need to get our business done here and go on our way back to Kansas as quickly as possible. Tomorrow, we will get right to the point when we see the chief, asking him bluntly if he or anyone else in his village knew anyone named David Peterson. OK?"

Robin could see that Molly was stressed, and he wanted to do all he could to make her feel comfortable. He nodded his head in the affirmative and softly said, "I agree fully with you, Molly. I'm missing the States, and I'm more than ready to go home."

Robin's gentle and agreeable words made Molly feel better. She was telling herself that Robin was really a darling, so kind and supportive, and worth loving. She then told Robin, "Thank you for hanging in there with me. I now want to undress and wrap a cloth around me, as I want to take my calabash bath. Can you please turn around while I change?"

Robin dutifully turned around, and Molly continued to speak while she undressed. "Robin, I think I will hang up my clothes to air out and wear the same clothes tomorrow. What do you think?"

"Sounds good to me. For sure, they are not dirty. I also see here that some people can wear the same clothes for several days. I will do the same."

Molly finished taking her clothes off and hanging them on the upright sticks that held up the mosquito net fastened above their beds. She wrapped tightly an African cloth around her naked body, just above her breasts. In a more happy tone, she said, "All done. It is now your turn."

Robin undressed and also hung up his clothes to air out. He took from one of his plastic bags an African cloth and wrapped it around his waist. He too was now ready to take a bath. They both sat down on their beds and looked at each other for a few moments, then Molly said, "I'm feeling tired. I think I will lie down until they bring the buckets of water for us to bathe."

Molly laid her head on the very hard, tightly stuffed kapok pillow. Without a word, Robin did the same. With a whistling noise, Molly exhaled strongly outward, saying, "Wow. What a day!" She then quickly drifted off into a light sleep. Robin felt like doing the same, but he felt that he needed to stay awake to guard Molly and let her know when the water for the baths had been delivered. It was a tough battle for him to stay awake, but he was determined to do so.

When the last rays of the day's sunlight were about gone, Robin heard a clapping of hands at the doorway to their room. He rose rapidly from his bed and walked in his bare feet to see who was clapping. He did not want Molly to be woken up. He pulled back the curtain to see a smiling woman say with a giggle, "Dear sir, your water buckets are ready for your bath."

Robin did not think this was a good moment to disturb Molly, so he decided he would take his bath first. He held tight his cloth around himself, grabbed the towel that was lying neatly folded at the foot of his bed, and tippy-toed out of the room, holding his rubber thongs in one hand. He found the two buckets of water at the entrance of the shower stall. He picked up one and placed it in the stall. He stepped inside the stall, took off his cloth, and draped it over the narrow entrance to the stall. He was happy to note that the water was warm, as the women had set the buckets on the dying embers of a cooking fire. He took the calabash floating on top of the water and began pouring water over his body. He then took the round ball of local soap made from cacao pod ashes and palm oil and thoroughly washed his hair and body. He then used almost all the remaining water to rinse the soap off his body. Before leaving the stall, he urinated, trying to aim at the small drain hole leading outside the back interior wall of the stall. He finished up by pouring the little remaining water along the area on the stall floor where he had peed.

The bath was invigorating. He felt good as he dried his body off and walked back to their room. He returned to his room to find Molly sitting on the edge of her bed with a pained expression on her face. Molly looked at the dripping-wet Robin and with a dour tone said, "Robin, I don't feel well. How was your bath?"

Robin happily replied, "The bath was great. It made me feel much better. I'm sure you will feel better too after you take your bath."

Molly slowly rose, picked up her towel, slipped on her rubber thongs, and headed toward the bath stall to repeat what Robin had just done. Robin held the curtain back to ease her exit. She adjusted her cloth wrapping to make sure it stayed in place as she ambled toward the bath stall. She entered the stall, and after a short time, Robin could hear faintly water splashing on the hard concrete floor of the bath stall. He assumed Molly was enjoying the same bathing experience that he had a few minutes earlier. He combed his hair and hung his towel over a wooden chair so that it could dry. He was going to lie down while he waited for Molly, but as he sat down on the bed, he heard her screaming for him to come. Robin grasped his body cloth and ran out the door to the nearby shower stall. He found Molly still calling him to come when he arrived. He quickly shouted, "Molly, what is it? I'm here."

"Robin, sorry to bother you and act so crazy, but my time of the month has come early. I don't have any sanitary napkins. The ones I brought with me were in my lost suitcase. I cannot come out of here until I have some pads. Maybe you can find some at Chez André's."

Molly's unusual demand put Robin in an unprecedented position. He had never before bought sanitary napkins, and it was the last thing he had thought he would have to do in Africa. Molly had placed him in an awkward position, but he had no choice but to try to help her. As nonchalantly as he could, he said, "Molly, I understand. Try not to worry. I will go now to search for pads."

Robin did not want to go himself to buy pads, so he approached one of the women in the compound to do it for him. He had a difficult time communicating to the woman that his "wife" was on her period and needed pads. He had to use some unsightly gestures before the woman finally understood what he wanted. She told him to wait. She talked with some other women in the compound, and one of them entered her room and came out with some red rags. She stuffed them into a flimsy plastic bag and handed them to the woman whom he had talked to in the first place. He was ready to receive the bag from the woman, but she said, "A man should not involve himself in such women's business. I will take this bag to your wife."

The woman walked past Robin and headed at a quick pace to the shower stall. As Robin was walking toward their room, he saw the woman walking back. He entered the room thinking that was the end of this dramatic and unanticipated event. But then he heard Molly calling for him to come again. He rushed to the shower stall, and he could hear Molly bawling as if her life had come to an end. She heard Robin arrive and yelled at him. "I said get some pads, not these red rags that have not been used in our country for a century. What am I supposed to do with these rags? Robin, this is serious. I need help now!"

Robin was quite concerned, as it seemed that this incident was like the straw that broke the camel's back and Molly was falling emotionally apart. He was very worried about her mental state and felt challenged as to what to do. He whispered in a soothing voice to Molly, saying, "I know this is very difficult for you, but they don't use the modern pads that you are accustomed to using. It is these red rags that they use here. I don't know what to do. Please try to use the red rags."

Molly was outraged, but after complaining loudly and cursing the gods that had brought her to Africa, she tried to restrain herself, saying, "In that case, Robin, go fetch my panties and bring them to me."

Robin did as instructed and returned with Molly's panties. He never thought he would be standing outside a shower stall in the middle of Africa handing Molly her panties. He called out to her, saying, "Here are your panties." She snatched the panties as soon as Robin stuck them to one side of the cloth hanging over the shower stall entrance.

Molly growled, "Thanks. Now, go away and leave me alone."

Robin returned to their room in a strange mood. He swore to himself that he would never understand women. He also thanked God that he was not a woman and would never have to suffer what Molly was undergoing. He sat on the edge of his bed as he waited for her. It became dark outside, and it had been a long time since he had left Molly in the bath stall. He was thinking he should take one of the kerosene lamps and go see if she was OK and lead her back to their room. Just as he was about to get up and go back to the stall, Molly came marching into the room in a testy mood. She took one look at Robin and said, "Sit where you are, and don't make a move or say a word."

Robin was worried. He had never seen Molly in such a fit. He did not know what to do except what she just told him to do. He tried to be calm and act as if everything were normal between them. He certainly did not want to do anything that would make her become even more contrary. He sat as quietly and as still as possible. After a few minutes of playing almost dead, Molly shouted at him, "Robin, what is wrong with you? Aren't you going to eat with me? Our dinner was served some time ago and is waiting for us just outside our doorway."

Molly's words helped Robin's spirits perk up, and he simply replied, "Let's eat."

They exited their room to find a miniature low table piled high with an assortment of tin plates. They sat down and placed a kerosene lamp near the plates on the only empty space left on the table. Molly pried off the one pale-green, bowl-like tin plate that had been superimposed on another plate and found some huge slices of something resembling an oversized potato. She uncovered another bowl and found the same kind of orange sauce they had burned their mouths with at the roadside food stall where they had eaten lunch. That was it. That was their first dinner in the village. They were happy to see two bottles of mineral water placed at the side of the table.

They grabbed their forks and began to taste small pieces of the boiled tuber slices. Their first bites of this starchy food were not bad, so they took larger bites. They found that what they were eating was a bit dry, forcing them to drink water after every bite. Robin volunteered to see if the sauce was as peppery as the one they had tasted at lunch. To his pleasant surprise, he found it was not spicy at all and began to dip his bite-size chunks into the sauce before eating them. He encouraged Molly to do the same. Oddly, they found this a pleasant, tasty food for hungry stomachs. They did not know that what they were eating were boiled slices of the indigenous yam tuber and that Cyprien had told the women to take the unheard-of measure of not putting hot peppers in their sauce.

With some food in her stomach, Molly was feeling a little better, and this prompted her to give Robin one of her sweet smiles and say calmly, "Robin, I'm sorry for the way I behaved. You must know one thing about me. I hate having my periods, and when I do have them, I'm not the easiest person to get along with."

Robin nodded and said, "Molly, I know. My older sister was the same way. When she was on her periods, I gave her a wide berth. I guess I can't do that to you now. Anyway, all is well, and I find our sitting here under the starlit sky with the flickering of a kerosene lamp almost romantic."

Molly managed a slight laugh, saying, "I imagine you can find anything romantic as long as it suits your purposes. I'm certainly in no condition for any romance tonight. And how can I have any romantic notions with all those insects attracted by the light of the lamp? There are bugs everywhere!"

They ate their fill, picked up their plastic water bottles, and returned to their room to fetch their toothpaste and toothbrushes. They stood outside on opposite sides of the entrance brushing their teeth with one hand and rinsing their mouths with water from the bottles they held in their other hand. They spit their mouth rinse out as far as they could on the empty ground near their room's foundation. Once their teeth-brushing ritual was over, Robin closed the door and locked it. They returned to their beds and wished each other a very good night and the sweetest of dreams. They were both exhausted and fell into a deep sleep shortly after lying comfortably on their beds. Not even the geckos scurrying over the walls or the mice scampering above the ceiling boards could disturb their sleep.

It seemed like a shorter night than usual. It was as if they had only been in bed a couple hours when the total silence of the night was broken by the nonstop crowing of a band of roosters that were located at various places across the village. Shortly after the roosters began their unending chorus, a sweeping sound invaded their ears as the women began to clean the compound from one end to another. While the sweeping continued, other women began making clanging noises as they assembled and washed all the tin plates used the day before. Robin covered his head with a pillow and tried to ignore all these sounds. Molly simply ignored the sounds. They both were telling themselves that it was too early to get up and they needed more sleep.

A little while later, they heard a sound they could not ignore. Someone was loudly clapping their hands in front of their door. Reluctantly, Robin got up to see who it was and why they were trying to get their attention. He opened the door slowly and spied in the early dawn's light one of the women. The woman said in an urgent tone, "You must get up now and eat your breakfast. The chief sent a message that he will meet you in one hour."

Robin did not need to awaken Molly, as when she heard the woman's words, she sprung out of bed and began preparing herself for what she and Robin had traveled over ten thousand miles to do. This was the day they would at long last find out what had happened to David Peterson from Kansas. Nothing could stop them now. They were certain that the truth they sought was just a short distance up the mountainside in the chief's compound. Their excitement rose to new heights. They were proud of themselves for having come this far to find the answers they needed about David Peterson from Kansas.

CHAPTER TWENTY-ONE
SON OF DAVID

Chief Gyasi arrived in the royal compound early in the morning to talk with Letivi. He was eager to hear the latest news about Letivi's mother—his daughter. He found Letivi sitting semi-naked on a small stool in front of his sleeping room. Delalia was tenderly washing his wounds again and applying the potent healing cream to each cut and bruise. Gyasi was alarmed to see his grandson in such a pitiful physical state. For him, Letivi looked as if he had been in a fight with a ferocious wild animal. It was painful for him to see Letivi suffering from so many cuts and scratches. His sympathy and curiosity about what had happened forced him to cry out, "In the name of all the gods and grandfathers, my dear Letivi, what happened to you?"

Letivi slowly raised his head so that his eyes met Gyasi's and said quietly, "Chef Gyasi, welcome. I am glad you have come. We need to talk, but first, allow Delalia to finish treating me."

Delalia brought a chair for Gyasi to sit down next to Letivi and then withdrew silently to complete her tender care of Letivi. When she had finished working on Letivi, she helped him put on a chief's gown that he wore only when receiving special visitors. Seeing Letivi put on this gown informed Gyasi that he would be seeing this morning the white couple who had requested the day before an audience with him. In a soft and obedient voice, Delalia excused herself in the customary manner of bowing her head, signifying high respect to royal authority.

After Delalia disappeared into the adjacent part of his multi-compound royal residence and was out of earshot, Letivi invited his grandfather to sit in more comfortable chairs located under the large neem tree that dominated the center of his private compound. Once they were seated, they allowed a short interval of time to pass so they could both adjust their moods to deal with the seriousness of the moment. Letivi spoke first. In a voice weaker than usual, he said, "Grandfather, do not worry about me. I am hurting physically and mentally, but I will recover and be all right. My wounds were caused by many scrapes in the bush that I endured when walking home in the very dark night. The dire conditions at my mother's place did not allow me to spend the night there."

It was difficult for Gyasi to believe that Letivi had taken the high risk of walking through the woods during a moonless night. He knew that undertaking such a risky walk did indeed indicate a catastrophic situation. He hesitated before asking about the welfare of his daughter, Letivi's mother, Atibona, formerly known as Celestine. He cleared his throat and with teary eyes looked directly at Letivi and dryly asked, "And what about my daughter?"

Letivi was debating within himself how much he should tell Gyasi. He knew it was best that he not describe in detail what he had observed, but he also knew he had to say something and say it well. After taking a deep breath, he exhaled and looked intently at his grandfather before saying in a serious, sympathetic tone, "My dear grandfather and cochief, I am deeply distressed by all that I saw. I would like to describe what I saw, but I believe what I observed was for my eyes only. All I can tell you now is that your daughter and her domain are no longer part of this world. They are gone from this Earth forever."

Although Gyasi had been expecting to hear this bad news, hearing his worst fears confirmed made him sick to his stomach, and he felt he needed to be alone.

Seeing how affected his grandfather was, Letivi reached over and put his hand on top of his grandfather's, saying, "Grandfather, please. We need to stay strong for our people. This is a very harsh blow for both of us, but we must not allow it to cause us to fail our people."

Gyasi nodded slowly and wiped the tears from his eyes as he said, "This is difficult for me, but it will be much more difficult for my wife. It will be very hard for me to break the news to her, but I must do so quickly before she goes again to see our daughter. We both knew this moment was coming, but now that it has come, we cannot help but be deeply affected."

"Yes, Grandfather, these are terrible times for us," rejoined Letivi. "I feel that key pillars of my world are dying at almost the same time. It is impossible for me to accept that the thousand-year reign of the ancient baobab is over at the same time as the demise of my mother's holy, centuries-old domain. Nothing can replace them. I ask myself why this is happening while I am chief and whether my being chief has anything to do with it. All I am left with now is the moon. I know the moon is forever, but is the moon enough for me to be all I can be for our village?"

Gyasi was touched to his very core by Letivi's words. He did not know what to say. He was also afraid that these events could hasten his own death. He knew his departure to the other world would leave Letivi very alone, making it almost impossible for him to cope with all the challenges facing him. The only words he could muster in response to Letivi's sorrowful laments were, "My son, you must make it so the moon is enough for you to lead our village to greater prosperity and happiness."

They sat quietly for a long time, allowing their thoughts to dwell on the new world landscape that now confronted them. They could have continued in this trancelike situation for a much longer time, but they were disturbed by loud clapping by one of Letivi's guards. The guard clapped many times more than normal before Letivi was able to acknowledge his presence by saying, "Come. I am here."

The guard approached within a few feet of Letivi and Gyasi and barked out, "Chief, I have come with the two white people you said you could see now. They are sitting in the outer waiting room."

Letivi thanked the guard and dismissed him by saying, "Tell them I will be able to receive them in about thirty minutes. After you see me entering the main meeting room, bring them to me."

Letivi then turned to Gyasi and said, "Before my mother left, she told me that the original name of my father was David Peterson. Now these two white people are coming from America in search of David Peterson. What do I tell them?"

Gyasi lost no time in saying, "I have always known that your father's American name was David Peterson because that is what your mother told us to put on the birth certificate we used to enroll you in school in Melomti. For sure, you cannot tell these foreigners what really happened to David. All you know is that he went away before you were born. We cannot tell outsiders any of our secrets about Bobovovi, who was born as David

Peterson in America. They must not even know that I am your grandfather. If you tell them you are the son of David, they must keep that a secret because the village knows you as the son of Chief Yofu."

It was easy for Letivi and Gyasi to see that talking with these two young Americans would be a complex task fraught with many potential pitfalls. They wanted very much to see people who came from David's country, but they were afraid that see-ing them could open up a can of worms best left closed. In any event, they had no choice but to receive them and handle as best as they could this much-unexpected encounter. Letivi rose from his chair, and Gyasi followed him to the meeting room.

The guard saw the chiefs enter the meeting room, and, as instructed by Letivi, he led a very nervous Molly and Robin to meet the chiefs. The first thing Gyasi noted when they entered the meeting room was that they violated tradition by not remov-ing their shoes. Letivi was not able to notice anything because of the transfixing effect Molly's appearance and her every move had on him. He had never seen a white woman up close before, and there was something about Molly that sent gentle shock waves rolling back and forth through his body. The effect Molly was having on Letivi made him struggle to come up with the words to welcome his American visitors.

Molly and Robin took their seats, which were located less than six feet directly in front of the chiefs. They saw before them an old African man and a young man with a light complexion that made him appear almost white. They believed they could safely assume the young man was the White Chief they sought. While they were very ill at ease, they were in a hurry to say their piece and see what this would produce in terms of answers about the disappearance of David Peterson.

Letivi forced himself to settle down and follow protocol by saying, "We welcome you to our village. We appreciate that you have come a very long way to see us. How can we help you?"

The melodic manner Letivi spoke his words threw Molly off her prepared script. She was confounded by the strong connection she felt with him. It took Molly a moment to regain her composure and say, "Thank you for receiving us. My name is Molly Peterson, and next to me is Robin Fletcher. We both come from small towns in Kansas in America, and we have been researching a David Peterson who mysteriously disappeared many years ago from another small town in Kansas. Our research tells us that years ago, David was a Peace Corps volunteer in your village. We have come here to find out what you can tell us about David."

Letivi almost did not hear what Molly said. He was captivated by her every gesture and was busy examining every inch of her body with his furtive, unmoving eyes. He had never seen a woman with such beautiful long hair and milky-white skin, and he had never seen anyone with blue eyes and red hair. And he was mesmerized by her thin lips, which moved in such a precise manner as she pronounced every word. He was surprised by the fluency of her speech. It was obvious to him that she had been to school.

Gyasi could see that Letivi was contemplating closely the presence of these two white strangers, so he took his turn to reply to Molly. "Yes, many years ago, we had in our village a Peace Corps volunteer named David. One day he disappeared and was never seen or heard from again. From that day almost nineteen years ago until now, we have never heard anything from him or about him."

Robin jumped in to say, "Is there no one in this village or in this country who can tell us what happened to David?"

Gyasi said, "No, there is no other person still alive who is in a better position than me to know anything about David. Many who knew David are now dead."

Molly continued, "Our research shows us that he was in this country. Then he came back to his hometown in Kansas and spent many years there before disappearing on the night of a full moon when some people reported a bright flash of dry lightning in the nighttime sky. He was known as JB at that time by all the people in his hometown of Gemini."

These words from Molly had Letivi and Gyasi looking at each other. For the first time, they were hearing that Bobovovi did go home to Kansas and that he must have left there on a moon-beam. They both knew that the old baobab had conspired with the moon goddess to have Bobo returned and buried within the interior of the baobab. But they could not reveal these secrets to anyone, let alone to white, foreign outsiders.

After a long pause, Letivi pulled himself together to say, "What you are saying is very interesting to us. This is the first time we are learning that the man we called Bobovovi did return to his home in America."

When Letivi spoke, something occurred to Molly that caused her to look directly at Letivi and ask in an almost rude tone, "What is your full name?"

Letivi was put in an uncomfortable position. He felt that Molly had some sort of psychic power over him and he was obliged to respond with only the truth to her question. Letivi meekly replied at some length, "My name is Letivi, which means I am a moon-child, as I was born under a full moon. I am told that my birth certificate states that my father's name was David Peterson, but I always thought that was done at the time because my mother liked this name. I have never known any David Peterson. My father disappeared before I was born, and my mother recently passed away. Officially, I am the son of Chief Yofu, my deceased predecessor. You must not say to anyone that my father is other than Chief Yofu."

Robin was confused and blurted out, "But who was Bobovovi? Was he also David Peterson? What does Bobovovi mean?"

Gyasi was not sure that Letivi should have said as much as he did. He now wanted to have more of a say in this sensitive conversation. He replied first to Robin. "Bobovovi means Tuesday's white child. This is the name we gave to David when we learned on the first day he was among us that he had been born on a Tuesday. It is only by that name that he is remembered. But please, never say that name because we believe Bobovovi is dead, and we never say the names of the dead."

Molly's feminine intuition was percolating within her, taking her way off her planned script. She looked hard at Letivi again and let the words boiling up within her fly out of her mouth. "Chief Letivi. Sorry. I can't help but note that you look like a Peterson. And, if you are, we may be related, as I'm a Peterson from my father's side. Are you sure you are not the son of David Peterson?"

Letivi did not know what to say. He thought that maybe the strong connection he felt with Molly was because they were indeed related by blood. Before responding to her, he needed to consult with Gyasi. He therefore said, "Madame, you are asking very difficult questions of me. Before I reply, I need to consult with my cochief Gyasi. Can you please step outside for a few minutes so we can talk in private? Thank you for your understanding."

Molly and Robin did as requested and quickly stepped outside. Letivi looked at Gyasi and said, "I think what she says is true. I feel deeply that we are connected by my father's blood. I do not see any other option but to admit that I am the son of David Peterson and a local woman."

Gyasi thought for a few minutes before replying, "I agree. I think it best that you say you are David's son. No use lying to these people about that."

While Letivi and Gyasi were talking, Molly was trying to convince Robin that she was sure that Letivi was David's son. She said emphatically to Robin, "Deep in my bones, I know Letivi is a Peterson. Nothing will make me think any differently!"

Letivi asked for Molly and Robin to return to their seats. Letivi looked at Molly and said in a soft, almost inaudible voice, "I share this truth for your ears only. My biological father was a white man from America. I was told by my mother, a local woman, just before she died, that his name was David Peterson."

Molly almost jumped for joy as she said in a loud voice, "I knew it!"

Robin smiled widely and said, "Chief Letivi, it is my pleasure to welcome you to the Peterson family."

This was a joyous moment for Molly and Robin. They had not discovered what had happened to David, but they had found his son, and for them, that was better than what they had originally sought. The main question now was what to do next. Did they just say their good-byes after taking a few photos with Letivi and leave it at that? Or was there more they should do?

Molly surprised everyone by abruptly standing up and saying, "As one Peterson to another, I feel obliged to invite Letivi to visit his many relatives and the birthplace of his father in Kansas. You must come to Kansas so you can see your people there, and they can see a Peterson from Africa. Don't worry about any of the travel expenses. I will cover all your costs. What do you say to that?"

Everyone in the room, including Robin, was astounded by Molly's invitation. The room became silent, as Letivi and Gyasi did not know how to respond to the unexpected invitation. Letivi broke the silence again by politely saying, "I thank you for your very generous invitation. This is a very big matter for us to consider. Since becoming chief over a year ago, I have rarely left our village, and I have never traveled outside our country. I will need time to discuss this matter with others. Perhaps we can take a break, and you can come back in the afternoon for our reply."

Robin moaned because doing as Letivi requested would require that they stay another night in the village. Molly was overjoyed with Letivi's response and said, "No problem. That's fully understandable. We'll be waiting for you to call us back. I'm thrilled about the prospect of Letivi coming to Kansas with us."

Molly stood up and shook Gyasi's hand. She also extended her hand to Letivi, who reluctantly lifted his hand to clasp Molly's. Letivi was afraid of touching a white woman who seemed to have unusual powers over him. When his hand did meet hers, it was as if electricity were generated by their touching. He had never experienced anything like this in his life. This brief touch made him forget all his woes and revived him from his state of depression. Earlier in the day, he had been feeling lost and bewildered. Now, he was feeling revitalized and full of hope. He did not want to lose that feeling.

After Molly and Robin had exited, Gyasi said to Letivi in no uncertain words, "My son, it would be a great honor for you and bring great prestige to our village if you travel to America. No chief in our village has ever traveled to another country. This opportunity to travel to one of the most powerful countries in the world should be accepted without hesitation."

Letivi was happy to hear the support expressed by his grandfather for his travel to America. He quickly replied with a renewed spark in his voice, "I am glad to hear you support a favorable reply to this invitation. I agree that this is not an opportunity I should miss. My main concern is that the president must approve my absence."

Gyasi interjected, "I am sure the president will feel about this just as I do. Call him now to ask for his blessing to travel to America for two weeks. Tell him that I will be here to act in your place."

Letivi did not like calling the president, especially as he had told him not to call him unless it was a dire emergency. Nonetheless, he took his mobile phone in hand and swallowed hard as he punched in the president's number. The phone rang only once before Letivi heard the gruff voice of the president. "Letivi, what do you want? Hurry, I am very busy."

Letivi quickly replied in as few words as possible to communicate what he wanted to say. "Mr. President, I have been invited to visit America for two weeks, and I need you to approve my travel."

The president surprised Letivi by responding in an unusually ebullient, wordy mood. "That's great news. You should go. I know you will make our country proud. It is good that you go to the country that will be helping us construct a cacao-processing plant in your village. Maybe you can visit USAID donor officials while you are in America and find new investors for our country. That would be wonderful. I will use photos we have of you to arrange for you to get an official government passport and obtain your visa from the US embassy. All should be ready within a few days. When do you plan to depart?"

Letivi replied, "Thank you, Mr. President. We depart in three days."

"OK. Leave the order before you go to cut down and clear away all the brush at the site where the cacao-processing plant will be built so the surveyors can do their job easily. Have a good trip. Call me as soon as you return."

Letivi quickly said before the president hung up, "Thank you, Mr. President. While I am away, Chief Gyasi will have the mobile phone, and he will be in charge."

The phone went dead, and Letivi told Gyasi, "The president fully supports my travel to America. Now, I guess all that remains is to gain the approval of the elders and clan heads."

Gyasi quickly contradicted Letivi. "We do not need to consult the senior council. All you have to do is to inform them of your travel plans. I know in advance that they will be delighted to learn you are having the good fortune to travel to America. I anticipate much rejoicing in the village when this good news is announced."

Letivi did not hesitate to say, "Therefore, we must hold a council meeting this afternoon with our two visitors present to attest to their invitation to me. We should call back our visitors now so I can accept their invitation and have them stay here until senior council members arrive for our meeting."

Letivi immediately summoned one of his guards and told him, "Have the two white people return, and instruct the town criers to inform the elders and clan heads to come to a meeting in a couple of hours."

The guard rushed away. Letivi and Gyasi began discussing all that Letivi would have to do to get ready to take his first plane ride to America. Letivi was both scared and excited about his trip. Thinking of his trip made him almost forget all the important losses he had recently experienced in his life. He wanted to leave as soon as possible. His only remaining worry was how Delalia would accept his absence. He also knew he needed to say good-bye to the remains of the old baobab and make sure the treasure buried below it was undisturbed.

Molly and Robin arrived out of breath. They had no sooner gone down the mountainside to their quarters than they were told to return uphill to the chief's compound. They entered the meeting room and took their places again in front of Letivi and Gyasi. Letivi lost no time in announcing, "We have completed our consultations, and I am happy to inform you that I am able to accept your invitation to accompany you to America."

Molly clapped her hands in joyous appreciation and said, "You will not regret your decision. You will have the best of times in Kansas."

Letivi asked, "Please let me finish. You need to know that I can only be away for two weeks. Also, I can travel only on the condition you do not tell anyone in this country that I am the son of David Peterson. I must have your word on this."

Molly immediately said, "Of course. You can count on me and Robin to do as you ask. All we want is for you to have the opportunity to see where your father came from."

Shortly after Molly finished talking, voices could be heard outside the meeting room. Senior village leaders were gathering in response to the chief's summons. Gyasi got up to go outside and see if enough men had arrived to commence their meeting. While he was outside, Molly told Letivi they needed to talk over all the travel arrangements with him. She also told him they needed to return to Melomti as quickly as possible in the taxi they had rented so they could obtain his ticket and anything else he needed to travel. Letivi told her his passport and US visa would be arranged by his government and should be available in a few days. He was careful not to mention the link he had with the president.

Gyasi returned to the meeting room, followed by the barefoot elders and clan heads, who sat on the floor. Molly and Robin were asked to move their chairs to one side. When almost thirty men were seated and impatiently waiting to hear why their chief would summon them on such short notice, Letivi tapped his wooden staff five times on the hard floor pavement. Upon hearing this sound, the group fell silent, and Letivi said, "Thank you for coming so quickly. I have some good news. I will be traveling to America for two weeks."

Everyone immediately clapped and cheered, thanking the gods and grandfathers for such good fortune. Molly and Robin were amazed and pleased at the joyous reaction of the group to this news. Letivi held his staff up in front of him, and the group became quiet again. Letivi continued by saying, "I present to you Molly and Robin from Kansas in America. It is thanks to their invitation that I'm able to travel to America."

Upon hearing about Molly and Robin's role in making it possible for their chief to visit America, all the men rose, and, one by one, they filed in front of Molly and Robin to shake their hands and thank them for inviting their chief to America. Molly and Robin were surprised to see that their travel invitation was such a big deal in the village. Letivi indicated again that he had more to say, and the group became quiet. "I also want to note that the president is aware of my visit, and he supports it fully."

Again, there were loud cheers. Letivi called for quiet one more time to say, "Of course, while I am gone, Chief Gyasi will act in my place. I know he has some news about our cacao-processing plant to provide you in the days to come. I plan to leave the day after tomorrow with Molly and Robin. I hope this news is received well by everyone in the village."

There were more loud cheers and praise songs as the men rushed out of the meeting room to spread the good news throughout the village. The chiefs knew that this news would be the cause of much celebrating all night long in the village. Gyasi told Molly and Robin, "A guard will escort you back to your quarters. I need some time alone now to talk to Letivi. Please come back tomorrow morning so we can discuss the details of your travel plans. Letivi will be ready to go early in the day after tomorrow."

Molly and Robin thanked Letivi and Gyasi and headed on their way back down the mountain to the room they had stayed in the night before. They also needed time alone to discuss all the ramifications of Molly's insistence on taking Letivi to Kansas. Robin did not think that bringing Letivi to Kansas was a good idea. Molly thought it was a great idea, but she could provide little in the way of substance to support her idea. Her intuition told her that it was the right thing to do. She also thought Letivi might tell them more about David after they got to know each other better when he was far from the village. Never had the futures of so many depended on the whims of one very determined woman.

CHAPTER TWENTY-TWO
LAST DAY IN ATAKU

Everyone in the village was happy about Letivi's travel to America except Delalia. She wanted her husband close to her and the baby growing in her stomach. She feared he would be attracted to the more sophisticated women he would meet on his trip. Already she had heard that the American woman who had come to Ataku was very pretty. She did not like the idea of Letivi spending so much time physically close to her. She could not help but be jealous of this woman and all the others Letivi would meet during his time away from her. She was also concerned that Letivi's health would suffer if she were not at his side to care for him. Above all, she was peeved because Letivi had made this decision to go to America without consulting her.

Letivi's thoughts dwelled on everything except on Delalia's cares and worries. He did not know it, but he was being very traditional in the way he was behaving with her. Without saying so, he took her for granted and expected her to agree with everything he did. For him, Delalia would always be there when he needed her. There was no doubt in his mind that he could always count on her steadfast support. Nobody else saw anything amiss with Letivi's behavior, as it was normal that a wife existed to serve the man and give him children. Delalia knew she could not complain and that she had to conform to her role as a good village wife. She could not do otherwise, since she had been molded her entire life into this role by an unrelenting socialization process that put a woman in her place and kept her there. There was no good escape from this gender trap—a trap of which only a few, if any, were conscious.

All this was fine with Delalia as long as her man was near her. Seeing him travel across the world to an unknown land in the company of another female was something for which her upbringing had not prepared her. She waited for an occasion to have a serious talk with Letivi about her concerns, but Letivi was immersed in the details of his trip, making it difficult for her to have a quiet moment with him. He was running around as if he were in a daze, doing all he believed he needed to do before traveling. He would find out later that all he was doing to prepare for his trip actually had no relation to what actually had to be done to travel to America.

For Letivi, the main things he needed to do was say farewell to the elders and clan chiefs, request the ancestors to bless his trip, visit the old baobab tree, and have a conversation with Gyasi to make sure they agreed on all outstanding business and actions to be taken during his absence. Thoughts about obtaining a suitcase and what to pack in it would be considered only at the last minute when he realized he could not travel empty handed for two weeks to faraway America. Again, he knew he could count on the help of the faithful Delalia.

On his next-to-last night in the village, Letivi barely slept. Delalia was desperate to talk with him, but she could see that his agitated state made it a bad time for conversation. As Delalia lay beside him, Letivi knew he should say something to her, but he did not know what to say, and, even if he did, he was not in the mood to do so. Delalia, like everyone else in the village, knew he was going to America with the two white foreigners, so what else was there to say to her? Moreover, he would only be gone for two weeks, so it really was not a long absence.

While Delalia was dying for some affection, Letivi tossed and turned all night long as he turned over in his head all the facets of his travel to America. He was possessed by the excitement of it all. All his personal problems and challenges faded into the background as he focused on going to the land of his father. He rose upon hearing the first crowing of the nearest rooster and abruptly told Delalia he would be away part of the day. Delalia quickly hustled about to bring him a bucket of bathwater and some cassava flour mixed with peanuts, sugar, and water to munch on. She knew better than to ask him where he was going, but she could see that it had to be important; otherwise, Letivi would not have risen so early.

The only words Letivi said to Delalia were, "I'm going. Tell Gyasi that I will return late in the morning to talk with village council members."

As the first rays of the sun were creeping over Mount Ataku's almost treeless summit, Letivi took off at a brisk pace to follow paths that would take him to the distant land of the ancient baobab. When he arrived at this place about ninety minutes later, full daylight illuminated a sad scene. The old baobab had been reduced to a massive trunk shorn of its branches. People had ceased giving offerings to this baobab since they had moved to worshiping the next-oldest baobab, located a good distance away. The mighty trunk, which rose over thirty feet into the air and measured almost ninety feet in circumference, stood as a testament to the great baobab that had reigned here for a millennium.

Letivi placed his hands on the huge stump to say his last prayers to the old baobab and ask for its blessing of his trip. He also said some words to his father, whose remains he had placed over a year ago inside the old baobab. He wanted his father to know that he was going to visit his home in America. He repeated his words many times in all the tree languages he knew, but he felt no response of any kind. He was deeply saddened to find the old tree dying and not to see any evidence of its past glory and the grandeur of this sacred place.

One undeniable fact known only to Letivi was the golden stool that remained buried below the decaying baobab. One central purpose of his visit to the old baobab was to ensure that the hiding place of the golden stool remained undisturbed. It was a heavy burden for him to keep this secret, but he knew that the secret must be kept if peace and stability were to be maintained among his people. Releasing knowledge of the golden stool would be like casting a malediction upon the village and all he was striving to do for his village. Letivi believed the stool had been buried over a hundred years ago by wise chiefs to protect the village from the negative fallout that knowledge of it would generate. He felt he was duty bound to safeguard this secret until the ancestors told him otherwise.

Letivi embraced the stump of the old baobab while saying good-bye. It was a teary-eyed moment, but Letivi knew he needed to be strong and face the world as it was and not as it had once been. As he headed back to the village, he was thinking about how all the knowledge and contacts he would make in America would enable him to lead better his village to a higher level of development so it could play a greater role in the politics of his country. He could see that he must use his visit to America to enhance the development of his village and his country.

When he returned to his compound, he found Gyasi and village council members waiting for him. Although his dress was inappropriate and his feet and ankles were covered by dust from the paths he had followed, Letivi immediately took his seat in front of the group, saying, "Excuse me for my appearance. Thank you for coming. The purpose of this meeting is to bid you good-bye again and to seek any advice you may have to offer for my trip to America."

The elders and clan heads could see that Letivi had been out walking along dusty paths. They wanted to know what he had been doing, but it would be improper for them to ask a chief such a question. They knew chiefs had to do things that were known only to them and had to be kept secret. The violation of such secrets could upset the ancestors and result in undesirable consequences. These traditional customs and attitudes made it easier for Letivi to keep his secrets.

The oldest elder stood up with the support of his much-worn, simple wood staff. In a crackling old voice, he said, "Chief, we have discussed in much detail among ourselves your marvelous trip to America. We support fully this important journey. All we ask is for you to go and return safely. We look eagerly forward to all you will have to tell us about your travels when you return."

Letivi thanked this man for his words and the support of all present for his trip. At that point, another man, a respected fetish priest, stood straight and tall to say, "We ask that you bring back with you two things for each clan fetish sanctuary. These two things are a pebble and a vial of water from a river in America. If you can, it would also be good to bring tiny amounts of earth from each place you visit. In this way, we may be able to enjoy some of the natural spiritual powers that exist in America."

Letivi quickly understood this last request, saying, "I will make it my duty to do as you request. I will be taking daily notes of my trip, and when I return, we will spend much time together so I can relate to you all I saw and did in America."

It was with great excitement and anticipation that all the men stood and clapped loudly while singing their chief's praises. They were overjoyed with the good fortune of having a chief who was going to America. They were convinced that nothing but good could come from such an auspicious trip. They knew Letivi's safe return from America would elevate the prestige of their village to new heights and they would be envied by the entire country. It was indeed a time of rejoicing and praise making.

***

The ebullient atmosphere in the chief's compound did not affect Molly and Robin. They had a sound night's sleep and were lying in bed much later than usual. They were unsure of how to spend the day as they waited for Letivi to arrange his things so he could go to Melomti with them early the following morning. A loud clap at their doorway made Robin jump from his bed, wrapping his sheet around his hips so he could go see what the person wanted. He slowly opened the door to see a smiling Cyprien. "Good morning, sir. Your guide is waiting for you. What should I tell him?"

Robin did not have a clue about what Cyprien was saying and was about to tell him to go away when Molly interjected from her bed, "Oh. I forgot. Someone asked me yesterday if we would like to climb the mountain, and I said yes. Let's get ready to go."

Robin was in no mood to go mountain climbing, but he could not refuse Molly. He reluctantly told Cyprien, "Tell the guide to wait. We are coming. But we need to eat something first."

Cyprien quickly replied, "OK. I will tell him. He will also be carrying food and water."

Molly and Robin went through their usual morning routine. They decided to wear their dirty clothes for the two-hour hike up Mount Ataku. They also put on the shoes they had worn for the long trip to Kotoku. Molly was looking forward to having fun on their mountain climb. She thought this would be a great way to pass the time and discuss with Robin all the details related to their trip home. Robin only wanted to stay in bed and do as little as possible. His only interest was getting out of Kotoku and returning to Kansas. He had had quite enough already of Africa and its lack of basic amenities.

They ate their breakfast of locally made bread, jam, and Nescafé and headed toward the exit of their compound to join the man who would guide them up and down the mountain. They found the man standing just outside the compound doorway. The man said, "Hello. My name is Stanislas. I am your guide. Please do not worry about anything. I have taken many white people up and down the mountain. I have everything we need in my backpack, including a first-aid kit. Are you ready to go?"

Molly gleefully replied, "We are as ready as we will ever be. Let's go, Robin."

They began their journey to the summit by walking back along the same wide path that led up the slope of the mountain and passed in front of the chief's compound. People on either side of the road cheered them along, and they were followed by a passel of young children laughing and singing songs about the white visitors who were taking their chief to America. They passed the last dwelling in the village. Farther up the path, they came upon the old church that European missionaries had built almost one hundred years ago. They took a photo of the church while Stanislas briefly told them about its history.

After the church, they continued their climb along slippery paths that led indirectly to the top of the mountain. The land around them was covered with cacao plantations and natural forest. At places, the path was quite steep, and they had to place their hands on the ground to steady themselves so they could keep climbing. After an hour of nonstop hiking up the mountain, Molly and Robin were becoming very tired. Stanislas noted their weakening state and told them to rest a bit when they arrived at a wide spot in the path with boulders protruding from the surface, which made for comfortable seating.

They looked around to see some farmers who were working their steep fields by tying around themselves ropes that had been attached to sturdy trees. This was something they had never seen before. Their lack of knowledge of cacao also prompted Stanislas to describe cacao cultivation and show them a cacao pod cut from a nearby cacao tree. They had difficulty believing that the chocolate they had enjoyed all their lives came from such pods. They were shocked when Stanislas told them that he knew nothing about chocolate and had never tasted it. All he knew was that their cacao beans were shipped to Europe to make chocolate.

After their brief break, they trudged upward on a steepening slope to the top of the mountain. Stanislas exclaimed, "We have arrived. Now, that was not so bad. Welcome to the old village of Akokoji, where our ancestors first lived before they went down the mountain to create settlements on the plain below. Here you can see the stone fortifications that were built to protect the people from warring tribes and slavers. When attacked, they would roll large stones down on their enemies. As you can see, the village is built on a series of stone terraces so that some flatland could be created. Let's go greet the village chief."

They walked through the quaint village dwellings to the chief's unimposing residence. Stanislas explained, "Everything is built from mud bricks. The absence of sand on the mountaintop prevents making concrete. It is not easy to live here, as everything has to be hauled up the mountainside on the heads of women. Also, the nights are longer here. The clouds and mist that gather around the mountain at night do not dissipate until late in the morning. We think the people living on the mountain are healthier, as it is never hot, there are fewer mosquitoes, they get lots of exercise walking up and down the mountain, and a late sunrise allows them to sleep more."

The chief of Akokoji was standing on the threshold to his house, dressed in all his royal finery. He warmly said, "Welcome to my village. We are happy you have come. My name is Adolph. Please enter."

They walked into an elongated meeting room with wooden benches placed on either side and a low ceiling made of stiff straw reeds that had been tightly bound together with strips of rawhide. The chief's large and very elegant hand-carved iroko chair dominated the room at its far end. The shutters were open on either side of the room, and a cool breeze and soft light flowed agreeably through the room. The walls were covered with enlarged framed photographs of previous chiefs, various posters, and some old maps.

Chief Adolph asked everyone to take a seat and welcomed them again. There was another man in the room. The chief introduced him, saying, "This is our village historian. He will rapidly recount to you the village's history from the time of its founding until the present day."

As their eyes examined their unfamiliar surroundings, they listened politely to the thirty-minute oral presentation. They did find it interesting how the original inhabitants fled a wicked ruler in the east to take refuge on the mountain, where they ferociously defended themselves from all enemies for decades. It was only when the white man came that they began to enjoy peace. In particular, it was when the white missionaries came that they were encouraged to leave their mountaintop redoubt and become Christians. They were also enticed by the white man's schools and the education they offered.

When the historian finished talking, the chief asked Molly and Robin if they had any questions. Immediately, up flew Robin's hand. He said, "Thanks for that interesting presentation of the history of your village. One thing I'm curious about is the chief's name, Adolph. I have not seen anyone use that name since the days of Adolph Hitler in Germany about fifty years ago."

Chief Adolph laughed before saying, "I understand your point, but for us the name of Adolph has a different significance. I will explain. The first white man to visit our village, in the late 1800s, was a German named Adolph. He came with many gifts. Since that time, it was decided that all village chiefs would take the name of Adolph in honor of the visit of this impressive first white man. Therefore, I am Adolph IV."

Chief Adolph continued, "We still have a few items this first white man left us over one hundred years ago. You can see on the wall over there a map, which at that time was the latest German map of West Africa."

The chief got up and walked over to a pedestal covered by an old German imperial flag. "Here we have the flag he left, and under the flag is our most prized possession."

He lifted the flag to reveal a shiny bronze military helmet with a spike on top that had been worn by the Kaisers' imperial guard almost a century ago. Lying next to this antique helmet was an equally antique German army bugle. The chief commented, "On very special occasions, I will wear this *pickelhaube* and blow the bugle. But those occasions are rare, especially as we want to preserve these treasures. Many white people who have visited us have offered large sums of money for these items, but we refuse to part with them at any price."

Molly and Robin were very impressed by the history lesson and the artifacts from German times that had been so well preserved. Robin liked hearing this story about the first white outsider to arrive in this part of Africa, but he was also curious to hear and see more about the local people's history. He asked permission to speak and said, "Thank you. This is all very interesting, but what more can you tell us about your own civilization before the arrival of white people?"

Chief Adolph chuckled when he heard Robin's query and said, "We would like to tell you more, but we do not have any written record to help us say more. We did not learn the concept and importance of writing until the white man gave us his learning. Still, many of us cannot read or write. All we have is our oral history, which has been passed down from one generation to another. We are not a people who produce artifacts that could survive in our tropical conditions. There were great civilizations elsewhere in Africa in ancient times, but not here."

Robin thanked the chief for his interesting explanation. Robin's thoughts drifted to the many museums he had visited in the States. These museums would show things that existed centuries before. Now, he understood that such a museum would be difficult to establish in Kotoku because much of its tangible history was of recent origin and not well recorded. He thought of the world his grandfather had lived in and compared it with the world in which he imagined Chief Adolph's grandfather had lived. He found there was nothing that was really comparable. If the past was truly prologue to the future, what past building blocks pointed the way to predicting Kotoku's future?

Stanislas interrupted to remind everyone that they needed to finish their visit to Akokoji, eat their lunch, and begin their descent down the mountain to Ataku before it became too late. Molly and Robin thanked Chief Adolph again and said their good-byes. Stanislas led them to an open place at the edge of the village that offered a vast scenic view of all that lay below the mountain. They sat on benches under the shade of a large breadfruit tree as they thoroughly enjoyed the dizzying vista. Stanislas opened two packages covered with brown wrapping paper. Inside each package were a few pieces of fried chicken and yam slices. Stanislas placed his hands under the paper with the food lying on it and offered one to Molly and another to Robin. As they placed the food on their laps, Stanislas offered two clear, small plastic bags full of purified water.

The climb up the mountain had made Molly and Robin very hungry. They found the chicken and fried yam slices very tasty. The chicken was small and tough, but it was savory. The yam slices were like French fries but thicker and with a more starchy taste. Both the chicken and the yams slices were very oily, making them look for something to wipe their hands on. Stanislas noticed that they wanted to clean their hands, and he offered them tissue paper from a small cellophane package he kept in his breast pocket. He also saw that they were having difficulty extracting water from the plastic bags, so he demonstrated to them how to tear one corner of the bag open with their teeth to create an opening through which they could squeeze water into their mouths.

Molly and Robin were enjoying the moment. It was as if they were on a picnic at some scenic overlook spot for tourists. They could see the ground in front of them was barren, and in the middle of the large barren patch was the trunk of a small tree with three stubby branches at its top. Cupped in the vortex of these three branches was a clay bowl. Molly was prompted to ask Stanislas, "What is this open place used for, and what does that tree pole over there symbolize?"

Stanislas tried to answer Molly's question without revealing any village secrets. He said dryly, "This place is used mainly for the monthly dancing and drumming under the full moon. Every full moon, the people from Ataku and other surrounding villages come to dance to the drums and drink their fill of palm wine. This has been a sacred place for traditional ceremonies since the arrival of our first ancestors. You are welcome to come and join the revelers at the next full moon."

Molly and Robin could not possibly know this was the place where Bobovovi was skewered over twenty-two years ago by a moonbeam and carried to his house in Ataku. None of the local people born since that magical time knew this remarkable story. The chief, Yofu, at the time had commanded everyone never to mention this miraculous event and to erase it from their oral history. This draconian measure was taken to protect the people from angry gods who flooded the village the night after this incredible ride on a moonbeam had occurred.

Stanislas threw their trash into the adjoining bush and said, "We must now start our walk down the mountain. Going down is easier and faster, but the chances of injury are higher. Therefore, I ask that you go slowly and be careful. Don't get in a hurry."

They started their descent at the same spot they had finished the upward climb and followed the same worn path down the mountain. They could feel their legs weakening, but they pushed on. They were happy when they began to see the church and the first houses of the village in front of them. Many people were aligned along the wide path to welcome them back. Everyone wanted to get a good look at the two white people who would be taking Letivi to America.

Molly and Robin could not wait to take a bucket bath and make sure Letivi was fully ready to depart with them the next day. It was already late in the afternoon, and they needed to know if all was in order for Letivi's travel. Before separating from Stanislas, they asked him to leave word at the chief's compound about their imminent arrival to check in with Letivi. Dutifully, Stanislas marched back up the mountain slope to deliver this message to the chief's guard, who always stood just outside the royal compound entrance. The guard grunted his acknowledgement of the message, and Stanislas headed to his home in a distant compound.

Standing near the guard when Stanislas left his message, but on the other side of the entrance door, was Delalia. She now knew the white woman would be coming, and she wanted to make sure she saw her up close this time and that Molly also saw her and understood that Letivi had a pregnant young wife. To make sure she did not miss Molly, she sat down next to the inside of the compound entrance and waited patiently. She told herself that she must see clearly the female who would accompany her beloved Letivi.

Molly and Robin arrived at the entrance of the chief's compound and requested permission to enter to see the chief.

Delalia immediately sprang through the entranceway and said affirmatively, "Greetings. I am Chief Letivi's wife, and I will escort you to his meeting room."

Delalia eyed Molly from head to toe as she tried to sum up what her intuition told her about this foreign woman. Molly, in turn, looked intensely at Delalia and wondered if it was true that Letivi had such a young wife. Delalia navigated them around a few goats, chickens, and sleeping dogs to the meeting room. All the way, every eye in the compound was riveted on Molly and Robin. The women in the compound could easily see that Delalia was making it clear she was the chief's wife. Delalia instructed Molly and Robin to sit down while she alerted her husband to their presence. Delalia felt satisfied that she had done well to underscore the point that Letivi was her man.

After a delay of about fifteen minutes, Letivi entered the meeting room, followed by Gyasi. When the usual greeting and handshakes were terminated, Molly could not wait to speak. "We enjoyed our time climbing the mountain, and now we are ready to depart early tomorrow morning on the first leg of our journey to America. Letivi, are you ready to travel?"

Letivi hesitated as he thought over his response. He said in a humorous manner, "I am ready, but I am not yet fully prepared. My main constraint is that I do not have a suitcase in which I can fit my clothes. For example, my royal chief's gown is so bulky it can almost fill a suitcase. I really do not know what to do."

Molly quickly replied, "Don't worry about a suitcase. We can buy you a new suitcase in Melomti. In fact, as the airlines allow for two suitcases per passenger, we will buy you two suitcases. But you should not bring too many traditional clothes. There will be few occasions to wear them. You will need to wear regular street clothes most of the time. Please keep in mind that America is a very informal country and most people wear casual dress."

Molly's words puzzled Letivi. He did not know what "street clothes," "informal," and "casual" meant, but he did not want to say anything that would reveal his ignorance of these terms. He paused a long moment before saying, "OK. I will bring only a couple of my traditional outfits. As I do not have any of the other kinds of clothes you mention, I ask that you help me buy clothes in Melomti that would be the most appropriate."

Molly recognized that this was awkward for Letivi. She smiled and said in a sympathetic tone, "All right. That will not be a problem. We'll buy you the clothes you need in Melomti. After we arrive in America, we can buy you more clothes, if needed. For sure, you'll need a warm coat. Winter is fast approaching in America."

The point about winter concerned Letivi, as he had never experienced cold weather. He was also not sure where they could buy a winter coat. He sheepishly admitted to Molly and Robin. "I have never known cold weather, and I do not know where we can buy the kind of coat you need for such weather."

Gyasi, who had been sitting silently, wryly said, "Dead people's clothes."

Letivi knew immediately what Gyasi meant and said happily, "Yes, we can find winter clothes among the piles of used clothes from America that are for sale in many places in Melomti."

He explained to Molly and Robin, "We call this used clothing 'dead people's clothes' because we believe nobody would give up such nice clothes unless they were dead."

Molly was primed to explain how people changed clothes often in America and gave the clothes they did not want any more to charity, but she saw no need to provide this clarification at this time. Wanting to move on, she skipped this thought and said, "Chief Letivi, please be ready early in the morning with anything you want to bring on the trip. We need to leave early so we can get a head start on making all the arrangements for your ticket and our travel to America."

Letivi raised his head, made a boyish grin, and looked straight into Molly's eyes before saying, "Don't worry. I will be ready to go when you are."

Molly had been looking for the opportunity to mention Letivi's young wife, and she seized this moment to do it. "OK. That does it. We'll see you in the morning. Make sure you say a nice good-bye to your wife."

Although Letivi was surprised to hear Molly mention his wife, this made no difference in the strong feelings he felt for Molly and his happiness about being able to spend the next couple of weeks with her. As for Molly, she discounted almost totally the attraction she felt for Letivi and made every effort to treat him in a businesslike manner. She sincerely wanted Letivi to benefit from his trip to America and for him to visit his father's home area, and that was all. She could not know that the journey she was embarking on would entail much more than she could imagine. In reality, transporting an African from his village to another world in America is no small undertaking. Nobody could possibly anticipate the profound consequences of Letivi's trip to America.

CHAPTER TWENTY-THREE
MELOMTI PASSAGE

Robin could not sleep. He tossed and turned. His sleeplessness mainly stemmed from the fact that he believed this final night in Ataku was his last chance to be intimate with Molly. His entire body was pulsating with a burning desire to sleep with Molly, hold her tight, and do as they had done a few days ago in their hotel room in Melomti. It was maddening for him to see Molly sleeping in another bed less than six feet from him. How could the beautiful Molly be so close, yet so far from what he desperately needed at this moment? He was torn between accepting his lonely fate or forcing himself on Molly. He was tortured by these thoughts. He knew any unilateral move on his part would not be welcomed by Molly, possibly doing permanent damage to their relationship. His pain and frustration were accentuated by the sound manner in which Molly was sleeping. He found it wrong and even callous that Molly could be so oblivious to his suffering.

Could Molly not feel the lust oozing copiously from every pore of his body, covering him and his bed, and painting the wall and floor in a brilliant scarlet color? Robin had never suffered such torment and believed he was on the verge of losing his mind. He struggled to control himself. He was afraid that in his delirious state, he was capable of doing harm. He growled and thrashed around on his bed, making noises that he hoped would awaken Molly so she could see his dreadful situation and give him the love he needed to heal. There was no moving Molly. She was either sound asleep or ignoring the stressed condition of her male companion. Robin became increasingly tormented by the cure for what ailed him being so close yet so remote. For him, this was inhumane cruelty.

Up the hill, there was another person who was not sleeping because her partner was not submitting as she wanted to her amorous desires. Delalia was determined to have sex with her husband, Letivi, before he departed on his trip to America. She wanted to make sure that his sexual needs were fully satisfied before he embarked on a trip in the company of a foreign woman. Letivi did not resist. Delalia did as she pleased. But his mind was far away as his head spun around all the details, real and imagined, that his trip to America involved. Delalia applied all her charms and proven techniques, but she could not bring the preoccupied Letivi to a climax. She spent much time doing the best she knew how to do, but nothing was working that night, as it usually did so easily. She finally gave up, but Letivi's inability to perform as always raised her level of concern about her relationship with her husband. Letivi tried to excuse himself by explaining, "I'm sorry, but my mind is so focused on my trip that my body is not functioning as it should. Maybe we can try again in the morning."

When morning was announced by the crowing roosters, Delalia found Letivi's side of the bed empty. Letivi could not sleep, so he had arisen before daybreak to begin necessary prayers in front of the oldest grandfather's house. He was joined there by his grandfather, Chief Gyasi, when the sun's first rays broke through the mountain mist. They both asked the grandfathers to bless his trip and to bring him home safe and sound. As they prayed, they poured ample libations of expensive imported schnapps on the ground in front of the miniature door to the grandfather's small house. When they had finished all these required ancestral ceremonies, Gyasi turned to Letivi and said in a solemn voice, "My son, this is the best time for me to say my final words to you before you travel. Please listen to me well."

"Yes, Grandfather. I need your final words and blessing."

Gyasi continued, "I will pray every day for your safety and uneventful return to our village. Your grandmother will do the same. The most important advice I have for you is to be very careful not to reveal any of the village's secrets or any truths about your father and mother. Most importantly, the magical and mysterious life of Bobovovi must not be talked about. Say anything you want, but do not say the truth about your father and your mother and her former domain. Know very well that outsiders would not understand any of these truths and will question the sanity of anyone who repeats them."

Letivi interrupted his grandfather. "Please don't worry. I know this very well, and all this special knowledge will remain with me and not be communicated to anyone. You can count on me!"

Upon hearing these words, Gyasi embraced tightly his grandson, whispering into his ear, "I love you, my son. Please travel well and come back to us an even better and stronger man. And never forget that Africa likes and needs you just as it liked and needed your father."

Standing quietly a short distance away was Letivi's beloved grandmother, Evelyne. She did not say a word but gave Letivi a long and endearing hug that said everything.

After these emotional moments with his grandparents, Letivi said, "I now must prepare for my departure."

Gyasi responded, "Good. The people are already waiting to bid you a good and safe trip."

Letivi handed to Gyasi the cloth pouch that contained the cell phone and its charger, saying, "Please keep the phone charged and with you at all times, as you never know when the president will call. I have the number of the phone, and I will try to call you in case of an emergency. However, I am almost certain that the president has enabled this phone only for communication with him."

Letivi returned to his sleeping room to find a sullen but dutiful Delalia with his breakfast and bath water prepared, as well as the cardboard box and plastic bags with the clothes he was taking with him. Also laid out on his bed were the clothes he would wear for his trip to Melomti. He would wear a simple chief's thin outer gown and his royal hat with many totem figures sewn into it. Each small wooden figure had a meaning and was carefully painted with gold lacquer. He ate and bathed, and Delalia helped him dress. She had decided not to do like all the other villagers and see him off in the taxi car waiting in the village center. She held Letivi's hands and looked deeply into his eyes, saying, "My dear husband. Remember these words. I'm your wife, and I'm with your child. Our lives depend on you returning to us as the man we knew when you left. Our baby will need a strong and loving father. Please come back as quickly as possible and be that father."

Letivi was moved by Delalia's words and said, "I will not forget your words. Please do not worry too much about me. I will be gone only two weeks, and you will always be my wife."

At that moment, Letivi stepped forward to give Delalia an awkward hug. He did not kiss her, as that was not their custom. Delalia managed to form a small smile as she called for the young girls in the adjoining section of the chief's royal compound to come and carry the chief's effects to the waiting taxi car. Delalia stood still as she watched her husband exit his sleeping compound and head toward the main exit and the throngs of people waiting to wish him a good trip.

When the loud hand clapping started at the door, the sleep-deprived and very restless Robin was already up, fussing with arranging for the trip back to Melomti. He gruffly told Cyprien, the person clapping, that he was up and they would be out soon. Cyprien called through the door, "OK. The whole town is up and waiting. The chief will be here soon."

Cyprien's words prompted Molly to sit up in bed and ask Robin, "Please go take your bucket bath while I arrange my things. We should hurry to bathe and eat so we can leave as early as possible."

Robin wrapped his towel around himself, noisily opened the door, and stomped out of the room without saying a word. His rough demeanor only made Molly laugh. Hearing Molly laugh only made Robin feel more depressed.

Molly could hear Robin returning. She was wearing only her panties. She did not rush to cover herself before Robin entered the room. She felt that she should soothe and titillate Robin a bit by playfully giving him a brief glimpse of her naked body. She wanted to make him feel better and show him that he was still very much a part of her life. As soon as Robin entered the room, he was stupefied by the sight of Molly's lovely feminine contours. Molly feigned her intentional nakedness by saying, "Oops. You are back so quickly." She then quickly wrapped the cloth around her body and headed out the door, brushing by a speechless Robin.

After Molly exited, Robin began having a talk with himself. He told himself that if he were a real man, he would have grabbed Molly and thrown her to the floor and had his way with her, in spite of the possible consequences. He could now see that thinking this trip could open up the possibility of making a life with Molly was foolish. He no longer cared about Africa and finding David Peterson. All he cared about was becoming Molly's man and having her love him as much as he loved her. He could see that he could never have a happy life if Molly was not his partner. He would not stop until he and Molly were in a permanent and fully committed relationship as a couple.

A cheerful Molly returned, saying, "My dear Robin, please step outside for your breakfast while I dress and arrange my things. I will join you briefly. I can hear the noise from all the people assembled to see us off. I guess early in the village is much earlier than our early."

Robin did as requested without murmuring a word. Molly quickly dressed and gathered her things together before joining Robin at the small breakfast table for their usual bread and jam washed down by Nescafé and bottled water. Just as they were finishing their breakfast and taking their antimalarial pills, Cyprien showed up to announce, "The chief is here, and everyone is waiting. We should go now."

Molly and Robin immediately got up, gathered their things, and followed Cyprien out of the compound. At the compound exit, all the women who had seen to their every need were lined up to shake their hands and wish them a good journey. Molly quickly dug into her bulging handbag to come up with a wad of gadis to offer the women a generous tip for all their services.

The distance to the car was short, but the compact density of the crowd made it difficult to forge their way to the car. They could see Letivi standing beside the car shaking hands with well-wishers as they passed by. The people were singing songs and loudly rejoicing over the fact that they had a chief who was going to America. Drummers were joining in with a nonstop beat used to celebrate the happiest of events. Molly and Robin had never before seen such a jubilant send-off by so many people. Even the odd Chinaman was standing on the steps of his establishment, shouting in indecipherable words and clapping loudly. He was happy to see Letivi go to a country that he and everyone else could visit only in their dreams.

Molly and Robin approached the car as they followed Cyprien in a single file through the very animated crowd. As they arrived near the car, they could see it had been decorated with palm branches and red bougainvillea flowers. They placed their things in the open trunk, noting that Letivi's cardboard box and big plastic bag were already there. Letivi looked impressive with his chief's hat and his closely shaven face and head. When they arrived at the car, they greeted Letivi.

Cyprien led Molly and Robin to the opposite side of the car and explained, "A chief cannot sit in the front seat. In our country, important people do not sit next to their drivers. The chief will therefore need to sit in the back on the right side. A woman also cannot sit in the front seat, so Molly will also have to sit in the back with the chief. Consequently, Robin, you will have to sit in the front with me."

Molly and Robin nodded their heads to acknowledge their acceptance of what Cyprien had said. Robin was unhappy with these seating arrangements because they would place him away from Molly. He saw this as only the first of many actions to come where Letivi's presence would make contact with Molly more difficult.

They were preparing to enter the car when Cyprien cried out, "Step back. The fetish priests are coming."

Several senior fetish priests arrived, and the crowd made room so they could pour blood dripping from the slit throats of white roosters around Letivi and the car. As they circled the car with their bloody chickens, they called out to the gods and spirits to protect their chief and the car and to bring their chief safely back to them. These traditional priests were followed by the local evangelical pastor who asked everyone to be quiet and bow their heads as he prayed to God and Jesus Christ their savior for the safe travels of their chief. The crowd immediately became silent, and most people dropped to their knees to pray along with the pastor. After the completion of these prayers, the crowd stood up and yelled out a rousing "hip- hip hooray" type of group cheer.

Following this loud cheer, Letivi was shown his place on the backseat. Molly was asked to sit next to him, and the front door was held open so Robin could take his seat next to Cyprien. The doors were closed. Cyprien started the engine and slowly let out the clutch. The car moved forward at the slowest possible speed. Everyone in the crowd was waving frantically as they chanted at the top of their voices a phrase invented for the moment. Over and over they sang, "Our chief is going to America, going to America." To Molly and Robin, it sounded as if they were singing something that was almost in tune with an old American folk song, "She'll Be Coming 'Round the Mountain."

Cyprien carefully navigated his car out of the village, trying to miss the numerous children running alongside the car, the sleeping dogs, and the meandering sheep and goats grazing freely in the village outskirts. As they left the village limits, Cyprien picked up speed, and soon they could no longer hear the people or see the village. In less than a half hour, they joined the asphalted national highway and were on their way to Melomti, about one hundred miles away. They had driven less than five miles when they stopped at the first roadside filling station so Cyprien could gas up. Cyprien asked Molly to pay for the gas because he did not have enough money. He told Molly to deduct it from his final bill. As there was not any electricity at this station and the fuel had to be pumped by hand, it took some time to fill the car's fuel tank. The absence of electricity prompted Robin to ask, "How can a country develop without electricity? Isn't the availability of afford-able and reliable energy a key ingredient of development?"

Robin was expecting Letivi to answer his question, but he did not. Letivi barely heard Robin because of the disconcerting effect his close proximity with Molly was having on him. Robin loudly repeated his questions, pointedly asking the chief if he had any views on the subject of energy and its relationship to the development process. Still, Letivi did not respond. Molly finally intervened, saying, "I'm sure Letivi has something to say on this subject."

Hearing Molly's words jarred Letivi into full alertness, and he replied, "Yes, indeed. Energy is important, and without it, we can't advance. We don't have any hydroelectric dams in our very flat country, and, thus, all our electricity is generated from expensive, imported generators. The fuel for these generators is also imported. The amount of electricity generated is insuf-ficient and available only to the richer people in some cities. I don't know what the answer is to resolving our huge electricity deficit."

Molly was impressed with Letivi's studious reply. She admit-ted to Letivi, "Before coming to your village, I had never lived without electricity. Everyone in America has electricity. You will see. America is a very well-lit country. I find it very dark here at night, even in Melomti, by comparison."

Robin was racking his brain to come up with an intelligent answer to Kotoku's electricity problems. He would like very much to demonstrate his brilliance to Letivi and Molly. He quickly ran through his mind such options as solar power and natural gas turbines, but he was not sure of these, particularly if no transmission lines existed. He almost regretted raising such a challenging subject, as he could not think of any viable solution. He was discouraged by the thought that Kotoku's people would always be poor because they did not have access to an economical and efficient form of energy.

With a full tank of gas, Cyprien started the car again and headed down the national highway that led to Melomti. They soon saw groups of people along the roadside clapping and cheering as they passed them. It appeared that the word about the White Chief's trip to America had spread quickly and everyone wanted to wish him a good journey. Never before had any traditional chief traveled to America, so Letivi's trip was on the national news. Cyprien was happy to see everyone knew about Letivi's trip because that would mean no police or customs officials would stop his distinctively decorated car at any useless roadblocks.

They made good progress as Cyprien drove at top speed. Letivi had never been in a car that sped along at such a high speed. He wanted to tell Cyprien to slow down, but he did not want others, particularly Molly, to know he was afraid. Perhaps his fear of high speed contributed to his urge to pee. He held his urine back as long as he could, but the time came when he could not wait. He quietly told Cyprien, "Please stop in a good place for me to relieve myself."

Robin interjected, "Good idea. I need to pee too."

Molly also needed to pee badly, but she did not want to repeat the experience of peeing in the open. She told herself she would rather hold back her urine and risk infection than pee again in the bushes. She said, "I'm OK. You guys go ahead. I can wait until we arrive in Melomti."

Cyprien found a quiet spot alongside the road where there were no people and plenty of bushes to hide behind. He came to a stop, and Letivi and Robin stepped out of the car and headed toward secluded places that were some distance from each other. Letivi decided to pee behind a nearby tree. Robin thought he was lucky to be able to hide behind a large earthen mound. Cyprien went to the other side of the road to relieve himself behind a clump of bushes. They were all far enough from the road, in positions that did not allow them to notice that several women and children had come walking down the highway. These people stopped at the car and tried to converse with Molly.

Molly did not know what the people were trying to say to her. She stared at the women, who were carrying large loads of firewood on their heads and small babies on their backs. She was quite impressed by how the women could maintain their balance and walk in such an easy and graceful manner. She worried about the way the babies were wrapped tightly with cloth stoles that the women tied around their bodies just above their breasts. It looked as if the babies' necks would snap. She also thought that this method of carrying babies could contribute to elongating their breasts. She did recognize that the way they carried babies was handy, as it allowed their hands to be free to do other things. She was also impressed that childbirth did not seem to slow these women down or keep them from doing their daily work tasks.

All the kids with the women were eager to reach through the car window and shake Molly's hand. Molly shook their hands and patted them on the head. She did this willingly in spite of her fear of contracting undesirable germs from these children, who were covered with a layer of dirt. She could see that one little boy had head lice and ringworm. Another boy had a pimply rash all over his almost-naked body (she could not know that this boy had a bad case of scabies). The children sang their usual little jingle, "Give me five gadis." Molly was convinced that they needed much more than five gadis. She thought that maybe any charity for these children should start was with the gift of a bar of soap so they could take a good bath. She had read somewhere that the frequent washing of one's hands could reduce significantly the disease burden. She was seriously tempted to give a small amount of money to the children, knowing full well that the excitement and pleasure her gift brought them would be fleeting.

The three male occupants of the car returned, and Cyprien yelled at the women and children, telling them to move on. When all were seated in the car, Robin was making fun of his peeing experience, saying, "I was really lucky to find such a good spot behind that odd earthen mound that was sprouting out of the ground. I enjoyed peeing on it."

Letivi was amused by Robin's unsolicited comments. Cyprien was less amused and wanted to educate this ignorant white man about the mound he had just pissed on. He bluntly said, "Look around you! Can't you see there are many similar mounds? You must know that these are termite mounds. Some are active, while others are abandoned. I wish you could be here at the onset of the rainy season so you could see how countless thousands of termites fly out of these mounds."

Robin and Molly appreciated this information. Robin was thinking that these mounds were made by the removal of unwanted soil from farmers' fields. Molly had been thinking that people had piled dirt in these places so they could plant some kinds of crops. The possibility of such large mounds being built by termites had never dawned on them. They also did not know that termites—flying ants—in Africa were a different species than those which damaged many houses in the America.

They had only driven a short distance when Molly saw something that made her shout, "What is that? There is a bare ground spot that is smoking. Maybe there is some kind of underground cauldron."

When Letivi and Cyprien heard what Molly said, they could not help but laugh. Molly was surprised and a bit irritated by their laughter and said, "Why are you laughing? What did I say that is so funny?"

Letivi sensed Molly's discontent with their laughing, so he took the lead in explaining, "The smoke is coming from the slow burning of small pieces of wood underground. Charcoal makers are at work here. They dig a pit and fill it with chunks of wood from the cutting of small trees. They set the chunks on fire and carefully cover the burning wood with green straw and earth. They seek to keep the fire burning with as little air as possible. In this way, they make the charcoal many people use to cook. You may have noticed the charcoal being used to cook your food in the village."

This explanation was clear, but Molly was having a hard time accepting it. The charcoal she had seen was much different from the charcoal used at home for backyard barbecues. Local charcoal was brittle and looked like pieces of wood painted black. It was very unlike the tightly compressed and well-formed charcoal briquettes in Kansas that she bought in triple-layered paper bags.

Robin spouted, "Good to see another form of energy at work, but this still involves cutting down many trees, and that has to have certain negative consequences on the environment. The use of natural gas for cooking would be much better, but I can see that such an option would be too costly for most families. It is indeed a shame that people cannot afford to improve their lives."

They continued to zoom past villagers and dismantled road-blocks, passing hundreds of well-wishers who lined the roadsides in every village. Molly and Robin were impressed that Letivi's trip to America had made him a national celebrity and top role model for the youth of the country. Every child wanted to be like Letivi and go to America, the land of plenty where everything was possible and available. This outpouring of support and envy for Letivi's trip made Molly feel very good about her decision to take him to Kansas.

They reached the broad savannah grassland that covered the coastal plain. The scent of the salty sea saturated the air and soaked everyone in sweat. Letivi's eyes were riveted on the much-worshipped groups of baobab trees that stood like tall and mighty sentinels guarding the entrance to Melomti. The car slowed to almost a crawl as they entered the chaotic and congested traf-fic. Molly directed Cyprien to take them back to the same hotel where they had previously stayed. Letivi was excited by being in the city where he had gone to school and the prospect of staying in such a luxury hotel.

They pulled under the Melo Hotel entrance canopy, and Molly led the way to the reception area. Letivi and Robin fol-lowed. Molly was in a hurry to make sure there were three rooms available. The man behind the desk easily recognized them and welcomed them back. Robin made an audible sigh when he heard that three single rooms had already been reserved for them. He knew this meant he would not be sharing a room with Molly as he had on their arrival. Hearing Robin sigh, Molly turned to him and whispered, "You know very well I cannot share a room with you while Letivi is with us." Robin now knew that it would be a very long and painful time before he would have Molly alone with him again.

Cyprien carried in their baggage. Following him were two men from the presidency who were demanding to see Chief Letivi. One man was very tall and skinny, and the other was short and rotund. They reminded Molly and Robin of Laurel and Hardy, but in another color. The tall man greeted them and shook Letivi's hand, saying, "The president has sent me to make sure you are well received in this hotel and that you have everything you need for your trip. He asked me to give you this envelope. The man with me is here to take the photos we need to make your official diplomatic passport and obtain your US visa. We already have your yellow health card. No need to take any vaccinations. All will be ready well before your departure tomorrow. We have also arranged for you to charge your ticket to the presidency at the Air Afrique agency. The reservations of your escorts have also been confirmed."

Letivi thanked the men and handed the envelope to Molly as he went with the fat man to have his photo taken against a nearby white wall. Molly peeked into the envelope. She could see it was full of hundred-dollar bills. She muttered to Robin, "There's a lot of dollars in this envelope. With this money and his ticket already paid for, I will not have to spend any of my money. That's good! It saves us from another horrendous trip to the bank."

Letivi returned to the reception desk to join Molly and Robin. The two men asked for Letivi's permission to leave and said, "A presidential vehicle will be here tomorrow to take you to the VIP lounge at the airport. All of you should be ready to depart two hours before your flight time. The airline will call us to confirm the time your flight departs."

After the men left, Molly approached Letivi. Standing on the tips of her toes, she whispered into his ear, "Please know that this envelope is full of money."

Letivi responded, "Yes, I know. When I was taking my photo, the man told me the envelope contained five thousand dollars in spending money for my trip. It is a gift from the president."

A delighted Molly said, "That's really nice. We'll save this money for use in America and use the rest of the gadis I have to pay for the night at the hotel and the clothes you need to travel."

Letivi shyly replied, "No need to pay anything for the hotel. The man told me the president has taken care of our hotel expenses, and we have all been given suites. Also, my ticket is in first class, and you have been given a free upgrade to first class. No need to do anything at the airline office. Everything has already been arranged. This is the president's way of showing how important my trip to America is for him and our country."

Molly and Robin were happy to hear this agreeable news. They now knew they were traveling with one of Kotoku's leading dignitaries. Even Robin was starting to feel it was a lucky thing to have Letivi with them. Letivi loudly cleared his throat and said, "But I still need that winter coat and other clothes to wear on the plane and in America."

Cyprien was standing by, waiting for instructions. Molly beckoned to him to come and told him, "Be ready to take us to where we can buy clothes for Letivi after we drop our things in our rooms."

Cyprien smiled widely and said, "Yes, ma'am. Always at your service." He was proud to be seen with such a well-known and highly respected person as Letivi. He could also see that he would be in line to receive a bonus for all his services. He would be something of a rich man after receiving final payment. He could not wait to celebrate his good fortune with his family.

The porter placed their things on a trolley and took them up the old Otis elevator to the top—fifth—floor. Letivi did not let on that this was his first time on an elevator. He was happy to get off at the fifth floor because he was afraid that a power outage could have stopped the aged elevator between floors. Letivi was shown the presidential penthouse suite and was blown away by its vastness and all the luxuries it contained. There was a well-appointed living room, a huge bedroom with a king-size bed, and a bathroom that was larger than any room he knew in the village. There were also a couple of things in the bathroom that he had never seen before: a bidet and a huge bathtub. He could not believe that he would be staying in such a nice room alone. Many families in the village could live comfortably in such a large space.

Molly and Robin were also very impressed with Letivi's ultra-luxurious accommodations. Yet they could not complain about their adjoining VIP suites, which were larger and nicer than any hotel rooms they had previously known. Also, their suites were as cool as Letivi's rooms. The porter told them that the president had installed a separate air-conditioning system to ensure the entire floor was always cool. This floor of the hotel was permanently rented and cared for by the president for special visitors to the country. Molly was thinking that they really did not need so much space and luxury, but there was no way they could decline what the president had so generously offered.

Molly made the porter's day by paying him a sizeable tip. They dropped their things in their rooms, locked their doors, and joined up in the wide hallway to take the creaky elevator down to the lobby. Cyprien was waiting for them in his car in front of the entrance. They took their places in the car, and Cyprien started the motor. As he pulled away from the hotel, he said, "I will take you to one of the best shops to buy the latest in European fashion." They did not know that the tall man had told Cyprien where to take them to buy Letivi's clothes.

Letivi knew this meant going to an expensive, elitist shop that served the very rich. He did not like doing that, but in this instance, he did not think he had a choice but to follow along. Letivi was given a royal welcome at a shop that carried the enticing name of 'Temptations.' It was obvious they were expecting Letivi. Molly and Robin were duly impressed by the attention the shop owner and his staff gave Letivi. They measured him and had him sit down in an expensive stuffed armchair. They almost ignored Molly and Robin, telling them to sit over at the side of the shop on a couple of flimsy folding chairs. They began showing Letivi pants, shirts, and shoes. Letivi called to Molly, "Please come and help me choose the clothes that will be the best for me to wear in America."

Molly left a disgruntled Robin sitting alone and fuming over all the attention Letivi was getting and how dependent he was on Molly. Most of all, he was put off by the way Molly seemed to enjoy taking care of Letivi. He was becoming jealous of the time Letivi spent with Molly and how they apparently enjoyed each other's company. He was worried because Molly seemed to have no time to spend with him anymore. He was hurt because it really did seem that two was company and three was a crowd.

Molly looked at the various samples of slacks and shirts they had brought out for Letivi to examine. She selected three outfits and asked if Letivi could try them on. Letivi was shown to a dressing room in the back of the shop. He awkwardly put on pants and a matching shirt and stepped out of the cubicle so Molly could see him. She could not believe her eyes. Letivi looked so unusual in his new, modern clothes. He seemed younger and more handsome. She was delighted by this new look of Letivi's. The shirt fit him well, but the waist and length of the pants needed adjusting. The shop attendants quickly noted that they could have their tailor quickly make the necessary adjustments and deliver the clothes to the hotel.

Letivi tried on one more set of clothes, and Molly approved. He was going to try on more clothes, but Molly said that was enough, as they could buy additional clothes in Kansas. One reason she was insistent on this point was that she could not believe the high cost of the items Letivi was trying on. They were five times the cost of similar items in America, and the quality was probably not as good as the clothes easily found in regular clothing stores in America. Molly reached into her purse for a large bundle of gadis to pay for the clothes. The store owner told Chief Letivi, "Please tell your white woman friend that your money is no good here. Also, I have something to give you from the president."

Letivi told Molly, "The man says we do not need to pay. Also, he is bringing from the back of the shop a gift for me from the president. I think this is one of the many shops that the president and his family own."

The shop owner returned, pulling a very expensive Samsonite suitcase. He opened the suitcase in front of Letivi and pulled out a winter jacket of the highest quality. He said, "The president knows you will need these things."

Molly and Robin were awed again by such unexpected generosity. Seeing the suitcase reminded Molly that she and Robin also needed suitcases. This prompted her to say, "It is a very nice suitcase they are giving you, Letivi. As our suitcases were lost on our inbound trip, we need to buy at least some carry-on bags."

When Molly said her last word, the well-dressed shop owner snapped his fingers and made a gesture to one of the attendants. He turned to Molly and said, "We would also like to help those people who have invited our Chief Letivi to America. Please pick out anything in the store you need while my attendant brings two carry-on bags for you."

Molly and Robin could not believe their good luck. They did need clothes and shoes. They immediately began looking for clothes for themselves and later joined Letivi to try on shoes. They felt as if they had won one of those prizes that allowed you to shop for free. Letivi asked Molly if the shoes he had selected were OK. She said they looked great. She asked Letivi if her clothes looked all right, and he said they most suited her. Again, Robin felt left alone. Molly did try to cheer up Robin by telling him his selection of clothes and shoes was a good one. After adding some socks and undergarments to their free shopping haul, they thanked profusely the shop owner and his team. Everyone was in a good mood and laughing as they loaded their suitcases into the trunk and took their seats in the car.

Only Cyprien was not laughing. He knew that after he dropped his passengers at the hotel he would be the end of his storybook travel episode with Molly and Robin. He looked forward to receiving his final payment, but he was sad he would not see Molly and Robin again. It was a very awkward moment after they arrived at the hotel and final good-byes had to be said. Robin shook Cyprien's hand at length, and Molly gave him a big hug. Cyprien's spirits rose sharply when he saw how much money Molly had handed him. It was much more than he had expected. Molly gave more because she had ended up with more gadis than she had anticipated. Cyprien felt as if he had gone from rags to riches. He could not wait to get home and celebrate his good fortune with his family, friends, and neighbors. He would be partying all night.

Before he separated from his three illustrious passengers, he asked Molly for the favor of taking a photo with her and Robin. Molly readily agreed and removed her camera from her handbag. One of the hotel porters came and took a photo of the three. Letivi also asked to be in a photo, so a second photo was taken of all four of them. Cyprien begged Molly to send copies of the photo back with Letivi. She and Letivi told him not to worry and that his request would be easy to honor.

Darkness was beginning to fall. Molly suggested they go with their things to the hotel restaurant to eat before going to their rooms. Letivi and Robin readily agreed. They walked over to the first-floor restaurant and were quickly shown a table reserved for special guests. Letivi felt awkward, as he had seldom eaten at a high dining table. Also, he did not know what to order from the menu. In the village, his food was brought to him and placed on a low table. He also ate using his right hand. Now, he would have to use a knife and fork. To keep things simple, he ordered a well-done streak and French fries. He was surprised that Molly and Robin asked for the same food. They all asked for Cokes to drink and bottles of mineral water to take to their rooms.

Their food was served, and Letivi asked the waiter to bring some hot chili sauce to douse amply on his fries and meat. He also surprised Molly and Robin by pouring mayonnaise and vinegar on his fries, which he called chips. Molly and Robin politely declined to follow his example. They did not want to experience ever again the effect of tasting local hot sauce. Letivi awkwardly cut his meat into bite-size pieces. This was not something he was used to doing. In the village, he would take the meat in his hand and tear off pieces with his teeth. His table manners were very different from what Molly and Robin had been taught. Both his elbows were on the table, and he held his fork in a full-hand grip as he stuffed his mouth so full he could not fully close it when he chewed. He was not in the habit of using a napkin and did a poor job of cleaning the food particles adhering to the area around his lips and on his chin. He also had the habit of smacking. Both Molly and Robin were taken aback by his table manners, but they were not sure what to say. They knew that in America, these kinds of table manners would be viewed negatively.

As they ate, Molly told Letivi about what to expect tomorrow at the airport, on the plane, and at every stop along the way to Wichita, Kansas. She said they would also have plenty of time on the plane to talk more about the places they would visit and the people they would see. Letivi listened attentively, acknowledging his understanding with some grunting sounds and by saying 'yes' several times with his mouth full of food. Molly and Robin knew that grunting was a way of talking in Letivi's country, but that doing this in America would raise eyebrows and be frowned upon.

They finished their food, and Molly left the waiter a generous tip, as she still had more gadis than she needed. Molly and Robin took their bottles of mineral water. Letivi said he did not need bottled water because he had marvelous clear running water in his hotel bathroom. They grabbed their things and headed to the old elevator. They entered the elevator, and Letivi excitedly asked to push the buttons. This was something he had never done before, and he did not want to miss the opportunity to do it now. He pushed the button for the fifth floor, the doors closed, and the elevator made scary groaning noises as it slowly climbed to the top floor. They all had kept their room keys and were ready to go to their respective rooms. They bid one another good night and sweet dreams. Molly said, "We can sleep late tomorrow because our flight doesn't leave until in the afternoon."

Once they were all in their respective huge rooms, they felt the same thing: loneliness. Robin took several cold showers to cool his body and ardor for Molly, but he tossed and turned, unable to sleep. Molly had never had any trouble sleeping, but this night she could not sleep. She could not get her mind off all the things she would do in America with Letivi. As for Letivi, he stayed up late playing with the plumbing and running water in his bathroom. He was also transfixed by all that was on TV. When he did go to bed very late, he rolled over many times, going left to right on his wide bed. He did not know how to sleep on such a large and soft bed. He ended up making himself a place on the thick carpet to sleep. He, too, was not used to sleeping alone, and this was the first time in his life that he had truly been alone. He missed his village already and was eager to finish his trip to America and return home. He knew he would not sleep well again until he was in his own bed in the village.

CHAPTER TWENTY-FOUR
GOOD-BYE KOTOKU

Letivi woke up early. He had not slept well on his floor pallet in the unusual surroundings of his palatial presidential suite. He did not know the exact time, but he could tell by the soft sunlight pouring through the sheer curtains on his windows that it must be about the time he usually woke up. His first impulse was to get up and get out. He was not used to being inside. He had spent a lifetime living mostly under the open sky, and he wanted to go outside now. In the village, about the only time he was inside was when he was in his sleeping room. He felt an urgent need to go outside.

He went to his well-endowed hotel bathroom and turned on the cold-water faucet, cupping his hands to catch water he could splash on his face and rub into his eyes. After he completed this quick face washing with plain water, he donned the same simple chief's robes he had worn the day before. He knew he should not be seen in his own country without his chief's attire. He walked swiftly out the door of his room and searched for a stairway because he was afraid to take the elevator alone. He could not find the stairwell, so he took a big swallow, upped his courage, and decided to venture on the elevator alone.

He pushed the elevator button, and he could hear it grudgingly coming his way. When it arrived, he hesitantly stepped inside. He pushed the button for the ground floor. The lift groaned its way safely down, and its doors opened as they should when it arrived at the ground floor. Letivi immediately stepped out, and its doors shut automatically behind him. Letivi found his first experience alone on an elevator so exhilarating that he decided he wanted to do it again. He pushed the outside button and stepped inside, pushing the fifth-floor button. He went all the way to the top and down again. He then decided to go back up again, stopping at each floor. He found that riding the elevator was thrilling. He could not get enough of going up and down. He was ready to continue his adventure, but there was a porter on the ground floor with another guest waiting for the elevator. They were bemused by Letivi's strange, childlike behavior.

Letivi confidently stepped out of the elevator at the ground floor, saying good morning to those waiting to use the elevator. He looked for an exit to go outside. He saw the front exit but did not want to be noticed, so he looked for a back exit. He could see that the hotel was very well decorated and made to be attractive to its patrons, but all the modern decorations were meaningless to him. He preferred being outside so he could see the sky, the sun, and all of nature's wonders.

He found the service exit in a far corner at the back of the hotel. He quickly darted through the exit to the outside. He was immensely relieved to be outdoors. His eyes feasted on the large grassy lawn and the many trees growing in the hotel's backyard. He could see an old man sitting at a low table near one of the outbuildings. He approached the old man and greeted him.

The old man looked up and was surprised to see before him the "White Chief" he had heard was staying at the hotel. He stood up as quickly as his old body would allow and said, after slightly bowing, "Welcome, Your Majesty. I'm honored by the presence of the White Chief whom I have heard so much about. My name is Emerson. How can I help you?"

Letivi was pleased to be with a humble and simple person and replied, "Please call me by my name, Letivi. And, for God's sake, please sit down. May I join you?"

Before Emerson could reply, Letivi was sitting down on a small stool on the opposite side of the low table. Emerson was delighted and asked Letivi, "May I serve you one of my special cups of coffee?"

"Thank you. That is very kind. Yes, a cup of your coffee is what I need this time of the morning."

Emerson disappeared inside a small building adjoining the grassy area where they were sitting. Letivi could hear him gathering some tin cups and plates. He could also hear that he had put on some music that his mom once told him she had liked when she was young. Emerson returned carrying a small tray with two cups of steaming hot coffee and some French bread slices with orange marmalade. He gently placed a cup of coffee in front of Letivi and regained his stool with his own cup of coffee. Letivi said, "Thank you. Do you have any sugar?"

Emerson quickly replied, "My coffee is already sweet, so you will not need to add any sugar."

Letivi found it curious that the coffee could be already sweetened, but after taking a little sip, he said, "Wow! That is good, sweet coffee. How do you make it?"

Letivi took the knife provided and smothered several slices of bread in a thick layer of marmalade while Emerson explained how he soaked coffee beans in molasses for weeks before drying and grinding them. Emerson continued to look intently at Letivi. He could not help but say, "My chief, excuse me, but I must say you remind me of a white visitor I had many years ago. You hear the old song, 'Dje Melisi,' I am playing? He told me that was his favorite Franco tune."

Letivi tried not to show any emotion, but Emerson's words made him think that the white visitor could have been none other than his father. In a very controlled manner, Letivi replied, "That is a nice song. My mother once told me she was fond of this song in the years before I was born."

Letivi was thinking that maybe his mother and father listened to this song together. He asked Emerson, "I'm curious. Tell me about the white man who visited you years ago."

Emerson happily said, "Not much to say. He enjoyed his coffee and asked me if I knew a place to eat. I indicated to him the location of the roadside eatery, One Hundred Percent, and I suggested he go to the big dance our hotel was having in the front courtyard that same night. I never saw him again, so I am not sure if he went to the dance. I can't remember his name. I don't think he told me his name. Hey, he might have said he lived in a village named Ataku. Is that not your village?"

Letivi steeled himself, trying not to reveal that what Emerson was saying was very earthshaking for him, saying simply, "Really? Are you sure about that? I have never known any white man in my village of Ataku. We do have a Chinaman, but no white man."

As Letivi was talking, Emerson was studying intently Letivi's facial features. He did not know if he should tell Letivi that in some ways he looked like the white man who had visited him many years ago. Just when he was about to say something, a loud feminine voice could be heard coming from the back door of the hotel. It was Molly calling. "Letivi, what are you doing out here? We thought we had lost you. Please come back inside so we can talk about our trip."

In front of Emerson, Letivi answered Molly in a snappy manner, as a chief should, "Wait for me in your room. I will be there shortly."

Letivi wanted to tarry longer with Emerson because he had once met his father. He finished his coffee, stood up, and shook Emerson's hand with a loud mutual snap of their middle fingers, saying, "Thanks for such good coffee. It was such a pleasure meeting you and learning that you had met once a white man who may have stayed in my village. I also enjoyed the music. As you know, I am traveling to America with two white people. I must go now. Thanks again."

Emerson was humbled by Letivi's generous handshake and became so emotional over the unexpected pleasure of meeting the much-talked-about White Chief that he could only mumble, "Chief, you have made this old man happy by honoring him with the unexpected pleasure of your visit. I wish you a good journey. God bless you."

Deep down inside himself, Emerson was wondering if Letivi was not the son of the white man who had visited him a long time ago. He was sad because he knew in his heart that just like that white man, he would never see Letivi again. He stood silently, feeling very old and lonely as he watched Letivi enter the hotel.

Letivi eagerly headed toward the elevator. He was proud that he was no longer intimidated by the elevator and felt he was now its master and not its servant. He arrived at the fifth floor and headed for Molly's room to let her know he had returned. As was the custom, he stood in front of Molly's door a long time clapping, but there was no reply from inside the room. He therefore resorted to the exceptional measure of knocking on the carved and well-varnished thick wooden door. After a couple of knocks, Molly opened the door wide, saying, "Oh, it's you. Please come in and sit down while I finish dressing."

Letivi's eyes were naturally attracted to all the curves and bulges of Molly's womanly body presented under a tightly wrapped African cloth. He was surprised she would invite him into her room while she was wearing so little clothing. He was trying to figure out if there was some meaning behind such seductive behavior. Molly grabbed her new clothes and went into her bathroom, saying, "I will only be a moment."

While Molly was dressing in her bathroom, Letivi gazed around her room. He was surprised that Molly left her panties and bra lying out where anyone could see them. In the village, women would usually keep any feminine articles out of sight. He also noted that her clothes were thrown about everywhere. He wondered if this messy, uninhibited behavior was specific to Molly or the way most Americans behaved.

Molly exited her bathroom dressed in some of the clothes they had picked up at Temptations the day before. Letivi was shocked at how different she looked in Western dress. She looked much younger, and her modern dress made him feel older and very traditional. Molly noticed how Letivi was staring at her and asked, "Letivi, what's wrong?"

"Nothing is wrong. You just look much different in your new modern clothes compared to the African clothes you were wearing."

"Yes, I know, but these are the clothes that will be comfortable for me to wear on the plane. If I arrive in America wearing my African clothes, people would look too much at me and ask me too many questions. What will you wear on the plane?"

Letivi replied, "I have no choice but to wear the same chief's robes and hat that I wore yesterday because many people will be waiting at the airport to wish me a good trip. They would not recognize me or appreciate it if I appeared in Western dress."

Molly gave Letivi an understanding look and said, "That's OK, but maybe you will want to keep a set of Western clothes in your carry-on luggage just in case you want to change before you arrive in America. Have you packed your suitcase yet?"

"No, I have not packed my suitcase yet. I needed to get some air first."

Molly offered, "If you like, I can help you pack. Have you taken your bath yet?"

Letivi was not used to being talked to in such a bossy, patronizing manner. He was becoming irritated by all of Molly's questions and raised the tone of his voice. "No, I have not taken a bath. Why do you ask? Do I stink?"

Molly tried to lessen Letivi's irritation by chuckling and saying, "Well, we'll be in planes and airports for nearly twenty-four hours, so it is a good idea to bathe well before we go to the airport. It's late in the morning, and we should eat an early lunch and get all our things ready so that when the president's men arrive, we can go."

Letivi stood up, saying, "OK, I will go take my bath and get myself ready. Maybe you should come to my room later to help me pack my suitcase and carry-on bag. See you later."

Letivi did not want to sound too cold because for reasons he did not understand, he was very attracted to Molly. Yet he was a chief and a man, and in his culture, a woman could not talk to him the way Molly was doing. Molly could also not understand that the way Letivi was behaving was because he had been brought up in a very different cultural context. They were both creatures produced by different worlds.

Letivi was trying to adopt the same informal behavior and manner of speech that Molly and Robin demonstrated, but his effort to do so almost made Molly laugh. She held back her laughter and said, "Very well. That is fine with me. See you in a little bit. By the way, I have already told Robin the same thing, and he is preparing to meet us for lunch in the hotel dining room. We skipped breakfast."

Letivi toddled off to his adjoining presidential suite. When he arrived at the door of his room, it immediately dawned on him that he had left his key inside the room. Luckily, a housemaid was standing nearby, and she could see that Letivi was unable to enter his room. She very courteously approached him and said in a tender voice, "Chief Letivi, allow me to help you enter your room?"

In a traditional authoritarian manner, Letivi grunted his assent to her help, refraining from looking at her. The young woman quickly opened Letivi's door and asked him, "Chief, is there anything else I can do to serve you? I am here because the president asked the hotel to keep a woman on guard to cater to your every need."

Upon hearing these words, Letivi looked at the woman from head to toe, sizing up her physical attributes. Although she scored high in terms of body proportions, Letivi told her, "No, thank you. I will not be in need of your services at this time."

The woman shyly thanked Letivi and said in a sad, sweet voice, "OK, but if you change your mind, please ask for me by my name: Freda."

Letivi knew it was customary to give the woman a gift of money, but he never carried money with him. As he did not have any money, he did her a favor by looking her in the eye, saying, "Very well, Freda. Thank you."

Letivi entered his room and pulled off his chief's gown and laid it over a chair so it could air out. He did the same for his undergarments, although he intended to wear the new pair of underwear and the white jersey he had received yesterday at Temptations. He stepped into the shower stall and turned on both knobs, for hot and cold water. He found he did not like any hot water, so he closed that knob and stood under a constant downpour of cold water. He was amazed that water just kept coming and never stopped, but he could not figure out how he was to wash with soap and then rinse himself. To take a bath as he usually did in the village, he needed a bucket.

As there was no bucket available, he took the metal trashcan in his bathroom and filled it with water. He then took one of the cups from the coffee-and-tea set in the main room to dip water from the trash can and pour it on his body. He wished the bucket was much bigger and the porcelain coffee cup was as large as his bathing calabash in the village, but he realized he could make do at a slower pace. He was very amused at the nicely wrapped but very tiny bar of soap with which he was supposed to wash his entire body. He was also missing the *akudja*—the village sponge—that he used to scrub his body. He never felt clean unless he scrubbed his body with an akudja sponge. He thought, "If this is how taking a bath is in America, I will be one dirty chief until I return to Ataku."

Letivi did like the big fluffy white towel provided to dry off. He wrapped the towel around his waist and returned to his spacious bedroom, which had an adjoining sitting room. He decided he would rest and dry while he waited for Molly to come and help him pack his suitcase. He sat down in one of the elegant wing chairs and was just about to doze off when he heard Molly knocking on the door, saying, "Letivi, it's me, Molly."

Letivi quickly stood up, threw his chief's robe over his naked body, and rushed to open the door for an impatient Molly. No sooner had he opened the door when a very agitated Molly burst into the room. She said, "We need to hurry. Robin is already waiting for us in the hotel dining room, and the people from the presidency have arrived early."

Letivi said, "No problem. I will finish dressing in my bathroom while you arrange my things in the suitcase. All I need is some of that new underwear we received yesterday. Can you help me chose the underpants and jersey I should wear under this gown?"

Molly quickly emptied the contents of the plastic bags sitting on the floor onto Letivi's bed. She noticed his bed was still made up. She asked Letivi, "Did you sleep last night?"

Letivi answered unashamedly, "Yes, I slept on the floor because the bed is too big and soft."

Molly glanced at Letivi and laughed. "You are something else. You have a nice bed like that and you sleep on the floor. Go figure. Here is the underwear."

Letivi stepped forward to snatch the underwear Molly was holding next to her side. At the same time, she moved toward him. Before they could stop their forward motions, they briefly found themselves inadvertently face-to-face with the full length of their bodies almost touching. For reasons beyond his control, Letivi was immediately aroused. Molly felt his 'arousal' touch her slightly. She quickly backed away as Letivi grabbed his underwear. He did a fast about-face and retreated into his bathroom. An overheated and embarrassed Letivi quickly closed the bathroom door.

Molly was working to catch her breath as she tried to understand what had just happened between her and Letivi. She now knew there was more between them than she could have imagined. As for Letivi, he was trying to cool himself down as he took off his royal gown and put on his new underwear. He looked at his half-stiff manhood and asked it why it was being so stupid. He slapped it once and commanded it to stop its nonsense. He put on his new white jockey shorts and jersey and donned again his gown. Before exiting the bathroom, he doused some cold water from the sink faucet onto his face. As he dried his face, he gave himself a serious talking-to in the mirror. Over and over, he told himself, "You are a chief. Act like a chief!"

Letivi exited the bathroom to find that Molly had neatly folded all his clothes and arranged them nicely in his suitcase. They both acted as if nothing had happened between them and he was indeed the chief and she was something of an administrative assistant and tour guide. Molly said, "You are the only one who will have to check a suitcase. Robin and I only have carry-on luggage. You need a lock for your suitcase. Do you know where we can get one?"

Letivi answered in the authoritative tone of a chief, saying, "I am sure the men from the presidency can get me a lock while we eat lunch."

Molly said, "I hope so. Let's take our bags and go downstairs to join Robin in the dining room."

Letivi quickly responded, "We should not be seen carrying our bags. That is beneath us. Leave the bags, and the hotel people will bring them down. All you need to do is take your purse."

Molly did not know why they could not carry their own bags, but she did not say anything and followed Letivi out the door of his hotel room, heading toward the elevator at the end of the hallway. When she arrived, Letivi had already pushed the button to call the elevator and was adjusting the position of his chief's hat on his head. The elevator doors sprang open, and Letivi told Molly to enter and allow him to operate the controls. He very much wanted to show Molly that he was now a master at conducting elevators.

As they exited the elevator, two men sitting nearby in the hotel lobby snapped to attention. These were the same men in black suits and sunglasses the president had sent yesterday. They had come again with the president's big black limousine to escort Letivi to the airport. With only the barest acknowledgement of their presence and without stopping, Letivi told them, "We must eat our lunch before going to the airport. While we eat, find me a lock for my suitcase and have the hotel porters bring our luggage to the lobby."

Letivi and Molly entered the hotel dining room to find Robin already eating chicken and fries and drinking a Coke at the VIP table. Robin smiled and said in a happy way, "Good morning— or is it good afternoon? Sorry, guys; I was too hungry, so I went ahead and ordered my food. This is a great day. I look forward to our departure for the good ol' USA."

Letivi and Molly were surprised to see that Robin was in an exceptionally ebullient mood. They could not know that he had been the beneficiary of Freda's natural gifts. He had thrown all cares out the window and ridded himself of his intolerable lust for Molly by submitting to the favors of Freda, the young local woman who had been on standby in the top-floor hallway to cater to Letivi's needs. When Letivi declined her services, she knocked on Robin's hotel door, and he allowed her into his room. It did not take long for her to work her sexy charms on the overly horny Robin.

Although he felt some shame for this naughty tryst, the physical relief he enjoyed made it seem worthwhile. Of course, this was something that must always remain his secret. One reason he was eager to get out of Kotoku was that he did not want to see Freda again. He was afraid she might tell someone about her time with the young white man. He was counting on her discretion, especially as this was something about which Molly must never know anything.

The waiter came with menus. Molly dispensed with the menu and said, "I'll take the same as my good friend Robin is eating and drinking."

Letivi also did not want to see the menu. Before he left his country, he wanted to eat the kind of food he would usually eat in the village. He told the waiter, "I need some good African chop. Can you bring me a nice plate of yam fufu with a spicy meat sauce?"

The short-statured, chubby waiter was at a loss as to how to respond, particularly as he was dealing with a chief he needed to obey. He had no choice but to say, "Chief, we do not make fufu here in the hotel, but I will arrange for a good fufu dish to be brought to the hotel."

Molly and Robin found Letivi's behavior curious but agreed that he should be allowed to eat what he wanted for his last meal before he left his country. They were surprised that the waiter returned with Letivi's food about the same time another waiter was serving Molly's plate of chicken and fries. Letivi's taste buds became activated as he opened the covered tin plates to reveal a mound of yam fufu and a peppery hot meat sauce. He could not wait to begin eating.

Before he could eat, a young woman came with a plastic bucket and kettle so Letivi could wash his hands. The woman used the kettle to pour water over Letivi's hands as he washed them with a small bar of soap. He then rinsed his hands and let them dry in the air. All the wastewater was caught in the bucket. Letivi made the sign of the cross and asked God, the ancestors, and all the spirits to bless his food.

Wide-eyed Molly and Robin could not take their eyes off Letivi and his eating habits. Letivi rolled up the right sleeve of his gown. Using the thumb, forefinger, and index finger of his right hand, he began tearing off chunks of fufu, forming them into a small ball, dipping them into the hot sauce, and placing them into his mouth. He swallowed each fufu bite without chewing it. For Letivi, he could not be happier. He was eating his favorite food in the traditional way. His only complaint was that the table was too high, unlike the low tables they ate on in the village.

Robin finished his food. Molly was too nervous about the trip and all that lay before them to eat much. Letivi devoured with much gusto every bit of fufu and the sauce that came with it. Molly and Robin were impressed that he could eat what he ate and consume it all. When Letivi finished his food, the young woman returned with the bucket and kettle of water; Letivi washed his hands and the area around his mouth. He turned to Molly and Robin, saying, "That was really good. I hope we can find food like that in America. I feel like a new man. Is everyone ready to go to the airport?"

Molly and Robin both excitedly responded at the same time, "Yes, let's go."

They left their table and headed toward the dining room exit. They found the hotel restaurant staff lined up at the door to wish Letivi a good trip. They clapped and cheered as they exited the dining hall. In the lobby area, the hotel staff was also lined up to wish Letivi the best of trips. There was again much clapping and cheering. The headman from the presidency stepped forward and said, "Chief, all is ready for you and your entourage to go to the airport. Your luggage has already been loaded into the car, and we have all the necessary travel documents ready. Your suitcase has been locked. I will give the key to your white female assistant. Please let us move forward and get into the waiting presidential limousine."

They bid farewell to the staff, exited the hotel, and entered the black and very sleek presidential limousine. Molly and Robin were concerned about verifying that their luggage was indeed in the vehicle, but they could see they would have to trust that all was OK because there was no way to stop the protocol of the moment. Molly and Robin were instructed to sit in the farthest black leather-covered backseat of the limo. Letivi was told to sit in the middle under a sliding roof door. The two men from the presidency sat up front with the driver. Once all were comfortably seated, the headman gave the order to pull out of the hotel entranceway.

As they exited the hotel grounds, there was a group of motorcycle police from the president's office waiting to escort them. With police lights flashing and sirens blaring, the motorcycle escort took up positions in front of and behind the limo. Molly and Robin were shocked to see that there was no traffic, and the streets were lined with well-wishers of every size, shape, and age. They learned later that the president had declared today a holiday for all the people in the city and had ordered all neighborhood chiefs to mobilize their people along the roadsides to say good-bye to Letivi. The president saw Letivi's trip as an opportunity to enhance his own image as a leader, and he expected Letivi's trip to pave the way for American investment in Kotoku.

The driver pushed a button on the dashboard that opened the sliding roof door. The president's headman told Letivi that they would be driving slowly to the airport so everyone could say good-bye to him, and he should stand up so he could be seen by the public. Letivi did as advised and found himself with head and shoulders protruding above the top of the limo. People cheered loudly when they saw him. He waved to the crowds on both sides of the street. It looked as if everyone in the capital city had come out to see him off. Some groups of people held banners and posters saying things like: "We Love You, Letivi," and "Letivi, Our White Chief Forever."

Letivi was astounded by the massive turnout of people who had come to see him off. He was both happy and fearful. Deep down, he was afraid of becoming too popular because he knew the president hated for anyone to be more popular than he was.

Molly and Robin could not believe their eyes. They knew there would not be any welcome for Letivi in America, and they had never heard of any celebrity in the States ever receiving such royal attention. They could not think of one instance when an entire city was shut down to see one person off. They wondered why a chief from a small village up-country would be treated in such a stupendous manner. Certainly, the travel of any small-town official from Kansas would not shut down the nation's capital. They were beginning to think that Letivi was more important than they had previously thought.

It took over an hour at a very slow pace to arrive at the President Nasungu International Airport. This was the first time Molly and Robin had noticed that the airport had been named after the father of the current president of Kotoku. The huge crowds at the airport had to be forcefully moved back by presidential guards so that the limo could drive past the main terminal and take its passengers to the VIP Salon. The limo stopped at the end of a long red strip of carpet that had been rolled out from the VIP Salon to a point about fifty yards away. The presidential brass band was all decked out and playing loud marching music. On both sides of the red strip of carpet were over a hundred high government officials and local traditional and clergy officials. They had been waiting under the hot sun for more than an hour to shake Letivi's hand and wish him a safe journey.

Letivi slowly stepped out of the limo to loud applause and cheering. On either side of him were the president's guards. Some distance behind Letivi trailed Molly and Robin like shy little sheep. Nobody shook their hands or said anything to them. They were ignored because they were extraneous to the event at hand. They were viewed as white outsiders who were only there to assist the White Chief on his trip to America. Their presence was not important, and, in any event, trying to relate to these foreigners would be awkward. All this was fine with Molly and Robin. They did not care for all the fanfare and protocol. They just wanted to get all the formalities over with and get on the plane.

Letivi did his best to play the politician and diplomat, engaging in a lively manner with each person waiting in line. He was happy to see the director of his old school had been invited, and he embraced him. His hand was hurting from so much hand-shaking and it was beginning to swell. As he arrived at the end of the red carpet, he walked up the few steps leading to the VIP Salon entrance and turned around to say one final good-bye to all those who had graciously come to see him off. He raised both his arms in a gesture of thanks. Seeing his arms lifted into the air, the crowd clapped and cheered loudly.

Just before the entrance to the VIP Salon, a group of the country's top fetish priests and clergy were waiting to bless him and his trip. The fetish priests chanted powerful words of magic as they blew smoke and fine powder over him. They placed around his neck a cowhide string with leather pouches attached. These pouches contained protective amulets. He was told to keep this protection on him at all times.

When the fetish priests had completed their rituals, Catholic and Protestant clergy dressed in their finest church robes asked Letivi to kneel so he could receive their blessings. Letivi readily did as they asked. They walked around Letivi swinging a thurible with burning incense while they took turns reading from the Bible and saying prayers. When they were finished, the oldest among them placed a gold necklace with a cross pendant around Letivi's neck. They told him to never remove this cross, as it had been sanctified by the Holy Spirit.

Molly and Robin were looking forward to entering the VIP Salon to get out of the humid heat and the crowds. They expected that they would be mostly alone in the salon and have time to regroup and think about their next move. When they followed Letivi and his guards into the well-air-conditioned salon, they were not happy about seeing a room crowded with top government officials and diplomats. The American ambassador was there to meet Letivi and wish him well. He also greeted warmly Molly and Robin and thanked them for making Letivi's trip possible. He said this trip was great for strengthening relations between America and Kotoku.

Nearly an hour passed as they socialized with this elite group. Champaign flowed freely, and caviar was passed around as if there were an unending supply. The diplomats used this rare opportunity to drive home their pet messages to key government officials and to sound out their diplomatic colleagues on various issues. In other words, the diplomats were working this event and would return to their respective embassies to write classified cable reports on what they had done and learned at this auspicious occasion.

If nothing else, these reports would ensure that Letivi's name would become widely known across the world and there would be much analysis of his potential political role in Kotoku. The diplomats concurred that the popular Letivi was someone they needed to follow in the future. Some ambassadors would make sure that his name was henceforth on their invitation lists and that he would be considered for official visits to their respective countries. Whether he wanted it or not, Letivi was becoming part of embassy bio files and watch lists. The diplomats now knew they needed to ferret out more background on this popular white chief. They sure did not want the Americans to get the inside track with a potential leader of Kotoku.

Robin had drunk too much champagne and stuffed himself with caviar. This was the first time Molly and Robin had tasted caviar. Molly feared the champagne would go to her head, so she only drank a few sips. After a few nibbles, she found the caviar too salty for her palate. Letivi was too busy talking and meeting people to partake of substances he considered foreign and distasteful. Letivi was not used to all the attention and talking with so many people he did not know. He was exhausted and wished that all this would come to an end. He was relieved when his presidential handlers told him it was time to go to an adjoining room and prepare for boarding the plane.

Letivi said, "I am glad to hear this, but before I go, I believe protocol requires that I say a few words to this group of high officials."

Upon hearing these words, one of the president's men beat loudly on a champagne bottle with a steel knife and asked the crowd to listen to Chief Letivi, who looked around the crowd facing him and pronounced a short speech.

"Thank you for coming to see me leave on my trip to America. I was not aware that important people such as you would be here, but I am happy that you did come. It has been a great pleasure for me to meet you and talk to many of you. I look forward to future opportunities to see many of you after I return. Now they tell me the time has come for us to board the plane. I have no choice but to say good-bye.

"Before I go, please allow me to present to you Molly and Robin from Kansas. It is because of them that I have the opportunity to travel to America. They came all this way in search of a man from Kansas. After talking with them, we discovered that maybe this man could have been someone who lived in my village a long time ago. Our trip is mostly about finding more information on this man. Of course, this gives me a great opportunity to know for the first time America. Thanks again. Good-bye. Until we meet again."

The crowd applauded enthusiastically Letivi's speech. The dean of the diplomatic community offered one last toast in Letivi's honor. There was one final round of applause as the president's men led Letivi and his two Americans into an adjoining room where the chief of presidential protocol was waiting for them. This man was dressed regally in the latest European fashion and impressed all with his professional demeanor. He told Letivi, "I have here all your travel documents and boarding passes. All of you will be sitting in the first row in first class. Chief, your suitcase has already been checked. You will find the baggage tag pasted on your boarding pass. A duplicate key to your suitcase is taped inside your ticket. Your hand luggage is already in the overhead compartments above your seats. All is in order. You have nothing to worry about. To whom should I give the travel documents?"

As the half-drunk Robin wobbled about, Letivi indicated the travel documents could be turned over to Molly. He thanked the protocol chief, who pointed to a side exit where the limo was waiting to take them to the plane. It was late afternoon, and the Air Afrique flight to Dakar was fully boarded, behind schedule, and only waiting for the chief and his party to board before taking off. They drove the short distance on the tarmac to the waiting plane. They exited the limo and followed the protocol chief through thick swarms of swirling traditional dancers and noisy drummers to the stairs leading up to the airplane door.

The protocol chief showed them to their seats and bid them farewell and safe travels. Letivi followed him the few steps back to the plane entrance. As he stood in the entranceway, he could see that a large crowd had gathered on the upper outside balcony of the airport terminal. He raised his right hand high in the air to wave to them. When the crowd saw him waving, it let out a thunderous explosion of cheers. Letivi kept waving as long as he could. He was profoundly seized by the moment. He could not believe he was actually leaving Kotoku for the first time.

When he saw airport workers moving the stairs away, he felt a tightening twist in his stomach that told him it was true; he was really leaving his country to travel to America. A stewardess kindly asked him to step back and go to his seat because she needed to close the door. As Letivi made his way to his seat, he heard the door close with a loud, muffled thud. For him, the heretofore unheard noise signaled a huge turning point in his life. He was bedeviled because he did not know whether this unanticipated part of his destiny's path was a good or a bad thing.

CHAPTER TWENTY-FIVE
GOING TO AMERICA

Letivi had not been on a plane before. From the moment he took his ample first-class seat next to Molly, he did not like being on a plane. He felt confined and a bit claustrophobic. His main reaction was to try to get off the plane and flee. Sweat began pouring down his forehead, and his body twitched nervously. His anxiety increased as the plane began taxiing down the runway. The thought that there was now no escape caused him to choke and be short of breath. In his traumatized state, he could not hear Molly saying loudly, "Letivi, sit back and fasten your seat belt."

When Letivi did not heed her instructions, Molly forcefully pushed Letivi back into his seat and buckled his seat belt. Letivi did not like be restricted like this and was trying to unbuckle his seat belt, but the roar of the plane's engine's made him stop fumbling with the seat belt latch. He clutched tightly Molly's left hand. As the plane picked up speed to take off, Letivi squeezed Molly's hand with his right hand while holding firmly in his left hand the Christian and fetish pendants hanging from the necklaces on his neck. He shut his eyes and mumbled prayers, beseeching all the gods, ancestors, and spirits for their protection. He was still talking to himself after the plane had taken off and the attendants had switched off the illuminated fasten-your-seat-belt sign. He was oblivious to the world around him.

From across the aisle, Robin was yelling at Molly to do something about Letivi's frightful condition. He handed Molly a vomit bag to keep at the ready in case Letivi threw up. Molly was quite concerned. Letivi's complexion had turned purplish. She was afraid that he was going to pass out. Molly raised her voice an octave as she repeatedly called out, "Letivi, are you OK? Please say something."

Letivi slowly stirred from his highly traumatized state. He began to hear Molly's voice. He then realized that he had a full grip on Molly's hand. Startled by the way he was holding her hand, he quickly released it. A few moments later, he found his voice and weakly said, "I think I am OK now. For a moment, I thought I was going to die. As you can probably see, I've never been on a plane before."

Molly said in a soothing voice, "Relax, and don't worry. Everything will be all right."

Letivi reached up to take off his chief's hat and was surprised to find that it was not on his head. Immediately, in a rather loud tone, he asked Molly, "Where's my hat? I can't go without my hat!"

Letivi became quite agitated over not being able to find the hat, which had been passed down from one chief to another for generations. He had to find and keep safe this priceless village heirloom. This chiefly hat had never been out of the country before. He kept trying to stand up so he could search for it, but he did not know how to unbuckle his seat belt. Molly told Letivi, "Just relax. I will find your hat for you. Sit still while I look."

Robin was amused by Letivi's loss of his hat. He offered to help look for it, but Molly was already up and looking around. She looked under the seats. She could see Letivi's hat lying on the floor behind his seat. Evidently, it had tumbled off his head backward while he was undergoing his takeoff trauma episode. She was afraid the passenger sitting behind Letivi would step on it. She quickly but very politely asked the man sitting behind Letivi, "Please, sir. The hat of the man sitting in front of you has fallen on the floor in front of your feet. Can you be so kind as to pick it up and give it to me?"

The bald-headed old white man smiled and awkwardly reached down. He grabbed the hat, and when he handed it to Molly, he said some words in a language she did not understand. Molly responded with a simple, "Thank you very much, sir."

Letivi heard the man's words and struggled even more to release his seat belt. Molly returned to her seat and told Letivi that she would put his hat in their hand luggage in the overhead compartment. Letivi briskly said, "That will be good. Can you help me so I can go talk to the man behind me?"

With the flip of one finger, Molly opened the metal latch on Letivi's seat belt, and he immediately stood up and passed in front of Molly to go see the man sitting behind him. Molly thought Letivi wanted to thank the man in person for retrieving his hat. She then heard Letivi speaking to the man in the same language he had spoken when he had handed her the hat. She stood up to look behind their seats, and she could see Letivi carrying on an animated conversation with the old man, who appeared to be enjoying immensely his exchange with Letivi.

Molly could not wait to ask Letivi which language he was using when he spoke with the old man. She waited much longer than she had expected, as Letivi spent almost thirty minutes talking to the old man. He returned to take his seat next to Molly when he saw the stewardesses handing out headphones. Once Letivi was seated, Molly blurted out, "Letivi, what on earth was that all about?"

Letivi calmly and in a matter-of-fact tone said, "The man is Greek. We spoke in Greek about nothing. I've always wanted to speak Greek with a Greek. I learned Greek in school, but I never had the opportunity to use this language until now. He said I speak perfectly the old form of standard Greek."

Molly was impressed. "How did you learn Greek and why?"

"I learned with the priests who taught at my Catholic boy's school in Melomti. I also learned Latin. I really like learning languages. I was so good in Greek that the priests called me Mousaios, after a legendary scholar and prophet in ancient Greece."

"I did not know that you were such a good student."

"I was the best student the school had ever had. I read all the books in the school library, the university library, and the National Archives. I helped many other students with their schoolwork and was invited to give speeches everywhere. That is why many people know me."

Robin was listening in and was intrigued that he and Letivi had a common interest in books. He talked across the aisle, telling Letivi, "I will be happy to take you to some libraries and bookstores in America. I'm sure you will be very impressed."

Letivi replied, "Thank you, Robin. I look forward to that. I love books. All I know is from books. The only thing I don't know is in the books I have not read. I miss reading. Ever since I became chief, I stopped reading. There is nothing to read in the village."

Robin was struck by Letivi's words about knowing only what is in books because that was exactly what his grandfather in Kansas used to say. Letivi turned to Molly and Robin to add, "When I was in school, bishops came from Rome to take me to a school in the Vatican that was reserved for the training of their best and brightest priests. I did not go because I had to fulfill my destiny and stay near my village so I could become chief."

Letivi did not tell them that he had to be in the village when his father, David Peterson, returned from Kansas. He could never tell them that. He knew they would question his sanity and be unable to believe that the old baobab had conspired with the full moon to snatch David from Gemini, Kansas, and, after a stopover in the spirit world, land him at the foot of the old baobab. That was really what had happened to the David they were looking for, but it was something he could never tell them.

Molly's and Robin's regard for Letivi was ratcheted up a few notches after learning about his academic prowess. Molly told Letivi, "That is very impressive. You know, both Robin and I have university degrees."

It was Letivi's turn to be surprised. He could not believe that Molly and Robin could possess university diplomas and be so ignorant of Africa and its ways. He had never previously met anyone with a college degree except his high-school teachers. This was the first time he had ever met a woman with a university degree. He wasted no time in telling them, "That is really something. Are there many people in America who have done higher learning?"

Molly responded, "Letivi, America is a big and rich country, and one of the things that makes it a powerful nation is that most of its people have finished high school and tens of thousands have done university work. Everybody goes to school in America.

There are schools everywhere. If you wanted, you could easily continue your studies in America."

Letivi was busy trying to imagine a country where everyone went to school and the difference that would make. He knew that in his country a high percentage of the population, particularly women, was illiterate. He was about to say something about this when he saw Molly put on her headphones to watch the TV suspended from the ceiling in front of him. This marvel stopped Letivi in midsentence.

He had never watched TV in this way before. He wanted to do like Molly. He managed to extricate the headset from the plastic wrapping in which it was sealed. He placed the headset on his head and put its spongy ends into his ears, but he could not hear anything. Molly noticed Letivi had not plugged in the earphones, so she showed him the two small holes at the end of the armrest where he should insert the two jacks. Letivi did as Molly had demonstrated and was immediately taken to another world.

Letivi's enchantment with the TV was interrupted by Molly telling him that dinner was being served and he needed to lower his serving tray. Letivi did not know what she meant. He fiddled with the ashtray receptacle embedded in the armrest and twisted awkwardly the service tray knob on the seat in front of him. He wondered if touching the light and stewardess call buttons above him would release the tray. Molly, who was having a hard time not laughing over Letivi's attempts to make the food tray appear, reached over to turn the latch. Robin was chuckling at Letivi's antics and leaned over into the aisle to tell Molly, "Looks like you can take the boy out of the village, but you can't take the village out of the boy. I guess you can't learn everything you need to know by reading books."

The stewardess arrived with her food trolley and asked Molly and Letivi if they would like beef or chicken. Molly took the chicken, and Letivi jumped at the opportunity to eat some meat. The stewardess smiled at Letivi and handed him his food tray. She did the same for Molly. Letivi stared at his tray, struggling to see the "food" on it. He did not recognize anything on the tray. Like a mother would help a child, Molly unwrapped the food items on Letivi's tray. Even after the unwrapping, Letivi remained stumped, as he did not see any food that he was accustomed to eating.

The "beef" was a few chunks of meat mixed with rice—not the thick steak he was expecting. He was about to dabble in the beef dish with his fingers when Molly gently told him that it was better to use the plastic fork and knife provided. He broke a tong off the fork as he stabbed the first chunk of beef. After that, he was more careful in the use of the fragile fork, but the food did not taste good to him. He explored the other little dishes on the tray, but nothing appealed to him. He did eat the little baguette of bread provided by dunking it in a glass of water. He did the same with a second piece of bread offered to him by the same smiling stewardess, who removed his tray, asking him if he wanted coffee or tea to drink. Unsure of what to say, Letivi shook his head.

Molly was appalled by Letivi's eating manners, but all she said to Letivi was, "You need to eat. This flight to Dakar is almost three hours long, and the flight from Dakar to New York is about nine hours. Then, from New York to Wichita, it can take six more hours. So you need to eat anytime you have the opportunity to do so. I know it's hard to change your taste preferences, but you will need to do that if you are going to be able to eat the food provided to you in America."

Letivi listened well to Molly's words. He knew that she was right. He responded by saying, "I wish I would have brought with me some cassava flour to munch on. I don't know why I didn't bring any. Everybody takes cassava flour with them when they travel."

Molly replied in a firm tone, "It's a good thing you didn't bring any. It would have caused us a problem with the US Agriculture Service when going through the port of entry formalities at JFK Airport in New York. They confiscate all agriculture products, and they sometimes apply fines."

Letivi did not quite understand what Molly meant. He did not know what to say. He reached into his gown pocket and pulled out a stubby tooth-cleaning stick that was frayed at one end. He began rubbing vigorously the frayed end of the stick against all sides of his teeth. Molly was observing closely this unusual use of what appeared to be a cutting of a tree twig. She found herself obliged to ask, "Letivi, what are you doing?"

Letivi stopped his teeth rubbing for a moment to reply, "I'm cleaning my teeth with an African toothpick. One reason we have such strong and white teeth is the use of such toothpicks."

Molly replied as politely as she could, "Letivi, please never do what you are doing now to clean your teeth when you are in America. In my country, such a habit would be frowned upon."

Letivi grunted acknowledgement of Molly's words and stopped rubbing his teeth, but he kept the stick in his mouth to chew on. He turned to look out the small window again, as he had been doing every few minutes. He could not understand why it was all black outside the plane. With his tooth stick dangling from his mouth, he asked Molly, "Why is it so black outside? I cannot see any stars or the moon, or any lights on the ground."

Molly cleared her throat and replied, "It is probably because we are flying in dense clouds. Letivi, can you please do me a big favor and take that disgusting stick out of your mouth?"

Letivi was somewhat shocked by Molly's demand, but he immediately took the stick out of his mouth and put it back into his pocket. Molly was thinking about all the work she would have to do to get Letivi to conform to behavioral norms in America. Letivi was getting ready to return to his immersion in watching TV when the plane shook as if it would fall apart. Letivi's rapid, involuntary reaction was to grab Molly's hand. The fasten-your-seat-belt indicator flashed on, and the captain informed all passengers over the intercom system that they should fasten their seat belts because they were entering a zone of turbulence. As Letivi was fumbling with the seat belt latch, Molly again had to help him fasten his seat belt. It was not easy to tighten the seat belt over Letivi's ample chief's robes.

The plane suffered some severe jolts. Letivi was afraid they would crash. He wished he had paid more attention to the presentation given by the stewardess before they took off about what to do in an emergency. He told himself if this was how flying was, he would never fly again unless it was absolutely necessary. He repeated the word "turbulence" over and over. This was a new word to him, and he liked the sound of it even though turbulence was now threatening his life. The turbulence gradually ceased, and the captain announced on the intercom, "We are now out of the zone of turbulence. But we are beginning our descent to Dakar, so keep your seat belts fastened."

The plane dipped its nose and began descending rapidly as it aimed for the Dakar Yoff International Airport. The plane burst through the cloud cover, and Letivi was pleased to see below the lights of ships at sea and villages along the shore. The plane slowed, and there was a loud cranking noise as the landing gear was lowered. This noise prompted Letivi to grasp Molly's hand again. He was genuinely afraid, particularly as he thought that landing was more dangerous than taking off. His heart skipped a beat as the plane made a bouncy landing on the tarmac. He released Molly's hand as the plane stabilized and taxied to a parking position on the runway in front of the airport terminal.

Letivi was very relieved. He loudly exhaled a big breath when the plane came to a standstill. He told Molly, "I am pleased to be in Senegal. I have always wanted to see another African country."

Molly quickly told Letivi, "You will not be seeing anything. When we get off this plane, they will put us on a bus and take us directly to our Pan Am flight to New York."

Before Letivi could express his disappointment, a voice announced over the public address system, "Thank you for flying with Air Afrique. For arriving passengers, we hope you enjoy your stay in Senegal. For transit passengers, we wish you a good onward journey. For those passengers going on the Pan Am flight to New York, we ask that you disembark to board a waiting bus. Please have your tickets and passports in hand. Do not forget anything in your seats or any of your hand luggage in the overhead bins."

With satisfaction, Letivi clicked open his seat belt and then stood up to join Molly and Robin in the aisle. Robin took down their three carry-on bags from the overhead storage compartment and handed Molly and Letivi their bags. When Robin handed Letivi his bag, Letivi hesitated because he did not know what he was supposed to do with it. Never before in his life had he carried his own bags or done much of anything himself that involved physical labor. Letivi wanted to fit in more, so he took his bag and placed the strap over his shoulder just as Molly and Robin had done. At that moment, it dawned on him that outside his own country, he was no longer a chief or anyone important.

Robin led the way off the plane, followed by Molly and Letivi. The attendants wished them a very good time in America as they stepped out and began to walk down the stairs. Molly had to help Letivi hold up his royal gown so he would not step on its bottom edges as he descended the stairs. On the ground, their papers were checked, and then they were told to board a nearby bus. Increasingly, almost everything was a new experience for Letivi. He had never been on a bus before, and he had never imagined a bus without seats. They and numerous other passengers stood, holding on to leather straps dangling from a round metal bar fastened to the top of the bus's ceiling. As soon as the last passenger boarded, the bus wasted no time in transporting them a short distance to where the Pan Am plane was parked.

They descended from the bus and were escorted to the plane's stairs by an attendant who repeatedly cried out for first-class passengers to board first. Letivi no longer felt like royalty, but Molly and Robin felt they were being given royal treatment with their upgrades to first class. They climbed up the stairs and were warmly welcomed by the attendant, who showed them their nearby first-class seats. They were in the same position as in their Air Afrique flight, but the seats were much bigger. Molly and Robin were happily grateful for their good luck in having such great first-class seats. Letivi was only seeing more challenges and felt faint as he thought of taking such a long flight. He prayed silently to the ancestors for the added strength he needed to survive another flight.

Robin collected their handbags and stored them in the overhead compartments. The attendant handed out newspapers and magazines, and then she offered drinks—champagne, orange juice, or water. Letivi played it safe and took water. Molly and Robin could not turn down the opportunity to drink champagne and clinked their glasses together. They were both happy to be returning home.

Letivi was too busy looking out the window at all the activity. He saw many planes—more planes than he had ever seen in his life. They were mostly very big planes with different words written on them in a variety of colors. He could see the world was a much bigger place than he had ever imagined.

As the plane was being readied for takeoff, Molly turned to Letivi and said, "This would be a good time to change from your royal chief outfit into your new clothes that are packed in your carry-on bag. It would be good if you arrived in America wearing your new clothes. Do you think you can change your clothes in the plane's restroom?"

Letivi responded, "I don't know. I have not yet used the plane toilet, but I do need to pee."

"We'll need to wait until after takeoff and the fasten-your-seatbelt indicator has been turned off. I will ask Robin to escort you to the toilet, and you can try to change."

The airplane attendants went through the usual drill of closing the plane's door, asking everyone to fasten their seat belts, and demonstrating what to do in case of an emergency. Letivi paid attention this time because he knew almost the entire flight would take place over the Atlantic Ocean. He had now mastered the seat belt latch and felt proud of this accomplishment. Letivi felt the same chill go down his spine when they closed the plane's doors. His heart beat faster as he clasped Molly's hand for the noisy takeoff. After the plane was well on its way, he let go of Molly's hand, breathed easier, and prayed for a smooth flight. In doing the latter, he was much like everyone else on the plane.

As soon as the fasten-your-seat-belt indicator was turned off, Molly told Letivi and Robin to hurry to the toilet to see if Letivi could change his clothes. Robin fetched Letivi's bag from the overhead compartment, and they both hustled down the aisle to the toilet stall. Robin opened the first vacant stall. He told Letivi to step into the stall, handed him his bag, and showed him the knob on the inside of the toilet door that he would have to shove sideways to lock the door and turn on the toilet lights. He closed the door and waited just outside for Letivi to finish.

Letivi had never been in such a cramped space. He looked around, and all he saw was alien. He did know he needed to pee, so he placed his handbag on the floor between his legs and began wrestling with the drawstrings on the cotton pants he wore under his royal robe. He would have to lower his pants and then gather his ample robe up in his arms so he could pee into the metal toilet. Doing all this was not easy, as the space was too tiny to allow his usual movements for such an effort. He did manage to pee, and he noticed next to the toilet a small blue lever with the word "flush." He pushed down on the lever and was startled by the loud sucking sound that it produced as it flushed the toilet with a whirlpool of blue liquid. The sound made him back up and slam into the door. The thud alarmed Robin, and he called through the door, "Letivi, is everything OK?"

Letivi replied, "No problem." He then tried to see how he could remove his royal clothes in such a cramped space. He tried in many ways to remove his royal outer garment, but there was just not enough room to stretch his arms fully so he could get the garment off. He stood on the toilet; he sat on the toilet; he turned around and around; but he could not get in the position he needed to remove his outer garment. His effort caused him to perspire profusely. He finally gave up and redressed himself in his royal clothes as well as he could. He unlatched the door and found Robin talking to the stewardess, who was asking if there was a problem, as other passengers were complaining that his friend had spent too much time in the toilet.

The tired and irritated Letivi did not say a word or look at anyone as he brushed by those passengers waiting to go to the toilet. Robin followed Letivi back to his seat. Letivi handed Robin his handbag and took his seat next to Molly, who was surprised to see Letivi still in his chief's clothes. The peeved Letivi said, "I'm sorry. The toilet room is too small for me to change my clothes."

Molly could see that Letivi was upset by not being able to change his clothes, so she said gently, "OK. That is not a problem. You can easily change clothes in the first big bathroom we come across in JFK Airport."

Letivi found his headset on his seat, but before he could put it on, the stewardess came with the drink trolley and asked what he would like to drink. He could see that she had beer, so he requested a bottle of beer. He was given one that he had not seen before, as it was American. He read the label but could not say the name. He asked Molly to pronounce the name for him. Molly said, "It is a Budweiser, or we refer to it just as Bud."

Letivi did not pour the beer into the glass provided. He took the bottle directly to his mouth and guzzled quickly its entire contents. Molly winced again at such unacceptable behavior on Letivi's part. Letivi wiped his mouth with his right hand and said, "That was good, but it was too watery. I could not taste the alcohol. In my country, the bottled beers have higher alcohol content. Anyway, I will ask for more beer."

After the drinks came the food trolley. Letivi chose the fish this time. He was again disappointed. The few pieces of mushy fish were marinated in a sauce that tasted awful to him. He asked for another beer and more bread. He toyed with his food again. He timidly tasted every food item to see if he could eat any of them, but nothing agreed with his palate. He thought he might enjoy the custard dessert, but it was far too sweet for his taste. He took the tinfoil wrapping off the soft French camembert cheese, thinking this might be a new food he would like, but the smell alone nauseated him. He did eat the crackers and licked the small patty of butter off its cover in one swipe of his tongue. He contented himself with bread, water, and his weak beer.

When he finished eating, he wiped his mouth again with his right hand. He did not know that he had on his food tray a napkin. He wanted to clean his teeth with his little twig but refrained from doing so because he knew Molly did not like that. He was eager to watch some TV and put his earphones on. He became so engrossed in watching TV that he did not notice when the food trays were taken away and the plane was darkened to allow people who wanted to do so to sleep. The thing that did take him away from his TV was the cold he felt penetrating his body.

He had never experienced such coldness. He looked at Molly and Robin and could see they were both sleeping under blankets. He finally spotted on the floor in front of him a blanket of the same color wrapped in a clear plastic bag. He removed the blanket and covered himself with it. The blanket helped, but he was still too cold. When the stewardess passed by, he asked her for another blanket. With two blankets covering him, he felt better and returned to watching a movie on TV.

As the night wore on, Letivi was among the few on the plane who did not try to sleep. Molly was in a deep sleep, and at one point her head came to rest on Letivi's arm. Letivi liked feeling Molly next to him. Not only was it nice to have a woman close, but her closeness made him feel warmer. He missed his own bed in the village and sleeping next to the always-agreeable Delalia. He was starting to think that flying in a plane was not so bad.

The hours wore on, and before Letivi could finish his second movie, the cabin lights were switched on, and an announcement was broadcast over the intercom that breakfast would be served and they were about two hours from JFK, where the local time was about four in the morning. Letivi wondered how the night had passed so quickly. Molly had said the flight was nine hours long, but they were arriving at JFK only a few hours later than their takeoff time in Dakar. He waited for Molly to wake up so he could ask her why the flight was shorter than she had said.

Robin was awake before Molly and was upset to see Molly lying against Letivi. He told himself that she should be sitting next to him, not Letivi. He was jealous of Letivi and all the attention he received from Molly. He recalled how tight he had been with Molly on the flight to Africa, and he couldn't get out of his head how they had slept together at the hotel in Melomti. He wished Letivi could disappear so he and Molly could continue building their relationship.

Molly awoke, and Letivi began to bombard her with questions. "How can we leave Dakar at about midnight and arrive at JFK just before sunrise? How can this be possible?"

A sleepy-headed Molly was in no mood to reply. She said, "Letivi, please let me wake up first. You must know that we went through many time zones, and New York's time is five hours earlier than Dakar time. It is also the following day here."

These words from Molly perplexed Letivi, and he continued to try to figure out why there was such a difference in hours. This was a phenomenon that he had never previously experienced. He was telling himself that there were many things that he had not read in books. Molly looked at Letivi's haggard face and asked him, "Letivi, did you sleep any at all?"

Letivi was bemused at Molly's questions and replied snippily, "No. I didn't sleep. Why? Was I supposed to? I was too busy enjoying television for the first time in my life."

Molly retorted, "You will regret not having slept. Be ready to experience a serious case of jet lag."

Letivi dismissed Molly's comment as not being important, especially as he had never heard of "jet lag." He was eager to eat his breakfast because he knew it would be composed of items with which he was more familiar. He gorged himself on croissants, butter, and jam, washing it all down with well-sugared coffee. He felt good and was eager to land in America.

The plane glided in slowly as it descended to JFK Airport. Everyone on the plane, especially Letivi, was excited to catch glimpses of downtown Manhattan and the Statue of Liberty. Letivi's eyes and brain were not capable of comprehending all he was seeing. One fear he had concerned landing in the ocean because he could see the airport landing strips were surrounded by water. He was pleased this time that the landing was very smooth, and he did not feel the need to hold Molly's hand. All the passengers clapped their hands and cheered when the plane landed. For Letivi, this was more like it, and he readily joined in, clapping hard and shouting some praises for the pilots.

Letivi gazed out the window as they neared the airport terminal. He could not believe his eyes. He saw a multiple of the number of planes he had seen at the Dakar Airport, and Molly told him this was only one part of the overall JFK Airport. As the plane was docking, Molly told Letivi, "Listen to me well. Stay close to me, and don't wander off. It is very easy to get lost here. There are thousands of people coming and going, sometimes in a very chaotic manner. I have all your paper work. Also, I have completed the customs forms that were handed out earlier on the plane for our entry into America. We must go through the formalities here, find our baggage, and take it to where it will be put on our next flight to Wichita. This can be very complicated, so stay close to me."

Letivi meekly replied, "Don't worry. I will be with you every step of the way."

They collected their handbags and debarked, walking quickly along one corridor that joined a wider corridor. There was a huge mass of people. Letivi felt as if he were in a fast-flowing river filled with a wide assortment of human beings. Everyone seemed in a frantic hurry. They followed the signs pointing to the hall where everyone must show their passports and, if not American, their valid US visas. They arrived at the vast hall, where Letivi was stunned by the large number of people waiting in lines. He had never seen more people in one place than he was seeing now. There were more people than lived in Ataku and perhaps his entire district. He was beginning to appreciate that America was a very big country. He was trying to suppress a gut reaction to run the other way.

They came to a men's restroom, and Molly told Letivi, "This is a good place to change your clothes and freshen up. Robin will go with you. I will go to the adjoining women's restroom. We should meet back here in fifteen minutes. We have three hours until our next flight, so we should have plenty of time."

Both Letivi and Robin nodded their heads and entered the spacious restroom. Letivi tried not to let on that he was over-whelmed by the large number of sinks, urinals, and toilet stalls. He wondered if there were this many modern flush toilets in all the public buildings in his country. Letivi entered one of the toilet stalls with his handbag and, after urinating, began the chore of changing from traditional clothes to modern ones.

While Letivi was changing, Robin used the toilet and washed his face and hands. He was very happy to be back in what he called "the good old USA." Ten minutes passed, and Robin asked Letivi, "Are you ready yet?"

Letivi replied, "Almost." He had changed his clothes but was having trouble tying his new shoes and stuffing his royal gown into his handbag. He finally managed to tie his shoes, but part of his gown had to remain sticking out of the open top of his hand-bag because it was too big for the bag. He stepped out of the toilet in his new duds. It was an amazing transformation! One kind of Letivi had entered the toilet stall, and a completely different Letivi came out. Robin could not believe the difference. In his eyes, Letivi looked so much better. Letivi looked in the mirror and was shocked by his new look. It would take some time for him to get used to this total makeover. He was not sure this was a better way for him to dress, although the clothes weighed less and were easier to wear.

Letivi turned on a faucet at one of the sinks, doused water on his face, and washed his hands with the liquid soap dripping from a chromium container on the wall. They exited the rest-room to meet Molly, who was already waiting for them. Molly was also blown away by Letivi's radically changed appearance. He could easily pass himself off as a well-to-do, handsome young man. She was sure he would catch the eyes of many ladies. They joined the line for American citizens. Molly told Letivi, "There is a different line for non-US citizens, but let's try to be accepted as a family." The long line of people snaked back and forth at a slow pace as they steadily approached the immigration agents who would examine their passports and custom forms.

After about thirty minutes, they arrived in front of one of dozens of booths where entry documents were being checked. Letivi continued to be impressed not only by the number of people but by the wide diversity of people. In his country, everyone was black. Here, there was every imaginable racial type. He was intrigued to see mixed-race people like him. Here, he was just a small fish in a large pond. In his own country, he was a big fish in a small pond. He did not like the feeling of being a 'nobody.' He felt like a fish out of water.

They were called forward by the immigration agent, and Molly led the way, placing all their passports and forms on the counter in front of the agent. He began examining their documents closely. He noted that Letivi should have gone to the VIP/Diplomatic line, but he could see they were traveling together. He asked Letivi to sign the customs form that Molly had completed for him. Letivi frantically tried to recall how he had signed his passport. He jotted down his unusual signature, which was unlike anything anyone would use in America. It looked more like chicken scratches than a signature. The middle-aged, Hispanic agent laughed at Letivi's weird signature as he stamped the form and Letivi's passport. He handed all the paper work to him, saying with a wide smile, "Welcome to America." It was at that moment that Letivi knew he was really out of Africa and truly on the way to the land of his father.

CHAPTER TWENTY-SIX
LAND OF MY FATHER

L etivi could not move. He was paralyzed by all he beheld in the baggage reception area. His eyes could not comprehend the vast scope of all the activity. There were a dozen baggage turntables receiving suitcases being ejected magically from the bowels of the airport to ride on mechanical conveyor belts. Letivi stood transfixed as he tried to figure out how things worked and what the people walking to and fro were doing with a kind of pushcart he had never seen before. He was struck again by the diversity of the people and the variety and heaviness of the clothes they were wearing. He had never seen people wearing heavy sweaters and coats. Letivi was feeling very out of place. He was asking himself, "What am I doing here in this strange world? I want to go home."

Molly and Robin did not understand Letivi's hesitancy. They were in a hurry to collect his suitcase, clear customs, and check his bag for their flight to Wichita. Molly spoke loudly so Letivi could hear her above the noisy clamor. "Letivi, what is the matter? We need to find your suitcase and take it to the drop-off point for our next TWA flight. We really have no time to lose. Let's go quickly to where your suitcase should be. Follow me."

Briskly, Molly led the way to where the suitcases from their flight were being unloaded. Letivi was surprised to see his suitcase moving along in front of them on the metallic conveyor belt. Molly and Robin thought Letivi would run forward and grab his suitcase, but Letivi stood still, marveling at how his suitcase had traveled so far and ended up here. He also did not know he was supposed to carry his own suitcase. Letivi's failure to take his suitcase off the conveyor belt exasperated Molly and Robin. They waited patiently for the suitcase to come around again to where they were standing. As soon as he spotted Letivi's suitcase again, Robin ran forward and snatched it off the belt. He yanked out the handle and pulled it behind himself on its rollers. Robin looked at Letivi and rudely yelled, "Let's go. Let's get out of here."

Molly and Letivi trailed behind Robin as he strolled to the exit. Agents were waiting to inspect their baggage and receive their custom forms. They moved swiftly past a customs agent and walked to where they put Letivi's bag on another long conveyor belt that would lead to its being loaded onto their next flight. Molly and Robin were moving too fast for Letivi. He wanted to walk slowly, as he was accustomed to doing in the village, so he could better take in this totally new world into which he had been thrust. The pace was too fast for Letivi. He felt like sitting down to recuperate from all the multiple novel shocks he was experiencing. He was also tired from carrying his handbag. He looked for a place to sit down, but he did not see any benches or chairs. He was unnerved by Molly and Robin's constant nudging and telling him to hurry. In his village, there was never any hurry, and it was bad matters to rush by others without greeting them properly.

Molly was examining their tickets and looking at a big-screen TV that presented all the departing flights. She was looking for the gate and terminal they needed to use for their onward flight. Once she got this information, she told Letivi and Robin, "Follow me. We need to get out of this terminal and catch a shuttle bus to another terminal. We must hurry, as we don't have much time."

Letivi did not know what Molly was talking about, but he had no choice but to follow along like a captured prisoner. Molly walked at a fast clip to board an escalator that would take them up to ground level. Robin kept gently nudging Letivi forward, but when they arrived at the escalator, Letivi froze. He had never used such a "moving stairs." He was afraid to step onto the escalator. A very frustrated Robin harshly told Letivi, "Stop acting like a child. Hold tightly to the banister and step squarely onto the first step of the escalator that appears in front of you."

Very hesitantly, a nervous and shaky Letivi stepped onto the moving metal stairs. At first, he lost his balance and almost fell down. Molly had already arrived at the top of the escalator. When she looked down and saw Letivi wobble, she emitted a muffled scream that resulted in all those around casting eyes on the scared Letivi. Everyone began laughing at the way Letivi was holding on for dear life to the hard rubber handrail. They looked at his new clothes and mistook him for a country bumpkin who was coming to the big city for the first time. Molly and Robin were feeling a bit embarrassed by Letivi's naive, childish ways.

Molly extended her hand for Letivi to grasp when he arrived at the top landing. Letivi almost stumbled when he was forced to step off the escalator. Robin stood closely behind Letivi to make sure he did not fall backward. Molly and Robin were seeing that taking Letivi out of his village and bringing him to America was fraught with unforeseen challenges. They forged ahead to the outside exit to wait for the shuttle that would take then to their terminal. As they opened the plate-glass doors and stepped outside, Letivi was surprised that they were outdoors. He had not realized that they had been underground. His body was shocked by the coldness of the weather. While Molly and Robin found it refreshing to be in such a cool clime, Letivi began to shiver and feel physical pain as the cold temperature penetrated his body. He had never experienced such cold before except when he once stuck his hand inside the freezer compartment of a refrigerator.

Molly saw Letivi shivering and his lips turning purple. She said, "For God's sake, Letivi, retrieve your jacket from your handbag and put it on."

Letivi did as Molly commanded and zipped his jacket all the way up to his neck and placing his hands in the side pockets. Their shuttle bus arrived, and Molly urged Letivi to board first. Letivi took the first available seat and was happy to feel warm air blowing out the vent next to him. He appreciated the warm interior of the bus, which quickly departed and began making its rounds to the other terminals. Letivi could not believe that JFK was a collection of many airports, each much larger than the national airport in his home country. He also could not believe how much concrete he was seeing. The roads, huge parking lots, and all the areas around the various terminals were paved with concrete. He was convinced that more concrete had been used at the airport than in his entire country.

Letivi was curious as to why they called the airport JFK, so he asked Molly, who was sitting next to him, "Why does everyone refer to this airport as JFK?"

Molly laughed. She thought everyone knew what JFK stood for. She calmly told Letivi, "I thought you knew that JFK stands for John Fitzgerald Kennedy, our thirty-fifth president, who was shot and killed on November 22, 1963. His assassination was a very traumatic event in our country. The airport was renamed in honor of him. You know he was this president who created the Peace Corps in 1962, which enabled your father to work in your village."

"Thanks for telling me this, Molly. I did know some of that but not all. It all happened long before I was born. I wonder how a president can be killed in such a great country. It would be very hard to kill a president in my country because almost nobody has a gun."

"Letivi, one thing you need to know about America is that many people possess firearms. They believe this is a right guaranteed under our constitution, which was written by our forefathers in the late 1700s."

Letivi pondered for a moment what Molly was telling him before saying, "I am surprised to hear that. If people in my country had guns, there would be too much killing."

The small bus stopped at the TWA terminal. They got off, passed through the cold air, and entered the warm terminal building. They stood for a while in a short line at an airline desk to show their tickets. The attendant who served them indicated the gate where their plane would be boarding shortly. Letivi noticed that among the many shops were restaurants. The smell of food made him hungry. He asked Molly, "Can we eat something? I am feeling hungry and thirsty."

"OK, Letivi. Maybe we can get some fast food and eat it at the gate. For sure, we don't want to miss our flight."

Robin quickly added, "It would do me good to have a good old American hamburger. I see a McDonald's. Let's go there."

As they stood in the line in front of McDonald's, Letivi looked around to see what other people were eating. He did not recognize any of the food, except for French fries. All the plastic and paper containers the food came in made it harder for him to see what people were eating. They arrived in front of one of the many cash registers, and they were asked for their orders. Molly and Robin immediately asked for Big Mac combos. Letivi did not know what to say, so he simply said, "The same."

They received their orders in one paper bag with three plastic cups of Coca-Cola with ice. Molly could see that it would be too difficult to walk to the gate with all these food items and their handbags, so she said, "Let's eat quickly here at one of these stand-up tables." They walked to one table and began to unwrap their food. Letivi closely watched Molly and Robin, trying to imitate them. He was not used to standing while eating. He saw them chomp into their Big Macs and munch on their fries after dipping them into ketchup they had squeezed out of small plastic packets. He did the same but did not like what he tasted. For him, the bread was unusually soft. He took the two bun slices, pressed them together, and ate them in three big bites.

He then took out the hamburger patty and scraped all the condiments off with his finger and ate the meat in two big bites. He did like the fries and stuffed his mouth full of them. He began to drink his Coke, but it was too cold. He pulled the plastic lid off his Coke cup and tried to remove the unusual pellets of ice. He did not know how people could drink such a cold drink, particularly as it was so cold outside. Failing to remove the ice, he shoved the Coke aside. He was wiping his mouth with his hand when a bemused Molly offered him a paper napkin. Letivi thanked her, saying, "This is my first time to see a hamburger. It is so little food. Why do they call it a meal?"

Molly could see that Letivi was thirsty, so she asked if he wanted to drink some water. Letivi replied, "Yes, that would be good."

Molly replied, "I see there is a drinking fountain nearby where you can quench your thirst with nice cool water."

They finished eating, picked up their trash, and placed it in a receptacle. This entailed another new experience for Letivi— picking up his trash and placing it in a bin. They walked over to the chrome-plated drinking fountain that was attached to the wall. Molly demonstrated to Letivi how to push the lever so that water would spring forth. Letivi had never drunk water in this way. Before trying to drink, he pushed several times on the lever. He finally placed his lips on the water stream, but he could not drink. Again, the water was too cold for his liking. He then resorted to his usual way of drinking water, cupping his right hand under the water stream and catching some in his hand to slurp it into his mouth. He found this a satisfying way to deal with the water machine, but Molly yelled at him, "Letivi, stop drinking like that. It is not allowed here! If you want to do like that, maybe next time when you use the restroom, you can drink the water from the sink faucets and then dry your hands with the paper towels."

Letivi replied, "That's a good idea, but is it safe to drink the water from the faucet? In my country, all piped water is contaminated."

Molly laughed again. "Letivi, in this country all water coming out of faucets should be safe to drink."

Letivi was amazed by this revelation and promised himself he would drink his fill the next time he found a water faucet.

They walked along a long corridor before they came to the designated gate. When they arrived, the plane was already boarding. They immediately got in line. They hurried to enter the plane and locate their first-class seats. Letivi noted that the plane was smaller than their last plane but very clean. Their seating arrangements were basically the same. Letivi was proud to show that he could now buckle his seat belt on his own. Before they had time to become comfortable, the doors were closed, and the plane began taxiing to the takeoff runway.

Molly advised Letivi, "This will be a much shorter flight than our transatlantic flight, but we do have a stop in Saint Louis before heading to Wichita. In any event, we should be landing in Wichita early in the afternoon. Please note that Wichita is one hour behind New York time."

Again, Letivi was puzzled by the constant changes in the time of day. In his country, there was only one time zone. He had just started his stay in America, and already he did not know how he would explain everything when he returned to his village. He could see it would be hard to describe so many things to those who had not seen them with their own eyes. There was too much that could not be compared to anything in his country. He felt as if he had no useful point of reference to guide his way and observations. It was like being lost at sea in another world in a small boat with neither sail nor rudder.

Their flight had a routine takeoff and quickly gained altitude. Letivi tried to get a glimpse of New York City again, but all he saw were the clouds in which the plane was enveloped. Snacks and drinks were served. Letivi ignored the snacks. He was feeling much more comfortable this time on his plane ride to the heart of America. He was looking very much forward to seeing his father's home area.

Without any coaching, Letivi stood up and went to the toilet. He easily locked the door. He found it easier to move in the cramped space in his new clothes. After peeing, he flushed the toilet without being surprised by the noise it made. He pressed the lever on the sink faucet and cupped his right hand to collect water to drink. He drank his fill of the warm water. He could not wait to return to his seat and tell Molly he had finally been able to drink some water. He exited the toilet and walked back to his seat. He sat down and told Molly, "That was a much better plane toilet experience, and I was able to drink plenty of water."

Molly reacted energetically without hesitation, "Don't tell me you drank water from the plane toilet's sink. That water is not potable. It is wastewater unfit for human consumption. Didn't you read the warning label?"

Letivi was shocked by Molly's words. All he could manage to say was, "But you said I could drink out of any water faucet in America."

The skies opened as the flight headed over the Midwest, and Letivi could see out of his small plane window wide swaths of farmland. He was surprised to see that there were so many farms and that the fields of cultivated land were so incredibly large. He turned to Molly and said, "The farms I see below are so big. How can people cultivate such large fields?"

Molly, who was becoming impatient with Letivi's incessant questions, dryly replied, "Letivi, one family here can farm a thousand acres. They use tractors and lots of machinery. They plant huge, dense fields, using a lot of pesticides, fertilizers, and the latest improved seeds."

Again, Letivi was having trouble processing all the information Molly was providing him. After some thought, he told Molly, "That's amazing. In my country, ten acres would be considered a large farm, and all cultivation is done by hand. There is not enough land to do bigger farms, and even if the land were available, there are not any tractors."

Letivi's words forced Molly to be the one who was thinking this time. She was wondering how a country like Kotoku could advance with such small farms and the use of only hand labor. She was concerned that Kotoku could never become less poor with only a national patchwork of small farms worked with hand tools. She reflected on the fact that America had started with small farms and progressively built up to large farms as the rural population declined and urban centers expanded rapidly. She asked herself why such a transition was not also taking place in Africa. As far as she was concerned, large farms were necessary to feed the fast-growing number of urban, nonagricultural producers.

While Molly was lost in her thoughts about how to get agriculture in Africa moving and keep it moving, the fasten-your-seatbelts indicator flickered on, and an announcement poured out over the plane's loud intercom system: "Please buckle your seat belts. We are beginning our descent to the Lambert Saint Louis International Airport. We wish those disembarking passengers a good stay in Saint Louis. All those passengers in transit should remain seated, as we will continue on to Wichita after a forty-five-minute layover."

Letivi was intrigued by the name Saint Louis, and he asked Molly, "Is this a French-speaking part of the country?"

Molly laughed—not only because Letivi's questions were funny, but because he was asking already another question. She looked at Letivi and smiled, saying, "No, Letivi. This is not a French-speaking part of our country. In the old days, this place was founded by French people who have long since departed.

You need to understand that America was settled by a large assortment of people who came from many other parts of the world. That is one reason it is called the United States and is often referred to as the melting pot."

The snide manner with which Molly answered his questions made it harder for Letivi to ask any more questions, but he could not resist. "Molly, sorry to ask so many questions, but can you tell me where the name Wichita came from?"

Molly knew it would be a challenge to answer this question in a way that Letivi would understand. She knew she had to keep her reply as simple as possible. She took a deep breath and said, "Letivi, many place-names used today are the same as those used by American Indians before the arrival of white people. When the whites first arrived, they used the names that the Indians used, and we still use these names today. Wichita is the name of the Indian tribe that was camped where the city of Wichita is today when the first settlers arrived over one hundred fifty years ago."

Letivi was perplexed. He had only the vaguest notion about there being any people in America before the white people arrived. He was very interested in America's Indians. Excitedly, he asked Molly, "I hope I can visit with some Wichitans. I would like very much seeing how they live and talk. They may have something in common with us Africans."

After hearing Letivi say these words, Molly felt like crying. She did not know how to tell Letivi what had happened to America's Indians, and she had no idea what to say about the Wichita tribe. All she could say was, "Letivi, Wichitans don't exist anymore. The history of America's indigenous people is very complicated. I think the best thing is for me to buy you a book to read on America's history."

Letivi wanted to keep quiet, but he was dying to ask, "What happened to the Wichitans? Where did they go?"

To make Letivi stop this line of questioning, Molly blurted out, "Letivi, many American Indians were killed in warfare or by disease brought by the white man. Some were absorbed by the white population. Many of the remaining Indians were settled in land reserved for them. Please don't ask me any more questions now on this difficult subject."

Molly's reply had Letivi thinking about his country's history with whites. He knew well that whites had exploited his ancestors, making them slaves and colonializing them. He knew his people had suffered much under the whites, but he also knew they continued to suffer under the corrupt and sometimes bloody leadership provided by their own brothers. Nonetheless, he was thinking it was a good thing that the lack of resources and a hot, humid, tropical climate discouraged whites from settling in large numbers in his country. He knew that whites could not survive malaria and other tropical diseases. Maybe his country was lucky because it did not have any natural riches, mild climate, or the large swaths of fertile land that attracted whites.

Both Molly and Letivi were buried in their thoughts as the plane prepared to take off. Robin had overheard every word Molly and Letivi had said from across the aisle, and he was also turning over in his mind all the various facets of their interesting exchange. He could see now that Letivi's visit would be a genuine eye-opener for not only Letivi but for Molly and him too. He was now less worried about losing Molly's affection than losing his ability to cope with all the ramifications of Letivi's visit.

After a brief interlude, the plane crossed the Kansas-Missouri border and entered into the airspace over Kansas. Molly softly said, "Letivi, look out the window now, and you can see Kansas below."

Letivi glued his eyes to his plane window, observing the wide, flat vista unfolding below him. He remarked to Molly, "Kansas is even flatter than my country. All I see is vast, endless plains."

"Yes, Letivi, Kansas is very flat, particularly its western half. In eastern Kansas, we do have some rolling hills, and you will see the spectacular Flint Hills, which pass close to my hometown of El Dorado."

As the plane prepared to land at Wichita's Mid-Continent Airport, Molly told Letivi and Robin, "I will call my retired uncle Harold when we arrive. He lives in Wichita, and I know he will be happy to drive us the thirty-five miles to El Dorado. My uncle Clyde in El Dorado would be pleased to accommodate both of you. There is not enough room at my house."

The plane had a smooth landing. There was no clapping this time. People exited the plane without any emotion or fanfare. Letivi could see that Wichita was a smaller city because its airport was much smaller than JFK. Yet, as small as it was in comparison to JFK, it was larger and much more modern than the national airport in his home country. They quickly exited the departure lounge and headed for the baggage collection area. While they were waiting for Letivi's suitcase to show itself on the conveyor belt, Molly fished out a couple of quarters from her handbag to call her uncle at a nearby pay phone.

Molly reached her elderly uncle. He promised to drop everything and drive immediately to the airport to meet her and her two companions. Letivi's suitcase found its way again to its owner, and Robin grabbed it, telling Letivi he would take care of it for him. Letivi and Robin joined Molly, who was about to go outside to wait for her uncle when Letivi asked, "Can we please wait inside? It looks very cold and windy outside."

Molly replied, "Of course. You wait here with Robin, and I will go outside and wait for my uncle. He'll be looking for me. When I see him coming, I will signal to you and Robin. Watch me through the big glass window and be ready to come when I give you the signal."

In less than fifteen minutes, Molly gave a hand signal to indicate that her uncle was approaching the pickup point in front of the airport. Letivi and Robin rushed outside to join Molly at curbside in the chilly weather. Molly's uncle arrived in his beautifully restored 1957 Ford Fairlane 500 Skyliner. This spry old man jumped from the driver's seat and ran around the car to give Molly a big hug and to shake vigorously Letivi's and Robin's hands. As he grabbed Letivi's suitcase and placed it in the trunk, he asked everyone to put their handbags in the trunk. He then said, "Please get into my car, and let's get out of here."

Molly told her uncle, "I will need to sit in the backseat with our special visitor, Chief Letivi from Africa, as I know he will have many questions. My good friend, Robin, can sit up front with you."

Uncle Harold replied in a deep Kansan drawl, "Well, welcome, Laddy and Robby. Good to see all of you made it all the way from Africa. Welcome to the Air Capital, the Wheat State, and the home of the Jayhawkers."

Letivi was puzzled by the way Uncle Harold talked and by everything he said. He also noted his bizarre dress of denim bib overalls and a plain blue shirt. He wondered if it was some kind of uniform. He told himself that he needed to buy a notebook to record everything he did not understand so he could discuss it later with Molly. He did not want to spoil Molly's homecoming with too many questions. He was impressed that the obviously elderly Harold was very active and able to drive. After they were comfortably seated in the spiffy backseat, Letivi whispered a question to Molly: "How old is your uncle?"

Molly hollered, "Uncle Harold, how old are you now? Our visitor from Africa would like to know."

"Why, darlin', I turned seventy-six last week. Never felt better."

Letivi had never seen such an old person who was so active and driving a car. He knew that most people in his country would never see such an advanced age. In his village, there were probably not more than a handful of people as old as Harold. He asked Molly, "Are there a lot of old people in America as active as your uncle?"

Molly could not withhold a little giggle before saying, "Of course, there are people of my uncle's age and even older doing a lot of things. You will see people like him everywhere."

Letivi was thinking that in his country, one never saw old people out in public doing anything. He could see that one sign of an advanced country was having old people being able to remain active. He lamented that too many people in his country died at a young age, and child mortality was too high.

They left the airport and drove onto the fast-moving, multilane Highway 54 and headed east to Augusta. Letivi had never been on a highway so big and wide, with painted lines and hundreds of cars that were mostly big and unfamiliar to him. He did not know how the speeding cars avoided ramming into each other. His breath was taken away by all the movement and what he observed along the sides of the highway. He was practically speechless. He did not see anyone on a motorbike or a bicycle. He wondered how poor people moved about. It was his first time to see billboards. He busied his mind with trying to read and interpret every sign they passed.

Uncle Harold broke the silence by saying, "I'd like to share with you my special collection of rock 'n' roll music from the 1950s. As I'm sure you know, I have restored this 1957 car to its original form. This was a labor of love that took several years and much expense."

Immediately, Harold turned on his tape deck, and loud music began flooding out of his souped-up sound system. Letivi had questions to ask Molly, but his voice was drowned out by the music. He was having a hard time believing he was in a car from 1957. There were not any cars this old in his country. Mechanics in his country were expert at keeping for years even the oldest junk cars plying the precarious, unmaintained roads, but no cars were this old. There was no such thing in his country as an antique car or restoring a car. Cars in his country were driven until they could not possibly be used anymore.

Molly pointed to the center of Wichita as they passed by it, indicating with hand gestures that they would return another day to visit the city. She wanted to show Letivi sometime later WSU, the university his father had attended. They sped past the Wichita city limits as they headed to the small town of Augusta. Letivi saw one unusual thing that compelled him to address yet another question to Molly. He cupped his hands over Molly's left ear and said softly, "Sorry, but I need to know what are those long metal arms with a pipe stuck in one end that are going up and down in many big fields we are passing."

Molly could see why this distinctive feature of the Kansas landscape would interest Letivi and whispered into his ear, "Those are oil pumps. Remember four important things about Kansas's history and economy: wheat, cattle, aircraft and oil. I also need to buy you a book about Kansas."

Letivi was mystified about how oil could be pumped from underground and he had more questions to ask Molly about what was done with the oil, but they had arrived in Augusta, and Harold had slowed down to obey the city speed limit. Letivi was surprised to see speed limit signs, as none existed in his country. He was also surprised that people obeyed the traffic signs, particularly as he had not yet seen a single policeman or soldier. He was also impressed that they had not yet encountered any roadblocks. Harold was singing happily along with his blaring music. He turned down the music and asked, "Are any of you world travelers hungry? There are many fast-food joints we could stop at here along the Augusta strip."

Molly quickly replied, "No, Uncle. I'm eager to get home and eat some of my mama's cooking. And we need to rest after such a long trip."

Harold said, "Right-o," and turned up his music as he exited Augusta and accelerated to the higher speed limit. He was headed for Haverhill Road, and then he would take a left turn and go the remaining ten miles to El Dorado. Letivi was getting a stiff neck because his head was constantly turned to the right to look out the window as he struggled to digest all the new elements he was encountering in his new world. He saw many farms and lots of strange-looking cattle grazing on ample pastureland. He turned to Molly once more and whispered into her ear, "Where is the wheat and what kind of cattle are those? Also, where are the sheep and goats?"

Molly whispered back, "It's November, and winter is coming. The wheat was harvested last June. Nothing grows in the winter. The cattle are mostly Angus and Herefords. People don't raise goats and sheep here. There are some people who raise pigs. All animals are fenced in or kept in pens."

Letivi continued to ponder Molly's words and all the new wonders he was observing. He wondered how people could live in the winter if nothing grew. It was obvious to him that people had to work hard and produce much during the summer months in order to survive in the winter. This was very different from his country, where people could go to their fields or into the bush at any time of the year and find something to eat.

They passed the southern city limits of El Dorado. Letivi was seized by the sight of a huge assembly of pipes, tanks, and burning smokestacks on his side of the road. He could not contain himself and excitedly exclaimed, "What in the world is that?"

Harold and Robin laughed at the way Letivi was so agitated after seeing for the first time an oil refinery. Molly calmly said, "Letivi, settle down. That is an oil refinery. It makes gasoline and other fuels. El Dorado is something of a refinery town."

"But why are flames spewing out of the top of the smokestack? Is that some kind of eternal flame for the gods?"

"No, Letivi, those flares are there to burn off any gas escaping the fuel-making process. These flames never stop."

Again, Letivi had received information that was beyond anything he could fully understand or believe. Before he could recover from the complex refinery scene, he saw a few people walking around a huge grassy area, and some were swinging at little white balls. He could not refrain from asking Molly, "What is going on over there in that big grassy field?"

"Letivi that is a golf course. Those people are playing golf."

That sounded simple enough to Letivi's ears, but he had never been exposed to golf before, so he really did not know what to think. They turned right onto Central Avenue and headed toward the center of town. Molly asked her uncle to turn off his music so she could give Letivi something of a guided tour of the part of El Dorado they would be passing through. She pointed to the left and said, "That is our roller rink. I went there often as a teenager, and my mom and dad met there." No matter that Letivi did not have a clue as to what she meant by "roller rink."

They proceeded east on Central Avenue, and Molly pointed out various houses and buildings. She noted the little confectionary, Westend, where she said she had hung out as a kid. They passed the Susan B. Allen Memorial Hospital, where Molly was born, and the old school buildings where she went to junior high and high school. They turned right on Star Street, just before the old Butler County Courthouse, which was constructed in 1909. Molly pointed out the Carnegie Library, which was built in 1912, and the youth center, the Cage, where she often went as a teenager. Letivi listened attentively, but there was so much he did not understand, and his knowledge of much of what Molly was telling him was so low or absent that he did not know how to formulate an intelligent reaction. He did know there were not any buildings in his country anywhere near the ages of the courthouse and library.

They proceeded south on Star Street to Molly's parents' house. Letivi observed the old wooden houses, which were very different from the mud-brick houses in his country. He was thinking that even if they could afford and construct a house like this in his country, a voracious variety of African termites would quickly decimate it. He could not believe how clean everything was. He had not yet seen any trash and garbage heaps. He wondered what people did to dispose of their trash. He also did not see any open sewers or street gutters. Where did all the wastewater go? His biggest impression was that in front of every house was a big grass lawn. He was puzzled why people were not planting food crops on such nice land. He was happy to see many trees, although none of the trees were like any he knew in Africa. With all those trees, there should be no shortage of firewood for cooking and charcoal making. He was amazed that he had not yet seen a single fly or other insect. There were pesky flies everywhere all the time in his country.

Letivi was forced to save his many questions as Harold pulled into the gravel driveway in front of Molly's parents' house and began to honk the horn to let everyone know he had arrived with his precious cargo. Robin quickly said to Harold, "Thanks for the ride and all the good music. I'm very happy to be home."

Harold replied, "Think nothing of it. The pleasure is all mine. I'm happy to see my lovely niece out of Africa and back where she belongs. I thank God that she has returned home safe and sound."

Letivi had no time to say anything, as Molly screamed to her uncle to let her out of the car so she could embrace her mother, who was running toward the car with other family members. Molly was in tears as she hugged and kissed her mom and the others who had come to receive them. Letivi and Robin sat still in the car, waiting for all the intense emotions of this joyous family reunion to subside. Letivi felt very alone and totally out of place. He wanted to flee, but there was nowhere for him to go. He was lost and a hostage to the goodwill of his father's people.

CHAPTER TWENTY-SEVEN
KANSAS HOMECOMING

etivi sat in the car as if he were a heavy stone. He was not in the mood to meet all the people waiting to see him. He felt lost in an alien world and wished there were at least one black person among those waiting for him to get out of the car. He knew they would be asking him many questions about Africa for which he did not have good answers. It was difficult to respond to questions from people about his home country when they had never before heard of it. He was certain that none of the people waiting anxiously to meet the man from Africa could find his country on the world map.

After Molly had completed her emotional hugs with all those family members and close friends who had been waiting all day for her arrival, she turned to her mother with an inquiring look. Her mother knew what the expression on Molly's face meant and said, "My dear daughter, please don't worry. Your baby is well and taking a nap. I know you are eager to see her, but I think it's best to wait until she wakes up."

Molly reluctantly nodded her agreement and rushed to her uncle's two-door car to open the door so Letivi could get out of the backseat. She firmly said, "Letivi, please come and greet my parents, family, and some of my friends."

Letivi slowly exited the car, braced himself against the chilly weather, and followed Molly to meet all those who had been patiently waiting to see him. She first introduced him to her mother, Della, and her father, Roy. Molly gracefully presented Letivi to all those assembled. "This is Letivi...pronounced let-tee-vee..., Chief of Ataku, a village in the country of Kotoku in faraway Africa. His Christian name is David Peterson, the same name as his father, whom we now know came from Kansas."

Molly's mom, Della, responded excitedly, "Let's all welcome David from Africa. Most of us here are Petersons, so we should welcome him like kin. Look at him! Doesn't he look like a Peterson in many ways?" Following these words, everyone applauded loudly.

Molly followed by saying, "Thank you, Mama. This is very cold, windy weather for our important visitor, so can we continue talking inside. I know that many of you have worked hard to provide us with an early Thanksgiving dinner."

Unexpectedly, Robin let out a loud "amen." He was very hungry and could not wait to chow down on some great American home cooking.

Molly's parents led the way up the wooden steps and across a narrow wood deck to the front door of their modest old Sears model house. Letivi followed closely behind Molly and her parents. He noted that her father was dressed in the same kind of uniform as her uncle Harold. This made him think they belonged to the same organization. Upon entering the living room, Letivi was amazed to see that almost the entire room was occupied by a table covered with the widest variety of food he had ever seen. Most of the food items on the table were new to him. He did not see any of the food that he ate in his village. He was very hungry, so he was hoping he would like some of the items on display in this feast.

Molly whispered to Letivi, "Please excuse the humbleness of my parents' house. They have never been well off and have had to work very hard all their lives for the little they have."

Letivi looked around and saw mostly things that were beyond the reach of anyone in his country and said, "If any person in my country had your parents' possessions, they would be considered wealthy."

Della called, "Please gather around, everyone, as we ask the Lord to bless our food."

Roy said a loud but short prayer, thanking God for the food and for the return of his daughter and the safe arrival of her friends. Following his heartfelt words, he said in a loud voice, "Let's eat!"

Letivi turned to Molly and said, "I'm impressed that your parents are so religious. I see several crosses on the walls and a picture of Jesus at the Last Supper."

Molly replied, "Letivi, just about everyone in Kansas is a firm believer of the Bible and goes to church at least once a week. My mom never missed Sunday church services for sixteen years while growing up. You probably also noticed the US flag flying in front of the house. Most people in Kansas are also patriotic."

"I saw the flag in front of many houses, but I was not sure what it was about. In my country, the national flag is only flown in front of government buildings."

Molly responded, "When we have more time, I will explain to you what our flag represents. Right now, we must sit down and enjoy this great meal before the food gets too cold."

Della insisted that Letivi sit at the head of the table and Molly and Robin sit to either side of him. When all were seated, Della tapped a knife against a glass to get everyone's attention and said, "As is our custom, our special guest, David, gets to choose which piece of turkey he would like to eat. David, what do you choose? Please tell us and my husband will carve the turkey and give you the piece of your choice."

Letivi now knew that the huge roasted chicken in the middle of the table was a turkey, something he had not seen before. Trying hard to be responsive, he said, "I'll take the leg."

Roy cut off a leg of the turkey and asked for Letivi's plate. At the same time, he said, "I was thinking you would take the breast so you could get the wishbone. Maybe it's just as well you didn't because in this family, we keep the wishbones from every Thanksgiving. We dry, sand, varnish, and tag them. We keep them in a special box to remind us of all the times we joined together as a family for Thanksgiving. I'll show you later this box full of wish bones."

Letivi did not have a clue about what Roy was saying. When he was served his turkey leg, he was told that as the guest of honor, he should began taking food from the dishes in front of him and pass them on to Molly, who was seated at his right. The only dish he recognized was green beans, so he picked up the bowl and, with Molly's coaching, helped himself to a few spoonfuls of beans. He then proceeded to load onto his plate items he did not know. He found cranberry sauce, mashed potatoes with gravy, stuffing, and candied yams. Each time, he asked Molly what food he was placing on his plate. The mashed potatoes reminded him a bit of pounded yams. He was confused when Molly said he was taking candied yams, as these yams were nothing like what he called yams. Molly said that these yams were really orange sweet potatoes, but that confused Letivi even more because they did not look anything like the white sweet potatoes he knew in his village.

They were all laughing and talking and gorging themselves except Letivi, who toyed with his food and remained silent. His thoughts were about Ataku and what people were doing there. He tried to eat his food, but the only thing he found that was palatable for him was the turkey leg. He impressed all those seated at the table by grasping firmly his turkey leg in his right hand and eating all the skin and meat right down to the bone. He then got everyone's attention when he cracked open the bone with his teeth and sucked out the nutritious marrow, making a loud, slurping sound. All eyes were on Letivi as he devoured the entire turkey leg, leaving a small pile of bone fragments on his plate. Letivi really enjoyed the turkey leg and felt like washing it all down with a beer. He turned to Molly, belched loudly, and asked, "May I have one of your American beers?"

Molly was obliged to reply, "No, Letivi, my parents are very Christian and don't permit alcoholic beverages in their house. They are what we call teetotalers. I think it best that you don't mention any African customs that involve drinking, magic, or sorcery, as people here would interpret these kinds of things as being anti-Christian. Letivi, you are not eating all the food on your plate."

To the latter, Letivi replied, "All this food is new to me. Please don't expect me to change my taste preferences overnight. My taste buds are used to eating my African food, and it will take some time for them to adapt to these new foods. Anyway, I am missing my African food."

The bit about her parents being "teetotalers" bemused Letivi because he and his people were devoutly Christian, but that did not prevent them from drinking alcohol. This kind of Christian interdiction of alcohol was a new concept to him. At that moment, Molly's mom stood up to offer a toast to Letivi. "Please let's all raise our glasses to toast having an African chief among us. Welcome again, Chief David. We hope your stay with us will be all you would like it to be."

Everyone then turned to Letivi to see what he would say. Softly, Molly advised Letivi that according to local custom, it was his turn to speak. Letivi looked around the room at the odd assortment of people surrounding him and wondered what meaningful words he could say to such a motley assembly of white people. He cleared his throat and looked at everyone and then said, "Thank all of you for such a warm welcome and all the good food. As you know, I'm new to this land, so I'm still trying to adjust to it and understand things here. I ask all of you for your patience while I get used to things. In the days ahead, I look forward to getting to know you and your country better."

Although many had a hard time understanding Letivi's different accent, everyone applauded enthusiastically. Molly called for quiet, as she also had a few words to say. "I, too, want to thank all of you for this warm welcome back home. As you know, I went to Africa with my good friend Robin Fletcher, who is seated across the table from me, to try to find out what happened to David Peterson, who disappeared from Gemini, Kansas, nearly six years ago. Our investigations led us to the village of Ataku in the country of Kotoku. We did not find what happened to David, the elder, for whom we were searching, but we did find his son, the David we have sitting with us today. We thought it would be a very good thing if we could bring this David back with us to visit where his father was born and raised. In the next few days, we hope to show David, Chief Letivi, where his father lived and where he went to school."

Many around the table did not really understand all that Molly said, but they knew if Molly said it, it must be good. A number of people were studying carefully Letivi's features and were talking among themselves about the way Letivi looked. Finally, Molly's dad, Roy, said forthrightly, "Well, there is one thing I can say for sure. The young man sitting at the head of the table is shaped like a Peterson." These words generated a number of affirmative nods and a few 'amen's.'

Letivi was squirming in his chair when one man asked, "Do you know any of your father's relatives? Who knows? We could be related to you."

Molly saw that Letivi was uncomfortable, and she replied, "All we know is that David's father was from Gemini, and his father had an older brother named Edgar. We plan to visit Edgar's grave in Gemini. We also know that his father went to Udall Rural High School and WSU. We also plan to visit those places. As it was Robin who did all the initial research about his father, I now ask him if he has anything to add."

Robin had enjoyed immensely the familiar food and company. He stood up and said, "I also want to thank you for this great reception. I should tell you that the thing that started us on this adventure was my discovery in Topeka early last September of a little book at the Kansas Annual Book Festival entitled *The Hero of Gemini*. That hero was David Peterson, the elder. This led me to go to Gemini to find more information about David. To make a long story short, as you all know, Gemini went belly up as a town, and this led me to look for its city records in the county courthouse in El Dorado. I met Molly at the courthouse, and she joined with me in my search. Together, we discovered that David had gone to Kotoku in Africa as a Peace Corps volunteer. We found that David had indeed lived and worked in Ataku, but we still don't know what happened to him. As Molly said, we were nonetheless very happy to find his son and bring him back with us to see his father's country."

People clapped as Robin took his seat. Letivi was feeling uneasy, as he knew very well what had happened to his mysterious father. But he could not say a word on this subject because he could not reveal the magical secrets involved.

Molly's mom was the next to speak. "I'm sure we all have questions to ask the young David who is with us today, but before you bombard the poor man with questions, please let me know who would like tea or coffee. We also have apple, cherry, and pumpkin pies for dessert."

Before Della finished noting beverage orders, a crusty old cousin of Molly's father asked the first question. "David, are you married, and do you have any children?"

Letivi did not expect such a question about his personal life, but he did not hesitate to reply, "Yes, I was married earlier in the year to a woman in my village, but we do not have any children yet." He did not want anyone to know that Delalia was pregnant.

The same man continued with another question. "Are you a Christian, and have you been baptized? Also, were you married in the church?"

Letivi replied quickly, "Yes, I am a Christian, and I was baptized by the Catholic priests at the all-boys school I attended for many years. I was married in a traditional village ceremony."

When Letivi uttered the word "Catholic," a palpable moan of disappointment permeated the room. Letivi could not know that this Bible Belt part of the world was filled with many Protestant fundamentalists who barely considered Catholics Christian. Indeed, most people in the room believed the Pope was something of an Antichrist. They also could not condone a marriage that took place outside the church.

After a brief pause, the old cousin said he had one more question, and that was, "Do you read your Bible?"

An increasingly irritated Letivi crisply replied, "I have read the entire King James version of the Bible several times, and I can quote many scriptures. I have also read many parts of the Bible in its older Greek and Latin versions. I know my Bible."

The last words from Letivi impressed all those present and put a stop to questions about his religious orientation. Of course, Letivi could not tell them that he also believed in the ancestors, many spirits, and a large pantheon of African gods. Molly stepped in at this point to say, "We were expecting you would like to ask David about Africa. I think we have heard enough about his religious beliefs."

One of Molly's aunts quickly raised her hand and asked, "Do you live anywhere near Tarzan?"

Letivi laughed. He knew the story about Tarzan. He simply replied, "No, ma'am. That is not possible because Tarzan is a fictional character."

The same aunt continued. "What about all the wild animals where you live?"

Letivi replied, "Sorry to disappoint you, but we do not have any of those wild animals you are thinking about."

Molly's father, Roy, was the next to speak. He said, "When my daughter left for Africa, I went to our public library to study up on that country, and I learned that it is very poor and underdeveloped. I look at you, and I see a very healthy and strong young man. I wonder how you turned out so well given the bad conditions in your country."

This was not an easy line of thinking for Letivi to respond to. He knew he had to say something, and he needed to show respect for Molly's father. It was obvious to him that it was almost impossible to explain anything about Africa to people who knew almost nothing about the continent. Letivi calmly replied, "Yes, compared to other parts of the world, Africa is less developed. Certainly, many of the things I see in your country we do not have in my country. Nonetheless, we work hard and enjoy living in close connection with other members of our community. Although we are faced with many challenges you do not have here in your country, we manage to survive and deal with life successfully."

Molly could see that Letivi was tiring of such uninformed questions, and she was also feeling very tired and in need of rest. She stood up to get everyone's attention and said, "We are very tired after our long trip of more than twenty-four hours, and we need to rest. I'm sure David would be happy to answer any further questions you may have in the days ahead. As you know, he will be staying with us for two weeks. Please let's call it a day and find our beds so we can rest."

Molly's mother gently interceded, saying, "Molly, I know that you are very tired, but we did not hear a word from you or Robin about what you think about your trip to Africa."

"Yes, Mother, you are right. I think that on this point we should hear from Robin."

Molly pointed to Robin and made a gesture with both her hands that he should rise and speak. Robin's mind was racing to formulate words that he could politely say about Africa. With much hesitancy obvious in his voice, Robin said, "Africa is hard to describe to anyone who has not experienced it. It is nothing like I imagined before going there. The capital of David's country has many modern buildings, and we stayed in a very nice hotel. In Letivi's village, there was not any running water or electricity, but people are living happy lives. Life is not as easy there as it is here, but people live full and good lives in tight-knit communities. I hope to write an article about our trip. I will try to put down on paper my major impressions of this eye-opening trip."

Letivi appreciated Robin's kind and positive remarks about his country. He knew Robin really did not like Africa and could have said many negative things about it. He was pleased that Robin's diplomatic remarks were positive and brief. A crackling voice came from a rocking chair in the back of the room. A very old man said, "Sounds to me that Africa is today just like it was here in Kansas when my family first arrived in the early 1900s. I grew up on a farm in a remote area on the plains, and we did not have running water or electricity, and we used an outhouse. My long-deceased wife was part Cherokee and born in a sod house in Oklahoma. Back then, some of the old-timers would tell us that they had even less and lived in sod homes. Many men's lives were defined by how much land they cleared and cultivated in their lifetime. My grandfather was very proud of the forty acres he had developed by hand from scratch. And I can tell you that the winters were just as cold as they are now, and the summers were just as hot. Look at me. I survived, and I'm over ninety years old. I think I turned out all right in spite of the lack of machines and all the deprivations experienced in my youth."

These remarks from an old-timer made people laugh. Letivi liked what the old man said, but he was thinking that maybe life in his country today was not as good in some ways as life had been for many in America one hundred years ago. He also wondered how people in America survived through the winters. He was already suffering from the chilly autumn weather, and he knew that the cold winter had not yet arrived. He could not see how his people could survive even the current cool weather. One blast of wintry weather would surely kill most people in his country. He told himself that he needed to leave America before colder weather set in.

At that moment, the muffled cry of a baby was heard. All heads turned to see the source of this soft sobbing on the stairs. Molly jumped up and walked quickly to take in her arms her beautiful two-year-old daughter, saying, "Don't cry, baby. Mama is home."

Almost every eye in the room was filled with tears to observe such an emotional reunion of mother and child. Letivi, and particularly Robin, were in a state of shock because Molly had not told them she had a daughter. Seeing Molly holding tightly her golden-haired daughter changed the way they thought about Molly. Letivi's respect for her grew because she was a mother and had thus proven she was capable of bearing children. Robin was upset because she had never told him she was a mother. He also felt a tinge of jealously for the man who had fathered Molly's child. The fact that Molly had a daughter somehow reduced the ardor of his strong feelings for her.

Everyone stood up to prepare to depart, saying their good-byes to Molly and her parents, and to Letivi and Robin. Molly brought her daughter over to introduce her to Letivi and Robin. In a soft, pleading voice, she said, "I hope you are happy to meet the love of my life and my only true treasure, my daughter, Elisa."

Robin tried to hide the awkwardness of the moment and the sense of disappointment he felt over learning that Molly had a child. Letivi's eyes locked tenderly on Elisa's, and they both reached out to each other. Letivi felt something magical when their hands touched. Molly was surprised when Elisa stretched her arms out to be held by Letivi. Molly's parents were also very surprised because Elisa never allowed anyone to hold her except Molly and her grandparents.

When Letivi took Elisa in his arms, a weird trance-like feeling enveloped him. He walked to the other side of the room, where he could talk to her in private. Elisa could not understand a word Letivi was saying, but she listened as if she were memorizing every word. Letivi quickly told her that she was a special child and related to her all his deepest secrets. For reasons he could not understand, he felt compelled by the ancestors and all the gods to say things to this child that he could not say to anyone else. For Letivi, the blue-eyed child with curly, golden locks was something of a cherubic angel sent by the gods.

Letivi carried Elisa to her mother. Before he handed Molly her child, Elisa gave a hug to Letivi and kissed him on his cheek. This gesture jarred deeply Letivi's emotions, and he became teary-eyed. This spontaneous kiss from Elisa told him more than anything else that he was indeed welcome in the land of his father. The only person to ever kiss him before in his life was his mother, Celestine (Atibona). He was overwhelmed by this instantaneous deep bonding with Elisa. He wrestled internally with all the possible implications of what this mystical contact meant. When he had time alone, he would definitely need to consult with the ancestors about the magical spell Elisa had cast upon him. For a moment, he thought his mother had returned in Elisa's body. It was not possible for him to cope calmly with this stunning, unexpected event.

Molly and her parents were amazed by Elisa's unusual intimate behavior with a stranger from Africa. They could not figure out whether this was a good or bad thing. Molly wondered why Elisa treated Letivi like the father she had never known. If her daughter reacted to Letivi in this way, how could she not like

Letivi too? Her relationship with Letivi had just become much more complicated.

Molly struggled to regain her composure so she could make a more formal introduction of her Uncle Clyde to Letivi and Robin. She said to them, "Please follow me to meet my Uncle Clyde. You will be spending the night with him.

"Uncle Clyde, please meet David and Robin. As you know, they will be your houseguests. I believe their bags have already been placed in your car."

The fiftyish Clyde shook hands with Letivi and Robin and said in his smooth Midwestern voice, "Very happy to have you boys as my guests. I don't live far away. I'm sure that you are looking forward to hot showers and a good night's sleep in a bed."

Robin said good-bye to Molly and her parents. Letivi's eyes locked again for an instant on Elisa's, as if saying, "See you again soon." Letivi nodded to everyone and turned without saying a word to follow Clyde and Robin through the nippy weather to the car. Molly called after them, "Please be here around eight a.m. tomorrow for breakfast. My dad will take us to visit Gemini." Elisa was waving vigorously good-bye to Letivi in a way she had never done before in her short life.

Robin yelled, "OK, see you tomorrow morning." He wanted to add, "Let's go, Wonder Boy," to refer to Letivi, but he refrained from doing so at the last moment. Now that his feelings for Molly had been torpedoed by the fact she had a child and the connections he had observed between her child and Letivi, he was thinking increasingly of extracting himself from this adventure and getting back to the life and books he had known before reading a book about JB and meeting Molly.

As expected, Letivi sat in the back of Clyde's new, beige-colored Ford Taurus station wagon, and Robin sat in the front.

Letivi was impressed by how nice the car was. He was seeing that America had many cars of many different types. He also noted that given the long distances between places in America, a car was needed. He was very pleased that all the cars he had been in so far had heaters.

They arrived in less than ten minutes in front of Clyde's simple wooden-frame house. Letivi was reluctant to step out into the cold again. For him, the gray overcast clouds and trees without leaves cast a ghostly pall over the town. He had never gone a day in his home country without seeing the sun. Since he had arrived in Kansas, there had been little sunlight, and all looked dreary to him. He told himself that on his next trip to America, he would return in the summer because he had heard it was very hot and sunny then.

After grabbing Letivi's suitcase in the back of the car, Clyde opened the car door for Letivi, saying, "Welcome to my humble abode. I have one spare bedroom with twin beds for you and Robin. I live alone. My wife died several years ago, and my grown children have moved away."

Letivi stepped slowly out of the car, and Clyde closed the car door behind him. He followed Clyde and Robin the few yards across the brownish grass lawn to Clyde's front door. They entered Clyde's small, spartanly furnished house, which was basically composed of a living room, a kitchen, a bathroom, and two tiny bedrooms. Letivi liked the smallness of the house. For him, the house was perfect, as it contained all one really needed—running potable water, reliable and affordable electricity, good sewage and trash collection, and TV. He also liked the fact that Clyde was dressed in another uniform he saw most people, men and women, wearing—blue jeans and a long-sleeve shirt with buttons that snapped on. This dress reminded him of the cowboy man he saw on Marlboro cigarette posters in his country.

Anyone with such a place in his country would be considered to be among the spoiled, wealthy elites. Those elites lived in luxurious mansions, but they did not have any of the basic utilities and services this house enjoyed. They also did not have nice paved roads and sidewalks. For electricity, each house depended upon costly home generators and concrete septic tanks feebly responded to their sewage effluents. The local water was also not potable, and there was no such thing as underground sewage systems and trash collection. Oftentimes, their palatial mansions were surrounded by trash and people living in abject poverty. Many of these people were homeless squatters who possessed only the most basic, makeshift kind of shelter. For him, America was indeed the land of plenty. This was something he felt he needed to tell everyone during his stay in America.

Letivi knew he could not share a room with Robin. He had to be alone to consult the ancestors. Letivi boldly said, "Mr. Clyde, is it OK if I sleep in your living room? I need to be alone to say my prayers."

Clyde gave Letivi a surprised look, saying, "I guess that is OK. I appreciate a man who prays."

Robin politely jumped in and said, "I also appreciate a man who needs to say his nightly prayers, and I think our African chief should sleep in the bedroom. I will use the sofa here in the living room."

Clyde said, "Either way is fine with me. The important thing is that you both get some sleep because you have a big day ahead of your tomorrow."

Letivi thanked Robin and told them both good night and entered the bedroom with his suitcase and closed the door.

Clyde and Robin gave each other looks to indicate that they thought the foreigner among them had a loose screw somewhere. Robin then remembered he had wanted to give Letivi the short book he had about his dad, *The Hero of Gemini*. He thought Letivi should look at it before going to Gemini tomorrow. He fished the book out of his hand luggage and knocked on Letivi's bedroom door, saying, "Letivi, I forgot to give you something."

Letivi slowly opened the door a crack to see what Robin wanted. "Here, please take this book and old newspaper article with a photo about your father. I have been meaning to give these to you for some time. You might want to read some of this before going to Gemini tomorrow."

Letivi reached through the narrowly opened door and snatched the thin book and article from Robin's hands, saying, "Thank you. That is very kind of you. I'm very tired. I need to sleep." Letivi was wondering why Robin had waited until now to share these things with him. He could not wait to examine the old newspaper photo of his father. He did not know that this was Robin's way of saying he was beginning to withdraw his involvement from this protracted case and prepare himself to go back to the life he had before he stumbled on a little book about the hero of Gemini at the annual Kansas Book Festival.

Letivi quickly and firmly shut the door and locked it from the inside. He would not be doing any toiletries or sleeping until he had finished reading what Robin had given him and communicated with the ancestors. He needed to ask the ancestors why things were the way they were between him and the baby Elisa. He found that his eyes were too tired to read, so he put the book and newspaper article aside until tomorrow and switched off the lights. He removed his clothes and sat on the floor next to his bed, wrapping a blanket tightly around himself. He worked himself into a deep state of meditation. He called repeatedly on the ancestors to reveal to him the meaning of his connection with Elisa. After almost two hours of deep meditation, a few words flashed through Letivi's mind. He interpreted these words to mean his mother's spirit was residing temporarily in little Elisa so she could be with her son during his visit to America. More importantly, her spirit had traveled to Kansas to be with his father's spirit, which had been returned to his birthplace. He knew then that Elisa must go to Gemini with them tomorrow. It was time for his parents' souls to be joined for all eternity.

CHAPTER TWENTY-EIGHT
THE SPIRITS OF DAYS GONE BY

L etivi was sound asleep. During the night, the cold drove him to get into bed fully clothed. He wore his winter jacket and covered himself with the all the blankets on the bed and the bottom sheet and mattress pad. It took him a long time to fall asleep, but when he did enter the land of nod, exhaustion caught up with him and pulled him into a deep sleep. He was so far away in an African dreamland that he could not hear the frantic pounding on his bedroom door. Molly's uncle, Clyde, was hammering on the door with his fist and shouting, "David, wake up. It is late. It is time to rise and shine."

With a start, Letivi opened his eyes wide and quickly remembered where he was. His ears began to capture the noise being made on the other side of his bedroom door. He struggled to get out of bed, wrapping himself in the old quilt bed cover. He waddled toward the door to hear better what was being said. It dawned on him that he was the David being told to wake up.

He was not yet used to being called David. He placed his mouth near the door and said in a shaky voice, "OK. I am up. Good morning."

Clyde replied, "That's good. Good morning to you too. All is well in Jayhawker land. I have left a towel for you on the floor in front on your door."

Letivi was curious to know what Jayhawker meant and made a mental note to ask Molly or Robin about this. He was surprised to see that he had left the lights on all night. He searched for how to turn off the lights and was delighted to flip the wall switch several times, turning the lights off and on. He liked the form of the American light switch. Without the lights, the room was too dark, so he went to open the curtains on the one window in the small bedroom. He pulled the curtains open and was pleased to see early morning sunlight pouring through the window. He was thinking that with all that sun, it would be warmer today. One thing that he did not understand was the sparkling white frost that covered everything outside. For him, it looked as if the sprits had magically dusted the land with a glistening white powder. This sight excited him. He could not wait to go outside to touch the magical white dust.

Letivi quickly opened his suitcase and removed the other set of new clothes he had been given in Melomti. He could see that he needed to buy more clothes. In particular, he needed a much warmer winter coat and a stocking cap. He headed out his bed-room door for the adjoining bathroom, picking up his towel as he went. He saw Clyde and Robin sitting in the living room and told them, "Good morning."

They both responded with a good-morning, and Clyde said, "We got a cup of joe ready for you." After Letivi entered the bath-room and closed the door behind him, Clyde and Robin both had a good laugh over all the clothes Letivi was wearing. They did not understand why Letivi was cold, particularly as they were perfectly comfortable wearing only their undershirts.

Letivi was puzzled about what drinking "joe" meant. He wondered if this was some custom where you drank the body fluids of a close relative. Before removing his clothes, he made sure he knew how to operate the cold and hot water handles and the bathtub drain. He closed the drain and opened the hot water faucet. The first thing he wanted to do was soak his very cold feet in hot water. After doing that, he would remove his clothes and take a bath. He removed his socks, rolled up his pants, and put his feet into the scalding hot water. He bit his tongue and immediately removed his feet. It was all he could do to keep from crying out in pain. He could not believe the water could be so hot. Even the water heated over a wood fire in the village was not that hot. He wondered how such hot water could be produced. He quickly learned to add cold water to the hot water so he could comfortably place his feet in the water. He was learning some things the hard way, but he was learning.

After his feet were sufficiently warmed up, he began removing his clothes as he allowed the bath water to rise. He was eager to submerge his entire body in the wonderful warm water. This would be a totally new experience for him. He filled the bathtub and turned off the water. He quickly entered the tub and sat down. He did not count on the water overrunning the tub after he got into it. He quickly rose to stop the water from flooding the bathroom. It took him some time to figure out how to stop the overflow. He opened the drain and allowed some water to exit. After lowering the water level, he again sat down and found he could even lie down without the water flowing over the top of the bathtub.

This was a heavenly experience for him. He wanted to stay submerged in the wondrous warm water as long as he could. His fingers were wrinkling, and the warm water was turning cold when he heard a loud rap on the bathroom door. It was Robin. "Letivi, are you going to stay in there all day? We're already late for Molly's house. Please hurry."

Robin's words stimulated Letivi to rise and say, "OK. I'm finishing now." He splashed some water from the bathtub onto his face and rubbed vigorously his eyes to remove all traces of his good night's sleep. He told himself that he did not need to soap his body because he had soaked off all his dirtiness. He unplugged the drain and stepped out of the bathtub. He grabbed his towel and dried his body thoroughly. He had forgotten his toothbrush in his bedroom, so he put toothpaste on his right forefinger and used it to clean his teeth. He opened the cold-water faucet on the sink to rinse his mouth but found the water too cold to touch. He mixed some hot water with it before catching some water in his cupped right hand for swishing around in his mouth. He checked his face out in the mirror over the bathroom sink and noted that he was getting too white. He told himself that he needed to sit in the sun to darken up a bit.

Letivi quickly put on his new set of clothes and his jacket, zipping it fully up. He gathered up his dirty clothes and opened the bathroom door, saying to the nearby Clyde and Robin, "I'm ready. Just let me put these clothes in my bedroom."

When Letivi disappeared into his bedroom, Clyde checked out the bathroom. He was upset to find water covering the floor and Letivi's towel lying on the floor. The bathroom rug was soaked. He pulled up the bathroom rug and laid it over the side of the bathtub. He used Letivi's towel to wipe up the water on the floor. He noted that the toilet tissue roll had been soaked, so he removed it and tossed it in the wastebasket. He walked out of the bathroom with the wet towel in his hand and said to Robin, "Your African friend is worse than a child. He left the bathroom in a total mess. Don't they have bathrooms in Africa?"

Robin laughed and said, "Nope. In general, there are no real bathrooms in his village. The American bathroom must be a real delight for our African chief."

At that moment, Letivi briskly stepped out of his bedroom and said, "I am ready to go."

Clyde jokingly asked him, "Did you make your bed?"

Letivi did not know what to say. He had never made a bed in his life. Robin jumped in to save Letivi from the awkwardness of the moment, "Letivi, Clyde is only kidding you. Let's go. Molly and her family are waiting for us. She just called to see why we are so late."

Letivi was puzzled about how Molly could call and asked Robin, "How did Molly call?"

Robin was tiring of Letivi's gross naiveté of American ways, He pointed to the black telephone sitting on a small end table and said, "You see that. That is called a telephone. Every house in America has one or more of those. You can call anywhere with one of these telephones if you are willing to pay the bill."

Letivi was astounded that everyone in America had a telephone. In his country, only the very rich and top government officials had access to telephones. Letivi politely said, "Thanks for your answer, Robin. Now, where is that 'joe' I am supposed to drink?"

"No time now. We must go. You can have your coffee at Molly's."

Letivi was again puzzled by what the relationship was between "joe" and coffee. He did not have much time to dwell on this, as

Clyde opened his front door and called on Letivi and Robin to go outside so he could lock his door. Letivi was eager to touch the shimmering white dust sprinkled by the spirits. Once he was out the front door, he was shocked that he could not see any of the white dust. He did not want to ask Robin, but it was important that he know about the white dust. "Robin, when I looked out my bedroom window this morning, I saw that everything was covered with some kind of white powder. What happened to the whiteness?"

"My dear Letivi, what you saw was frost, which is frozen granules of moisture. When the sun came up, the temperature rose, and the sunlight burned off the frost. Wait until you see your first snow or ice storm. That will really blow your mind."

Letivi was severely stressed to cope with all these imponderables so early in the morning. He also did not know it, but he was suffering from jet lag and escalating cultural shock. He took his place in Clyde's car, and they started on their way to Molly's house. They had to cross through the middle of town, and Letivi was all eyes, as there was much to absorb. At one point, Clyde stepped hard on the brakes to slow down to avoid a person crossing the street. He rolled down his window and yelled at the person, "Damn jaywalker! I almost ran over you."

Letivi was surprised by Clyde's unruly behavior, but he was thankful for learning what a Jayhawker was and he said, "Oh. I see. A Jayhawker is someone who crosses in the middle of the street."

Upon hearing what Letivi said, both Clyde and Robin let out loud sighs. They knew how tough it would be to explain these terms to Letivi. Robin tried to keep it simple. "No, Letivi, a jaywalker has nothing to do with a Jayhawker. The former is someone who illegally crosses a main street far from the designated crosswalk, but the latter is a nickname for people who are from Kansas. When I can, I'll show you the colorful mythological bird symbol that represents a Jayhawker. By the way, did you have time to read the book and article I gave you last night?"

Letivi, who was lost in a ton of thoughts, mumbled, "No, I was too tired to read. But I am eager to read all I can about my father and will do so as soon as I can."

Although Robin gave Letivi a good explanation, he was still stumped. He was thinking that maybe the Jayhawker was some kind of ancient totem for which the people had forgotten its true meaning. He was intrigued by the fact that his father had been a Jayhawker and how this made him half Jayhawker. This made him want to get one of those Jayhawker symbols for himself. He was lost in his thoughts when they pulled up in front of Molly's house.

Clyde opened the front door of the house without knocking and shouted out, "We're here. We are a bit late, but here we are now."

They entered the warmth of the living room, and Letivi immediately began looking for Elisa. Molly's mom came out of the kitchen to welcome everyone, saying, "I hope all of you are in top form on this beautiful sunny day. How's our African chief doing today?"

Letivi timidly said, "I am fine. Where is Molly?" He really was looking for Elisa, and he thought she would be with Molly.

Della replied, "Molly is in the laundry room, just behind the kitchen, washing some clothes."

Letivi excused himself and immediately headed toward the kitchen and the laundry room. He found Elisa at her mother's feet in the small laundry room. Elisa immediately got up, ran to Letivi, and jumped into his arms. They embraced, and Letivi whispered words of his love for her in her ear. Molly was again taken aback by the close connection between her baby daughter and Letivi. Words exploded from her mouth. "Letivi. Welcome. Please tell me. What is this 'thing' going on between you and my daughter?"

Letivi could see that Molly was genuinely concerned. He attempted to respond to her concerns by saying in a sympathetic voice, "Molly, I am as surprised as you are by the special relationship your daughter and I are having. I do not have a good explanation for why this is happening, but I feel it is a good thing. Maybe in time, the reasons for it will be revealed."

Elisa interrupted in an uncharacteristic way, saying in an almost adult voice, "Mommy, please don't worry. It's all right."

Molly could not believe how clearly her daughter spoke. She did not know what to think. She turned to continue loading clothes into the washing machine. Letivi was staring at her and following her every move. Molly noticed Letivi's constant staring and asked, "Letivi, what is wrong? Why are you looking at me like that?"

Letivi quickly replied, "Sorry. I am not looking at you. I am looking at that machine you are putting clothes into. What is it for?"

Molly found humor in Letivi's words and laughed before saying, "Letivi, this is a washing machine. It washes your dirty clothes. Every house in America has a washing machine. You should bring your dirty clothes here so we can wash them. And next to this washing machine is another machine for drying clothes after you have washed them."

Both machines were true wonders for Letivi. He had never seen such machines before and doubted if anyone in his country possessed such miraculous machines. He could see that for such machines to operate, one needed a reliable supply of electricity and high-pressure water. There was little electricity in his country, and piped water was rare. Moreover, even those who had piped water did not enjoy constant water flow and pressure. He thought it would be a very long time before the conditions were met in his country to allow the widespread use of washing machines. He did not think people would ever be able to afford such machines. People would have to continue for decades to wash their clothes by hand and dry them in the plain air. He knew then that his country would never be fully developed until most of the people had washing machines.

Molly could easily see that Letivi was very impressed by the washer and dryer. She wanted to help make Letivi understand that these machines had not always existed, so she said, "Letivi, I can see these machines interest you very much. I know you have never seen anything like them in Kotoku. It takes a long time to reach the development stage where the use of such machines becomes possible. While I have known these machines all my life, my mother was young when she first experienced the use of such a machine. My grandmother never knew such machines and washed all her clothes, including the cloth diapers of her seven babies, by hand and dried all the clothes on wire lines set up near one side of her house."

Molly's words helped Letivi understand, but he was still concerned that his people would be stuck for a very long time, or forever, in the situation Molly's grandmother had found herself in seventy years ago. He was feeling very discouraged about the development prospects for his country. His visit to America was showing him that there were many limits on development in his country that would be difficult to address, even if they had stability, peace, the best management, and good governance.

More than ever, he could clearly see that as good as his country tried to be, and as hard as its people worked, the realities of the situation obligated a lowering of their expectations in terms of their future development prospects. He could see that his people needed to learn how to remain content with the little they had and the meager gains they might be able to achieve in the future. He was afraid his people would want more than they could possibly have. He feared the younger generation was unwilling to accept the poverty experienced by their parents. They wanted more. But was more really possible?

Molly could see Letivi's worried expression and wondered how seeing a washer and dryer could depress him so. She had in mind to give him a tour of the kitchen and all its gadgets, but she did not want to add to his overload of information. Little Elisa was still in Letivi's arms. She playfully tapped his cheeks, saying, "Hey, you. Where are you? Say something."

Letivi snapped out of his deep thoughts about the welfare of his country and said, "Sorry. Somehow these machines made me think of how far we have to go in my own country to eliminate poverty."

Molly said, "Letivi, allow me to show you our kitchen and all its gadgets. Then, let's eat our breakfast so we can head for Gemini and Udall. Tomorrow we'll go to Wichita to see the university your father attended."

Holding little Elisa in his arms, Letivi tagged along with Molly to take a mini-tour of an American kitchen. Molly was proud of her parents' kitchen and said, "Letivi, my parents recently remodeled and updated their kitchen, replacing all their appliances. Here you can see their big new refrigerator, which has a large freezer compartment and makes ice. Next to the fridge is their new four-burner gas range, which lights automatically. We previously used matches to light the stove. We now just push a button, and an electrical spark is emitted to light the stove. I will show you how this is done."

Molly was talking too fast for Letivi. He was having a hard time taking in how the fridge and the range worked. He had never seen such before in his life. Molly turned the knob for one burner and pressed a button to light it. A circular blue gas flame appeared. Letivi took a step back. This was true magic for him. How could there be such a cooking fire in the house? He asked, "Molly, please explain to me where this fire comes from and how it works."

"Letivi, in America, natural gas is piped into the houses for cooking and heating. I saw in your country some people using small gas canisters. Here, gas is piped underground to all the houses, which pay for the service, and the stoves are hooked up to these gas lines. If you don't pay your monthly gas bill, they will stop your supply of gas. Some people have electrical stoves, but the same principles apply."

Letivi tried hard to understand, but it was all too new and complicated. He knew this was something they could never have in his country because they did not produce any natural gas. And, again, even if they did, who could afford it? Also, what about the risk of fires and explosions? There was one thing Molly said that prompted him to ask a question. "Molly, where do people go to pay for their electricity and gas bills?"

"They pay by mail. They write a check, put it in an envelope provided by the company, and give it to the mailman who comes by their houses almost every day, or they drop it in a mailbox or take it to the post office. We do much by mail in this country."

This information about the mail service floored Letivi. For him, mail delivery at home was just not possible and something that could never work in his country. There were too many practical and security obstacles. And again, who could pay for it, and who could be trusted with its operations and money? If having an efficient national mail service that delivered mail daily to your house was what being developed meant, his country may never be considered developed.

Molly then pointed at a white box with something like a TV screen and said, "Here is the microwave my parents recently purchased. It can cook and warm food in just a few minutes using sound waves."

Letivi was listening well to Molly's every word, but what she said just could not be possible. "Molly, can you please show me how this machine works?"

Molly poured some cold water from the sink faucet into a ceramic cup and opened the microwave door to place the cup in the middle of the circular rotating tray. She closed the small door and pushed a few musical buttons, saying, "Just wait one minute, and you will see the water in the cup is very hot." After about a minute, she withdrew the cup of water from the microwave and showed Letivi that it was cool on the outside but hot on the inside. Letivi was in total disbelief. For him, this was indeed some sort of powerful magic about which he needed to learn more.

Molly moved around the kitchen to the sink and said, "We don't have much time. Our breakfast is getting cold, and my parents and Robin are waiting for us at the table. I only have two more things to show you: our dishwashing machine and our garbage disposal." Molly slid open the washing machine and indicated to Letivi how it worked. Then she ran some water in the sink and turned on the garbage disposal. She explained to Letivi how these two modern conveniences worked. She also told Letivi that her parents had decided against buying a trash compactor. This latter statement prompted Letivi to ask, "OK. Whatever that means, but what do people do with their trash here? Everything looks so clean and neat."

Molly spoke at a fast clip. "Twice a week, men come with a big garbage truck and collect our trash and take it to the city dump, which is located far from town. On those days, we put our trash in a required refuse receptacle and set it at the curbside in front of our house so the men can easily pick it up and place it into the dumper mechanism in their truck."

Letivi was beaten into silence by all he had heard and the amazing wonders he had just witnessed and could barely say, "Thanks, Molly. I hope to see one of those garbage trucks someday. Please know and appreciate that all you have said and showed me is new to me in spite of all the books I have read. I also hope we can find more time to experience these wonderful machines so I can understand them better. I also need to get a notebook to write many things down."

"Sure, Letivi. We'll be very busy these first few days, but after that, we'll have lots of time to do anything you would like to do or talk about. Let's go eat breakfast now."

As they were entering the living room and finding their places around the table, a bell sounded. This bell startled Letivi. He had never heard such a thing. Elisa immediately asked to be put down so she could join her grandmother to see who was at the door. Letivi was also curious. He slowly followed Elisa to the door. Della opened the door to greet a man in a gray uniform. Letivi instinctively hid behind the door because he thought the man might be a crooked policeman. When Della saw Letivi doing this, she said, "David, you have nothing to fear. It is only the mailman delivering me a telegram that is addressed to you."

Letivi was delighted to see firsthand how the mail service worked, but he was now very concerned about receiving a telegram. He did not know how he could receive any messages because nobody knew where he was. Della handed him the telegram, and he said, "How is this possible? Nobody knows where I am."

Molly piped up, "Letivi, before I left Ataku, I gave Chief Gyasi my parents' address. I guess the telegram must be from him. Please open it quickly so we can know what it says."

Letivi carefully opened the telegram and read its brief message: "Call me when you can. Gyasi." He repeated the message out loud so all could hear it. He knew that he must find a way soon to call his grandfather, and that meant breaking their agreement about not using the cell phone the president had given them.

Molly gently said, "Do you think this means there is some kind of emergency?"

"No. If it were urgent, he would have said so in the telegram. I need a day or two to think. Then we should try to call him."

Everyone could see that Letivi was troubled by the unexpected receipt of a telegram from his fellow chief in Ataku. Molly urged Letivi to sit down and eat his breakfast. She asked him, "Would you like cream and sugar in your coffee?"

Letivi replied, "I think I would like to try joe.'"

Molly laughed. "Why, Letivi, coffee and joe are one and the same thing."

"Oh. In that case, I would like milk and sugar in my coffee."

"OK. Come and have some bacon and eggs and a stack of my mom's nice, fluffy pancakes. Choose what you want, and we'll warm your plate in the microwave."

Molly's dad, Roy, was trying to be polite and make conversation with Letivi. He asked Letivi, "Well, how is it going for you so far in America?"

Letivi politely replied, "It is OK, but I have a lot to learn, and the weather is too cold for me. It will take me a while to adapt. Maybe by the time I am getting used to things, it will be time for me to return to Africa."

While Molly, her mom, and her toddler were in the kitchen warming Letivi's food and fixing his coffee, Robin gave Letivi a preview of what they planned to do today. He said, "We will leave town and take a nice drive along part of the Flint Hills and go to Gemini. You need to know that when your father lived in Gemini, it was a thriving little town. Since around your father's disappearance, the town's oil refinery closed, and most people moved away. Today, it is like a ghost town, and only a few residents remain. One of those residents is Granny Rebecca. I have met her, and I would like you to meet her. She knew your father. The only other thing to do is visit the grave of your uncle Edgar and his wife, Gladys."

Letivi listened intently and said, "Thanks, Robin. Sounds very good to me. It is important that I see the grave of my father's older brother."

Molly returned with Letivi's breakfast and a cup of hot coffee. Letivi took a sip of the coffee and found it tasted almost as good as the coffee Emerson had offered him at Melo Hotel in Melomti. He liked the taste of the pancakes and the sweet maple syrup that covered them. He also found crisp American bacon to his liking, and the fried eggs tasted better than any he had eaten in his country. He could easily see that the best meal for him in America was breakfast.

While he ate, Robin continued his rundown of the day's agenda. "After we finish our visit to Gemini, we'll find our way to Udall to see where your father went to high school and his foster home. The most important stop for us in Udall will be to visit with Mr. Rankin, one of your father's former teachers, who remembers your father well as the best student he ever had."

Letivi thanked Robin for his preview of the main events of the day, saying, "Very good, Robin. Everything you and everyone else are doing to support my visit is much appreciated. Let's stay flexible and see how things go. Are we ready to go now?"

Roy replied, "Well, your driver and his car are ready. Clyde wanted to go too, but he said he had something else to do today and left."

Roy opened the front door, and everyone put on their coats—except Letivi, as he had never taken his jacket off—and said their good-byes to Molly's mom and headed out the front door. Once they were outside, Letivi looked around and did not see baby Elisa. He stopped walking and turned to ask Molly, "Where is Elisa?"

Molly could see that Letivi was seriously concerned about Elisa's whereabouts and said in a kind tone, "Elisa is staying home with my mom."

Letivi surprised Molly when he said in commanding voice, "Elisa must come with us!"

Molly was perplexed and tried to explain. "Letivi, please understand that it is a lot of trouble to take a two-year-old on a day-long trip. She won't sit still in the car and asks to make many stops."

Letivi quickly answered, "She will not be any trouble. Bring her. I can't go without her."

Molly was a bit upset by Letivi's demand that Elisa accompany them. She also found his demand very odd. She did not know what to say or do. She finally said, with a tinge of annoyance in her voice, "OK, Mister Big Chief. Have it your way. I will go and fetch Elisa. Please go wait for us in the car with my dad and Robin."

The wait in the car was long enough to prompt Roy to start the engine so he could run the heater. About fifteen minutes later, Molly came out of the house with Elisa all bundled up. She carried a bag full of the things Elisa would need during the day. Molly's mom was not happy because the main reason she was staying behind was to take care of Elisa. Now she would be left home alone.

Letivi got out of the backseat and opened the rear door on Roy's old four-door, light blue 1983 Buick Skylark sedan for Molly and Elisa. As they passed by him, he winked at Elisa, and she winked back. That exchange of winks told him he had done the right thing to insist that Elisa come with them. As soon as everyone was settled in the backseat, Roy said, "Here we go. We'll follow the yellow brick road. Elisa, you have to sit still and be a good girl."

Elisa surprised everyone by saying in a way she had never done before, "Yes, Grandfather. I will be a good girl."

Molly gave an inquisitive look at Elisa, saying, "Sweet baby. Where are you getting all those words?" As soon as Molly stopped talking, Elisa worked her way out of her mother's lap to sit very still on Letivi's. Molly was again surprised by the strange attraction Elisa had for Letivi.

Within minutes, they were past the city limits and driving north to Haverhill before turning east on State Highway 400. Once they were on the latter highway, they passed Leon and began to go through vast open spaces filled with rolling hills covered by brown, tall bluestem grass. It was all open land dotted here and there with cattle and windmills. Letivi was impressed with the vast vistas of unending prairie. He was thinking that there was much space for many more people. He also wondered why he did not see more land cultivated. He asked, "How many people are in Kansas? How big is it? This part seems so empty. And the road is not yellow."

Robin replied from his position in the front seat, "Kansas has about two million and five hundred thousand people, and it covers just over eighty-two thousand square miles."

Letivi began crunching in his own mind a comparison of these statistics with similar ones for his own small country. His country was about one-fourth the size of Kansas, but it had almost four times the population, and that population was divided among over twenty distinct ethnic groups, each with its own language and customs. This complex diversity of ethnic and linguistic groups presented formidable development challenges and represented a huge obstacle to nation building. Ongoing ethnic tensions served to create an unstable environment. Adding to this volatile mixture was a deep divide between agriculturalists and herders. Things were not made easier by a fast-growing and youthful population—nearly 60 percent were under twenty-five years of age. Every twenty-four years or so, the population of his country doubled, and some of the faster-growing urban centers doubled in size almost every ten years.

Letivi asked another question. "What is the per capita income for people living in Kansas?"

Robin replied, "I'm not sure, but I recall reading somewhere that the average family of five people made around $40,000 per year."

Letivi knew that that average family size in his country was much higher and that the average per capita income was nearly $400 per year. This would mean that a family of ten people had an average annual income of about $4,000. That was less than a tenth of the average household income in Kansas for a family half the size.

All these statistical comparisons vividly communicated to Letivi that closing the income gap between his country and Kansas was akin to *Mission Impossible*. Poor people in Kansas would always be much richer than the average person in his country. He tried not to dwell on this subject, as it made him sad for his country and his people. This trip was opening his eyes to many difficult considerations. He was almost regretting learning firsthand how large the development gap was between his country and America. Perhaps he would have been happier not knowing what he knew now. These daunting facts were of much torment to Letivi and were the underlying cause of his growing state of depression about the fate of his country.

They passed the turnoff to Beaumont, and a few miles later, just before arriving at Piedmont, Roy began slowing down the car to take a left turn off Highway 400 to go a few miles north to Gemini. There was a rusty sign standing alongside the road at the turnoff with a barely visible arrow pointing in the direction of Gemini. The old county road covering the few miles to Gemini was pockmarked with potholes. It was obvious that the road had not been maintained for several years. When they arrived in the small former town of Gemini, Letivi was surprised that it looked better than Robin had described. He found that even the unmaintained road was better than many roads in his country. He knew that Roy's low-riding Buick could not make it over Kotoku's rough roads. He could see that everything was crumbling and unkempt, but with a little effort here and there, and some cleaning up, the town would be habitable. Certainly, even in its current run-down state, squatters from his own country would find Gemini attractive. The only reason a town would be abandoned in his country would be if the people believed a diabolic spell had been cast over it.

Clyde dodged the many potholes and the random debris in the streets as he followed Robin's directions to Granny Rebecca's house. Clyde stopped the car in front of Granny's house. Robin was surprised to see the condition of the house; it had greatly deteriorated in the couple of months since his last visit. He looked for Granny's dog, but it was not to be seen. He told everyone to wait in the car while he went to the house to see if Granny was home. He slowly walked up to the house and knocked loudly on the front door, saying, "Granny, are you home?"

Robin knocked repeatedly and called for Granny to come to the door. He expected to hear her old dog bark, but there was nothing but an eerie silence. He gave up trying the front door and circled the little old house, trying to peer into its windows for any sign of life. He could not see or hear anything. He was headed back to the car to inform the others that nobody was home when he heard someone loudly whistling an old Perry Como song, "Round and Round." He turned to see an old man in a raggedy white T-shirt and faded baseball cap briskly walking down the street and whistling as if this were the happiest day in his life.

He waved at the man and hollered as loudly as he could, "Hey, mister. Good morning. Can you help me?"

The man continued walking and whistling up a storm, continuing on his way as if Robin did not exist. Robin ran after the man, calling for him to stop. The man kept going and paid no heed to Robin, who ran up to the man and placed himself squarely in front of the man. Upon seeing Robin a very short distance in front of him, the man became frightened and said, "Please don't hurt me. I'm old, deaf, and penniless."

Robin smiled and acted in a way to show the man he was not of any harm to him. When the man saw that Robin was friendly, he reached into his jeans pocket and pulled out a hearing aid. He turned it on and placed it in his left ear. He stretched out his hand and said, "Hello. My name is Peabody, last mayor of Gemini. I think I'm the last person to reside in my town. I'm sorry. I shut off my hearing aid since there is nobody around, and I whistle better without it."

Robin immediately responded, "Very honored to meet you, sir. I'm here with my friends to visit with Granny Rebecca. I met with Granny a couple months ago, and she gave me information that helped me find David Peterson's son in Africa. You may recall David better as JB."

Mayor Peabody's jaw dropped. He stammered as he tried to say, "Really? That's amazing. I did not know JB like Granny did, but I was the mayor in charge of the investigation of his disappearance. I was also in charge of the discovery and burial of the corpses of his older brother and sister-in-law."

"Thank you, Mayor. That is very interesting. I think I saw your name in a little book I read, *JB, Hero of Gemini*."

Mayor Peabody lit up and said, "Is JB's son in the car with you? I'd really like to meet him. Does he know what happened to his father?"

"Come with me and meet the young David Peterson from Africa. He does not know what happened to his father, but his existence does prove that JB had been to Africa."

They walked to the car, and Robin rapped on Roy's car window. Roy lowered the window, and Robin said, "Hey, everyone. Get out of the car and meet Mayor Peabody, last citizen of Gemini."

Everyone exited the car, and there was a cordial round of greetings and handshakes as they introduced themselves to Mayor Peabody. Letivi held on to the Mayor's hand as he studied his face, asking, "Did you know my father?"

The mayor replied forthrightly, "No, my son, I did not, but I can honestly tell you he was a much-loved figure in this town. People were very depressed after he disappeared, and our town has suffered severely. Look around you. There's very little left of the Gemini your father knew. Ever since your dad disappeared, Gemini started to die."

Letivi took pity on the old man and said, "I'm sorry for the demise of your town and the way my father left you. I wish things could have been different. Did you know his older brother, Edgar?"

"No, son, I'm sorry that I did not know Edgar, but I'm the one who arranged to give him and his wife a proper final resting place in our town cemetery."

Letivi could see that the mayor really did not have anything more he could tell him about his father, so he asked, "Can we see Granny Rebecca? Is she around?"

"I'm sorry to tell you and your friends that Granny passed away about a month ago. She was the last woman to live in Gemini. Her dog died the day after she did. You can see her grave in the cemetery at the end of this road."

All the time Letivi was talking to the mayor, he held Elisa in his arms. Elisa surprised everyone by saying, "Thank you, Mr. Mayor."

The mayor laughed and said, "You have a beautiful little daughter. She is quite a spark plug. I hope you can excuse me. I need to get home to feed my cats and take my heart medicine. It was great meeting you folks." He turned around and started walking toward the way from which he had come. He shut off his hearing aid and began whistling another golden oldie, "Be-Bop-a-Lula."

They watched the aged mayor walk slowly off. It was a sad and melancholy scene. He was an old man near the end of his time in a town where he had once been a highly respected official. Now he was a 'nobody' and all alone in a forlorn place. It was as if there were only ashes remaining where there had been once a raging fire. One could sense the end of an age and, for better or worse, the passage of time. Only the older Roy could truly sympathize with the painful predicament of Mayor Peabody's long life. Roy was teary eyed when he said in a hushed voice, "I really feel for the mayor. He has lost everything, including his town. I know well those songs from the 1950s that he is whistling. For my generation, there was no better time to be alive than the 1950s. Growing up in a small town back then was the best thing ever."

Molly piped up and said, "I guess there is only our visit to the cemetery that remains. Let's go."

They piled back into the car, and Roy drove the short distance to the shabby cemetery. It was easy to spot Granny Rebecca's grave, as the earth covering it was still fresh and it was near the small parking lot at the cemetery entrance. Robin led the group deeper inside the cemetery to Edgar's and Gladys's tombstones and the granite slabs covering their graves. Seeing where his uncle's and aunt's remains lay incited much emotion within Letivi. He asked in a solemn voice, "May I have a moment to pray over my uncle's and aunt's graves? Thank you."

The group backed away and gave Letivi the space and quiet he needed to say his prayers. Letivi handed Elisa to Molly and then walked to Edgar's grave and knelt. Little Elisa squirmed free of

Molly's grip and ran to kneel next to Letivi. Molly was surprised by this behavior, but she could see that the moment required giving in to her daughter's determination.

Letivi placed his hand on the granite slab before him and said with a forceful intensity, "Uncle, it is I, your nephew, son of your younger brother. I come from Africa to visit the home of my father, David Peterson. I pray that your time in eternity is one of happiness and peace. If you can, please, dear Uncle, give me a sign to indicate whether or not the spirits of my father and mother are with you. I believe my father's spirit wanted to return to his birthplace to be with his blood relatives." Elisa mimicked Letivi, placing her hands on the slab and mumbling her own words. The hearts of those observing this sight were deeply touched.

A few moments after Letivi said his last word, a strong gust of wind came out of nowhere, blowing dust and leaves so hard that they all had to cover their faces. Only Letivi and Elisa did not cover their faces. They allowed the wind to strike every part of their bodies. Then the wind stopped as quickly as it had started. Roy commented, "That's Kansas for you. You can get a 'blow' across the plains at any time."

For Letivi, the "blow" was quite a different matter. It was a clear sign to him that his prayerful inquiries had been answered and his father's and mother's spirits were happy to call this place and the heavens above it their eternal home. He felt an unprecedented peace in his heart. He turned to tell the group, "It was a very good thing that I came here. I will never forget this place and the importance it has in my life. I am ready to go now."

Little Elisa ran from Letivi and joined her mother, saying in a child's sweet voice, "Mommy, I'm your baby again, but I will always love Letivi." Molly did not know what to think of Elisa's words. She was not aware that she knew Letivi's name. She could not fathom why Letivi was more to her daughter than a simple David could ever be. She was both afraid and happy about this mysterious tie between her daughter and Letivi. She told herself that as long as her daughter was happy and healthy, she had nothing to worry about. She was fine as long as she refused to acknowledge her inner feelings about an unknown fear.

CHAPTER TWENTY-NINE
COUNTY ROADS

Nobody said a word in the car. All was quiet as they left the bumpy road from Gemini and regained state Highway 77. Roy broke the silence. "We'll need to backtrack a bit and get on a county road to Atlanta and then take another secondary road to Udall. We should be there in less than an hour."

All those in the car remained silent as they thought over the events that had already occurred that day. Elisa had fallen asleep in Molly's arms. Robin was taking notes in his journal. He thought that someday he would write some articles about his search for JB. Letivi asked Robin, "Do you have some paper and a ballpoint I can borrow? I also would like to jot down some notes."

Robin tore a few pages out of his journal and passed them and his spare ballpoint pen to Letivi, who began scribbling immediately on the pages.

Molly tried to peek at what Letivi was writing, but she could not make out a word of his curious penmanship. Her curiosity finally got the best of her, and she asked Letivi, "What language are you writing in?"

Letivi replied, "I make my notes the way your third president, Thomas Jefferson, did. I write backward in English. My notes can only be clearly read when held up to a mirror. I got the idea by reading a book a long time ago about the life of President Jefferson. He got the idea about mirror writing from Leonardo da Vinci. He also could write with both hands, as I do. I am really left handed, but teachers required me to write with my right hand. Also, in our culture, you must eat with the right hand. I like President Jefferson because he had mixed-blood children like me."

Molly was doubly impressed. She was surprised that Letivi knew who Thomas Jefferson was and amazed that he could teach himself to write the English language backwards so easily, from right to left. She could see there was much about Letivi she did not know. She told herself to be patient. She was confident that in due time Letivi would tell her much more about himself and all he knew.

They reached the road to Atlanta and turned south. Letivi was expecting to see an unimproved road, but instead, the county road was nicely paved and well maintained. He was impressed that this little-used road was better than the national highways in his own country, which were under constant, heavy use. He was surprised that such a good road passed through an isolated area where another person or vehicle was rarely seen. There were many large population areas in his country that suffered greatly because they did not have access to any all-weather roads. He knew that road infrastructure was needed to enable a country to progress, but were roads really needed in such sparsely populated areas?

Letivi could not believe how clean the roadway was. He did not see any litter. In his country, there would be all kinds of litter along the roads, especially plastic bags. Here in Kansas, it looked as if the roads were so clean that you could eat off them. He could not help but ask Molly, "How do you keep the roadway so clean?"

Molly lost no time in replying, "It is against the law to litter, and heavy fines are imposed on those caught littering. People generally keep their trash in their cars and discard it when they come to a designated receptacle."

Letivi thought that such a law was a very good thing, but he did not know how it could be enforced in his country. He asked Molly, "How do you enforce this law? I am surprised that I have not yet seen a single policeman or soldier. In my country, you see armed security forces everywhere."

"Letivi, most people in my country are law abiding, and they appreciate law and order. The police go where they are needed and make regular patrols elsewhere. If you have a problem and need the help of the police, you call 911, and they will come immediately to your location. As for the military, they stay on their bases. They are not used for internal matters except when they are called on to help with major disasters. Their main role is to protect our country's interests outside of America. I note that America has one of the largest and most powerful military forces in the world."

Letivi could not argue with the importance of law and order in a progressive society, but he knew well that in his own country, there was much chaos and corruption, as everyone at all levels tried to manipulate things in their favor. In his country, money and the power that came with it talked louder than any laws. Everyone and everything had its price. The wealthy and politically well-connected could act with impunity. Court verdicts could be bought. Nobody really knew what was legal and what was not, and few cared. Survival was the name of the game, and you did what you needed to do to buy yourself and your family more time.

Letivi could never see the law being applied fairly in his country. He was convinced that there could never be a workable 911. He could see that maybe it would be good to have an international type of 911, whereby outside assistance could be called to help save a country from its leaders and put it on the right track. Even when people had a problem in his country that required the intervention of the police, they would not involve the police because they were often more of a problem than any criminal. Letivi could see that they really needed a fair and honest justice system in his country, but he could not see how such a system could develop amid the extreme poverty of the masses and corrupt, greedy leadership.

America's large but almost invisible military force stood in stark contrast to the situation in his country, where gun-toting, ragtag security forces were seen everywhere. The role of the military in his country puzzled him. His country had never been in a war and would probably never be in a war, so he wondered about the utility of an oversized military force that cost the national budget as much as key sectors such as education and health. At the same time, he knew that it was very dangerous in his country to meddle with the military's privileges.

Letivi took note of a big sign alongside the road that said, "Buckle Up, It's the Law." He immediately squirmed around in his seat to find the seat belts. Thanks to his airplane experience, he knew what to do. He wrapped the seat belt around himself and buckled it. He saw that Molly was watching him closely. He looked at her and said, "Molly, should not you and Elisa buckle up? It's the law. You told me everyone obeys the law in America."

Molly took a deep breath. She knew this would be a tricky one to explain to Letivi. "Yes, Letivi, it is the law, but only those sitting in the front seat are required to buckle up. As you can see, my dad and Robin are using their seat belts. For safety, we should also buckle up in the backseat, but we usually don't. In this regard, we are in violation of good safety rules but not the law. I note that this is a relative new law and many people in Kansas are not yet obeying it. Many people don't see any reason to buckle up on the kind of county roads we are using because of the absence of any traffic.

Letivi was confused about what Molly just said. Nonetheless, in spite of this curve Molly had thrown him, he decided to keep his seat belt buckled. Letivi's good example prompted Molly to also buckle her seat belt and hold tightly her precious daughter.

This seat belt subject and many others had Letivi's mind working overtime as he gazed across the endless plains on a sunny day with a light November wind. He began observing fields that he could see had been cultivated and other fields with huge lumps of straw. He asked Molly, "What crop has been planted here?"

"That is wheat stubble left from last year's crop. As I think you know, Kansas is referred to as the Wheat State because it produces much wheat each year. Harvest is generally in June. If you come back to Kansas at that time, you'll observe ripe wheat as far as the eye can see. Oh, see that bird sitting on the barbwire fence over there? That is a meadowlark, Kansas's state bird, and growing in the roadside ditch are sunflowers. The sunflower is Kansas's state flower."

Letivi cogitated over how big farms were in Kansas. One field of wheat or corn could produce enough food to feed his village for at least a year. It was nothing here for someone to farm a thousand acres. He noted again that in his country the average family farm seldom exceeded ten acres, and those acres were all worked by hand. He could not see any possibility for farm sizes in his country to be ever as large as in America. The thought of large farms in his country scared him because over eighty percent of the population depended mostly on subsistence farming. He asked himself, "If large farms took over in my country, where would all the people go?"

Letivi commented, "Farms are very big in Kansas."

Molly replied, "Yes, they are, and crop yields are among the highest in the world. Did you know that about two percent of America's population is composed of farmers, but they are able to feed a national population of nearly two hundred and fifty million and also export hundreds of thousands of tons of food each year?"

Upon hearing Molly's words, Letivi was again feeling sorry for his poor small country and its population of nearly twelve million. Farmers in his country worked very hard, but they rarely produced enough food to feed themselves for an entire year. Furthermore, producing enough food was becoming a more difficult challenge because the population was growing very fast. At the same time that there were more mouths to feed, food was becoming more expensive, as the dependence on food imports was rising. Letivi could see that family size was an important factor in terms of providing good nutrition to all family members, particularly children. He asked Molly, "What is the average size of a family in Kansas?"

Molly said, "I don't have in my head any firm statistic for that, but it seems that most couples have two to three children. Almost everyone here practices birth control, so they can choose the size of their family."

Letivi did not know a couple in his country who would accept such a small family size. Couples in his country would normally aspire to have as many children as possible. It was not unusual to find many families with eight to ten children or more. As many children died before achieving the age of five, couples would end up with fewer grown children, but that number would still be more than two to three. Modern birth-control methods were almost unknown, and Letivi doubted such methods would ever be widely accepted in his country. At the same time, he did worry about how the capacity would be developed to educate, care for, and employ such a fast-growing and youthful population.

Letivi was bemused by the fact that Kansas had a nickname and a state bird. He thought that was a cute custom, but he could see no practical application for it in his country. Given the diversity of dozens of ethnic groups and the variety of ecological zones in his country, there could never be agreement on a state flower or bird. And, given the artificial way the colonial powers had divided up Africa, it would be difficult to choose a bird or flower that was not also prevalent in a neighboring country.

Letivi kept seeing grassy fields with huge mounds of straw scattered about the landscape, so he asked, "What are those big bundles of straw I am seeing in many fields?"

Molly simply replied, "Those are prairie hay rolls. The hay is cut, and a bailing machine rolls it into a huge cylindrical roll. These rolls can weigh over one thousand pounds. Farmers will take the hay away as they need it for feeding their livestock during the winter months."

That answer left Letivi with no more questions for the moment. Roy interrupted the question-and-answer session by jokingly saying, "Here's the Atlanta metropolis." In reality, Atlanta was a very small town of less than three hundred people. They turned right and headed west on another county road to nearby Rock, an even smaller town. They turned south and, upon reaching Rock, they turned right on Highway 15 for the short drive to Udall.

Letivi had noticed a couple of other things that intrigued him. He saw some sort of flimsy wooden fences made of slender strips of wood standing upright behind the barbwire fences along the roadsides and wondered why two fences were needed. He had also observed several signs indicating nearby historical markers, and he did not know what this was all about. So he again asked Molly about these two observations. Molly was brief in her reply. "Those other fences you see are to prevent snow from drifting over the road in winter. The historical markers are to indicate the occurrence of some famous event that occurred in this locality."

Letivi was not satisfied with her response. He could not imagine what she meant by "snow drifting," and he had a hard time believing that someone would go to all the trouble and expense to construct historical sites. He had seen sand drifts in his country, but he did not think they could be stopped by such fences. For sure, it had never snowed in his tropical country. He was certain that there were no roadside historical markers in his country, and, even if there were some historical events to mark, he doubted that there would ever be such markers in his country.

At the Udall city limits, there was a large sign welcoming them to "America's Safest Town." Letivi immediately asked Molly why Udall was so safe. Molly quickly explained, "A tornado wiped out the town in 1955. When they rebuilt the town, they constructed many storm shelters so that people could be safe whenever a tornado struck again. The threat of tornadoes is a big menace, especially in this part of Kansas, which is located in what is referred to as Tornado Alley."

They were entering Udall, so Letivi did not have much time to reply. He said, "I don't know what a tornado is. In my country, we don't have tornadoes. That's good because they sound like very bad and destructive things. You'll need to tell me more about tornadoes some other time."

As they crossed the railroad tracks and drove onto the main street of the small town of Udall, population about eight hundred people, something caught Letivi's attention that prompted him to ask, "What is that tall structure that sits next to the railroad tracks? I have seen a number of these types of buildings, but I do not know their use."

It was Robin's turn to respond to Letivi's endless series of questions. "Letivi, that is a grain elevator. Farmers truck their grain harvest here for storage and sale. It is loaded into boxcars and hauled away on trains. Comparatively, that is a very small grain elevator. Maybe we can take you someday to Hutchinson and see a good number of the largest grain elevators in the world. I believe Wichita has the world's largest grain elevator."

Letivi was again bemoaning the fact that even the smallest thing in Kansas was bigger than what existed in his country. There were not any large grain storage units in his country. His government did store some grain bags in a warehouse for food shortage emergencies, but the quantity was less than could be stored in this small-town grain elevator. He was certain that the capacity of this grain elevator was sufficient to store enough food for all twenty villages in his district for a year. He was impressed that there was a train in this small town and that it could transport grain a long distance. He lamented the fact that they did not have a railroad in his country.

They turned off the short main street and passed through the sparsely populated small town, heading toward the high school that Letivi's father had attended. Letivi noted again that all the houses, no matter how small, had huge lawns and there were no walls between the houses. He was puzzled as to why there were no walls between people's properties. To protect one's property and secure it from thieves, it was essential in his country to build a high wall around one's property. In the cities, modern houses were surrounded by high concrete block walls that were often topped by barbwire and shards of broken glass. He explained this aspect of his country to Molly, and she replied, "Interesting. The only places in our country with walls like that are prisons."

They parked in front of the high school. Roy asked Letivi, "Do you want to go in? Classes are in session, so we would have to get permission to visit the school from the principal's office."

Letivi took a few minutes to stare intently at the school. He told himself this was where his father had gone to secondary school many years ago. He finally replied, "No. I don't need to go inside the school. I do not wish to cause a disturbance. I'm interested in seeing Mr. Rankin, who knew my father, and visiting the foster home where he lived."

"Okey-dokey," replied Roy. "Let's go pay a visit on the elderly Mr. Rankin. Robin, please show me where to go."

Robin said, "Turn around and go two blocks the other way. We passed near his house on our way in."

While they turned around, Letivi commented to Molly, "I can see the schools here are very nice and full of students. Most schools in my country are not so nice and jam-packed with children. Also, many children do not go to school."

Molly quickly retorted, "It is the law that every child go to school, and the legal consequences are quite heavy for parents who don't send their children to school. It is also required that class size doesn't exceed twenty students. Almost all children graduate from high school and many of those who do graduate go on to college."

It dawned on Letivi what really made America strong as a country: most of its citizens received a quality formal education. In his country, the illiteracy rate was still very high, particularly among women. Families still preferred sending their sons to school instead of their daughters. There were tens of thousands of children who were not in school. At the same time, public primary school classrooms often had a hundred or more students, making it more difficult to ensure a quality education. Many children did not complete all six elementary school grades, and it was not unusual for children who finished the sixth grade to not be able to read and write correctly. If they forced families to send all their children to school, there would not be enough classrooms, teachers, and school supplies. Letivi was asking himself, "How can a country advance when the majority of its people have not benefited from a good-quality primary school education?"

They parked in front of the large grassy lot that fronted on Mr. Rankin's small white house. Robin volunteered again to see if Mr. Rankin was home. He strode across the wide front lawn and rapped gingerly on the front door several times. All was very quiet. He waited a couple of minutes and knocked again. While he was waiting and listening for any noise coming from within the quiet house, a shout rang out from the street. "Hey. What do you want?" These words came from a short, gruff old man who was dressed in a black and red checkered woolen hunter's shirt, walking his little black Scottish terrier in the street.

Robin yelled back, "We are looking for Mr. Rankin. Is he home or around in town somewhere?"

The man laughed crazily before saying in a booming voice, "You just missed him. You can now find him just east of town in the county cemetery. He died last week."

Robin was saddened to learn that Mr. Rankin had passed away. He had enjoyed his previous meeting with him and was thankful for the information he had provided on Letivi's father. It was this information that had led Molly and him to WSU, where they discovered that David Peterson Sr. had joined the Peace Corps and gone to Africa. Without saying another word to the weird old man, Robin rushed back to the car to inform the others.

He climbed into the car and shut the door, solemnly saying, "Mr. Rankin is no more."

There was a long moment of silence before Letivi said, "I'm sorry not to see Mr. Rankin before he died. It seems that everyone who knew my father well is dead. Let's go see where my father lived when he went to high school."

They drove a few miles out of town to a small, hardscrabble quarter-section farm. There was not much to see, and they were intimidated from getting out of the car because a man was sitting in a rocking chair on his front porch with a rifle lying on his lap. It was difficult to imagine where David had slept in such a small house. The old red barn was small and lopsided. There were a few scrawny cattle in the feedlot next to a barn, which was located a short distance from a small pond. It was obvious that this was a relatively poor farm occupied by people with relatively little means. This desolate scene generated many impressions in Letivi's African mind.

Letivi knew that white people were viewed in his country as being well off and successful. No matter how poor and uneducated a white person was, he or she would be highly regarded just because of the color of his or her skin. He had always believed his father, who was exalted in his village and elevated to demi-god status, came from a special, holy place. He could not believe that his father had come from such austere environs. He almost wished he had not seen where his much-worshipped father had originated. In any event, he told himself it was not his father's origins that counted but where his final destiny took place in Africa. His father's unpretentious beginnings were not important. Only what had happened to him in Africa truly mattered.

Letivi said in a soft, barely audible voice, "I have seen enough of this place. Where do we go next?"

Molly replied, "I guess we head back to El Dorado. Maybe we can stop along the way in Augusta for a bite to eat."

Her dad said, "Fine with me," and started the car, turned it around, and drove along the short stretch of gravel road they had come on, returning to rejoin Highway 77. They crossed over the Walnut River and headed back through Rock and on to the town of Douglas before arriving at the larger town of Augusta. For most of the way, all was quiet. Elisa was now awake and saying, "Mommy, I'm hungry. Can we get some Chicken McNuggets?"

Molly informed all present that Elisa had decided where they would eat. "Elisa wants chicken McNuggets, so we will be going to the McDonald's in Augusta."

Everyone let out a loud shout. "Great choice, Elisa!" Letivi did not say a word. He did not understand what either McDonald's or McNuggets meant. He decided not to ask any questions about this and would wait to see for himself what all the fuss was about. He was surprised that a baby could decide where they were to eat. That would rarely happen in his country. He began to think that little Elisa knew more about America than he did. As they drove along, Letivi's eyes continued to be glued to the side window as he tried to take in everything he saw. He was wondering if Kansas had a state snake. He did not think so because he had not yet seen any snakes or lizards. He asked Molly, "Do you have any snakes or lizards here?"

"Yes, we do. We have several kinds of snakes, and a number of them are poisonous. Sometimes you see them cross the road, but this time of year, you will not see any because they are hibernating. I have never seen a lizard in Kansas, although there may be some."

Letivi replied, "We have many snakes in my country. They are all bad. We hate snakes. When we see them, we kill them. We eat some kinds of snakes. We have several kinds of lizards. They are everywhere. We even have gecko lizards, which run around on the walls inside our houses at night. They are harmless. We do not eat them." He wanted to add that some people feared the gecko lizard and chameleon because of their spiritual powers, but he refrained from mentioning it because it would be something difficult to explain.

Molly rejoined, "You know there is a time of the year in our state when there is what we call a rattlesnake roundup in some towns. The rattlesnake is the most prevalent poisonous snake in Kansas. A large number of people participate in this roundup to find and kill as many rattlesnakes as possible. At the end of the roundup, the snakes are skinned and grilled for a huge snake-eating feast. People say rattlesnake meat tastes like chicken. I don't know because I have never tried it."

Letivi liked what Molly was saying. It made good sense to him that people should get together and kill and eat poisonous snakes. He happily said, "I would like to see one of those roundups."

The car slowed down to the town speed limit, and Roy kept an eye out for McDonald's golden arches. Elisa was the first to see the arches and began to clap her hands and chant repeatedly, "McDonald's!"

Roy turned left and found a parking place. They had decided not to use the drive-thru lane because everyone needed to go to the toilet. They got out of the car and headed for the door. Letivi closely followed Molly and Robin in case he needed help in handling this strange new eating world. He stood behind Molly in the food-order line. Molly told Letivi, "Relax. Look at the pictures showing different kinds of food combinations and see if there is one you would like to eat."

Letivi did not know what to order. He had doubts about ordering again a hamburger, as he shied away from eating pork, so he thought he did not want anything with "ham" in it. The only thing he recognized was chicken, and this made him think that he should get the same McNuggets that Elisa had ordered. He timidly told Molly, "I will take Chicken McNuggets and a Coke."

They placed their orders. Roy had already found seats for them while they waited for their order number to be called. Letivi was feeling uncomfortable because people were looking at him. Somehow they could see he was not from Kansas. He felt like an outsider who was looking in from a vantage point that was far outside the world in which he found himself. He longed to be back in his village among his own kind. It also dawned on him that there were not any black people in the crowded dining room. He had lived his entire life among black people, and now he found himself constantly surrounded by more white people than he had seen in his entire life. His discomfort prompted him to ask Robin in a hushed voice, "Are there any black people in Kansas?"

Robin immediately grasped why Letivi would ask such a question. He could easily understand that after having spent a week in Africa where he had been a lonely white face among a sea of black faces, Letivi was now feeling the reverse effect. He replied, "Letivi, we have black people in Kansas, but there are few in this area, and their presence is generally low. I think that less than six percent of the state's population is black."

One of the cashiers called out their order number. Robin told Letivi to sit still with Molly and Elisa. They would go and bring back the food and drinks. Robin and Roy returned with the food trays and placed them on the table. Molly began sorting out the food. She served Elisa first, using the paper wrapping from her hamburger and pouring Elisa's McNuggets on it. Elisa began quickly nibbling on her McNuggets and sucking Hi-C on her straw. Molly then gave Letivi his ten-McNuggets box and his Coke. She also offered him some small barbecue and ketchup packets. Letivi looked to see how Elisa was eating this new food. He did as she was doing, except he added the tasty barbecue sauce. Molly showed him how to open the sauce packets. He found the McNuggets to his liking, and he liked the sweet sauce. He looked at Elisa and winked. Elisa said with a giggling laugh, "Good, ain't it?"

Letivi nodded his head in agreement with Elisa. Out of the corner of his eye, he was watching how the others devoured a variety of hamburgers and their French fries. He found the plastic shiny tables, benches, and trays of interest. He was amazed when he was told you could drink as much as you pleased without paying extra. He was having trouble drinking his Coke because he was not used to ice in his drink. This was not used to drinking from a paper cup. He did not like drinking with a straw, as he had never used one before.

Elisa wanted to go to the inside playground, but Molly said they did not have time for that today. Letivi wanted to get more

McNuggets, but he did not say anything. He also wanted to see for the first time a playground for children but kept his thoughts to himself.

Everyone stood up to leave. Letivi began to step away from the table, but he was halted by Robin, who asked him to help carry the trays and trash to their places. Letivi immediately noted that you had to clean up after yourself. He carried the tray with his and Molly's trash and empty cups and followed Robin to the trash bin. He imitated Robin's every move, placing the trash in the bin and the tray on the shelf. Letivi was beginning to feel he could adapt to this American way of living. He was also thinking that it would be nice to have something like McDonald's in his country.

When they dumped their trash into the large bin, Letivi noticed that many people had not finished their food and had thrown it away. This surprised him because in his country, no food was ever discarded. There was always someone around to eat any leftovers. There was never any waste of edible food. This observation had Letivi wondering about how much unconsumed food was wasted in America. He turned to Robin to ask, "Robin, I see that many people did not eat all their food and tossed it into the waste bin. Does this kind of thing happen often in America?"

Robin quickly understood what Letivi was driving at and bluntly replied, "There is too much food in America that is thrown away. Maybe all the hungry in Africa could be fed if there were a way to recover and preserve all the uneaten food in America and distribute it in Africa. Certainly, the quantity of food wasted at the thousands of McDonald's in America would be sizeable. We also feed our pets too much, and perhaps Americans spend more on the feeding and care of their pets than Africans spend on their food. I would guess that the total annual amount spent by

Americans on their pets is a multiple of your country's GDP, and that only a handful of African countries have a national annual GDP larger than this amount."

Once they were back in the car, Molly said, "Our next stop should be the Walmart in El Dorado so we can buy Letivi the additional clothes and winter coat he needs. It will be also good that he see what a big store in America looks like."

Roy uttered his usual "Okey-dokey," started the car, and headed east out of Augusta on Highway 400. Elisa was squirming and demanded to sit on Letivi's lap. When she got onto Letivi's lap, she kissed him on the cheek and said, "I love you, Letivi."

Again, Molly was mystified by the connection between her daughter and Letivi and her ability to say so distinctly his name. They arrived at Haverhill and turned north on a county road to El Dorado. Letivi recognized that this was the same road they had used when he came from the Wichita Airport.

They arrived in El Dorado and went left on Central Avenue to go to the Walmart Store. Molly explained to Letivi, "Many people in town don't like Walmart because ever since it was built, many shops located downtown had to close because they could not compete with the giant Walmart chain. I'll be interested in knowing what you think about this store."

Roy found a parking place in the huge parking lot not far from the store's front entrance. Letivi followed the group like a docile sheep through the automatic opening doors. He turned to see how the doors closed by themselves. Robin grabbed a big shopping cart. For Letivi, it was as if he had entered a town within a town that had been created for the purpose of selling anything one would need. He could not see from one end of the store to another. The line of cash registers seemed endless. He was thinking that there were more goods for sale and cash registers than all the stores put together in his country. There was far too much to examine. He whispered to Molly, "I really need a lot of time to see everything in this big store. I hope we can come back when we have more time so I can slowly walk around."

Molly placed Elisa in the cart's child seat. She said, "I have to go to the toy section to get something that will keep Elisa entertained. Then we need to go to the men's clothing section to buy some more clothes for Letivi."

Roy asked Molly, "Do you need any money? I brought my Walmart card."

Molly said rapidly, "No, Dad. Letivi brought a lot of money, and I will use some of that."

Letivi continued to be ensnared by the spell the retail nirvana had cast over him. When he heard Roy mention a card, he regained enough consciousness to ask, "You mean you can pay with a card?"

Roy responded, "Yes, my son. In our country, we use many credit cards, such as the Walmart card I'm holding in my hand. You pay with the card and then pay the company when you receive your monthly bill."

Letivi was thoroughly confused. For him, it was some kind of scam that permitted you to pay with a plastic card. This would never work in his country. Everyone would be trying to cheat the card system or steal someone's card. Moreover, without a mail service, you could never pay your bills. He felt compelled to ask, "How do I get one of these cards?"

Roy said, "Well, first, you would need to reside somewhere that has an address and have a local phone number. Most of all, you would need a bank account and a job. You have to have a good credit rating and maybe some references."

Letivi thanked Roy and again mulled over how a credit card system could work in his country. He concluded it would not be workable in his country except for a handful of the elites. Very few people had addresses and phones. He did not know anyone in the village who had a bank account. Not having a national mail service was a real constraint to many things.

Roy and Robin separated from the group and went to have a coffee. Letivi followed Molly and Elisa to the toy section. He kept getting farther behind, obliging Molly to stop and wait for him. There was so much to see that he could not go any faster. They finally arrived among the rows of toys. Molly put Elisa down so she could find a toy she liked. Elisa called to Letivi, "Come and help me find a toy."

Elisa took Letivi's hand and led him through row after row of toys. Letivi felt like a child. He had never experienced before the joy of having toys. He had never possessed a toy, and few children in his country had ever had a manufactured toy. Most people did not have money to buy such nonessential items. Spending money on toys would be considered a waste. There was no place for toys in the daily survival scheme. Children made their own crude toys from whatever materials they could scavenge. Letivi saw that the possession of toys by children could be a development level indicator.

Elisa picked out a little black baby doll. Letivi was surprised at her choice. He said, "Elisa, are you sure you do not want to get a white baby doll instead?"

"No. Mommy said that in your country, there are only black people, so I want a black baby."

Molly was standing nearby and watching intently Elisa's choice of a baby doll. She did not know what to think, but somehow Elisa's choice brought tears to her eyes. She forced herself to regain her composure by saying in a broken voice, "Hey, you guys. We need to go buy Letivi's clothes."

Letivi turned to Molly and pleaded, "Can you go and choose clothes for me? You know what I need. If I need to try on anything, I can do that later. I really need to look around this gigantic store. This is the most spectacular thing I have ever seen."

Molly replied, "OK. Be careful. Do not break anything. I will take Elisa and meet you in front of the exit in about forty minutes."

They parted ways. Letivi shuffled off to explore the rich bounty of the store. He walked as if he were in a trance. He did not know in which direction to go. There was too much in any direction he looked. He toddled off toward the electronics section. The sights, sounds, and display of goods in this section captivated him. He could have easily stayed in this section examining every item, but he knew he did not have much time, and he wanted to see some other sections before he had to meet Molly. He knew he could not see everything well in the short time afforded him. He would ask to be left at Walmart for an entire day so that he could take his time to see everything. He also wanted to see what he might buy for gifts to take back to the village.

Molly, Elisa, Roy, and Robin had been waiting for Letivi for a long time in the front of the store. Elisa had fallen asleep in Molly's arms, clutching tightly her new baby doll. Molly was becoming impatient. She fumed, "Daddy and Robin, can you please go and find Letivi?"

Roy and Robin began looking up and down every aisle in the store. They started at one end and began working their way to the other end. They were beginning to get worried that Letivi had disappeared from the store. Just when they were about to give up, they found Letivi in the grocery section counting how many different types of ketchup and mayonnaise were on display. They called out, "Letivi, where have you been? We've been looking everywhere for you. What on earth are you doing?"

Letivi did not react to their urgent cries and kept counting the items in front of him. It was as if he were on an important mission of discovery and the information he was gathering was essential for the report he would give to his village. Roy and Robin raised their voices. "Letivi. We need to go now. We can bring you back here another day and give you all the time you need to complete your study of the store."

Letivi finally came to his senses and meekly said, "OK. Let's go. But I do need to come back. There is so much for me to study and learn in this store. I can see that many secrets about the genius of your country are embedded in the realities of this store."

They quickly escorted Letivi back to where Molly was waiting for them. Molly had lost her patience. She was not in a good mood and snappily said, "I've already paid. We can go. Letivi can try on his clothes at home. If they don't fit, we will bring them back for exchange."

Letivi quickly inquired, "Do you mean you can bring clothes back after you already bought them?"

"Yes, Letivi. Here in America, you can return clothes if they are not damaged and you have your original receipt."

Letivi could not believe his ears. Again, something that would be impossible in his country was very possible and already being done in America. As they walked out of the store and across the parking lot, Letivi could not wait until they were all in the car so he could share some of the things he had learned in the store. Once they were all seated in the car, Letivi began bubbling over about the enlightening experience he had had in Walmart. He firmly stated, "I now know what makes your country so great: everything you need is readily available and up to date. When a country can have a store like that and most people can go into it and buy what they need, what more can you ask? What my country and other poor countries need is a well-stocked Walmart in every town with a population that has the purchasing power to benefit from what Walmart has to offer. The day we have all that will be the day we know we have succeeded in our development process."

Everyone in the car looked incredulously at one another. Letivi's words had them thinking in ways they had never thought before. Letivi was not yet finished. "Maybe you do not need so many varieties of such items as ketchup, mayonnaise, and sanitary napkins, but it is good that people have plenty to choose from, and the products are fresh. In my country, too many times, the little our small shops have to offer is old and expired."

Everybody was genuinely impressed that Letivi had gained so much from his short visit to the local Walmart. Letivi's impressions made them think hard about all those things they took for granted. They could see that compared to Letivi's country, they did indeed live in the land of plenty and, consequently, should not complain so much and be thankful for all they had. As they drove north into El Dorado along Central Avenue, Letivi was again all eyes as he beheld the large lawns and nice sidewalks running along the street. It was rare to find such nice sidewalks in his country. But there was one thing that puzzled him, so he felt obliged to ask, "Where are all the people? I see the nice sidewalks, but it is rare that I see any people using them. In my country, there are few sidewalks, but the roadsides are covered with people. Also, where are the people on motorbikes and bicycles?"

Robin was impressed by Letivi's observation and said, "Letivi, people in our country mostly use cars and walk only for exercise. Few people ride motorbikes and bicycles, and, if they do, it is for recreational purposes. Also, keep in mind that this is a small town."

Letivi thanked Robin for his reply. He could see that in a wealthy country where everything was located long distances from where one lived, a car was the best way to go. He was challenged to think of how wealth could be created in his own country so that someday most people could own and drive a car. As things stood now, cars and the fuel needed to operate them were very expensive in his country. The cost was well beyond the budgets of all except a few.

As they pulled into the driveway at Molly's parents' house, Molly told Letivi, "You can try on the clothes I bought for you while I help my parents fix dinner. If there is time, you might also want to watch TV."

Letivi said, "That sounds good. I need time to write up my notes on the essential ingredients of the development process. I would also like to try to call Chief Gyasi to see what he meant by that telegram."

They got out of the car, and Molly put Elisa down so she could walk to the house herself. She then said to Letivi, "This is not a good time to call your country because it would be very late in the night there. The best time would be to call Chief Gyasi early tomorrow morning before we go to Wichita."

Letivi replied, "Oh, I keep forgetting about the difference in time zones. I still find it interesting that it can be late at night there and still afternoon here. I'm OK with that, but I have one more question. Why are all those black and gray plastic barrels sitting alongside the streets?"

A very tired Molly replied, "Letivi, as I explained to you, those are trash receptacles. People set them out late in the day before the garbage truck comes to collect their contents early tomorrow morning."

Letivi was dumbstruck again. Another of America's many marvels had been revealed to him. He could only mutter to himself, "Only in America."

CHAPTER THIRTY
BROKEN HEART

Letivi was busy scribbling notes about his observations. He particularly wanted to make a list of all the advancements in America that would be good to achieve in his own country. His head was swirling with ideas, and he was worried about overlooking some important points. He wrote furiously with his left hand, from right to left. Robin was impressed by Letivi's efforts and provided him with more paper and an old magazine upon which to write. Without looking up, Letivi thanked Robin.

Robin sat opposite Letivi in a comfy stuffed armchair. He could not keep his eyes off the intensity with which Letivi was writing. He wondered what he was writing about, but he did not want to interrupt him. He could not have imagined that Letivi was at that moment writing about how clean America was and how such good sanitation reduces the disease burden. He was noting that you could not raise animals in the city limits, littering was prohibited, peeing in public was unheard of, and spitting on the sidewalk was punishable by a fine. There was none of this in his country, where filth and rubbish abounded. He did not know how any of this could be achieved in his country, but he knew that these were good things to do for his people because they would help create a healthier environment.

He also noted the absence of flies and mosquitoes and the role winter played in suppressing germs. If they could only increase the control of disease vectors in his country, his people would be less sick and more productive. Moreover, young children would live longer, and average longevity would increase from fifty-five years to something near America's life expectancy of about seventy years. If they could only find a way to control the mosquito vector, they could lower the incidence of malaria, the major killer of children and the main reason for clinical consultations. He knew doing all this would require massive efforts to vaccinate children and educate the people, a high degree of political will, and a huge amount of funding to clean up the country and keep it clean. He was eager to return home to begin working on schemes to achieve these noble goals.

Letivi looked around for a moment and then returned to making notes about the importance of good infrastructure and communications. He noted that every house had a TV and a telephone. He enumerated everything he had seen in Molly's kitchen. He especially underscored the need for affordable and reliable electricity. He noted that since he had been in America, he had not once observed an electrical power outage, and in even the most remote community, there was electricity. Most of his country was without electricity and remained in the dark at night. Not a day would go by in the capital city of Kotoku without several lengthy power outages.

The high cost of electricity made it beyond the financial wherewithal of almost everyone. Letivi worried his country could never have steady electricity, and this would limit its development prospects. Expensive and erratic electricity, along with other factors, made doing business in Kotoku too expensive. And having natural gas piped to every house in his country was beyond the realm of even the wildest imagination, especially as most houses were built of mud bricks in unimproved areas and covered with straw or a simple tin roof. More importantly, most people could barely afford to buy firewood or lumpy local charcoal to cook. Letivi could see that using natural gas would help conserve the environment, which was negatively affected by deforestation caused by the need to produce increasing quantities of wood and charcoal for cooking.

Roy stepped into the living room and said, "Let's watch the evening news." He turned on their big TV screen, and Letivi was immediately seized by the images that flashed before his eyes. He had never before seen TV news. He was engrossed by all the happenings in the world that were reported. He was not aware that so much was happening in so many places around the globe. In his village, he did listen to the news on his radio, but he had never seen any news on TV. He followed closely all the world, national, and local news. He was happy to see that sports got much attention. There was more news than he could possibly absorb. There was too much news about things that would not be news in his country.

Letivi did appreciate that there was national political news on more actors than just the president. In his country, the news communicated via radio and TV was almost totally about what their president was doing, whom he had met with, and what he had said. The powerful state media was dominant and primarily used to promote the president's popularity. Letivi liked the fact that in America, there were many candidates who competed for votes from the people. His president was the son of the previous president, and, if elections were held, he would be the only candidate. The president was able to do as he pleased because he had the full backing of the military, which was managed by well-heeled officers loyal to the president. His president also had the wherewithal to buy off any opposition, and if he could not buy them off, he would get rid of them or force them into exile.

Following the news broadcasts was something Letivi had never seen or heard: the weather report. There were not any weather reports or forecasts in Kotoku. This was interesting to Letivi, but he could not see the utility of weather forecasts in his country because the seasonal weather was highly predictable. In his country, people watched the skies and felt the wind to know how the weather might change. It was invariably wet or dry, hot or hotter. Not much to report on there.

For Letivi, the weather report was boring. He looked over at Robin and could see he was dozing. He also felt unusually sleepy. He wanted to write some more before dinner, but he was enveloped by a heavy sleepiness he had not felt before, especially at this time of day. He dropped his paper and ballpoint and fell into a deep slumber.

Roy looked around and saw both Letivi and Robin fast asleep. He got up and went to the kitchen to see his wife, Molly, and little Elisa to announce, "Hey, the two boys are in a deep sleep. I don't think they can eat. It will be hard enough to get them into the car and take them over to Clyde's."

Molly and her mom both let out a loud sigh. They were disappointed that the food they were cooking would not be eaten by Letivi and Robin. Molly exclaimed, "Looks like jet lag finally caught up with them. Let's try to get them in the car and take them to Clyde's house so they can sleep. They can eat a big breakfast tomorrow. We better give Clyde a call so he knows we're coming."

Little Elisa piped up. "I never see big people sleep before me. Letivi looks like a baby waiting for his mom to take him to bed."

Roy woke Robin up and asked him to help him get Letivi into the car. A woozy Letivi was able to walk with their help. Molly came trotting behind them with two big bags full of the clothes she had bought for Letivi at Walmart and his paper and ball-point pen. She told a wobbly Robin, "Make sure Letivi tries on his clothes before he comes to breakfast, and if anything does not fit, please bring the receipts and clothes back with you. Sweet dreams to both of you."

Clyde was waiting for them in front of the house when they arrived. Robin headed straight into the house. Clyde and Roy helped Letivi into the house and took him into his bedroom. Letivi sat down on the bed as he struggled to clear his head so he could undress and go to bed. Clyde returned with Letivi's bags of clothes. Clyde said, "Goodnight. See you tomorrow." Clyde gently closed Letivi's bedroom door as he shook his head over the idea of someone going to bed at suppertime. He returned to his living room to find that Roy had departed and Robin was fast asleep on the sofa. He shook his head again. He was puzzled as to why Robin and Letivi both had some kind of unusual sleeping disorder.

The dark small town night was icicle cold and quieter than a tomb. Letivi had crawled under the covers fully clothed. He fell into a deep sleep and found himself in an African dreamland almost before his head touched his pillow. It was as if the drummers and the old chiefs were waiting for him. The drums beat emphatically their ancient welcoming tune. The same old chiefs who had given Letivi his chiefly ancestral initiation stood high and majestic. They looked benevolently down upon Letivi from some lofty place in the other world. In perfect unison, they chanted repeatedly in one voice, "Chief Letivi, do not forget your solemn oath to lead your village. You are destined to be a great chief, and your son will follow you as chief. Stay strong and come home to Ataku, where you belong. Your village and your country need you." All night long, these words were drilled into Letivi's heart and mind.

Letivi awoke before sunrise, switched on the ceiling light, and sat for a long time on the edge of his bed contemplating the words of the ancestors and what he had read in the book and article about his father. He missed the deep sense of community and belonging that he felt in his village. He also missed the communal spirit that prevailed in his village and the slower pace that permitted him ample time to chat and interrelate with his people. He knew that he must bring his visit to America to a quick end and return to Ataku. He felt rising within himself a growing urgency to call Chief Gyasi. All of a sudden, he was in a hurry to get his visit over with and talk with his grandfather. He rushed to try on the clothes Molly had bought for him. He was pleased that they all fit him well. He liked most the heavy winter parka and woolen cap. After trying them on, he did not want to take them off.

As Clyde and Robin were still sleeping, Letivi quietly left his bedroom and entered the bathroom. He finished his bath and slipped furtively out of the bathroom and was about to close his bedroom door when he heard Clyde say in his gravelly voice, "Son, are you up already?"

Letivi timidly responded, "Yes, I am. I need to go to Molly's house as soon as possible to call home."

Clyde cleared his throat enough to reply, "OK, son. We'll try to get a move on it. I need to go out back and feed my dog first. He has his own little house in the backyard."

Letivi dressed in his new brown corduroy pants, put on his thick woolen socks, blue flannel long-sleeve shirt, and a gray sweater, and then enveloped himself in his heavy parka. He felt toasty warm and protected from the exterior elements. He sat on the edge of the bed thinking of what he would tell his grandfather, Chief Gyasi. He made sure he had in his pocket the small strip of paper with the number of the president's cell phone that he had entrusted to Gyasi. He knew he was not supposed to use this cell phone in this way, but Gyasi's telegram and his dream compelled him to call.

It took some time for Clyde and Robin to prepare themselves. Letivi passed the time deep in thought and looking around his bedroom and outside the window at the dreary winter landscape. He retrieved his notepaper and began adding to it. His first additional note was about how warm it was in the house no matter how cold it was outside. He also noted that it was the same in the cars. He was told that during the hot summers, the same machines that produced heat could produce cold. For him, being able to control the internal temperatures was an achievement of the highest order. He was convinced that he would not live long enough to see anything like this in his village. He also added to his notes that many people had pets and expended much time and money to care for them well. He speculated that America's household pets were better nourished than many people in his country. He quickly added to his notes that people in America also spent much money on cosmetics and sporting events—all things that were luxuries only rich people could afford in his country.

Clyde called out loudly, "Chief, let's go."

Letivi folded his notepaper and placed it with his ballpoint in his big parka side pocket. When he came out of the bedroom, Clyde and Robin could not help but laugh when they saw him all bundled up. They were wearing light jackets, while Letivi was dressed for the most severe winter weather. Robin blurted out, "Letivi, aren't you too hot with all those clothes?"

Letivi quickly shot back, "I feel just fine, thank you."

They left the house, and Letivi was happy that he felt the bitter cold much less than the day before. He was pleased that he had conquered to a large extent his biggest concern: Kansas' cold, windy winter weather. He told himself that he should dress like this for the rest of his time in America. He could not wait to thank Molly for buying him clothes that fit and such a wonderfully warm winter coat.

They arrived at Molly's, and Letivi wasted no time in getting out of the car and rushing into the house. Little Elisa was the first to greet him. "Letivi, you look funny. Why you dressed up like an Eskimo?"

Letivi smiled and said, "Because an African needs to keep warm."

Molly overheard this exchange and asked Letivi, "How did your clothes fit?"

Letivi happily replied, "All the clothes are nice and fit perfectly. I especially like the coat. Can we call Gyasi now?"

"Yes, we can. But first, let me talk about breakfast and our program for the day."

Letivi replied, with a tone of urgency in his voice, "OK, but I really need to talk to Gyasi."

"I understand, Letivi, but what I have to say will only take a few minutes. Is it OK to warm up the T-bone steak we fixed for you last night and put it with the fried eggs we know you like?"

Letivi found this to be an odd question because in his country, meat was welcome at any time of the day. All the Africans he knew were most definitely carnivores. He did not think there could be such a person as an African vegetarian. He replied, "Of course. I welcome the meat with my eggs."

Molly continued, "Today, we will go to Wichita, Kansas's biggest city, to visit your father's alma mater, WSU. I have been in contact with one of the political science professors I had when I attended WSU. He would like you to say a few words to one of his classes. After our visit to WSU, I thought you would like to see the Wichita-Sedgwick County Museum. You can learn much about the history of this part of America at this museum."

Letivi said a quick, "OK, but can we call now?"

"Letivi, let's eat first. Then, we can call. OK?"

They entered the dining room. Letivi and Robin found that skipping dinner the night before made them very hungry. Letivi immediately sat down and consumed in a few bites his three fried eggs and with a few large bites finished his hash browns. He always kept his mouth stuffed. He then picked up his T-bone steak in both hands and gnawed it methodically down to the bone. He sucked on the bones and lifted his plate to lick it clean. He followed this remarkable eating show by swallowing his cup of hot coffee in a few gulps. After draining his coffee cup, he confirmed his satisfaction with a loud burp.

He looked around to see all eyes watching him. He did know that eating in the way he did was not the usual practice in America. For those observing him, he was quite a sight, dressed in his parka and guzzling his food and drink. Roy felt he had to say something to clear the air. "I like to see a hungry man eating with so much energy and gusto. Well done, son." Somehow, these sarcastic words caused everyone to laugh.

Letivi could not comprehend what all the fuss was about. He wiped his mouth on his coat sleeve and said, "I'm thirsty for water. May I get my own water from the kitchen sink?"

Molly responded, "Go right ahead. Take your glass with you."

Letivi enjoyed turning the sink faucet off and on. For him, it was something of a miracle to see how easily clean and plentiful water flowed from the kitchen sink spigot. Not a single house in his village had piped water. People sometimes had open wells in their home compounds. More often, women and children were required to search for water in streams or communal wells, which were often located far away. One of the main daily tasks of women and children was to carry water in buckets and basins on their heads from water sources to their homes. The water consumed was seldom potable and often too dirty to be used for cooking or washing. Waterborne diseases were common. If clean water for everyone was a development prerequisite, it would be decades before his country would be able to satisfy this most basic of human needs.

Letivi returned to the dining table to make some notes about the wonders of clean running water. Molly interrupted him to say, "We can try to call Gyasi now. Can you give me his number?"

Letivi dug deep into the side pocket of his parka to retrieve the thin strip of paper with Gyasi's number written in pencil. He handed the paper to Molly, who said, "Thank you. I will look in the phone book for the country code."

Letivi was amazed to see a phone book with the names and addresses of all residents. He took note of this impressive feat. Molly found the international access number and country code for Kotoku and called, "Letivi, come into the living room and sit by the phone. I will try to dial directly without the assistance of an operator."

Molly told everyone to be quiet. She instructed little Elisa to be still and sit down. She made it known she was calling Africa. She slowly pushed the buttons on the beige house phone. She finished entering the numbers and held the phone close to her ear to see if the call went through. She waited a couple of minutes. She could hear an odd ring tone, and then there was a broken voice. She quickly handed the phone to Letivi.

Letivi spoke loudly in a quick, staccato manner, "Grandfather, it's me, Letivi. I'm fine. I got your telegram. What's the news?"

The line was not clear. Gyasi could barely hear Letivi. All he knew was that it was Letivi calling him and he must speak fast to try to avoid any notice by the president. He was sure the president's people monitored all calls on this phone. He spoke as fast, loud, and affirmatively as he could. "Listen well. Do not come home. You are popular. Wait—" The line cut. The few words that Letivi heard made him feel as if the wind had been knocked out of him. He dropped the phone and stared straight ahead without muttering a word. Everyone could see that he had not had a good phone conversation.

Molly broke the silence by saying in a concerned voice, "Letivi, what is it? What did Gyasi say? Why do you look so disturbed?"

Letivi slowly said a few fragmented words. "The connection was bad. I could not hear him well. I will need to try to call him again tomorrow." Letivi did not want to reveal that Gyasi told him not to come home. He needed time to think about why his grandfather would say such a thing.

Molly was puzzled by the way Letivi was acting. She was surprised to hear Letivi call Gyasi Grandfather. She was asking herself, "How could Gyasi be Letivi's grandfather when he succeeded the previous chief, Yofu, who was his adopted African father?"

Molly knew that this was not the time to ask Letivi anything, but she could not hold back a question that jumped from her throat. "Letivi, I didn't know Gyasi was your grandfather. How can this be?"

Letivi mumbled, "He is my mother's father. Please, I do not want to talk now. We can talk later. Should we not depart for Wichita now?"

Letivi was trying to keep a stiff upper lip and act as if nothing had happened in the brief exchange with his grandfather. He wanted to carry on with today's program, but inside the deepest part of his inner being, his will to carry on was beginning to crumble. He could not stop thinking about why his cautious grandfather had told him not to come home. How could that be? He tried to hide his state of shock and his mental turmoil. He was able to function only because he was denying that his grandfather had said what he said. He needed more time to think about the real meaning of his grandfather's words.

Robin was becoming impatient. He had not tuned into Letivi's torment and just wanted to get through today's agenda. His concerns were about his own future, and that meant finding a job. He was toying with the idea of finding the courage to call his former boss in Chicago about getting his old job back. For sure, he needed some way to support himself and pursue his career as a journalist. He jovially said, "Hey, guys. Let's go to Cowtown."

Roy joined in. "Yes, indeedy. We need to go if we are to do everything planned for the day. I need gas, so the first stop will be the nearest station."

Elisa popped up. "Yeah, let's go." Then she ran and jumped into Letivi's lap. Letivi whispered some words into her ear, and she sprang out of his lap and grabbed her grandmother's hand, saying, "No, I'm not going. I'll stay home with Grandma."

Elisa's surprising good behavior made Molly want to know what Letivi had told her. Molly got up, grabbed her coat, and walked toward the front door. "Let's go, people. The Air Capital awaits us."

Letivi tried to be funny by saying, "Wait a minute. I object. I won't budge until somebody explains to me what is meant by Cowtown and Air Capital. I thought we were only going to Wichita."

Letivi's words gave everyone a good laugh and helped lighten the pervading glum mood. Robin chuckled as he said, "Letivi, all these words are different ways of referring to Wichita. Let's get into the car, and I'll explain more about this to you."

Roy told everyone to get in the car while he closed his garage door. Letivi now could see why Roy did not park his car in the garage—it was full of all sorts of stuff. For him, the contents of Roy's garage represented a real treasure. There were things in the garage that people in his village could only dream about owning. Roy noticed Letivi eyeing his garage bounty and said, "Yes, I got too much stuff. I need to have a garage sale to get rid of most of what you see."

Letivi commented, "You mean you will sell your riches?"

"These are not riches. Most of these things are excess junk. I will sell it cheap to other people who need or want to add it to their own pile of junk."

Letivi said nothing further about this, but he noted that garage sales were another thing that rich people had the luxury of doing. There were not any garage sales in his country because almost nobody had a garage and it was rare that anyone had any excess possessions they wanted to sell.

Elisa energetically waved good-bye as the four travelers pulled out of the driveway and headed west on their forty-minute trip to Wichita via what was commonly called the Kechi Road. There was silence in the car. Everyone was deep in his or her own thoughts. Letivi's head was splitting as he continued to ask himself why his grandfather would tell him not to go home. Why would he say such a thing, and why would he interject something about his popularity? He must return home to continue to lead his people and respect the promises he had made to the ancestors. He was the guardian of the secrets conveyed to him during his indoctrination with the ancestors during his secret chief's initiation ceremony. He was also the only one who knew about the existence of a golden stool buried beneath the old baobab. It was inconceivable to him that he would not go home.

Roy stopped to get gas, but hardly anyone noticed. Letivi did manage to take note that the price of gasoline was about a third of what it cost in his country. He could see that relatively cheap and plentiful fuel supplies supported America's economy. As his country did not possess any sources of fuel, they had no choice but to pay high prices for fuel imports.

Letivi resumed his torturous thoughts. Why was he too popular? Why did that matter? He did know that the president did not like anyone to be more popular than he was. Was that it? That was ridiculous! He did not have any political aspirations. He did not represent competition for the president. His only interest was to assist the people of his village to improve their situation and move to a higher development stage. He concluded that he would have to take the risk of calling his grandfather to get to the bottom of why he should not return home. He had no other choice if he was going to be able to maintain his sanity.

Letivi was so bogged down in his thoughts that he did not realize they had passed the Wichita city limits and were almost on university grounds. Molly had been providing him some information on the university, but Letivi was too buried in his excruciating thought patterns to hear any word she said. Letivi finally emerged from the depths of his internal cross-examination of every word he had heard Gyasi utter on the telephone when

Molly gently nudged him as she asked, "Letivi, what is wrong with you? Please pay attention."

Letivi struggled to formulate a few coherent words to say to Molly. "Sorry. I am still dwelling on what Gyasi said."

Molly treated Letivi with a no-nonsense attitude, saying, "Well, you better snap out of it. We are now on the WSU campus and headed for a parking spot near the Political Science Department. I hope you know what you are going to say to my professor's class."

Letivi sighed internally. The last thing he wanted to do now was to talk to anyone. He desperately needed time alone to think and decide what to do about the serious gravity of what Gyasi had said. He could see that the WSU campus was expansive and contained more modern buildings than the largest towns in his country. Although he had been told that there were many universities in America much larger than WSU, he was sure that WSU's student population exceeded that of most towns in his country and that its budget was far greater than any of those towns. He could also see that Wichita was a large city that covered more surface area than the capital city in his country, although Melomti had four times the population. He imagined that the city budget of Wichita was bigger than the national budget of his entire country, which had about forty times the population of Wichita.

Roy parked the car, and they exited into the cold but sunny November day. They walked slowly the couple of hundred yards to the Political Science Department building. Letivi had his parka hood pulled closely around his head, and his hands were deeply buried in its ample side pockets. He could not wait to get inside to enjoy that great American heating. They entered the plate-glass doors and found Professor Johnson waiting for them.

The professor enthusiastically shook everyone's hands. He especially shook Letivi's hand as he asked, "Are you the African?"

Letivi could not manage a smile, but he was able to loosen his tense face muscles enough to say, "Yes, I am the one."

Professor Johnson asked them to leave their coats in the cloakroom near the entrance. Letivi was reluctant to remove his warm parka, but Molly encouraged him to do so. She told him, "You need to remove your coat to speak in front of the class. It is the proper thing to do."

At that moment, Letivi did not care anything about what was proper. He continued to wrestle with the thought that he could not go home. This thought dominated his thinking and was pushing him toward a psychic abyss he had never known before. He fought an urge to collapse on the spot. He drew on every fiber in his trembling body to right himself and to think of some remarks he could say to students who knew nothing about Africa.

Loud applause greeted them as they paraded into Professor Johnson's packed classroom. Robin, Roy, and Molly sat at school desks aligned near the door. The professor took Letivi's hand and led him to a position in front of the class. He asked everyone to be quiet and said, "Thanks to one of my former students, Molly Peterson, I'm pleased to introduce to you Chief Letivi from the African country of Kotoku." His words elicited an even louder applause in spite of his awful mangling of the pronunciation of Letivi's name and the name of his country.

"As I know all of you want to hear what the chief has to say, I will take my place among you and turn things over to him." After saying these words, Professor Johnson took a seat in the front row, and all eyes were riveted on the odd-looking, young half-caste man standing in front of them. Many were wondering what was so special about this young man who was about their age. Besides feeling on the verge of collapsing, Letivi was feeling very awkward, small and insignificant in front of this class composed of almost all white college students. Again, he thought about how in his country he was a big fish in a small pond. Here, he was a small fish in a very large pond. Here, he was nobody.

Letivi knew he had to say something that was understandable and appeared to be intelligent. He stood motionless for several minutes. The students were wondering what was wrong with him. Some students thought that maybe he could not speak English or he was very shy. All doubts and questioning among the students were dissipated when Letivi said in an unusually loud voice the word, "justice."

Somehow Letivi had managed to tap an inner source heretofore unknown to him to say to the class the following words: "Justice is what we need the most. Without justice, there cannot be the peace and stability needed to pursue prosperity. Consequently, our fast-growing population will continue to suffer too much, and the battle against poverty will never be won. But even if this battle cannot be won, we believe with competent and committed leadership, the high level of misery can be reduced by making the struggle for daily survival easier."

"Your country is very rich. My country is very poor. In both our countries, we have good, hardworking people who deserve a better life and many unsung heroes doing their best to help others. Your country consumes a large percentage of the world's wealth, while my country consumes a negligible percentage. Where is the justice in that?"

"Is it fair that in your country, everyone enjoys their basic rights, while in my country, having all your rights satisfied is only the stuff from which dreams are made? Most of the people in my country live at an absolute low level of poverty, and that in itself is a violation of one's rights. We all have a right to enjoy our basic needs. These needs include access to health and education services, nutritious food, clean water, good sanitation, and decent shelter. We know we do not have to be rich to be happy, but how can people so desperately poor be happy?"

"We would like democracy too, but it is only good as far as it helps secure our basic needs. Perhaps most of all, we need honest, competent leaders who put the best interests of their people first and who do not act as if they are above the law. We do not want leaders who have blood on their hands and large bank accounts abroad".

"The development gap between your country and mine is too large. The biggest moral challenge in the world is narrowing the gap between rich and poor countries. Everyone needs to think of how they can contribute to doing this."

"I know I have not told you anything about my country or Africa. My country alone would be very difficult to explain to anyone who has never experienced it firsthand, and describing the large, complex diversity that exists on the African continent is not possible. As I hope you know, Africa is an indescribable mosaic of fifty-four countries composed of hundreds of ethnic groups speaking a countless number of languages and dialects. There is no way to sum up Africa, and I will not try to so today. Thank you for your attention. That is all I have to say today."

When Letivi finished speaking, there was only silence. The students could not figure out whether they had just heard a brilliant, brief speech that taught them more than they had learned thus far in their college career or some bizarre words from an unimportant chief from a remote village in Africa who was visiting America for his first time. Professor Johnson broke the uneasy silence by clapping loudly. His students immediately joined him in giving a loud and prolonged applause to a visibly shaky Letivi.

Professor Johnson sprang to his feet and thanked Letivi for his very instructional words and then turned to the class and asked if there were any questions for Chief Letivi. Many hands flew into the air. Letivi knew he was in not any condition to remain much longer in the classroom to reply to questions. He felt weak in the knees and queasy. His head was aching so much that he thought it would burst. He hardly noticed what was going on around him when Professor Johnson called on the first student to pose his question.

This over-excited student stood and said, "Mr. Chief. Can you tell me if you have personally ever met Tarzan and Jane?"

Everyone in the classroom laughed. Professor Johnson told the student to sit down and not ask any more questions that were not relevant. He asked for a show of hands for any more questions. This time there were fewer hands. The professor called on one student, who asked, "Why do you have those small scars on your cheekbones?"

This harmless question reminded Letivi of his sacred responsibilities as a chief, and his head began to spin and perspiration began pouring off his forehead. He became uncontrollably dizzy and suddenly fainted in front of a shocked classroom. Molly rushed to see what was wrong with Letivi while everyone in the classroom gasped and stood up to see what was happening. Molly quickly explained to her professor, "I'm sorry. He has not been feeling well. I guess all the pressures of his trip have finally caught up with him. We should have gone more slowly in introducing him to America. He'll be all right. We just need to get him out into the fresh air."

Robin and Roy placed themselves on either side of Letivi, picked him up, and carried him to the exit. A concerned Professor Johnson turned to the students and said in a calm and reassuring voice, "Please sit down and be quiet. Apparently, Chief Letivi is suffering from a case of physical exhaustion brought about by the heavy demands of his long trip and his experiences thus far in America. I'm sure he will be all right. Thanks to everyone for coming. Please return to your regular class schedule now."

The cold winter air revived Letivi, and he said he was all right. He felt embarrassed and disoriented but managed to say, "Sorry about that. I don't know what came over me. I think I am OK now. We can continue our visit."

Molly helped Letivi zip up his parka and held his arm as they followed Robin and Roy to the car. She had had enough excitement for the day and made a mental note to call Professor Johnson to apologize. Molly was thinking they should cancel their visit to the museum and return to El Dorado so Letivi could rest. When she suggested this, Letivi interrupted. "No, please. I am OK. I would like to see the museum."

Robin and Roy were not interested in seeing the museum, but after what Letivi said, Roy had no choice but to head toward downtown Wichita, where the Wichita-Sedgwick Country Historical Museum was located on old Main Street. The museum was housed in the old city hall building that had been built in 1892. This building was referred to as the Palace of the Plains. Molly softly explained all this to Letivi, who was forcing himself to stay on track and think straight.

When Molly said the building had been built in 1892, his interest perked. Again, there was no building in his country anywhere near that old. America may be the new frontier, but in many ways, it was old when compared to what modern Africa possessed. He wondered what a museum in his country would exhibit. There was little that could be displayed, since his country had gained independence thirty years ago in 1960, and he did not know what it could exhibit from the prior colonial period. Anything of importance had been hauled away by the colonists and was sitting in European museums. He wished his country had a museum that contained many things his people could be proud to display. His country's history was too short and there was too little remaining worthy of a place in a museum.

Roy was frustrated, as the street he wanted to take was blocked, and he had to follow a detour route. Letivi was curious as to why the street was blocked and quietly asked Roy, "Why can't we go on that street?"

Roy responded without hesitation, "You see that tall building over there? They are preparing to demolish it with explosives. Within the hour, that building will be turned into a pile of rubble that will be trucked to a landfill somewhere."

Letivi was astounded. He commented, "Why is a perfectly good building being destroyed? That building is bigger and nicer than most buildings in my country. It is a shame we cannot somehow move that building to my country."

Meanwhile, Letivi was feeling another kind of explosion growing in his head. The sounds of incessant drumming and the voices of the ancestors pleading with him to return to the village were increasingly wrecking his mind and damaging his spirit. He could not reconcile these urgent pleas with his grandfather's instruction not to come home. He could feel his mind and heart beginning to break into fragments. He fought back, but he became helpless and slumped lifeless in his seat as the car parked next to the museum.

Molly stared at Letivi and sounded the alarm with a loud scream. Robin and Roy quickly turned to look behind them and saw Letivi passed out and leaning against the backseat in front of him. Molly shook Letivi vigorously, demanding, "Letivi, what is wrong with you! Please, you can't do this!"

A very agitated and tearful Molly cried out, "This is an emergency. We need to take him to a medical clinic immediately."

Roy gunned the engine, turned on his blinking emergency lights, and raced to the Wichita hospital with which he was most familiar. Within fifteen minutes, they were at the emergency entrance at Wesley Hospital. Roy fetched a nearby wheelchair, and he and Robin worked to place an unconscious Letivi in the chair. They rushed through the emergency entrance doors as fast as they could go, telling the first attendant they saw that their friend had passed out for unknown reasons. The physician on duty was called, and Letivi was taken away.

Molly, Robin, and Roy waited in the reception area for someone to come and tell them how Letivi was doing. They waited over an hour before a nurse came and told them that the young man they had admitted was awake and calling for someone named Molly. "That's me," said Molly as she rose to follow the nurse to the room where they were keeping Letivi for observation.

Molly found Letivi lying flat on his back and staring at the ceiling. The nurse excused herself, promising to return in a few minutes. Molly said in a soft and tender voice, "Letivi, it's me, Molly. I'm here."

Letivi turned his head and stared deeply into Molly's eyes as he sputtered slobbery words out of his almost-paralyzed mouth. "Molly, I'm sorry. I'm broken because I can't do my duty and return to my village. When Gyasi said I was too popular, that meant the president sees me as a threat to his power. The president is afraid the military could get behind someone as well known and popular as I am in my country. I must return home, but I can't, and that is driving me over the edge."

Molly reacted immediately with some emphatic words. "Letivi, this can't be. I have always seen you as a good leader of your people and a potential future president of your country. We must help you find a way to return to Kotoku."

Letivi could no longer hold on to his sanity. He felt himself slipping into a darker world where nothing made sense. His bonds with Molly and her daughter were strong, and he wanted to be able to say more. With his last ounce of logic, he whispered to Molly, "I don't want to be president. I only want to do my duty as chief of Ataku. I can never be president because once the people know I am not circumcised, they will not want me. I have more to tell you, but it's over now. Good-bye, Molly. I love you and Elisa."

Molly could not believe what Letivi said about circumcision. She was now convinced that he had become mad. She watched him as he stared at the ceiling with drool dripping from the sides of his mouth. He kept mumbling something, and she placed her face next to his so she could better hear what he was saying. She thought she heard him repeating over and over, "I'm a fool." She wept when she heard these words because she did possess great affection for Letivi, and the last thing she wanted was to see him become mentally deficient.

The nurse returned and asked her to come with her to speak with the doctor about Letivi's condition. She met with the doctor in a small side room. The doctor was in a hurry and lost no time in saying, "Please sit down. This will not take long. Your friend is suffering from the sudden onset of some kind of psychotic disorder. He needs to be taken to a specialized clinic for observation. Does he have health insurance coverage?"

This situation was becoming too much for Molly. She was afraid of fainting. With an uncommon tightness in her throat, she replied, "He is from Africa. He is visiting with me and my family for only a couple of weeks. He does not have any health insurance."

The doctor said pointedly, "In that case, he can only be attended by a state hospital. I will arrange for him to be admitted to the Winfield State Hospital. He will remain there until the cause of his illness is diagnosed and treated."

Molly was not prepared for these unexpected, dramatic events. She could not bring herself to believe that Letivi would not be returning home with her. She felt like she was on the verge of having her own breakdown. The doctor could see Molly's profound anguish and counseled her, "Young lady, I know this is difficult for you, but we have no other option. Your friend needs a psychological evaluation and treatment for whatever ails him. Once he is better, you can visit him. We'll be sedating him now for the trip to Winfield in one of our ambulances. You will need to complete some paper work on him before leaving."

A sobbing Molly approached her father and Robin and attempted to convey to them Letivi's situation. Robin and Roy were shocked by the news that Letivi was being admitted to the Winfield State Hospital. They all knew about this hospital located on a hill outside the town of Winfield because when they were children, they were threatened with being sent to one of Winfield's three hills. Located on one hill was an orphanage, on another was a prison, and on the third was the state mental hospital. They could not believe that they were actually sending Letivi to "third hill."

Molly completed the paper work the best she could, leaving her contact information as the person responsible for Letivi. She entered Letivi's name as David Peterson and noted that he was a relative. The drive back to El Dorado was filled with an awkward, stony silence. The car felt empty without Letivi's presence. Molly did not know how she would explain what had happened. She knew her mom would cry. She worried that Elisa would never understand and would sob unceasingly. She knew they would all be depressed for many days and weeks to come. She wondered how she would communicate this sad news to Chief Gyasi.

Letivi was revived from his heavily sedated state by the dazzling rays of a full moon pouring onto his face through the barred window of his room at the Winfield hospital. The magic of the soothing moon rays caused a crooked little smile to form on his face. The brilliant rays generated in his mind a vivid vision of the old baobab covered with joyous miniature white birds singing a loud and touching chorus that animated hundreds of red-headed chameleons to dance in a synchronized manner around the trunk of the ancient tree. This happy scene under the light of the full moon calmed Letivi's spirit and gave him some hope for better days ahead for himself and his village. He began to feel deep in his broken heart that he would return to help his village find a better way forward.

While Letivi's soul was rejoicing in the moonlight, the night nurse seated at her desk down the hall was examining under an antique desk lamp some old hospital records. She found it interesting that another David Peterson had been hospitalized in their institution about twenty years ago for similar symptoms. She wondered if these two David's were related. She saw that the older David had been born at Wesley Hospital, the same hospital that had referred the younger David to them. The main difference between these two cases was the words the younger David kept repeating over and over, "I'm a fool." The nurse was intrigued by these words. She asked herself, "Yes, David was nutty, but why would he say so?"

The nurse and all the doctors could never know what really afflicted David. They did not know about the ancestors, the old baobab, the powers of the full moon, and the influences brought to bear by the other world. Could they ever know and believe that the elder David had ridden a moonbeam and was returned to Africa by the full moon to be buried under the old baobab that had once swallowed him? Could they ever know that the young David was not mumbling, "I'm a fool," but, instead, he was saying, "Golden stool?" Letivi knew he was duty bound to safeguard the stool. This sacred duty and his love for his people obliged him to return one glorious day to his beloved village of Ataku deep in the heart of Africa.

www.ingramcontent.com/pod-product-compliance
Lightning Source LLC
Chambersburg PA
CBHW052347020726
47503CB00001B/148